EARLY ONE MORNING

Also by Robert Ryan

Underdogs
Nine Mil
Trans Am

EARLY ONE MORNING

Robert Ryan

review

First Published in 2002
by Review

An imprint of Headline Book Publishing

10 9 8 7 6 5 4 3 2 1

British Library Cataloguing in Publication Data

Ryan, Rob
   Early one morning
   1.World War, 1939-1945 – Secret service –
   Great Britain – Fiction 2.World War, 1939-1945 –
   Underground movements – France – Fiction
   3.War stories
   I.Title
   823.9'14[F]

   ISBN 0 7472 6872 X (hardback)
   ISBN 0 7553 0093 9 (trade paperback)

Typeset by
Letterpart Limited, Reigate, Surrey

Printed and bound in Great Britain by
Mackays of Chatham plc, Chatham, Kent

HEADLINE BOOK PUBLISHING
A division of Hodder Headline
338 Euston Road
LONDON NW1 3BH

www.reviewbooks.co.uk
www.hodderheadline.com

For Jack Cameron Bond

Early One Morning is a novel inspired by the lives of
Robert Benoist, William Grover and Eve Aubicq

'It was simply terrific: 112mph and still accelerating over the crossroads past the Barn – and the road cluttered with the usual Friday-evening traffic. Along the next stretch we did 122mph and I thought, under the circumstances, that was enough, and said so in no uncertain fashion. Thereafter we "cruised" along at a mere 90–95mph, and doing just over 100mph in third gear . . . it was the most alarming experience ever, yet Williams drove superbly, absolutely at ease and complete master of every situation . . .'

– C.W.P. Hamilton describing his test run of an Atlantic in England with Williams at the wheel, 1937, quoted in *Bugatti, The Man and The Marque* by Jonathan Wood

Prologue

DUBLIN, OCTOBER 1926

They took him with embarrassing ease. The young man had left his rooms to attend the meeting at six thirty in the morning, well before the majority of workers would be out and about, and walked through a damp, drizzly Temple Bar deserted but for the odd bundle of slimy rags that marked the street dwellers' stations. He emerged next to the looming edifice of the Bank of Ireland and was about to cross Dame Street, hesitating only to let a cart and a slow-moving Riley pass, when he was aware of a man standing too close behind him. As he turned, he was sandwiched by a second figure who stepped into the gutter. Both were big, stocky men, wearing heavy tweeds and bowlers. The one behind produced a revolver, and quickly they had him in the back of the car down on the floor behind the driver and a coarse blanket, smelling of fresh horse, was thrown across him.

Twisted into a near-foetal position in the grey gloom, a heavy boot resting on his back, his heart flapping in his chest, the young man tried hard to calm himself as they progressed through the city. He was sure that they were following the river, familiar as he

1

was with the distinctive jarring rhythm of the oversized cobble-stones, and he fancied he could smell, even over the heavy equine musk, the yeasty aroma of the brewery, but soon the sounds of motor traffic fell away, and from the bucking of the Riley he guessed that they were on country roads.

By the time they stopped he was biting his lip, trying to contain the agony of the terrible pins and needles that were shooting up his legs. The blanket was pulled back and he was unfolded from the tiny space and allowed to stretch and stamp until circulation slowly, painfully returned. The driver didn't even look his way, and the kidnappers looked bored as he paced up and down the yard, pulling the wet air into his lungs.

He looked around for clues to his whereabouts. They had come down a long track to a cottage, once small, now badly extended with a lean-to at one side. A country drinking establish-ment of some kind he reckoned, where the parlour simply grew an additional space to welcome local farmers. No customers at this time of day, though. Although the road was well rutted and led off to a series of paddocks, there were no other vehicles visible, not so much as a tractor, and high hedges and a line of lime trees prevented him from checking beyond the farm for landmarks. He had no idea where they had brought him. It had been well chosen.

Satisfied his circulation had recovered, the pair pushed him inside the cottage and closed the door, leaving him alone in a gloamy half-light. The sour-smelling room was square, low ceilinged, blackened by cigarette and peat smoke, with a serving hatch crudely carved into the wall at one end, a single table, and a motley assortment of mostly home-made furniture. There was one rather grand armchair, probably the perch of the grandfather or grandmother who would hold court over this shebeen in the evenings, but now a rather dapper man was occupying it. His host was in his mid-thirties, he would guess, with a pencil moustache, immaculate brilliantined hair, well-cut suit and long, manicured fingers gripping the arms of the chair.

The stranger smiled, stood and held out his hand as if they had been introduced at his St James's club. 'Slade,' he said in plummy English. 'How do you do?'

The young man didn't take the proffered hand, but Slade wasn't fazed at all, turning his palm upwards in a please-yourself gesture. 'Sorry about the transport arrangements. Doesn't do to be seen to get into a CID car these days. Not in your line of work. Take a seat.' Slade sat down and produced a pack of cigarettes. 'Smoke? No?'

'What's going on?'

Slade lit his cigarette. 'Oh please. The accent. You don't have to do all that top o' the morning bog-trotter rot for me. You're as English as I am, man.'

It wasn't true. He was half-French and the English part of him had a hefty dose of Irish on his paternal side. It was tracing that branch of the family that had led him to this place. However, Slade was right about the accent, he had deliberately let his vowels soften and slur over the last few months. English voices closed as many doors as they opened these days.

'For goodness' sake, sit down, there's a good fellow. Nothing to be gained by standing there glaring at me. If I had wanted you arrested I could have you shipped north and imprisoned under DORA or for membership of a proscribed organisation.'

Defence of the Realm Act. Slade was British Intelligence. Reluctantly Williams grabbed a chair and lowered himself into it gingerly, as if it might collapse under his weight. 'What is an Englishman doing with Dublin CID men?'

'Just helping our Irish brothers.'

He snorted.

3

'Trying to make sure the Irish Free State has a chance against . . . well, against your new chums. O'Malley, isn't it?' Then slowly, savouring each name, he continued, 'Clarke, Mellows, O'Donovan, Lemass, MacBride, Carroll, O'Higgins, Kenny . . . nine in the flying column. Ten with yourself.'

Informer. The word flashed across his brain, illuminated in flaming letters. How else could a British spy know about all those people?

'Now, we have reason to believe.' Slade stopped and laughed at himself, a metallic, staccato sound, devoid of real humour. 'Sorry, force of habit. We *know* that you drove the getaway vehicles on the night of the Knockadore Garda station attack, the Crumlin Barracks, the Dundalk Post Office and the Ballinakill bank raids. That you stole the cars for these actions. That most of them are probably at the bottom of the Liffey right now.'

He said nothing.

'Let us take a magnanimous view of all that. Let us say that these were legitimate acts of war.' He opened his mouth to speak and Slade raised a hand. 'Please, I am not in the market for rhetoric. I have heard it all before. The Irish can be so poetic when their entrails are hanging out of their arse.'

'Is that a threat?'

Slade sighed with a surprising weariness. 'No. Just an observation. So, police stations for revenge, army barracks for weapons, banks and post offices for funds, driving the odd gun shipment up from Cork. I can see all that. But why the moneylenders?'

'I—' I have nothing to do with that, he had started to say, realising that it would be a confirmation that he knew something about the other matters.

'You what?'

'I don't know what you are talking about.'

'Is it because they are mostly Jews? Is that it?'

Although he had heard some anti-semitic remarks, especially from Kenny, he had always assumed the systematic harassment was a political action, not racial. However, he had made it clear to Sean he wanted nothing to do with the savage beatings and intimidations that the column had handed down these past weeks, no matter what the motives, and Sean had respected that.

'It has to stop. I have here a letter for O'Malley, who I believe is your commander.' From his inside pocket Slade produced an envelope and offered it. The young man stayed stock still, as if accepting it was a certain admission of guilt.

'Why would you be worried about moneylenders?' he asked Slade, knowing that the IRA had killed or shot at plenty of soldiers and police in the last twelve months.

'That's our business. What is in here is a . . . peace offering.' He shook the letter. 'Take it.'

Williams hesitated. Even talking with this man could earn him a death sentence from the column. Delivering messages made the bullet to the head almost inevitable.

'I know what you are thinking. You'll be all right. In there is the name of the informer within your flying column.' He felt his jaw drop. 'As an indication of our good faith. With the evidence to back up the accusation.'

Slowly the young man stretched across and took the document, half anticipating it would burn through his fingertips. He slid it into the pocket of his jacket and fancied he could feel the incendiary contents reddening his skin. 'What kind of game is this? The Brits giving up one of their own?'

'No game. I want the moneylenders left alone and I am willing to deal.'

The penny dropped. People desperate enough to use money-lenders were vulnerable, corruptible. It was at the moneylenders that men like Slade did their recruiting for the army of informers that plagued the city.

'My chaps will take you back, drop you off somewhere appropriate. Best you go under the blanket again, though. Just in case.'

Slade stood up and so did the young man. 'I can see you aren't convinced.'

'Why should I be?'

'No reason. No reason at all, Mr Williams.' So they even knew his real name. Everyone else in Dublin knew him only as Grover. 'Except you have my word as a fellow Englishman that I am telling you the truth.' He held out his hand again. 'You must trust me on this.'

After a moment's hesitation the young man took the hand and felt Slade's long white fingers close tightly over his own.

Part One

One

AUSTRIA, OCTOBER 2001

John Deakin glances across at his passenger and wonders when she is going to speak. The old woman is sitting stock still and upright, the bony hands crossed on her lap, staring out at the backdrop of Alpine scenery. For a moment he thinks she must have fallen asleep, but he catches a movement as she blinks, a long slow stroke of a blue-veined eyelid across watery, opaque eyes. The old lady has barely said a word since Salzburg where he picked her up off the plane, other than a thank you when he helped her into the hired Mercedes.

He sees the sign for the lake and makes the right, carefully feeding through the Autobahn traffic heading east towards Linz. Habit makes him check for a tail, but nobody else pulls off and there is nothing ahead on the road snaking up into the high glacial valley where the lake sits. They have the route to themselves. At this time of year, after the summer walkers have gone, the cows brought down from pasture and before the first snows fall, the mountains and lakes get a little peace. Except for Lake Senlitz. It will not have any for a few months yet.

Not for the first time that day he wonders about the old woman next to him. Fly out to Salzburg and await instructions he was told. He'd barely been there a day when the message came from the Consulate that he was to pick up one Dame Rose Miller. Extra–VIP. Deakin hadn't argued. The phone call that followed from Sir Charles, no less, was very clear. She deserves our respect and our thanks and she won't be with us much longer. Indulge her this once.

And, if he was honest, it was nice to be back in the old firm, even if this time it was a UDA. Ten thousand for a week's work. Pretty good money. Better than he got organising security at corporate events. It had been four years since they had said, sorry, Deakin, too many spies, not enough enemies. Not a bad severance package, but he'd been only thirty-eight. Hardly the age he had expected to be put out to grass.

Deakin has asked around, made some discreet calls, trying to get some operational background but the truth about his elderly passenger came from well before even his time. Fifties, possibly sixties, about the time of the real scandals, your Blakes and your Burgesses. Then finally he'd tracked Seagrove on a secure line and he'd admitted he'd heard the old girl was involved in a UDA back in the immediate postwar period. Berlin, Vienna, somewhere like that. Unofficial Deniable Actions. Off the meter, as they used to say in his department.

'It's about another twenty kilometres.'

Her thin voice may lack power but it still makes him jump.

'Yes, ma'am.'

She turns and looks at him, fixing him with those cloudy eyes. 'Deakin isn't it?'

'Yes, ma'am.'

'When we get there I should like to stay in the car. Not up to messing about in boats.'

'As you wish, ma'am.'

'Not ma'am, please. Makes me feel dead already. Rose will do, Deakin.'

He nods, knowing he will never be able to bring himself to call this dignified and scary old lady anything of the sort.

She reaches into her handbag and extracts a pair of Zeiss binoculars. 'Just park me so I can keep an eye on things, Deakin, eh?'

'Yes, ma'am.'

'And ring me.'

She hands him a card with a mobile number on it. Not such a relic of the past after all. 'Of course.'

Then, from the bag, Rose takes a Cartier watch, and Deakin gets the impression of great weight, and catches the sparkle of diamonds. She slips it on to her wrist, ludicrously large against the shrunken flesh clinging to the bones. She catches him staring and says, 'Lovely, isn't it? It's coming home, Deakin. At long last.'

Then, after being a silent companion, she turns positively garrulous.

Deakin pulls his coat tighter as he crunches down the gravel path from the makeshift car park to the mirrored waters of Lake Senlitz, its surface glinting like polished obsidian. It may only be autumn, with the hills and mountainsides still dappled with delicate yellow and purple flowers, but Senlitz exists in permanent winter, deep and icy and forbidding, the chill it exudes lowering the temperature in the valley by a couple of degrees. Below him, on the edge of the inky water, he can see Simon Warner, the Chief Archivist of the Imperial War Museum.

Warner looks to Deakin like a slumming Oxford don, a man who would be more at home in tweeds and an egg-stained knitted tie than the blue overalls and green wellingtons he is currently wearing. Behind Warner, out on the lake, are a pair of low, functional dive barges, hoists spouting from each side, with black inflatable Zodiacs zipping around like worker bees feeding the queen. On the very far shore, standing on the low cliffs that ring the southern end of the lake, is a derelict cottage with a dangerously crooked chimney. Around a kilometre from it to the west squats a large steam-powered crane, its jib hanging over the water, a hawser disappearing into the liquid night below.

Deakin reaches Warner who stands, clearly an irritated man, but one whose sense of good manners overrules any other considerations. He holds out his hand and says without much expression, 'Mr Deakin? Simon Warner. Imperial War Museum. Welcome to Lake Senlitz.'

Deakin takes the hand with his firmest grip and says, 'Hello. Thanks for waiting for me.'

'Six days. It's a long time.' Yes, thinks Deakin, he's pissed off. The Department has put a block on his activities for close to a week until they could rustle up him and Rose. He'd warrant Warner would be even more angry before the day was out. They were about to take his baby away from him.

'I know, I know. My people are very grateful.'

'Talking of which . . .' says Warner.

Deakin hesitates, gets his drift and shows some ID, hastily arranged by the Consulate to bring him on-side.

Warner nods. 'So why are you chaps so damn' interested? When we were trying to get funding for this, we were told by the FO and all its many, many departments that this was ancient history.'

'That was before your divers stumbled across some of our property. Shall we go?'

'Your—?' he begins, but Deakin is off, striding over to one of the black rubber Zodiacs. Without being asked, he clambers inside, wrinkling his nose at the smell, a combination of fetid water and the synthetic skin that suggests a thousand condoms fused together. Warner starts the engine and they putter out on to the lake, heading for the nearer dive barge.

By way of conversation, Warner asks, 'Do you know what else we are doing here? Other than recovering *your* property?'

'I know it probably isn't Nazi gold.'

Warner smiles for the first time. 'Yes, it's always Reichsgeld, isn't it? At least as far as the newspapers are concerned anyway. What we have got are the plates that the Germans created to flood Britain with forged currency. Do you know that by the end of the war up to a quarter of the five-pound notes in circulation were thought to be fakes? That's why they had to be changed.'

Deakin knows, but he just grunts. Let the man show off.

'Plus there is believed to be a lot of the money itself. More importantly there are also records of several concentration camps. Sachsenhausen among them.'

Deakin is interested now. 'Really?'

'Really,' and he adds pointedly, 'that is why we have some financial help from the Holocaust Center in New York.'

They pull level with the dive barge. A few figures wave, including what looks like a policeman. Warner catches Deakin's puzzled expression.

'Austrian police. It's their lake now, so we have to observe certain protocols. Keep them in the picture, basically.'

A thought occurs to Deakin. 'Won't it all be rotten? The money and the records?'

'Not at all. Very cold, very anaerobic down there. If the containers were properly sealed, no reason why everything shouldn't at least be legible if treated properly. That's why we have that.' Warner points to a large marquee on the shoreline. 'To preserve the material as soon as it comes out of the water, by whatever method is appropriate.'

They are around a hundred metres from the far shore now and Warner heaves to. He takes a mobile phone from inside his overalls, dials, and tells the crane operator he can begin, adding, with a sarcastic sneer, now that their VIP has arrived. Deakin glances back to the car park, the Mercedes a small outline now, but fancies he can see the binoculars trained on them. He can certainly feel Rose Miller's stare, even at this distance.

The crane engine starts a rhythmic thumping and belches black smoke. The hawser twitches, like an angler's line when the bait is taken by something large and unseen, then tensions and finally starts to move. Off to the left a pair of divers surface in a flurry of bubbles to witness their handiwork.

The steel line reels in and in, starting to swing a little as the object gains a little buoyancy, then tightens again as a bubble of long-trapped stale air escapes from the hidden treasure. The main hawser ends in a large ring and sends off four sub-divisions, each cable connected to the corner of the sunken bulk. Finally, like the back of a metal cetacean, a curve of rust appears, then the full roofline of a car.

'It's a Humber, we believe,' says Warner, 'although there was quite a lot of sediment over it. Probably a British staff car.' Deakin says nothing. Of course it was. Dame Rose has told him what to expect.

The remains of the windows have cleared the surface and black water starts to pour from within, receding in a rush, revealing the shattered windscreen and, grinning the strange mocking rictus of the human skull, a de-fleshed head, peering over the driver's side door.

★ ★ ★

It takes an agonising two hours to get the Humber across onto a stable platform, for the Austrian police to take their photographs of the body in situ and for a scene-of-crime team to arrive from Salzburg. The SoCs set to work with a desultory air. Old skeletons – old British skeletons judging from the tattered great-coat cloaking the bones – don't seem to push their enthusiasm buttons overmuch.

Deakin walks away from the activity and finally rings the old lady, imagining her digging in the bag for the mobile, the claw-like fingers trying to find the tiny buttons. But instead she is on the line immediately.

'Can you see it, ma'am?'

'Very well, Deakin, very well. Taking their time, aren't they? But I can't read the number. Is it still there?'

From his notebook he reads off the faded, barely legible serial number from the side of the bonnet.

'Yes,' she says, softly, 'that's mine. That's my car.'

'And that's him?'

'Open the trunk.'

'The police are treating it as a crime scene, ma'am.'

'Bugger the police,' she snaps. 'You hear me? Sort it out, Deakin. Remember who you are.'

He rings off, feeling admonished. Bugger the police. Remember who you are. Fine when you're sitting on the other side of the lake playing at being Queen Victoria. We are not amused, get on with it. He takes a deep breath, walks around to the boot of the car and, before anyone can stop him, yanks it open. A thin stream of gritty water sploshes down onto his trousers and he curses. Inside is more silt, wrapped around what was clearly a trunk of some kind. Warner comes round to see what he has found.

'Should you be doing this?' he asks priggishly.

15

Deakin ignores him and uses a finger to scrape away at the top of the trunk, revealing the ghostly imprint of the famed Louis Vuitton pattern, now bubbled and split. Riveted to the front is a brass name plate with a single word in copperplate writing, still clear after all these years.

Williams.

'Well,' says Warner, looking up as the Austrian pathology team slowly lever the bony remains from their resting place behind the wheel, 'at least we know who he was now.'

Two

VERSAILLES, MARCH 1928

Williams was halfway up the stairs to the main salon with the bottle of Margaux when he heard the insistent hiss behind him. He turned to find Eve making a series of strange faces at him, as if trying to settle on a suitable expression.

'Wait. You can't go in there looking like that.'

Williams looked down at himself and studied his dark woollen chauffeur's uniform. It was freshly cleaned and pressed, and the brass buttons shone proudly. True, it was the second-best winter outfit, but smart enough for most formal occasions. 'What's wrong, Miss?'

From the salon above came a peal of laughter, and he recognised the tone. One decanter down already, another on the way. It was going to be a four or five bottler.

Williams checked as surreptitiously as he could that his fly buttons were fastened, then repeated the question. 'What's wrong, Miss?'

Eve advanced two steps and shook her ringlets from her face. Although, as usual, she wore no makeup, she appeared to have rouged her cheeks. Williams looked closer. No, she was blushing, something he had never seen her do in the months he had worked for Sir William. And he had seen her in positions that would make a brothel madam colour up. She nodded at the silver tray and its contents.

'Can I take it in?'

'You?'

A second more piercing laugh. The guest.

'Do you know who that is in there with Bill?' Eve Aubicq always insisted on speaking English to him, even though she knew his own French was word perfect.

'No.'

'You'll never guess.' Williams wasn't even going to try. Sooner or later they all came by, from David, Prince of Wales down-wards, all the great and the not-so-good, seeing if they could get themselves Orpen-ed for posterity. Eve lowered her voice and in a hoarse whisper she finally told him: 'Charlie Chaplin.'

'Chaplin? Here?' Chaplin was a massive star in France and the city had been flattered by his full-length film *Woman of Paris*, possibly the only place where it received unanimous praise. 'Is Chaplin after a portrait, Miss?'

'From what I hear Orps doesn't have a canvas big enough to accommodate his head.'

Williams smiled and handed over the wine, glasses and cork-screw. 'And now is your chance to find out?'

She nodded eagerly. 'I'll let you know.'

Williams wondered where Eve stood on the subject of Lita Grey, the young wife whom Chaplin had married at sixteen and who three years later sued the star for insisting she performed 'abnormal, unnatural, perverted and degenerate' sexual acts. The French avant garde had rallied to the Chaplin cause, with one magazine claiming the act of fellatio was 'general, pure and

18

defendable'. Williams then realised the strange sound in his ears was his breathing and he had best stop thinking too closely about Eve's attitude to such things.

He retraced his steps downstairs to his subterranean rooms next to the wine cellar, changed into coveralls and headed back up for the front drive, where the Rolls stood.

This was the time of year when the big car earned its keep, gliding between Dieppe and Longchamps and the Champs Elysées, ferrying Orpen and Eve from one point on the French social carousel to another, occasionally dipping off into the dark sidestreets of Pigalle and along Raspaill for an invigorating – to Orpen at least – taste of the seamier side of Paris. It was a beautiful car, a six-cylinder Phantom 1, not two years old, but it required plenty of love and attention if it was to perform at its finest.

Williams had reached the top of the stairs when Eve reappeared in the hallway, her face still flushed, but now a darker colour, as if her skin had been bruised.

'Are you all right, Miss?' he enquired cautiously.

She spluttered for a second before blurting, in French this time, 'He asked if I had a younger sister for him. Younger.'

She pursed her lips to show her deep irritation and stomped upstairs, her heels clacking on the polished runners. Williams waited until she was two floors up before he allowed himself to smile.

Sir William Orpen grunted to himself as he traced the line of Eve's breast. Still not right. So hard to capture the complex shape, the muscles and fat and tendons, the way the right one rested on the rumpled sheets, the beautifully delineated curve running from her left armpit, the glorious blush of pink at the tip. He'd done her twenty, twenty-five times, and on each occasion he reached this stage where he was convinced he could no longer capture Eve's beauty. He had to work through it. He always had before. Now she was no longer a teenager, it was getting harder. The unlined, guileless, still-pubescent body has been simple. In her late twenties, she was becoming more complex, more interesting, more of a challenge. More beautiful. He could see it in the new lust in the eyes of his friends, even if not in Mr Chaplin's.

When he had taken Eve as a mistress at nineteen, his circle had just considered it the sad sign of an aging roué, and they treated her as a child. Now, though, they could see what Orpen had been feeding off all along, a luminescence, something ethereal that took your breath away. Now they were jealous. Some, he was sure, wondered how long before she grew bored of a fat, wheezy old man losing his teeth and hair, and moved on to someone else. Like themselves, perhaps.

'Bill.'

He looked up from the canvas, across the squalid clutter of the studio, over empty champagne cases, discarded palettes, abandoned portraits, to the bed where Eve reclined in all her glory.

'Bill.'

'Shush.'

'Bill, I am freezing.'

Orpen made a harrumphing sound. He had his overcoat on, and was sweating, but maybe she had a point. He'd put weight on these past three years, an extra layer of insulation. Perhaps too much. His small frame didn't suit it, and his once chiseled face was beginning to soften and sag around the edges. But there was one noticeable benefit of keeping the studio cool. 'As Orpsie always says – it makes y'nipples stand up.'

'It'll make them drop off unless you put some heating on.'

The phone made its ineffectual rattling sound at him and he

snatched it from the cradle. 'Hoi-hoi? Antoine. Yes. That '25 Margaux you got me. Got any more? What do you mean? I drank it. Don't be ridiculous. Lay it down, my arse. It's for drinking, man, not mollycoddling.' He watched Eve wrap the sheet around her. 'Just get me two more cases, quick as you like. As you were, love.'

'Not without a bit of warmth.'

Orpen considered this for a moment and finally yelled: 'Williams, *Williams.*'

The door opened a fraction and he could see the top of his chauffeur/valet's head. 'Williams. Put some heat on in here, will you, there's a good fellow? Oh, and bring me some more wine. Bit of cheese. You know the drill.'

The door closed again. Orpen heard the whoosh of the boiler and the gurgle of pipes. 'Happy? Come on then, be like a furnace in here before long and your tits'll go all droopy.'

Eve obligingly rearranged herself on the bed, and Orpen made some speedy adjustments to the line of her breasts on the canvas, rationalising that it was deliberation that was causing him to get it wrong. Go with the moment, the impression. Sure enough the fast lines began to capture her perfectly.

There was something slightly off, though. He had run out of the soft rosy red, the blush that Chenil in Chelsea did so well. Must get some more sent over, he thought. Stuff from Barbeux just not the same. He flopped off his stool and stood back to admire the likeness.

As if he had been waiting for the interval, like a patron late for a concert, Williams entered with a tray bearing bread, cheese, olives and red wine. He cleared a space on the paint-encrusted table and proceeded to ease the cork from the bottle, careful not to look at Eve. Orpen caught her playful smile as she spoke.

'I'd like a glass, Williams.'

'Yes, Miss. I brought two glasses.'

'I'll have it over here.'

Williams hesitated. He poured three big glugs into each goblet, glanced at the smirking Orpen, and crossed the minefield of a studio to the bed, keeping eye contact all the time. As he handed her the drink, Eve raised herself on one elbow and opened her legs slightly.

Williams couldn't help it, his eyes flicking down to the blond tangle of hair. He felt himself redden, and heard Orpen guffaw. As he left Orpen shouted: 'Careful, Williams, men have got lost in there,' then ducked as an empty paint can whistled by his ear.

Williams turned around and looked at the ruddy-faced painter. 'Don't worry, sir, I'm like Theseus. Always carry a ball of twine.' As he closed the door he heard an explosion of joy burst forth from his diminutive employer.

The following day Orpen was still wrapped in his dressing gown at midday, coughing and spluttering. Eve had donned a knee-length dress in *velours frappé*, the embossed velvet currently sprouting up across Paris shops, with simple black pointed-toe high heels. As always the face was scrubbed, devoid of any trace of powder or lipstick, and the only jewellery was a simple crucifix. While Williams stood mute in the corner she towered over Orpen, who seemed to be shrinking down into the winged armchair.

'Come on, Bill. I promised Sylvie. She wants to meet a racing driver.'

'Bloody stupid sport,' he rumbled. 'All that noise and smell. Eh, Williams?' He looked over for support. 'Oh, forgot. You like that kind of thing, don't you?'

'I shall take Sylvie myself,' said Eve petulantly.

'Off you go then. I'll finish you off from my imagination.

Should know what you look like naked by now I suppose.'

Eve thumped him on the arm and swept past Williams. Orpen looked balefully after her. 'You'd better go, Williams, or she'll try to drive the damn' Rolls. Then we'll all be in trouble.'

Thanks to Orpen's vacillation, they were a good forty minutes late for the premier race at the Montlhery circuit. The grandstands of the banked track were full, most of Paris having turned out to see the last race of Robert Benoist, former world champion, before he took up a post as sales manager for Ettore Bugatti.

Williams was forced to park the Rolls in a field some considerable distance from the entrance, and worried as he felt the wheels of the giant vehicle slip and slide on the mixture of grass and mud that was the legacy of a long, wet winter.

When he finally switched off the engine, happy they were on solid enough ground to give him traction when it was time to leave, Eve opened the door, peered down at the ground and sniffed.

'Williams. What is this?'

'What, Miss?'

'Where is the . . . car park? The Tarmacadam? The gravel. This is . . . this is mud.'

'And I have white shoes.' Sylvie was a willowy brunette with a high-pitched voice and a rather skittish, nervous manner. If she had been a horse Williams was certain she would have been a bolter.

Williams felt his boots squelch as he stepped down and looked at the flesh-coloured stockings the women were wearing. There was no doubt what contact with the field would do to them. He rolled up his sleeves and held out his arms.

'All right, then. Who would like to go first? Miss?'

★ ★ ★

Having seen the two women to the VIP box, Williams had his boots polished by one of the gnarled old men – a 'ruined face' from the war – touting for business around the car parks then took to the tunnel and walked through to the central grassed reserve of the track. Passing through the damp concrete tube he could feel the vibrations from the cars above, and as he emerged the raucous noise assaulted his ears. Now he could smell the fumes, the stink of benzol and the acrid stench of burnt rubber. Twenty cars were out there, Talbots, Alfas, Maseratis and Bugattis, hammering around the oval track, engaged in a mechanical dance, positions swapping with each lap, some passing on the straight, others taking the dangerous 'big lick' around the banking at each end.

Williams shook hands with a few of the other chauffeurs, turned and surveyed the track once more. Down here, the noise was intense, amplified by the giant horns of concrete created by the banking, boxing their ears as the cars screeched and growled their way around the track.

Williams could not make much sense of the race. He sought out and found Robert Benoist, the man who should be out front, but unless he was behind a couple of very fast back markers, he was trailing.

Williams borrowed a pair of binoculars and scanned the crowd. Eventually he found Eve and her friend Sylvie over by the finish line, in the cordoned-off area where champagne and canapés were getting more attention than what was happening out on the track. To the people in the VIP enclosure, motor racing was just another backdrop to the social calendar – it could be horses, shooting, opera, the scenes changing as if it were theatre. The two women were attracting a coterie of admirers, emboldened by the absence of Orpen who, he was under strict instructions not to reveal, was actually suffering from gout, rather than a hangover.

Williams spent a few seconds studying Eve, and switched back to the track and his struggling hero.

Robert Benoist was a great driver but clearly in decline. A former world champion, a World War One fighter ace at the age of twenty, a man with as many mistresses as cars – and he had a lot of cars – he was manfully struggling with his Delage. The company were about to withdraw from racing – like so many other small outfits, the economic situation was forcing them to retrench. So both man and machine were bowing out, but not as gracefully as they would have liked.

Williams removed his cap, pushed back his oiled hair and repositioned the binoculars. As he did so he thought he saw something. Benoist seemed to be on fire.

Robert Benoist was convinced he was on fire. Smoke was drifting up through the cockpit to his nostrils. At the moment it was rubber and canvas, but he could tell from the pains shooting across the soles of his feet that flesh would be next. He tried to lift them away from the glowing metal of the footwell, but the revs dropped alarmingly. He had always complained about the heat from the exhaust that ran along the outside close to his shoulder, but that was nothing compared to this. Someone had come up with the bright idea of lowering the driving position to enable the car to be more streamlined. Now he was virtually driving with his feet on the engine block. As he neared the pit entrance he yanked the wheel to enter.

As he skidded to a halt at his station, mechanics surged forward to begin refuelling and Robert leapt out and signalled to his brother. 'Maurice. Here. Now!'

Maurice was recounting his tales of Verdun, and the heroic story of how he got his limp, to the exquisite Annie Dubrey, and was slightly irritated by this interruption. Then he noticed that Robert's feet were smouldering.

Maurice held up his palm to Annie to show he would continue his heartbreaking exposition shortly and ran down, exaggerating his disability as he went. 'Your hat.' Maurice hesitated. Robert had a perfectly good white racing helmet on. Why should he want his prize felt trilby with the silk petersham band?

Robert snatched it from his head, ran to the water barrel and plunged it in. 'Robert. It's new, damn it,' whined Maurice.

Robert climbed back in and placed the limp hat over the accelerator pedal. 'I'll buy you ten, brother.' He roared away, savouring the temporary sense of cold bleeding through the ruined tread of his racing boots. All he had to do now was keep off the glowing brake pedal.

Williams watched Benoist wiggle out of the pits, lunging with the power full on, giving him a back end dangerously close to breaking away and spinning him. He felt a little prickle at the back of his neck. Maybe he's not such a slow old man after all. For twenty minutes he watched Benoist reel in the rest of the pack, until he swept past the leader in a big arc, right up the banking, his outside wheels threatening to grab nothing but air, before he swooped down and almost removed his opponent's radiator.

Williams looked up at the VIP enclosure, to where Sylvie and Eve were clearly leaving, not even waiting for Benoist to take the flag for the final time. Reluctantly he pulled himself away and headed for the car park.

As the chequered flag flashed by in a blur Robert Benoist felt himself deflate, his bones turn to rubber, and he had to fight to stop himself slumping over the wheel. Finished. Over. Getting out on a high note, that's what he liked. Or at least, that is what he had convinced himself.

He raised an arm in salute as sections of the crowd began to stand and applaud, more for the last decade, he knew, than any performance over the last hour or two. Robert pulled over into the pits, holding out his hands to try to keep the well-wishers back. A few camera bulbs detonated and he tried to remember to smile with his mouth closed – oil-specked dirty teeth looked so unattractive in the newspaper.

He took off his helmet and goggles and searched the faces for his brother. And there he was, behind one of the new hand-held cine cameras, his precious toy, making hand signals, as if he expected Robert to dance.

'Maurice, turn that damned thing off, come over here.'

Maurice limped to his side, the signal for others to press in, thrusting programmes for Robert to sign, photographs, scraps of paper.

'Sorry about your hat.'

Robert reached down and brought up a few crispy strands of felt, stiff like over-cooked bacon. He wondered how his feet had held up, but was frightened to look. They felt as if they had been flayed and then toasted.

'Ettore Bugatti has organised a welcome-to-the-firm dinner for you. But you may want to make your excuses.'

'Why would I want to do that?'

Maurice whispered in his ear. 'Your friend Françoise has come from Nantes. She wants to see you.'

Robert laughed. Maurice knew he would have to take his wife to any dinner, if only for appearance's sake. 'Where is she?'

'At the Hotel Plasse.'

Robert paused to sign a few more souvenirs, desperate for a drink and a bath. 'Can you get a message to her?'

'Of course.'

'Tell her to wait up for me. I am sure I shall need an early night after all this exertion.'

Before Maurice could answer a snapper barged his way through. 'Gentlemen, could I get a picture of both of you? For *Paris Life*? The retiring driver and his younger brother.'

'Older brother,' corrected Robert, poking Maurice in the ribs.

'Just a second,' said Maurice. Maurice arranged himself on the side of the car and there was a flash and detonation.

'Now, can I get out?' asked Robert.

Maurice moved out of the way and pushed the crowd back. Robert eased himself out of the cockpit and swung his legs out. As his feet hit the ground a powerful column of pain shot up his limbs, exploding in his cerebrum and expelling all consciousness as he slumped into his brother's arms.

Williams had to repeat the trick of carrying the two women over the muddy field although now they were full of champagne it was rather trickier, as both kept wriggling.

'Keep still. I might drop you, Miss,' he said to Eve, trying not to think about the lithe body – or the rustling silk chemise – under the velvet dress.

'And then Orpsie will sack you for sullying his little Evie. "Gee, honey," he will say, "did Willie boy hurt my little peach?"' She smiled and Williams wondered about letting her fall into the gloop anyway. The baby talk that Orpen affected was irritating at the best of times, but recently he had begun to sprinkle it with Americanisms. The constant stream of writers, journalists, negro dancers and jazz musicians appearing in Paris had made US slang the affectation of the year. There were rumoured to be fifty thousand Yanks in total, and they appeared to be in the habit of all turning up in the same place at the same time. The attraction was obvious – a devalued franc gave them twenty-five to a dollar, and the very idea of prohibition was anathema to the French.

Eventually both women were installed, more or less stain-free, in the rear of the car and Williams slammed the door on them. He started the engine, set the advance-retard, selected a higher gear than normal and eased the Rolls out of the muddy grooves it had settled into. Eve spoke in a loud voice, making sure it carried through to the driver's compartment.

'I'm sorry you didn't get a man, Sylvie.'

'Oh, don't worry, I'm going off them anyway. Present company excepted.'

They giggled and Williams glanced in the mirror to see if they were talking about him.

'Oh, never with the staff, darling,' insisted Eve, wrinkling her nose.

'Why ever not?'

'Because you never know where they have been.'

Williams had negotiated the worst of the mud and was easing on to the metalled section of the car park, now full of cars being cranked and pushed.

Eve continued in a yet louder voice. 'He turned up six months ago. No references to speak of. Couldn't use a knife and fork properly. Wasn't even a very good driver—'

Williams floored the big beast and the giant engine responded with astonishing liveliness. The Rolls leapt forward, and Williams began to swerve through the crowd streaming out of the stadium, fishtailing as the wheels flicked up a spray of sharp stones. Eve and Sylvie fell together in a heap in the back, squealing with a mixture of fear and delight.

Clear of the people, Williams began to fling the machine harder, and there was another loud exclamation as limbs tangled and dresses rode up, to reveal elasticated silk garters. Williams

29

glanced into the rear-view mirror as often as he dared. He managed to spin a one-eighty-degree turn and head for the exit when, from the corner of his eye, he saw the blur of blue bodywork and stamped on the brakes, rotating the wheel as hard as he could until the Rolls broadsided, two wheels lifting off the ground, leaving several tons of metal perched daintily on two tyres before it flopped back down and buried itself deep into the gravel.

The Citroën with the fold-back roof slowly pulled level. Williams recognised the driver, Maurice Benoist, and felt himself redden when he saw his brother in the passenger seat, two bandaged feet on the dashboard.

It was the latter who leaned across and wagged a finger at Williams. 'Who do you think you are? Robert Benoist?'

The two brothers pulled away in an insulting spray of muck, their laughter caught by the slipstream and thrown back into Williams' face.

Three

PARIS, APRIL 1928

Chauffeuring, Williams had decided soon after joining the Orpen household, wasn't so much about being able to drive as being able to wait. The evening had begun with him waiting for Orpen and Eve to get ready, waiting while they picked up Jessop, the young American writer who was on his way south and had been so for more than a year, then waiting on the Champs Elysées near Fouquet's while the trio had an early supper, then, swollen to a quartet by Raymond Berri, an industrialist who was after having his portrait painted by Orpen for his boardroom, waiting while they had taken in a show at the Bobino. Then they had completed the group by picking up yet another American, this one called George, from the Majestic.

Now Williams was killing time once more while they all drank Aquavit at Select among the crop-headed lesbians in their mannish *le smoking* suits who had struggled to keep their monocles in place as Eve swished by in her asymmetrical gold mesh dress with the deep v-neck line. Even Madame Select, as usual counting the cash in her fingerless gloves while her husband supervised the endless stream of welsh rarebits, had looked up from her arithmetic to see who was causing such a stir.

Orpen had imbibed prodigiously and from where he stood Williams could hear him on the terrace, seated as close as possible to the stove, buttonholing Barley, another young American sent abroad by his parents to gather a few rough edges. Orpen was doing his best to oblige.

'So I was there when they brought her in. Beautiful she was. Eighteen. French. The Belgians were convinced she was a spy. They tried her, sentenced her to death by firing squad.'

'And you saw her shot?' asked Barley, his jaw almost on the table.

Williams could see that several women had joined the party, including Sylvie and a rather imposing woman who towered over her.

'Had to. Official war artist. Orpsie saw some terrible things. Terrible. So she was asked if she had any last requests and the girl says, I would like to die in my mink coat. Okey-dokey, said the Belgian officer and it was delivered to her cell. Another round here. Yes, another set of drinks. So, come the morning, first light, she is led out to the execution wall, in her mink coat. Six Belgian soldiers stand there. The officer says, shoulder arms, take aim, all that, and just as they are about to fire she drops the mink coat off her shoulders.' There was a pause while Orpen knocked back a drink. 'And there she was totally bloody naked as the day she was born.'

'Gosh.'

'Gosh indeed. That's what we all said to ourselves. Gosh. Should've seen those Belgies' rifles shake. End of the barrel going up and down like they had St Vitus's dance.'

'What happened?' asked Barley.

'Happened? They shot her. She was a spy.'

Williams allowed himself a smirk. He had heard the story a dozen times, and knew it was pure fiction. Orpen had spun it round one of the first portraits of Eve he had executed of her in her late teens, when he caught her bare shouldered and innocent, with her curly blond hair falling on to that angelic skin. He had made the mistake of repeating the tale to someone at the War Office and a whole inquiry into the ungentlemanly conduct of the Belgians had been launched. Orpen was obliged to admit he created the whole story to up the value of the painting by a few thousand guineas.

Williams instinctively straightened his slouch as he saw the two-man police night patrol approach on cycles. These were the watchdogs of nocturnal Paris – Madame Select was famed for her readiness to summon them in the case of the slightest fracas – and were of a different order to most cops, seeming to consist mostly of rough, resentful Corsicans. Williams instinctively checked he had his identity card with him, but the pair cycled by, one of them even giving him a respectful nod, as if in workers' solidarity.

Ten minutes after the end of the execution story the party were out, with Orpen in the vanguard, weaving as he approached, hanging on to Eve's arm, his bulk forcing her to trace the same sinuous pattern on the pavement as him. 'OK, Williams, we have to squeeze eight in now. Including Hettie there.' He indicated the towering woman with the rice-powdered face at the rear of the group, a Lilly Dache cloche hat pulled down over her ears and a red squirrel fur coat. 'The tallest transvestite in Paris. Off to the Jockey Bar. Apricot cocktails. Then *dancings*. And Barley here wants to try Chez Hibou.'

The group all guffawed and young Barley managed a good-sport grin, even though all had clearly neglected to mention that Chez Hibou, on rue St Apolline, was a leading licensed brothel, one, if the rumours and the portrait above the mantelpiece were to be believed, which once had regular, if anonymous, royal patronage in the form of Edward VII.

One of the party, though, made his excuses. 'Thanks for the drinks and tall stories, Bill, but I gotta go.'

'George,' protested Orpen. 'Come on. Be fun.'

'I've got work to do.'

'Work. Call that bloody awful racket you write work?'

George laughed good naturedly and adjusted his glasses. 'Unless I do something I'll be just like every other American in Paris. A bum.'

'You can write as much of that jazzy stuff as you like, George. You'll always be a bum to me.'

George smiled, waved a hand and disappeared in search of a cab. Orpen looked at Williams. 'He thinks I'm joking. Have you heard his stuff? All right, off to Hibou.'

Williams sighed as he opened the door for Orpen. Heading for the discreet pink light of Chez Hibou meant more waiting, even though Orpen, Eve and the *travesti* would spend the time in the bar, paying for the naked girls to drink a harmless mixture of lemonade and grenadine while they sipped overpriced iced *mousseux* and tried to slip some into the *poules'* drinks whenever the eyes in the back of the fearsome Madame Hibou's head blinked.

Williams looked the fresh-faced American up and down as he climbed in beside Eve, and noticed the slight nervous tremor in his hands, the moist upper lip. A dizzying mixture of more alcohol, dancing with the *tapettes* and *dinges* at Bal des Chiffoniers, then on to choose from the flesh rack at a brothel. Boy was out of his depth. Eve caught Williams' eye and winked. Perhaps the wait wouldn't be too long at Chez Hibou after all.

34

Williams had grown used to Orpen's bouts of melancholy. Sometimes late into the evening when Eve was off with her own friends or visiting her father in Lille, Orpen would ring the bell and summon Williams with a bottle of Johnnie Walker or, if he was feeling homesick for Ireland, Jameson, and invite him to sit and chat in the living room in front of the fire.

Two nights after the Chez Hibou episode – when the Barley boy had finally figured out what was going on and fled, leaving the rest of them to go on to Bricktop's and hear the flame-haired negress sing Cole Porter songs – Orpen did just that.

He was in his cardigan, worn as usual over a waistcoat in place of a jacket, shirt with bow tie, spectacles on the end of his nose, swirling the drink in his glass, when he asked a startling question. 'How much d'you think I earned last year, Williams?'

Williams sipped at his own whiskey, eking it out. He was rarely offered a refill. 'I have no idea, Sir William.'

Orpen sniffed. 'Have a guess.'

'I really—'

'Have a guess, man, damn you.'

'Twenty thousand.'

Orpen smiled. 'Forty-six thousand, three hundred and ninety-four pounds.'

Williams raised a cautious eyebrow. 'Very good, sir.'

'Good? Bloody marvellous. And you know what?'

'No?'

'I'd give it all away if I could stop being a portrait painter. I hate bloody portraits. All little Orps gets to do is one pompous fool after another.' He paused and considered this for a moment. 'No, they are not all fools. Chamberlain I liked. Asquith, too. And Berri's not a fool. Except he wants to pose with a falcon. Told him he'll have to get his own. Get it stuffed. Not having a live falcon in here. Against the terms of the lease. No birds of prey in the house. Must say it somewhere.' He winked just to underline the jest.

He handed a piece of paper across. 'Look at this. Chaplin.'

Williams looked down at the drawing, a caricature of the Little Tramp, signed and dated. 'Man comes to my studio . . . *my* studio, greatest portrait painter in Europe, the world. Comes to my studio and does his *own* fucking portrait. Ha.'

Orpen drained his glass and refilled. 'Just three fingers, as the Yanks say. Forty-six thousand. I should be happy shouldn't I? But look, my wife hates me. Mrs St George never writes to Orpsie boy now.' This, Williams knew, was a former mistress, a long-standing affair that had soured some time ago. 'And I hardly see my children. Have you heard Kit play? Bloody good pianist she is. I'll get her to play for you when she comes over.'

Williams steeled himself for a long, slow ramble. Any minute now they were going to hit the how-life-should-have-been section, and this was open ended, a long improvisation on his woes. He snapped out of it, and even refreshed Williams' drink – just the one finger he noticed – and said jauntily, 'Forty-six thousand, eh? How about we go to Dieppe at the weekend and see if we can lose some of it?'

That night Eve lay in bed, listening to the tidal snoring of Orpen, a great nasal gush as air came into his tubes, a softer whistling as it ebbed. He had announced earlier in the evening that he would be heading off for London in a couple of months in time for his daughter Kit's series of concert recitals. There was no mention of Eve accompanying him.

Which is just as well, as she probably wouldn't have gone. The last time had been a disaster, as Orpen spent his time in male-only clubs and she searched in vain for some hint of levity in the grey, drizzly capital, so lifeless and buttoned-up after Paris.

When they did go out together, Orpen's fellow artists treated her as some kind of prize specimen, a lurid professional model and mistress like Kiki de Montparnasse, whose over-cooked memoirs they had all devoured.

It was hard to explain to outsiders why she was with this corpulent, somnambulant man. That ever since he captured her horrendous experiences at the hands of a German soldier at the age of fourteen on canvas, she had been smitten by his intuition, his generosity, the kindness, albeit attributes increasingly buried under hangovers and sore feet, but still alive and well at his core. Perhaps she'd buy a dog while he was away. Or two. She would love a dog, but Orpen hated canines, and would certainly order its destruction upon his return. No, not worth it.

To cap it all, Orpen was slipping away from her as a lover. Too tired, too fat he would complain. Eve could hardly remember the last time. She had to sit astride him now, because his tendency to flop, unannounced, his full weight on her could break a girl's ribs.

Her hand sought out between her legs, trying to conjure up some erotic image to initiate the proceedings, but none came. She heard the muffled slam of a door far downstairs, either Cook or Williams, and she felt a little electric spark. Not her type, but he'd do.

At that moment Orpen made an alarming barking sound and threw a stubby arm across her chest as he rolled over. She suddenly felt herself pinned and constricted, the limb as solid as a fallen tree trunk. She eased her hand away from her groin. Ah well, something else that will have to wait for another day.

Four

FRANCE, MAY 1928

Summer arrived quickly that year, turning Paris warm and golden. The casino at Dieppe was finally completed, and so the twice weekly exodus from Paris began in earnest, Williams motoring Orpen and Eve plus their companions of the week up to Rouen, where they sometimes took lunch at La Toque, partly because it tickled Orpen to be dining overlooking the very spot where the English burned Joan of Arc, and partly because he was slowly reeling in the flamboyantly moustachioed chef as a model for a portrait he wanted to execute.

Then it was an appearance, an entry, no less, in Dieppe, a long slow drive along the Esplanade, as if Orpen were royalty inspecting Dieppe's parade of grand mansions and apartments, then a few hours at Charlie's Bar, before the main business of the evening, a burst of intense gambling. Outside, as always, was Williams.

That day, the entourage consisted of Orpen and Eve with Raymond Berri, the chemist, Nick Jessop, the saturnine American writer, and his rather fey friend Patrick, a professional hanger-on from Philadelphia who had managed to pick up Louisa, one of the half-starved, but fully drunk artists who hung around the Dome hoping to hitch their wagon to a passing patron.

Jessop insisted that he was trying to pull himself away from the crowd that ricocheted from La Coupole to the Dome, Select, Falstaff's and back. He was complaining to whoever would listen that the scene was infected with a fatal lethargy. Except for those licking up what he called the 'literary vomit' at Gertrude Stein's famous gatherings. Rather than worship at the foot of a grim old lesbian in a circus tent, Jessop declaimed, he wanted to write and he needed discipline. He had been in Paris fifty-eight weeks, he protested, and had written only two dozen words. Williams wasn't sure that hooking up, as Jessop would have it, with Orpen was a passport to productivity.

Williams watched them slowly crank up the alcohol levels between Café Pirouette and Charlie's Bar, Orpen and Berri sticking to his habitual whisky and Eve to grenadine, the others moving through increasingly florid cocktails as they switchbacked from Sidecars to Cablegrams to Crystal Bronxes, Silk Ladies to Southsides, Picons to Ping-pongs.

Williams took a light dinner at the Bistro du Pollet – the monkfish livers followed by a sea bream fillet – with a handful of other drivers and sat out a sudden summer shower by indulging in a rare after-dinner brandy. By the time he emerged to stroll back to the car the rain had left the streets of the port shiny and streaming, the last heat of the day making the atmosphere delightfully Turkish bath-thick.

Williams took up his place at the car, lit a Salambo, cursing the useless French matches which were all spark and no flame, and read the latest issue of the *Light Car*, with its appreciation of Robert Benoist, starting with a smattering of war stories (including the time he was put on a charge for wearing a lavish foxfur

39

collar while strolling down the Champs Elysées in full Air Force uniform) and a critique of his driving skills. Sphinx-like the author called him, a man difficult to read until it was too late and he had struck, leaving his opponent breathing in his benzol. A man who, the article concluded, was, above all, loathe to walk away from any challenge. Williams lit another cigarette, his last.

He looked up as he heard a familiar clack of heels on the steps of the casino, heading down from the vast baroque doorway of the wedding-cake building towards him. Eve, hips swaggering, suggesting she'd moved from grenadine to something more potent.

She crossed the street, stretched out her arms and did a little twirl on her gold-barred kid shoes, the scalloped hemline of her skirt lifting as she did so.

'It's so stuffy in there,' she said by way of both greeting and exclamation. He could smell aniseed on her breath, which made it warm and intoxicating.

'I would imagine, Miss.'

'Have you never been in?'

'Casinos, yes. Dieppe casino, no.'

She grabbed his arm. 'Well, come on.'

Williams looked down at his uniform, the summer lightweight wool one, and shook his head. 'Hardly dressed for it, Miss.'

Eve nodded and stepped away. 'Oops. I was forgetting your position.' She let the last word slur. 'May I have a cigarette?'

'It's my last I am afraid, Miss.'

'We'll share.' She took the cigarette from his lips, inhaled deeply, tipped her head back and blew a long stream of smoke up towards where the gulls whirled in the dusk sky.

'How is it inside, Miss?'

'Oh, everybody has eyes for Babette.'

'And how is Babette dressed?'

She smiled. 'Mostly as Vander Clyde.'

For the past few years Babette, with her high wire and trapeze act at the Cirque Nedrano on Boulevard de Rouchechouart, was the only serious rival for Josephine Baker's crown as darling expat American of Paris. Under the blond wig, however, Babette just happened to be a Texan male called Vander Clyde, which he demonstrated by tearing off his hair at the climax of each performance.

'Tell me, Williams, what's a man like you doing here?'

He smiled and sidestepped the question. 'What's a man like me?'

'Ah, that's another question. What is a man like Williams? English but excellent French. None of that ugly, grating accent.'

'French mother,' he explained.

'Good driver, despite what Mr Benoist says.'

He nodded, not sure whether it was a compliment.

'Handsome in a kind of . . . English way.'

'What way is that?'

'Oh, more direct and conventional than the French I think.'

'And?'

'And you are young. You should be ruining your health with absinthe and ogling the dancing girls at Le Palermo. Yet for the last six months you have spent your days and nights waiting on Orpsie's whims. What is your secret, Mr Williams? And don't tell me you haven't got one.'

'Eve.'

The familiar rasping bellow, now slurred and rounded by whisky, carried across the street and bounced around them. 'Get in here. Don't worry about Williams.'

She turned and raised a hand to Orpen, who ducked unsteadily back in. She handed Williams the remains of the cigarette. 'Sorry. Seem to have done more than my fair share.' Eve smiled and turned around, affording him a good look at the oscillation of her hips accentuated by the low sash on the dress.

Three hours later, and Orpen was facing a chilling sobriety as fifty thousand francs crossed the roulette table to the croupier in half as many minutes. Eve tried to coax him away, but he grew more irascible with each spin of the wheel.

Berri was playing *chemin de fer*, and Jessop, Patrick and Louisa, the skin-and-bone Bohemian, had spun off into an argument about Dostoevsky and James Joyce, which was way over Eve's head and, she suspected, theirs as well. She could feel the slow drip of alcohol into her system over the last twelve hours souring her liver and the pall of smoke that rolled around the gilt fittings was beginning to sting her eyes. The atmosphere reeked of sweat and desperation. The night was slowly turning rancid. She had to go. Eve hovered over Berri as he won a couple of hands, then bust on the third and solicited his help.

'Ray, I'm tired and Orps is on one of his losing streaks. We should leave.'

Berri smiled. He knew they were in for a long night, no matter what Eve said. 'I'd get a room if I were you. He'll stay till he's winning again or broke. And broke'd take quite some time.'

Eve pouted at what she took to be a refusal to assist and stalked through the thin smattering of punters to the roulette table where Orpen was cursing the croupier under his breath. 'Y'slippery bastard. I know the owner y'know.' Then louder: 'OK, on the black this time, my friend.'

'Orpsie, come on. Enough.'

He swung his diminutive frame around and snarled. 'Enough? You mean this man here has enough of my money? Only just started, Evie.'

She tried to keep the petulance out of her voice but failed. 'I want to go home.'

'Go home then. Take Williams. I'll get back one way or another or take a room and he can come and get me tomorrow. Come on, come on, spin the damn' thing.'

As the ball clattered into the blurring wheel, Eve turned and walked off, glancing over her shoulder to see if Orpen acknowledged her departure. She was vaguely aware of Jessop rising as she brushed past his table at the perimeter of the gaming area. 'Eve.' She carried on walking.

Outside she sucked in the warm air, still deliciously damp with the last of the evaporated rain and skipped down the steps towards the Rolls. She could see Williams in the front, hat pulled down over his eyes and she let out a shrill whistle using two fingers that almost woke the entire town. Williams calmly pushed up the peak of his cap and pulled at his uniform to correct himself.

'Eve.' She felt the hot brandy-laden breath of Jessop on her neck. 'You're not leaving are you?'

'I'm tired, Mr Jessop—'

'Nick. It's Nick.'

'Don't worry, Orpsie won't leave you high and dry. He never does.'

'No. I wanted a chance to talk to you. Patrick and I are pushing off for Spain in a few days . . .'

She hesitated, trying to decode what this meant. 'It's an interesting country I hear.'

'Patrick has a commission to write a piece for *American Mercury* . . .'

'What about Louisa?'

Jessop hesitated. 'What about her?'

'I thought she was rather sweet. Shame to leave her.'

'She's bisexual,' he said dismissively.

'Are they mutually exclusive then?'

'I guess not,' he laughed at himself. 'Rats. I'm not going very well here, am I?'

She laughed at his hitherto unheard admission of fallibility and walked towards the Rolls as Williams slipped out to open the door for her. 'Nick, I would love to sit and talk, but I am very, very tired.'

Jessop's voice quavered as he said: 'Let's go to bed then.'

Eve didn't stop or break stride at this proposition, just made a slight huffing sound, a hiss of displeasure. She stepped into the car and Williams slammed the door. Jessop tapped on the glass and she cracked open the window a few centimetres as the car moved off.

'I can pay you know.'

It only needed a minuscule flick of the wheel and Williams managed to take the full weight of the Rolls over Jessop's foot as he pulled away, crushing several toes. Eve spun round as he shrieked and watched him hopping on one leg, his eyes screwed up in pain, bellowing that he would 'fix that man's clock'.

'Good God, Williams. Will he be all right?'

'Eventually, Miss. A few days. One shouldn't get too close to machinery. It can be dangerous.'

Eve looked back again as Jessop hobbled for the casino steps and began to laugh. 'The poor man.' She could feel the staleness of the casino clinging to her and sniffed at her arm. She shuffled her dress up to her hips and pulled it over her head with a grunt, aware of the driver's eyes flicking into the mirror. 'Williams,' she said firmly, 'I need a swim.'

Eve directed them west, towards St Valery, and down a narrow lane that snaked along the small valley that bisected the coastal cliffs. There was something of a moon, but not enough to aid navigation of a big car along a tiny track, and Williams was grateful for the large saucer-like headlamps of the Rolls. Eventually the track gave out to a small cove, where several boats lay beached and neglected on the crescent of sand.

Williams bumped the big car down the launch ramp on to the soft, gritty surface, hoping it was solid enough to support the weight. Sensing his tentativeness, Eve said, 'It's quite safe, Williams. I've done this before. Take it to the water's edge.'

'Yes, Miss.'

Williams did as he was told and stopped within ten yards of the sea, not wanting to risk the treacherous shoreline where the retreating water had so recently been lapping. He turned off the engine and for a few seconds listened to the faintest of ticks as it cooled down.

'Lights, Williams.'

'I'm sorry?'

'Put on the headlamps, please.'

'I'll have to start the car again to get the dynamo going. Otherwise we risk flattening the electro-chemical cells.'

'Whatever you need to do.'

Williams re-fired the engine, which turned over with the merest mechanical fuss, and stepped out to open the rear door. Eve came naked, her skin ghostly pale in the thin moonlight, already goosebumping. 'Won't it be cold, Miss?' he managed to ask.

'I expect. Get the whisky ready, will you?' With that she ran in, squealing as the water rose above her knees, then arcing into the frothy waves, disappearing for a second, gasping as she surfaced, air exploding from her lungs.

She struck out a few yards from the shore, framed in the yellowy orbs of the lights as if this were some extravagant Folies

Bergère number. 'It's . . .' Her teeth chattered and she had to clench them before she could speak again. 'It's not too bad, once you get used to it.'

She began to propel herself up and down within the illuminated patch of sea, first a crawl, then breaststroke and finally she turned on her back.

Williams positioned himself at the front of the car, rug in one hand, Orpen's emergency hip flask from the glove compartment in the other.

'Come in,' she shouted, her voice drifting away into the surf.

'I can't swim, Miss.'

Eve laughed, a full-throated sound that made his skin prickle with embarrassment, rolled on to her front and produced several long, powerful strokes, which torpedoed her way out of the yellow ellipse of the Rolls' lights. For a few moments he could hear the sound of her limbs breaking the waves and then nothing, just the soft burble of the car engine and the hiss of the ebbing waves.

Williams waited a decent interval before his first tenuous shout. 'Miss?'

His voice sounded tiny and ineffectual against the sea, as insignificant an event as throwing a pebble into the waters.

'Miss?' Louder, harder, trying to keep the panic from his voice. He thought about removing his boots. Should he wade in?

'Eve?'

There was a rope in the boot of the car. He could use that if she was out there with cramp. But first he should use the headlamps to scan the water's surface surely.

'Yvonne.'

That was it, Williams decided, he'd search by the lights of the Rolls and then summon help. He turned to step into the car and felt the slap of her wet skin against him.

'Nobody calls me Yvonne any longer.'

She pushed against his uniform, trying to catch some of his body warmth. He could feel her shaking, a deep, muscular contraction as her body sought to generate enough heat to push up her plunging core temperature. Williams flung the rug around her and began to rub as vigorously as he could. 'Whisky?' she asked with castanet teeth.

'Not yet. Too dangerous. What the hell did you think you were doing?'

'Having fun. Hold me.'

He grasped her to him but continued massaging her back.

'This'll ruin my reputation,' she said.

'And my uniform.'

As warmth and sensation returned she pulled away from him, looking up into his eyes. 'What are you thinking?'

'That the car will overheat soon. We must leave.'

'Ah. The ever-practical Williams. Yes, of course we must go.' But she made no movement. Williams lifted the wet hair plastered across her face, pushed it to one side and they kissed, a soft, unhurried, gentle touch of the mouths, a preliminary skirmish. He pushed his hips back, just in case she could feel the effect she was having.

'Are you hungry?' he whispered.

'Starved.'

'I'll cook you something.'

Sir William Orpen whooped as the tiny ball landed on the number twelve and his losses toppled, at last, over into winnings. For the first time in hours he looked at his watch and realised dawn wasn't too far away. Berri and the others had retreated to the bar, running on his account, no doubt, but what the hell. It wasn't the money that mattered here, it was walking away with

47

your head held high. He just wished Eve had a little more stamina for the long run, that was all. He was meant to be the ancient one, after all.

He tipped the croupier and headed for the bar for one last whisky before gathering up his waif and strays. He was sure they would find a driver somewhere, even at this hour.

When he got there the two Americans were face down on the table, asleep, and Berri and the girl deep in discussion with a chap he had never seen before.

Orpen slammed the chips down on the table. 'Fifteen thousand ahead, Ray. We should settle up and go. One more drink.' He signalled to the barman for his usual Johnnie Walker and waited for the introductions.

Berri said; 'Sir William Orpen, Josef Halken. In the same business as me. Degesch. Chemicals. Makes paints and dyes. Hamburg, isn't it?'

Halken nodded.

'How's business?' asked Orpen more out of politeness than anything else. His animosity towards the German people, stoked by his experiences at the front, had faded in the last decade, but was not extinguished entirely.

'Good, now. We have had a few bad years, as you know. Shameful. And dangerous. But since this new dye process—'

'Excellent,' said Orpen, heading the man off before he gave them a lecture on the finer points of the synthetics industry. 'Ray, see if you can summon up a car and driver. Eve's taken the bloody chauffeur.' Orpen scooped up his chips, ready to head for the cashier. 'Can't wait to see her face.'

Williams brushed the hair from Eve's face yet again, a face flushed from exertion and pleasure and she rolled off him on to the thin strip of bed left to her. 'God,' was all she said.

The first rays of warming sunlight were creeping through the shutters of the room, and Williams listened as a motor car chuffed along the lane outside, followed by the clop of a horse-drawn carriage. Versailles was waking.

Eve slid off the bed and paced, shaking her limbs, stretching, unabashed as he leant up on one elbow to watch her. It was nothing he hadn't seen before, but now it had changed. It was as if all those times in the studio he had kept his feelings, his thoughts and desires shut behind lock gates, barriers that had tumbled some time during the last few hours. Now he could finally acknowledge a connection, that, as the little voice in his head had wished for all these months, she was finally in his bed.

Eve put another *boulet* into the small stove, having kept the place heated all night after her chilling experience in the sea, even though it meant they sweated as if they were in the tropics during the lovemaking and looked around properly for the first time.

The room was simple, a square semi-basement with high windows, a bed, a dresser and a wind-up gramophone with Sidney Bechet on the turntable. She stopped at the little display of his worldly goods on the dresser. Lined up in a row, a small clockwork race car, two silver hairbrushes, a photograph of Williams on a car bonnet, some hair oil, a man's grooming kit and a silver trophy of a winged nude. Two neat stacks of thrillers – Agatha Christie, Marjory Allingham, Leslie Charteris – bookended the collection. After a moment's hesitation Eve picked up the photo.

Williams was perched on the bonnet, one leg on the floor, and around him, holding up a flag as a backdrop, were four badly dressed young men, smiling gap-toothed at the camera. With a shock she realised one of them was cradling a tommy gun.

'What on earth is this?'

'I was young,' Williams said with a yawn.

She looked at the face in the picture and back at Williams. 'Not that young. What were you playing at?'

'I was playing at being Irish,' he said eventually.

The flag was a tricolour. She finally pieced it together. 'A getaway driver?' She laughed. 'How romantic.'

Williams looked across at her standing there, naked, her stomach an erotic protuberance pressing against his furniture. Yes, that was what he had fallen for. The idea of the IRA as a noble cause, a group of Robin Hoods striking the occupiers and speeding away in stolen cars. Then the reality had sunk in. 'Only from the outside.'

'Is this your secret, Mr Williams?' She picked up the trophy. 'Or this? Number one, La Baule, Brittany?'

'A sand race. Borrowed car.'

'So. On the one hand, maybe a man on the run from Irish gangsters. Or the British? Huh? Orpen gives you shelter and a job while you . . . what's the term . . . ?'

'Lie low?'

'Aha. Yes.' She pointed to the pile of books. 'Just like your Agatha Christie. I have the solution. Or maybe . . .' She held up the trophy. 'Maybe you just want to drive. Anything you can get. Be Mr Robert Benoist.'

He snorted. 'Do you know how much a Bugatti costs?'

'So . . .' She put down the photograph and trophy. 'Let's see what else we have.'

Before he could stop her she slid open the drawer and saw the pair of stiff-backed blue passports. She picked them up and opened each in turn, her jaw slack with wonder. 'Mr Grover. And Mr Williams. Which is it?'

'Grover-Williams,' he said, 'Siamese twins. But we were separated at birth.'

She threw a passport at him and he caught it. The Grover one.

50

His given name. The one who shrugged off a stiflingly boring family and went in search of his wild, free-spirited Irish relations and found more than he bargained for. The Grover who had ended up with another man's life in his inside pocket, a letter that meant a bullet in the neck and a body thrown outside the police barracks at midnight. So after meeting Slade that morning Grover had gone back to his room and burnt the missive, unopened, and the reckless young man with a lot of growing up to do had skipped the country.

'I give up,' laughed Eve. 'You are even more of a mystery than when I started. Come on, tell me the answer.'

He put his arms behind his head and smiled, considering how much to tell her. Then a door slam reverberated through the whole house, and they both heard the fall of heavy, tired footsteps on stair treads. Coming down.

'Shit.' Eve dived under the covers just as the door burst open, and Williams managed to arrange himself so that the shapeless form crammed at the bottom of the bed looked like an extension of his own body. If he was eight feet tall. And multi-limbed. He just hoped his employer was too bleary eyed to notice.

'Williams. Ah, you're awake. Good. Did it. Got the money back. And more. Where's Evie?'

Williams couldn't answer. Eve was starting to nuzzle him under the covers, and he knew every word would come out two octaves higher than it should. He shrugged.

'She'll turn up. I'm off to bed. You can take the day off.'

As he turned Orpen heard the squeak from under the covers. He took three paces back into the room and pulled the blankets away in a great flowing crescent, revealing the curled-up Eve, eyes tight shut, as if because she couldn't see Orpen, he would be unable to see her.

Five

FRANCE, JULY 1928–JANUARY 1929

Williams sat outside the Floreal café on the corner of Boulevard Bonne Nouvelle, watching the weekend's entertainers arrive as he sipped at a chicory-laced coffee and smoked his last Celtique under the watchful glare of the smoker on the giant hoarding opposite, whose six-foot-long cigarette puffed out a thin stream of smoke advertising the very brand he had between his lips. At night the face glowed a blue-ish neon, bright enough to illuminate the four corners of Williams' tiny – or compact, as the concierge had it – room.

The first of the evening street bands was warming up on the wide pavement, a *baratineur* selling hats was practising his patter, half singing the praises of his cheap Princess Eugenie-style headwear that was currently going out of fashion all over central Paris. Here, though, in the second arrondissement, an area of honest artisans, dentists and furriers and dishonest vice, there might still be a market.

A light breeze occasionally carried the biting ammoniacal smell from the local *vespasienne*, a particularly ornate example of the type, spiral like a snail's shell, which was prone to blockage and overflowing and was, in the small hours, the venue for brief and sordid sexual acts by the lowest of the street girls.

Near by a gypsy guitarist picked a mournful refrain, some paean to his dead horse no doubt, that did little to lift Williams' mood. He dug out his last few sou and tossed them over to the guitarist and asked for some hot jazz. The man smiled, revealing teeth like piss-stained stalagtites and upped the tempo to sluggish. Now it sound like a paean to a dead horse who quite liked Django.

Seeing the transaction, one of the burly flame swallowers headed over, but Williams raised a hand to indicate he wanted no private show. A street band finally started up, playing 'Madame la Marquise'. The guitarist redoubled his efforts against the vulgar brassiness from across the boulevard.

It had been an eventful few weeks since Orpen's discovery of Eve's perfidy, as he denounced it. Williams had, of course, packed and left, which put him at something of a disadvantage. Drivers normally moved with cars – a chauffeur went to whoever bought the vehicle. But now he and the Rolls had been split asunder he really did feel like a recently parted Siamese twin, as if a large section of him was missing. He could still feel the wheel, the clutch, the advance-retard, but they were phantom sensations, coming to taunt him.

He had taken a few stand-in jobs, sitting in one of the *restaurants des chauffeurs* around rue des Favourites in the fifteenth, where news of vacancies, or whichever driver on the circuit was taking a holiday or ill, rapidly circulated over the huge plates of *bouef gros sel*, with mounds of leeks and carrots, the traditional driver's fuel.

He knew the positions would dry up come August, when Paris, and the restaurants, closed and the chauffeured classes moved south or north to the coast. There were other options. He could rejoin his father in the long-distance driving business – if he'd have him after that jaunt in Ireland – or he could get a regular non-driving job. Or he could go and see Constantini or Benoist and tell them that he was the man to move Bugatti and its race cars forward.

The latter fantasy make him smile and he took up a newspaper discarded on the wicker chair next to him and scanned it for a jobs section, but couldn't find one. He looked at the front cover. Gringoire. Some right wing diatribe was spread across the front, lamenting the paralysis, both intellectual and industrial, that gripped the country at the moment. The *années folies* were over, it claimed: France was about to pick up the tab for its decadence and plunge into turmoil.

Williams threw the rag back on to the seat and picked up the new detective paperback he had bought at the bookstore on rue de l'Odeon, opposite the one run by the strange American woman who published unreadable novels. Georges Simenon might be a Belgique, but he knew Paris well – in fact Orpen and the author had dined together at Maisonette Russe and the Château Madrid, the upper end of the social milieu. But in the novel the Belgian had captured the other, grittier end of Paris, not that of slumming, allowance-fed Americans in St Germain, but the cafés along the Canal St Martin, the slaughterhouses at La Villette, the market traders at Les Halles, the marshalling yards beyond the Batignolles and the ateliers of rue St Charles, the seedy nightlife of Pigalle, where the whores flap at tourists like crows, and the *truants* of rue de Lappe – those who, for whatever reason, would prefer not to see the inside of Police Judicaire.

Williams had just immersed himself in the tale of a country girl come to a sticky end when he heard the soft tattoo of elegant heels – glued, not nailed, as was the new style – crossing the paved street. Eve, dressed in a simple navy blue suit and carrying a large valise, which she placed on the floor. She signalled for a coffee as if this were a pre-arranged meeting and smiled broadly at him.

'How did . . . ?'

'Joe the Bum.'

'Ah.' The waiter at the Falstaff, a man with a Brooklyn accent so thick it came out like soup, had long acted as a letter drop for his regulars. 'Then the concierge at that horrible building you inhabit.'

He laughed. 'I can see the Rex and the Baths of Neptune from my balcony.'

'And the whores,' she said sniffily.

It was true. There were some *hotels de passe* – the far end of the sexual scale from the brothels that Orpen sometimes frequented – on the rue de la Lune, just up the steps at his side, where the amiable but low-fee prostitutes bantered with prospective clients and each other.

The waiter delivered her coffee and Eve said, 'And two Aquavits.' She nodded at the discarded paper beside him. 'Looking for a position?'

'Yes. Driver wanted. Must fuck employer's mistress behind his back.'

She laughed. 'Feeling guilty?'

'Aren't you?'

'No, I did it with the entire staff. Every week.' It took a moment before he realised she was joking. 'I particularly like gardeners. All those calluses.' She shuddered with mock pleasure.

'It still felt like betrayal.'

Eve nodded but didn't say anything for a moment. It had happened because it had happened. She felt the hand of inevitability in it. Just as all Orpen's other mistresses had had a natural lifespan, so her tenure had all but run its course.

'Betrayal? We all betray each other.'

Williams leaned forward and whispered: 'If you were mine I'd never betray you.'

Eve tried hard to stop giggling at his seriousness. 'Ha. Am I hearing some happy-ever-after fantasies here?'

He reached over and picked a strand of hair from her face. 'How could I hurt a beautiful woman like you?'

Eve hurled back her Aquavit and pursued her lips. 'Show me a beautiful woman and I'll show you a man who's tired of fucking her.'

Williams let out a roar of laugher, causing the guitarist to falter. 'So why did you do it? Was it me, or could it have been anyone?'

'How can you ask?' she said indignantly. 'I could have done it with Mr Jessop and been paid into the bargain.'

'Because I'm insecure.'

She looked into his eyes and saw it was true. He was like a sixteen year old, nervous, indecisive, daring himself to believe what was happening. She realised she hadn't told him why she had sought him out.

'Orpen is going back to London. Not permanently, but to renew ties with his family and no doubt Mrs St George.' Adding, in case Williams didn't know, 'One of my predecessors.'

'I'm sorry.'

'Don't be. It was amicable.'

'Even after . . .'

She grinned. 'I suspect you didn't get your sense of morality from your French mother. Orpen only raged for a day or two. You would have been forgiven. But you wouldn't wait. Too English by half.'

Williams had mostly been raised in France, but there were still prayers for the home country and God Save The King at the dinner table. Although only a boy when Edward VII died, he still remembered the black-draped portrait and the household that spoke in whispers for weeks and weeks until he was certain they were losing the power of speech and every now and then he would cycle down the road so he could shout at the top of his lungs. After sipping his drink for a while he said: 'I didn't want to be forgiven. I couldn't have gone back to how it was. Not me servant, you mistress. There are times when it is best to move on.'

The guitarist came over, his hand outstretched, but Williams shooed him away, his pockets empty. The gypsy went back to his more plaintive pluckings.

'Bill said,' she lowered her voice into a gruff whisky-soaked Orpen impersonation, 'I expect you are going to live in some cold garrett with that damn' chauffeur and starve.'

Williams smirked at the accuracy. In a way he missed the old soak. 'And are you?'

'Not quite.' She reached down to the valise, unzipped it, and brought out a wad of large denomination notes with a gummed band around it and threw it at Williams. He caught it just before it hit his chest, but he missed the second and the third and the fourth. He tried to catch his Aquavit, but it fell, rolled over and smashed on to the pavement.

'Not quite,' she repeated, standing and upending the valise on the tables, scores of packets, millions of francs cascading over the table, laughing at the way Williams' eyes bulged in his sockets.

Aware of a mournful gaze a few yards down the street, Eve picked up a thin bundle and tossed it to the guitarist who deftly plucked it from the air and burst into rapid fire chords of explosive joy.

'Dinner at Maxim's?' she asked.

'On you?'

'On us.' She leaned across the mound of cash and kissed him.

57

★ ★ ★

Eve could not sleep. The supposedly furtive noises she heard from outside were as loud as claps of thunder, the detonation of guns, the fireworks on Bastille Day. The men outside had promised to be as silent as ghosts, but they were the clumsiest spirits she had ever encountered. Still Williams slept on. Since the day on the Boulevard Bonne Nouvelle, several months ago now, Eve had pulled together several strands of her life plan. She had bought a converted watermill on the River Vie in the Pays d'Auge, Normandy, complete with ·kennels for her Scottish terriers, an apartment in Paris and enough money in the bank to see them through for the foreseeable future.

But Williams, she hadn't forgotten Williams in her master plan. He deserved something from all the money that came her way after the split with Orpen, a split she now began to suspect Orpen had somehow engineered. He had certainly picked up a new mistress with indecent, and suspicious, haste. And had showered embarrassing riches on Eve with a guilty fervour, as if it was him that had been found in bed with the chauffeur.

Williams had worked hard. He had fixed the place up, pruned the neglected apple trees in the orchard with the intention of making his own cider and calvados one day, built the kennels, helped choose the dogs – they settled on specialising in black Scottish terriers and white West Highland terriers – with an enthusiasm that surprised her, and ingratiated himself with the local village cafés and bars – scrupulously rotating his custom – and the *marie*, important conquests for newcomers to any rural area. Especially unmarried ones.

Winter's thin dawn chorus had come and gone by the time Williams opened his eyes and rolled over, a sleepy smile on his face. Light headed and exhausted from her long vigil, she kissed him on the cheek, enjoying the rough feel of stubble. 'Happy birthday, darling.' Williams kissed her back. 'I know I should get the breakfast, but would you mind getting the coffee?'

Williams got up, stretched, and wrapped a robe round himself. He threw open the window and looked over the valley floor, to the pastures and orchards of the fertile land, glistening with winter frost, and wondered why the view didn't make his heart sing quite as much as it should. Possibly the thought of the long months to spring, till the scene blossomed and plumped with fresh greenery. But no, he had to admit even now it had an austere, diamond-hard beauty.

Maybe it was another birthday. Thirty was coming over the horizon fast. By which time he wanted to have made his mark at something other than having a rich lover, no matter how beautiful. Maybe Eve had been partly right. Not that he'd grown tired of fucking her, but somehow it wasn't enough, there were still missing pieces to the jigsaw puzzle.

Williams went downstairs, selected two large bowls and placed a sugar cube in the bottom of each. He poured in the thick black coffee and then crushed the cube with a spoon. That would be enough for Eve, but he hadn't quite shaken off the very English need for milk in the morning. He tried the wire-fronted larder, but there was none. Two of the porcelain containers, but empty. Which meant going outside to the cool shed across the courtyard.

Eve paced out his actions in her mind, timing him. Put on coffee, get bowl, fetch sugar, pour coffee, crush cube, discover no milk, go outside, take two paces and . . .

Williams' whoop must have been heard in Caen, a window-rattling scream that conveyed disbelief and delirium all in one rush of air from his lungs. She heard him run back, halt, retrace his steps and then a sound like tearing calico, sweeping to a deeper throb as the engine revved.

Leaving it ticking over, Williams sprinted up the stairs and threw himself across the room into her arms and smothered her with kisses.

'Is it the right one?' she asked disingenuously, as if talking about a hat or a shirt.

'A Thirty-five B? Absolutely gorgeous.' He looked very serious. 'There is only one thing.'

'What?'

He listened to that rasping engine note as if something mechanical was bothering him.

'What?'

He stepped closer. 'The colour. Blue. Bugatti Blue. It'll have to be British Racing Green.' He puffed out his chest with mock pomposity. 'I am, after all, an Englishman.'

Eve reached up and grabbed him and outside the beautiful sleek Bugatti racing car chugged on, alone and neglected, for another twenty minutes until the new owner came down to take it for a spin.

Six

Trials Day, Monaco, April 1929

Robert Benoist sat on the terrace of the Café de Paris and watched the cars come round the Casino Square as they powered through the gap between the casino itself and the Hotel de Paris, checking the braking and handling of each one, paying particular attention to the Bugattis. Trial day, the first time most of the cars had run this new street-racing circuit. Already it was taking its toll – Benoist had seen two cars limping round, their mechanicals or engines unsettled by such a low-revving, convoluted and bumpy course.

Benoist wasn't convinced by this circuit. He liked big sweeping autodromes, like Montlhery and Avus in Germany, where the driver could go flat out. Here, he doubted if any of them could get into top gear, and rattling over cobblestones and tram lines put extreme stress on tyres and chassis. He as much as anyone would concede that Ettore Bugatti was a genius, but mechanical reliability was not his strongest suit when it came to race models. He knew there were other dissenters, too – the *Autocar* magazine had editorialised that such a Grand Prix was 'astonishing' and 'dangerous'.

Behind him his brother Maurice scanned the crowd, the faces at the hotel windows, those on the makeshift grandstand across the way and played his own running commentary.

'Josephine Mannion. You know all about her. I think that is her sister with her. Very different proposition. They say you need a car jack to get her legs apart. Ah, look, Kiki with some ugly artists. I hear Mistinguett is coming tomorrow. See, Noghes has got a few famous faces down here.' Antony Noghes was the cigarette tycoon who had bankrolled this attempt to start the Monte Carlo season early by running what he hoped would become the most fashionable motor race in the world. Maurice lowered the glasses. 'And shouldn't you be in the pits?'

'Ettore banished me. Says I intimidate the drivers.' Maurice laughed. He could just imagine his brother, eyes so piercing you felt as if he could see into your soul, making the young blades feel uneasy, as if they weren't up to the job of filling his shoes. Which, as far as Robert was concerned, they weren't.

A light drizzle had started and Robert watched the big seven-litre Mercedes of Rudi Caracciola roar into the square, pass the Hotel de Paris and slide into the bend, with Rudi having to steer it like a boat. Robert wondered how Rudi was coping with the Station hairpin and the demanding Gasworks bend.

As if to show how it should be done, a Bugatti came into view, power as full on as the driver dared in a fresh fall of rain on cobbles, and nimbly took the bend, straightening and flooring the pedal up the Avenue des Spellugues towards the downhill zig-zag to Monte Carlo station. Perfect. But something wasn't quite right with number 12. Then it struck him. It had been green. Not blue. It was a green Bugatti 35B. How could Ettore allow this?

Robert looked at Maurice. 'Who is that?' But it was gone. 'Number twelve.'

Maurice consulted his *liste de engages*. 'Williams. Englishman.'

'Do we know him?'

'Some talentless peasant.'

Robert brooded until, three minutes later, Williams came by again and he watched the same mix of looseness and precision guide the car through the bends. 'Peasant maybe . . .' he mused.

'Look. Over there. In navy blue.' Maurice's attention, as usual, was elsewhere.

Robert picked up his binoculars and scanned the sparse crowd on the opposite side of the square. 'Where?'

'At the top. Blonde.'

Robert focused on a mass of curly hair framing a face made even more beautiful by its lack of makeup. 'That's his woman.'

'Whose?'

'Williams,' said Maurice in triumph.

'And what do we know about her?'

'Sucks like a nanny goat.'

Robert lowered his binoculars and gave Maurice one of his powerful stares. 'Meaning you have tried and got nowhere?'

Maurice grinned. 'Something like that.' In fact, nothing like that. He'd introduced himself and been greeted with a I've-just-stepped-in-a-dog-turd expression from the woman.

Robert raised the glasses again, but she had gone, off to find another vantage point. Robert watched the Alfas, Maseratis and Bugattis come round one more time, followed by Rudi's Mercedes, now making its way through the field as its talented driver got the measure of the track. 'Where are they holding the draw for the start positions?'

'The Salles Touzet in the casino. Tomorrow night.'

Robert ordered another glass of wine and thought about the blonde. 'Make sure we're there. I'd like a closer look.'

63

Seven

RACE DAY, MONACO, APRIL 1929

One hundred laps. One hundred and ninety-seven miles. Sixteen cars.

Eve positioned herself near the pits, under the trees, just before the Ste Devote bend, right behind where their two ad hoc mechanics, Bernard and Jacques, hired, cajoled and flattered from the village garage and trained in the art of refuelling and tyre changing in the yard at the Normandy house, had set up shop. A large board in front of each station proclaimed the name and number of the driver. She tried not to dwell on all those hours ahead, hours in which her lover would try to drive as quickly as humanly possible through streets designed for horses and trams.

A lap of honour by Prince Louis, Antony Noghes accompanying, beaming. A year of hard work. Lobbying the International Association of Recognised Automobile Clubs, the Automobile Club de Monaco, the drivers and the manufacturers. Now, a happy man.

Robert and Maurice were positioned further along behind the

Dreyfus pit stop, with Ettore and his son Jean Bugatti. Maurice could not fail to notice that, even at the start when the tension mounted as Prince Louis did a lap of honour and the crowd cheered his vision and generosity in allowing the race, Robert's attention wandered along to where Williams was making frantic adjustments to his car, and Eve looked on, concerned and nervous.

Two laps of warm-up and the cars shuffled their way on to the grid under the watchful eye of Charles Faroux, the hard-bitten race organiser. Engines, gentlemen please.

The mechanics cranked the handles, engines fired, each one emitting its distinctive note, the low thrum of the Mercedes, the haughty cough of the Maserati, the piercing scream of the Alfa in the upper register and the strange tearing-fabric sound of the Bugattis. The drivers raised their hands one by one as the cars caught.

Williams watched Faroux move to the starter's podium, his sombre face showing none of the excitement he must feel, at least if he had a human bone in his body, which, to be fair, many doubted. Williams tried not to notice the thousands of pairs of eyes raking the field, to concentrate on the clutch, the accelerator, the brake, the gear lever on his right-hand side, on the co-ordination that would be needed to get this car round the first bend. He started to breathe as Rudi suggested, purging the heart-flapping chemicals from his blood, remembering his words. Calm. Clinical.

At the back of the field, thanks to a terrible draw, with a sea of metal in front of him, mostly Alfa red and Bugatti blue, Rudi also began the process of clearing his mind, reducing his world to the immediate vicinity only, stripping away the background like so much scenery in a music hall, flats to be taken away. Everything shrank to the vibrating microcosm of the cockpit and the next straight, bend, gear change, chicane, tunnel, uphill, downhill, round.

The flag raised.

Williams reached up and swivelled his flat tweed cap so the peak pointed towards the rear and pulled down his goggles.

The flag dropped. Away.

Rudi saw the stalled car just in time, yanked the wheel to the left, felt himself clip the bodywork, corrected. He pressed the accelerator and listened to the noise of the car, straining his ears for a sign, a torn cowling, a shredded tyre, a bent drive shaft. Tell me, tell me. It told him. No damage. Fifteen cars. Fourteen ahead of him into the first sharp bend with its deceptive kink at the far side. Lot of work to do, Rudi, he thought. Lot of work.

Eight laps gone.

It was a sight to make Ettore Bugatti's heart leap. Out of the tunnel towards the chicane they came, four of them, powering majestically down the incline like ships of the line. One, two, three, four. All Bugattis. In the lead, Williams, bringing the pack home, having snatched the vanguard from Lehoux in a daring manoeuvre along the Quai. But even without seeing that distinctive green, Ettore would have known which car it was by the engine note. So he had no trouble pinpointing number twelve, especially as Williams, this unknown Englishman, was adding something to the usual staccato roar of the engine, with gear changes so smooth as to be almost sensual, precise, yet delicate. Even Bugatti had to admit he was making the little car sing.

And then he saw the white shape and the familiar helmet. Rudi. Fifth. Fifth in a car that should have needed first gear and a team of horses to get round the hairpins, and here he was having bullied and pushed and sweated his way through the entire field to be a contender. Ettore watched the white behemoth close on Dreyfus and as they disappeared from view he knew Caracciola wasn't going to let his Bugattis have it all their own way.

Lap 25.

Williams felt him before he saw him. As he entered the mouth of the tunnel the scream of the supercharger became a bouncing banshee, smacking off the multifaceted rock face. Then, almost subsonically, came the deeper whump of Caracciola's Mercedes, the lazy 7.1 litre seeming to fire once every fifty metres, but delivering a magnificent amount of torque.

As number twelve exited the tunnel, the wail receding, Williams could feel the SSK looming behind, could hear the bassy boom of its big bore exhausts boxing his ears. He looked in the dancing mirror, and saw Rudi edge out, starting to probe.

Down the hill they accelerated towards the twitch of the chicane, until Caracciola could almost touch the shapely tail of the Bugatti. Now along the Quai, a glance at the open-mouthed crowds, their cheering unable to penetrate the gruff roar of the engine, instruments blurring as he braked for Tabac, down through the gears for the left hander, then back on the throttle, worrying the feisty little Bugatti all the way to Gasworks. Then he felt the slide, the wheels slither on the road surface, scrabbling for grip, and the back swing wildly. Trouble.

A rattle over the tram lines and up the hill now, and Rudi saw the Bugatti twitch on the oil-slicked surface. Rudi dived to the right, gambling on how the Englishman would correct his line, saw the supercharger of the twelve car vent smoke and flame through the hole in the bonnet, knew he had him, corrected his own back end as a wheel caught the oil slick on the cobbles, and was away powering up towards Ste Devote, in first place.

Lap 35.

Eve covered her eyes as Williams bravely stormed after the German, could feel his despair as the Mercedes rounded the bend first. She hated this, hated it. The next thing she knew Williams was in, grinning, face blackened by oil and smoke, urging Bernard on as the villager tipped fuel into the filler cap behind his head. He raised a hand to Eve, waited for the tap on his shoulder to tell him refuelling was complete, and floored the accelerator.

Eve looked across at Ettore and wondered who was the man next to him, calmly meeting her gaze. Then she had him. Robert Benoist. Looking right at her, those piercing eyes fixing her, a hint of a smile playing about his mouth. Eve had smiled back then turned her attention once more to the track, counting the seconds till Williams reappeared. He did. With Caracciola on his tail this time. She hated it.

Lap 75.

Eve watched as Rudi came rumbling into his designated pit slot and his white overalled mechanics leapt out at him. Rudi was out of the car and pointing furiously. New tyres. He needed new tyres. The strain of those corners had torn through the tread, leaving tendrils of rubber hanging down. The mechanics set about the wheel change while Rudi himself poured fuel into the thirsty monster. He looked up in despair as Williams rocketed by, willing the petrol into the tank, sloshing it carelessly over the bodywork and ground. Finally it was done and Rudi climbed back in and, grim faced, rejoined the battle. Eve looked at her watch. Over four minutes. Too slow, she knew. Far too slow.

Lap 100.
Close to four hours after the start the chequered flag came down on Williams. He had averaged 49.83 mph, round the 1.97 mile course, and had the fastest lap – 2 mins 15 seconds, at 52.69 mph. He came home 1 minute 17.8 seconds ahead of Bouriano's 35C. An exhausted Rudi came home third, his arms numb from the exertion of handling the Mercedes.

As Williams pulled in after his lap of honour, the crowd surged forward. Antony Noghes struggled through with the cup and managed to thrust it into Williams' hands, while flashes detonated all around. Williams saw Eve and beckoned her over. He kissed her, leaving a black smudge on her nose, which he made worse by trying to wipe away.

'How does it feel?' she asked him.

The grin that threatened to bisect his face said it all. Eve produced the gift with a flourish, holding it above his hand and while Williams snapped at it like a hungry dog, mesmerised by the way the diamonds caught the light. Theatrically he snatched it away and looked at it. A beautiful Cartier. He turned it over, but the steel back was unadorned.

'Don't worry, darling,' she said. 'We'll get it engraved. First in the first.'

Then she lost him as everybody else pressed in to claim their piece of the day's hero.

Robert watched Williams and Rudi pose, the weary combatants of the race. Maurice had been talking to Ettore and scuttled back as fast as his limp would allow.

'Good gossip, brother. She is, or was, the mistress of Bill Orpen. The painter. He . . . you will like this . . . he is the chauffeur. The chauffeur.'

'Really?'

'Yes and apparently the money is all hers. He's a kept man.'

'Lucky chap.'

'But Ettore reckons that was one of the best drives he has seen. Says the man has star quality. He's invited him to Molsheim. Going to offer him a team drive.'

'Is he now?'

'He thinks he could go all the way. Champion.'

Robert watched as Eve appeared at Williams' side, now clutching a small dog in her arms, and posed for more photographs, then he turned and slipped away into the crowd.

Sir William Orpen had, of course, heard of Robert Benoist, all of France had, but he had never met the driver before. So he was rather taken aback when Robert came visiting him at his studio and asked to see some of his work with a view to purchasing one. However, as he was crating up to ship back to England, he would be more than pleased to offload a few canvases.

Orpen waited as Robert flicked through the stacks in the studio until he had found what he was looking for. As he suspected. 'Beautiful, isn't she?' declared Robert, redundantly.

'Hhmm.'

'How much is this one?'

'It's not for sale, alas.'

Robert lifted it out, tried to imagine what it would be like in a frame rather than on the primitive stretcher, admired the graceful

70

curve of the reclining nude, the playful smile on the face. 'Why not?'

'I'm rather fond of it. It was my last portrait of her.'

'Two hundred and fifty thousand?'

Orpen coughed. 'Two-fifty? Done.'

Robert smiled and they shook on the deal. 'I'll have it picked up tomorrow if that is convenient with you.'

'Absolutely. Just get your man to call in advance. I'll have it properly packed. To protect her.'

Robert stepped back and admired his purchase, 'What's it called?'

Orpen, already regretting his hasty decision, murmured quietly: 'Early One Morning'.

Eight

FRANCE, JUNE 1929

Williams drove one more race at Montlhery after Monaco – a spirited second place in an all-Bugatti field, with fellow English-man Lord Howe winning – before the journey to Molsheim. He and Eve decided to drive in their new Peugeot, heading north west from Paris, stopping at Rheims, Verdun, site of the most famous battle of the Great War, at least in France, Metz and arriving in Molsheim, to the west of Strasbourg, early on the fourth day.

Eve couldn't help but notice how relaxed and happy Williams was, as if a great weight had been lifted from him. Having proved he could actually race and win, some inner calm had finally taken over. Although she now knew him well enough to suspect that, like a slow drip, the need for excitement would build up again gradually. For the moment he had nothing to prove. He was up there with the élite.

They were astonished to find Molsheim was less a works than a grand estate. Even the factory seemed like an extension of the house, spotlessly clean, with a relaxed, friendly workforce building cars – including a mock-up of the fabulous and gargantuan Royale, rumoured to be one of the most expensive vehicles ever produced – boats and the prototype railcars that Bugatti had designed using petrol engines and pneumatic tyres. Eve and Williams put up at the small hotel that had been built for customers who wished to stay over, and were then invited to join in the shoot.

'What's in season?' asked Williams.

'Pigeons,' said Ettore.

In the large pasture behind the factory twenty or so people had gathered to take turns at what the Americans called skeet shooting. Bugatti had installed a system that could hurl ten clays up at a time if required, to try to duplicate the mass explosion of birds from the undergrowth. Of course, when all ten were used it made sorting out who had hit what rather difficult.

Ettore pointed out some of the other guests. 'Bradley. English motoring journalist. Philippe de Rothschild. Banker, of course. Fine driver, too. Next to him, my son Jean. I'll show you some of his designs later. Very good. Robert Benoist I believe you know. No? I'll introduce you. Next to him, his brother Maurice.'

Bugatti was interrupted by a mass discharge of guns as the discs came arcing through the air, all but one exploding into tiny shards.

'Holtschaub. Customer. Dumas from the Ministry of Transport – here about the railcars, naturally – Meo Constantini, my race manager—' A second detonation of shotguns, more innocent clays pulverised in mid air. 'Would you like a try?'

Williams nodded and was found a place and a gun. He discovered the whole process oddly satisfying. No living creature suffered, there was an element of skill – although the line of flight was more predictable in the clay than with avian flesh and blood targets – and he found he was really rather good. Except when

73

Eve decided to tickle him or surreptitiously slid her hand across the front of his trousers.

Robert broke his gun and watched. Maurice sneered, 'I told you she was a slut.'

Robert smiled. 'Jealous?'

'Only all of me, brother.'

Lunch was called and they strolled back to the house. Ettore fell in beside Williams and Eve. 'How is my Bugatti?'

'I think one of the ends has run.'

'How do you know?'

'I can hear it.'

Ettore raised an eyebrow, surprised. It wasn't the quietest engine in the world when it was blown by a supercharger, and he thought nobody else could pick up every metallic nuance like its designer. 'We'll have to strip it down.' He looked at Eve. 'Expensive.'

'I had assumed as much,' she said with an affected weariness. 'Dogs are so much cheaper.'

'Well, there might be another solution,' Bugatti replied enigmatically and veered off to talk to Jean before either of them could ask exactly what that solution might be.

Lunch was held in the grand salon of the house, a feast of Alsace delicacies, with a foie gras pot-au-feu, spaetzle, baeckeoffe, kugelhopf and a vast assortment of sausages. The language in the room switched rapidly between German, French and English, with Ettore occasionally using his native Italian to emphasise a point. Robert and Maurice sat opposite Williams and Eve, with Bugatti at the head of the table.

Ettore did the introductions at their section, and Robert looked at Eve and said, 'Ah. Bill Orpen's muse.'

'Ex-muse,' Williams said quickly.

'I have a fine example of your musing.'

Eve stopped short of sipping her pinot noir, puzzled. 'You do, Mr Benoist?'

'Robert, please. Yes. "Early One Morning".'

Eve felt Williams shift uncomfortably, trying to figure out where this was going. 'Really? Bill said he'd never sell it.'

'I made him an excellent offer.'

'I'll match it,' said Williams.

'With what?' retorted Maurice. Eve glared at him and he went back to his plate of snails.

Robert waved a fork airily, as if distracted. 'No, it really isn't for sale now. I do admire it so.'

Aware that some kind of tension was building Ettore interrupted. 'Williams' car needs a re-build. I was thinking of giving him a team drive. What do you think, Robert?'

'You have a place?'

'Yes. You know we do.'

Robert took a mouthful of Gewürztraminer before saying, 'I thought I might have that.'

A silence fell. Constantino began to say something and then fell silent when Robert flicked a fierce glance his way.

Ettore said quietly, with a hint of flint in his voice, 'I need you in the Paris showroom.'

'I can do both,' insisted Robert. 'We can do demonstrations before races.'

'That wasn't the agreement,' said his employer, trying hard to keep the irritation from his voice. 'Now I have two would-be drivers, one place.'

'I have an idea,' said Maurice brightly. 'How about a challenge? Twenty laps of Montlhery—'

'That's unfair,' objected Eve. 'You have raced there dozens of times, Mr Benoist. Will just once.'

75

Williams touched her arm. 'That's all right, Eve. A duel? Why not?' Williams watched Robert's grin broaden. Time to find out if it was true the man never backed down from a challenge. 'But let's throw in the painting. Just for the sport.'

Williams could see Robert's brain working furiously. To refuse the wager would seem churlish, cowardly even, a vote of no-confidence in his own skills. He couldn't think of a way out that would save face. Eve felt Robert's eyes bore into her as he laughed at Williams' audacity and said: ' "Early One Morning"? Why not? Just for the sport. Ettore – name the day, I'll be there.'

Bugatti hesitated, wondering if he should be part of this, then noticed Jean signalling furiously. It was a second before he understood what his eldest son was saying. Finally, he nodded his consent.

'Excellent.' Robert stood up and clicked his fingers at Maurice. 'We have to take our leave. We have a few days in the country.' He hesitated and finally shifted his gaze from Eve to Williams. 'Does anyone know where I can find a decent chauffeur?'

Nine

MONTLHERY RACETRACK, JULY 1929

The early morning sun glinted off the brace of Bugattis sitting
out on the concrete, the last tendrils of a damp mist curling
around the eight-spoked aluminium wheels. Both were painted in
the Bugatti factory blue, each had been beautifully prepared,
overseen by Jean, who had watched every last rivet being ground
down, strengthened the drive train when he thought it too
delicate (a source of friction with his father, who always thought
his designs perfect) and tuned the vast sixteen-cylinder engines to
perfect pitch.

Next to the machines, on an easel, a protective cloth thrown
over it, was the prize, the one Williams wanted above all. He
would always find a way of getting a drive, whether he got the
Bugatti seat or not. He wanted that painting back where it
belonged. With Eve.

He sat in the pits, alone, slowly emptying his mind, reminding
himself of his golden rules. You can only be sure of winning if
you start a race absolutely calm, your hands not sweaty. The juice
in the bloodstream can come later, but there, on the start line, up

to the first bend, too much means a stalled car, a bad line, an over-ambitious out-braking into the curve.

No Robert, as yet.

Williams emptied his pockets into the small wooden container he always used. Already superstition and ritual were entering his racing life. Cigarettes. Lighter. Wallet. Change. All into the box. Next, the dressing routine. Shoes off. Overalls on. Soft kid racing boots, laced. Gloves, tucked into belt. Tweed cap. Goggles. Ready. Where was Robert?

The faint buzz entered his consciousness at that point, and he knew exactly where his opponent was.

The noise grew louder, angrier, and all heads turned upwards, eyes shaded against the sun. The bright red biplane appeared over the far side of the banking, the rotary engine screaming as the plane dipped, coming in on a collision course for the two Bugattis, sending mechanics and spectators scattering. At the last second it rose up, fixed wheels almost touching the metal of the cars and sideswiping the painting, the engine straining to claw into the air once more, the propeller wash peeling back the cover off 'Early One Morning', sending it tumbling down the track. Williams could see Robert at the controls, the trademark grin across his face.

The biplane gained height, circled, did a single, lazy roll and then came in to land on the far straight, taxiing off on to the central grassed reservation. Robert leapt out and bowed to the smattering of relieved applause.

He strode over towards Williams, stripping off the heavy leather gloves, jacket and helmet as he went, to reveal his racing suit underneath. He collected his white canvas helmet and goggles from Maurice and slipped them on. 'Ready?'

Williams nodded and they went to their respective cars.

'I hope you drive better than you fly.'

Robert laughed, knowing that was nigh on impossible. 'We'll see. One last look?'

Williams stopped before the naked form of Eve in the painting and then glanced over at the real thing, who blew him a kiss. Robert signalled for the portrait to be removed and stepped into his car. With one leg in he froze, extracted himself, walked back and held out his hand. Williams took it. 'I forgot. Goodbye, Williams.'

With no further explanation Robert got behind the wheel, the mechanic cranked the engine and sixteen cylinders fired in an exuberant explosion of power. Williams followed suit, heart racing with anticipation as the engine responded to the tiniest throttle pressure, watching Ettore and Jean tussle over who would drop the starting flag. Le Patron won, of course, and took his position on the low starter's podium.

Stay calm, thought Williams. Get the heart rate down. Don't worry. He may be more experienced, but he is older, slower, less hungry. Bugatti held the flag aloft and hesitated. The engines started to protest as the rev counters crept round to the red line, the intricate mechanical innards chattering away, blurring the instrument panel. The flag twitched. Williams reached up and swivelled his tweed cap backwards, pulling the goggles in place with a fraction of a second to spare. The flag cracked down and the world around Williams became a rocketing blur.

Two cars and two drivers each perfectly matched. Glued together the Bugattis powered round the track, a mechanical *pas de deux*, sweeping along the straight and up the banking, as if choreographed, occasionally one inching ahead, but never for very long, as if afraid of hogging the limelight, the thirty-two cylinders all firing on cue.

Even Eve, who thought this whole thing a theatrical sham, had to admit it was exhilarating and beautiful.

As she watched another neck-and-neck lap she became aware of someone at her side. Maurice. He offered her a Celtique cigarette and, after a slight hesitation, she took one. 'Peace offering?'

'Are we at war?' he asked.

'I had the impression you didn't like us.'

'No, no, no. Far from it. My brother is a great admirer.'

'And you?'

Maurice shrugged. 'Haven't you heard? I like what my brother likes.'

Williams in the lead now, edging ahead, and a slight frown flicked across Maurice's face.

'Why do you say something like that?'

'Oh, it's always been the same. I am the elder, but Robert . . . in the war I was stuck in the mud at Verdun,' he slapped his gammy leg, 'while Robert was the fighter ace. After the war when we took up racing . . . well, the leg again. I am one of those miserable creatures Josephine Baker despises so much.' He said it with a smile in his eyes.

Eve shook her head. The silly Baker woman had told a journalist how war deformities made her feel nauseous, a statement she quickly withdrew after the scandalous outrage that followed. Still, being the scantily clad toast of Paris she was quickly forgiven. Except by those she defamed. 'You shouldn't believe anything Americans say.'

Maurice glanced back at the track and stretched his collar. He was fashionably dressed in a wool suit, with waistcoat, shirt and tie and the brown suede shoes that the Americans had made acceptable, but it was not the best ensemble to be wearing in bright sunshine. Eve was glad she had chosen a simple cotton dress and brimmed cloche hat.

'You know,' Maurice said in a low voice, 'no matter who wins out there, I can think of two losers.'

'Who?'

'Us.'

He stood up to cheer as Robert came home to take the flag and Eve felt her heart sink.

Williams took it well. He pulled over and climbed out to the thin applause and shook hands with Robert. Jean wanted to press him on how the car had behaved, but he strolled over to see Eve, with the young Bugatti in tow, hectoring him with technical questions.

Maurice popped the champagne and handed Robert a glass. 'Still got the old magic, I see.'

'Only just.'

'What do you mean?'

Robert stripped off his helmet and took a sip of the drink. 'How many Grand Prixes have we raced?'

'Forty . . . fifty?'

'Seventy-two. And Williams?'

Maurice shrugged.

'One. One proper race and a handful of secondary events. Yet I beat him by this much.' He held his arms out to show a metre, slopping his drink. 'Next time this much.' He narrowed the gap to half that distance. 'Then.' He handed his glass to Maurice and clapped his hands with percussive force, causing Maurice to jump. 'I don't like it.'

Robert retrieved and gulped back the remaining champagne before walking over to Eve and Williams, who were talking to Jean near the Orpen painting, its protective wrapper back in place. Jean said: 'Congratulations, Robert. Williams here was just saying he could feel a vibration at around five thousand revolutions. Front left wheel. Did you feel anything?'

Robert shook his head and a concerned Jean pulled Williams

off to examine the two cars. As he stepped away Williams hesitated and asked Robert: 'What was the goodbye for? At the start?'

'Don't you know that? All factory Bugatti drivers always say goodbye to each other before a race . . . it's good luck.'

Williams went off with Jean.

'Sounds more like pessimism, Mr Benoist,' suggested Eve.

There was a sudden squeal of rubber on concrete and a cloud of acrid smoke as Jean took out Williams' car for a few laps.

'It's like "break a leg" in the theatre. We don't mean it. Anyway, your husband is a fine driver. I suspect he doesn't need luck.'

'That might be true. But he isn't my husband.'

'Really?' he said with feigned surprise. 'I would do something about that. Or he should.'

Williams returned, wiping his face with a cloth. He held out a hand belatedly to Robert, who took it. 'I was just saying, you're not bad for a chauff . . .' He stopped himself. Time to drop that. 'Actually, not bad for anyone.'

'Bugatti says he'll build another Thirty-five C. So there's two places. One each if we want it.'

Robert threw back his head and laughed. 'Wonderful. I bet the old rogue had two places all along. I was also just saying, Williams, you should marry this woman quick, before someone else does. And I have the perfect wedding present.'

He walked over to 'Early One Morning' and yanked off the covering, leaving Eve's flesh tones glowing in the sunlight. Robert looked at the representation, the subject and finally at Williams before saying quietly, 'She's all yours.'

Ten

It nagged at Williams every time he saw the painting. 'Early One Morning' hung at the head of the stairs in the Normandy watermill, and, like any everyday fixture, he quickly became habituated to it. Every so often, however, maybe once a day, he saw it afresh, and felt that grip round his heart when he realised that the beauty lying naked on the rumpled sheets was his. All his.

It was at that point he wondered why the man had done it.

They were at Bricktop's in Montmartre when he finally got around to asking him. He and Robert had spent the weekend at Molsheim testing new cars, all business-like and professional, so it hadn't been the place. On the Monday Williams stopped over in Paris en route to Eve, and after a dinner at Paquin's and drinks at Le Grand Duc they had crossed over to the hole in the wall where Bricktop, the red-haired hostess, had kissed Robert on both cheeks and ushered them to a corner table, jammed between the bandstand and a coterie of Americans.

They ordered brandy and Robert frowned at the clarinettist on the stage, playing a breathtakingly fast 'Cake-Walking Babies

83

From Home'. Robert wrinkled his nose. He wasn't sure about Bechet, especially the small, straight saxophone he sometimes played; he found it coarse and wailing.

When Bechet finished there was a commotion at the next table. One of the men had his wallet out and was trying to tip the player twenty dollars. His wife was trying to stop him. As usual, Bricktop refereed, gliding over and giving Bechet five, but then confiscating the wallet of the patron. 'Don't worry, Scott, I'll keep the tab running.'

The wife smiled gratefully, and the Scott character slumped down in front of his whiskey. 'Sing for us then.'

'Later, lover, later,' and she waddled off, pushing her ample frame among the tightly packed customers, schmoozing and kissing and shaking hands as she went.

Williams' head had a faint buzz to it now, and he knew he was relaxed enough to broach the subject that had been worrying him. The band, minus Bechet, had begun playing a blues.

'Robert, there is something I've been meaning to ask you.'

'Why I am such a good driver?'

'Not quite. Well, that as well.'

Robert stretched his arms expansively. 'How long have you got? I could talk about myself all night.'

'Why did you give the painting back?'

Robert narrowed his eyes and Williams felt himself sweat a little. A glare from Robert was one glare too many. 'Wedding present. Which reminds me. When are you getting married?'

'Soon. Very soon. So is that all it was?'

'Rubbish.' The voice boomed over the patrons from the bar. 'Keep the rhythm, man. You're all over the place.'

Williams looked round. It was Bechet, at the small bar at the rear of the room, verbally abusing his own band. They carried on, ignoring him.

'Horace, that is some terrible bass playing.'

Horace let the big instrument fall to the stage with a reverber-ating crash that shimmered around the room. From his inside pocket he produced a revolver and waved it towards his employer. 'Sidney, you dumb fucker. Just shut up. Go home.'

There were squeals as people realised exactly what he was wielding in such a cavalier fashion, and heads hit tables and arms folded over them as if they could protect them from bullets. One or two patrons slithered off their seats to sit it out on the floor.

The first shot caused a puff of masonry to bloom from the stage. It was then Williams realised that Bechet had a gun of his own. Robert reached over and gripped his arm. 'Don't move.'

'I wasn't planning to.'

The exchange lasted five seconds, a fusillade of rapid fire, booming around the confined space, rolling clouds of cordite mixing with the cigarette smoke. It ended when Bricktop took the gun from Bechet's hand and slapped him about the head with it, careful to avoid his mouth. Last thing she needed was a star with a ruined embouchure.

'Sidney, go home. Go on. Out. Horace, gimme that thing. Here. Now.'

Sheepishly the big man handed over his Gat, Sidney was packed off, it was confirmed that, miraculously, nobody had been hit and Bricktop decided it was time to sing 'Miss Otis Regrets'.

Robert let out a breath. 'They are such terrible shots. Best place to be is where they are aiming. Aaah,' he said as Bricktop launched into a smoky-voiced Cole Porter medley, 'this is more like it.'

They ordered a second round of drinks. 'So it was a wedding present?' persisted Williams. 'Nothing more to it than that?'

'I said. Yes. Why are you so interested all of sudden?'

'I'd never have given it away.'

'No, I can see that.'

'Then why did you?'

Robert gripped Williams' hand and pulled him closer. 'Two things, my friend. One, you won that race and if you ever tell anyone I said that I'll rip your tongue out.'

'I didn't. You won it.'

'It wasn't fair. Eve was right. I have raced Montlhery dozens of times. If you knew that course, knew the line, like I do . . . you'd have won.'

'And the second?'

Robert smiled, a big, warm, regretful grin. 'I realised to have that painting, to have that woman on the wall and not have the real thing to touch and feel and love . . . I realised, Will . . . that way, madness lies.'

They married the following year. Deliberately low-key, because there were those in the village who had never realised they weren't already married. Just a discreet service, a few of Eve's family and a celebratory lunch.

It turned into something of a wake. Eve had just finished organising the food when the letter arrived, informing her that Orpen had died. She cried for much of the morning, and Williams offered to cancel the day, but she decided the last thing Orpen would want was people to stop drinking and enjoying themselves on his behalf. So the wedding lunch was served in the courtyard at a long table, and the racing drivers and the dog breeders seemed to get on remarkably well once they passed the couple-of-glasses-of-wine-each mark, and it was only after the heat was starting to fade that Eve realised that she had lost her husband.

She excused herself and wandered down to the river, following the sound of heated voices until she was sure it was Williams and his cantankerous friend. She found a vantage point and, feeling just a little guilty, settled down to watch and listen for a few minutes.

'You are a very stubborn man,' said an exasperated Robert. 'I think you just lack the fire in the belly.' He pointed at his own stomach and was infuriated when Williams laughed and turned away.

Robert grabbed his arm, softening his tone. 'Don't do that. I didn't mean to insult you. Not on your wedding day.'

Williams shrugged. 'None was taken.'

'I didn't mean you are a coward. I know you are not.'

'Robert, I don't expect you to understand.' He put his hand on the other man's shoulder, a gesture Eve found oddly intimate. 'You have a wife, a mistress—'

'Two, if you don't mind.'

'A doting brother. Ettore thinks of you as his eldest son. You have the showroom, your customers . . . but it's not my life. Mine is different. I am what I am.'

'And what is that?'

'Oh God, you sound like Eve now.'

She coughed to reveal her presence and they both looked round. Williams came over, kissed her on the cheek and said, 'You try and explain to him. I need another drink.'

She walked over to Robert, his hands firmly in his pockets, jaw jutting out. 'Your husband . . .' He turned to look at her. 'Your husband makes me mad. Mad.'

'Why?'

'He wants Wimille to drive in his place at Monza. But Wimille has a benefactor, he will buy a car. We don't have to give him one.'

She had heard of Jean-Pierre Wimille, a young, phlegmatic driver who Williams reckoned had astonishing natural flair. 'Why does he want him to have the place?'

Robert blew out his cheeks. 'He says the Fifty-four we want to sell Wimille is not good enough. Will also says . . .' This was clearly the part that made Robert mad. 'That Jean-Pierre is a better driver than him.'

Eve sat down on the river bank, almost out of shock. Admitting that there might be a better racer, to these men, was tantamount to owning up to poor sexual performance. 'Is he?'

Robert knelt down next to her, his knee touching her shoulder, possibly accidentally. 'Wimille is . . . Wimille is a great driver. Or at least will be. One day. Will . . .' Robert tore a reed from the river bank and began to shred it while he marshalled his thoughts. He flung strands ineffectually towards the swans gliding regally by, who returned a stare worthy of Benoist himself.

'It is as if God gives some people this gift, to be able to control machines. Will has the best ability to read a car I know. To pinpoint what is wrong, how to fix the roadholding, the corner-ing. Wonderful. But God, being God, decides that there must be a system of checks and balances. To offset such a marvellous gift. In Will's case . . . he's lazy.'

Eve watched the sun filter through the leaves and play on the water's surface and considered this. It didn't add up. 'You think Will is lazy?'

'Not lazy as you mean it. I've seen the kennels he has built. Seen him strip down engines and gearboxes. Not physically, but here.' He tapped his temple. 'You see, he wins a race, it is enough for him. He has proved something for a while. The best of them – Nuvolari, Chiron back there, Rudi . . . maybe even I in my prime, we have to go out and do it the next day and the next and the next. Will, he comes home to his new wife and plays with his dogs.'

'You make that sound like a crime. I would say that makes him a better human being.' And, she wanted to add, a better husband, but thought Robert might take that personally.

'You are right. Except at Bugatti, we don't want human beings. Too troublesome.' He laughed. 'Will thinks too much.'

'What is Jean-Pierre's flaw?'

'Wimille? He wants two things: glory and money. Wants them so, so bad. Then again, that probably isn't a flaw in this game.'

Robert stood up and tossed the last of the reed into the water, watching it spiral away in the eddies.

'And yours, Robert? How has God cursed you?'

Robert rested a hand briefly, lightly, on her head and laughed. 'Me? I fall in love too easily.'

Eleven

LAKE SENLITZ, AUSTRIA, OCTOBER 2001

The old lady sits in a canvas chair in the marquee they have hastily re-erected next to the recovered Humber. On the wooden pallet in front of her sits the trunk, scuffed and swollen and damaged. By narrowing her eyes she can see it as it was – swish and elegant, in that hotel room near Berlin, the day she packed it.

Hovering around her and the Vuitton are Warner, his technician, a bored Austrian policeman and Deakin. Rose can sense a sort of irritable excitement in Warner. He wants to see inside the trunk as much as anyone, but dislikes the way this woman has taken control in such a matriarchal manner.

'OK, Deakin. Let's take a look.'

Deakin unclips the trunk and, with great difficulty, levers the two halves apart. As the front cracks open, a thin stream of slimy water snakes across the floor on to the pallet. The technician hovers, forceps in hand. Deakin waves him back.

She can smell the long, slow decay within. As with herself, the years have taken a toll. How much of a toll though? Deakin

90

works his fingers into the opening and pulls the two sides apart so it gapes like a razor clam.

Deakin thinks at first there is nothing but mush inside, but as he pulls the rotted fabric aside he realises it is only the top layer on each side that has emulsified, the clothes closest to the perished seal. Deakin peels off the remains of a man's suit, opening the jacket to read the label. James Pyle. It means nothing to him. He hands it to the technician who carefully places it on a trestle table.

Underneath, still shimmering after all these years, is a beaded dress, the once luminous material flat and dissolved in places, but still clearly something special.

'Odd choice for our Mr Williams. Did they have, what are they called, cross-dressers back then?' he asks her.

'It's a Molyneux,' she says tartly, as the technician lays it next to the suit and takes a photograph, the flash making her blink. 'Very expensive. Or was.'

The items start to come out thick and fast. A pair of silver-backed hairbrushes, hair oil, Lobb shoes, a Hermès belt, some women's underwear, a faded photograph album and a heavy object wrapped in greased paper. Gingerly Deakin unwraps it. A gun. A Colt .45 automatic pistol, still glistening with its sheen of protective oil. All are laid out and photographed before being labelled and bagged by the technician.

Finally one other object, right in the far corner, a piece of metal, a cylinder, maybe forty centimetres high. Deakin levers it out from its nesting place, where a film of rust has cemented it to the lining. There is no top, and poking out are the slimy remnants of bundles of money, French and English. A lot of money. Enough to want to kill someone for, he thinks. At least, back when it was worth something.

'Let me see that.'

Deakin hands over the container and Warner comes across to take a look. 'Please be careful,' he pleads.

'Of course.' She looks up at him. 'But it is mine.'

'What do you mean?' snaps Warner.

'Well, I put it in the case.'

Warner opens his mouth to speak but thinks better of it. He knows his chances of getting a straight answer from a spook – even an old spook – are pretty slim.

As she carefully wipes away at the slime with a tissue, the small group huddled around her see there is a thin, fragile paper label wrapped around the outside of the canister. A skull and crossbones slowly emerges. And just to hammer home the point, the legend 'Danger de Mort'.

'Is it safe?' asks Deakin.

'Oh yes. Emptied a long, long time ago. May I have a cloth?'

The technician obliges and carefully she scrubs away the final blobs of mud, revealing the stencilled details of the contents, the name of the producer and place of manufacture. She feels gratified at her little piece of theatre when she hears the collective intake of breath. They all know what it means. Still shocking after all these years. Good.

Rose hands the canister to a technician who holds it as if it is a bomb. Which it is. 'Can you clean that up and preserve it for me? So the label remains legible? There are some chaps I want to show it to.'

'Of course.' The man gets to work with chemical sprays and preservatives.

'Bloody hell—' starts Warner, but Rose raises a hand to silence him.

'Help me up will you, Deakin?' she asks. 'I need to take another look at the car.'

Deakin assists her out of the chair and they shuffle, slowly, out of the marquee and into the darkening afternoon light of Senlitz. Clouds are gathering over the mountains, and they seem to have taken on the black, threatening hue of the water.

Rose lets Deakin guide her round the ruined vehicle, and she squints in the windows, shaking her head. Finally, at the rear of the car, she asks him to open the boot once more and peers inside, holding her breath against the acrid smell of rapid, oxygen-driven decomposition.

She points a bony finger at a leather loop on the rear bulkhead.

'Pull that down for me will you, Deakin?'

He reaches in and tugs. The handle snaps and comes away in his hand. Rose raises an eyebrow, a silent instruction to continue. He traces the edge of the thick cardboard partition until he finds some leverage and tugs.

Deakin can't help it, he screams, or at least something halfway between a scream and a gasp emerges.

The body, trapped in the compartment for all these years, away from aquatic scavengers, has remained remarkably intact, so he can still see that it is, or was, a woman. The skin has mummified, stretched and wrinkled over the underlying bone, and there is still a mess of dirty blond hair attached to the skull. Slowly it topples over and hits the floor of the boot with a thump, sending up a sickly shower of ancient flesh particles.

'Fuck,' says Deakin quietly.

Rose, playing nervously with the elaborate watch on her wrist, nods and says, almost to herself, 'You know, I always wondered what became of her.'

Twelve

FRANCE, FEBRUARY 1937

Eve is dreaming, remembering in lurid details how they had made her husband so unhappy, so very unhappy. After all he had done for them. In reality they had been at Maxim's when it happened, but in the dream they are in a cellar, a cellar lit only by red lights that give everyone a devilish glow. Maurice is telling a convoluted joke about Satan and sex, when Robert enters, his eyes dark coals.

He orders a couple of Pernods and gives one to Williams, almost forcing him to gulp at it.

'Will. I have spoken to Ettore. He says yes. Le Mans. We can have two Tanks.'

Williams beams and Eve feels for him. The Tanks, the Type 57, are big beautiful alloy-clad racers, like something from the movie Things To Come *or* Metropolis, *which Williams has spent hours making super-reliable for an assault on the 24-hour race.*

It is at this point Robert's voice becomes oddly metallic, inhuman, as if a speaking weight machine were saying the lines.

'Ettore appreciates what you have done, Will. Without your breaking the endurance record at Montlhery, he wouldn't consider this . . .'

Williams seems to shrink, his voice growing smaller. 'But?'

'But France needs a victory. Badly. If you were to win, it would be an English victory . . .'

'In a Bugatti? Surely it's the car, not the driver. At least, that's what Ettore's always said to me.'

Robert takes a deep breath. 'He wants me to drive with Wimille.'

Williams nods, knowing that by championing Wimille he has been the instrument of his own downfall. 'And the second Tank?'

'Veyron and Labric.' Two more Frenchmen.

Williams blinks hard, downs the Pernod and leaves, squeezing Robert on the shoulder as he goes. Robert looks across at Eve and shrugs, unhappiness written across his entire face.

'How could you do this to your friend?' Eve screams at him and runs out after her husband, but the wet glistening streets are empty, just a few wraith-like wisps of smoke left hanging in the air.

Eve felt something move lightly through her hair, tickling her scalp and sat up, fearing a mouse. She squealed when the creature ran down the side of her face. Williams stepped back. 'Sorry. I frightened you. You were asleep.'

Eve looked around, momentarily disoriented. She was at the kitchen table, and had been lying with her head in her arms. The dogs lay in the dark corner, panting, having given up on supper.

'God. I was dreaming . . .'

'What about?'

'About how you should have raced at Le Mans.'

He shrugged. He was past caring now. The team had won, a French victory when the Germans were taking everything else in sight. Eve shook her head to try to clear the image of that cellar. 'What time is it?'

'Ten.'

She stretched, trying to shake off the heavy weariness of sleep.

'I thought you weren't back till tomorrow.'

'We have a customer in England. Interested in an Atlantic. I'm taking one over.' The Atlantic was Jean's astonishing sleek coupé, very low, very fast with a strange fin riveted down the back, giving it the air of some super hero's pursuit vehicle than a road-going motor. 'Coffee?'

She nodded. 'Are you going?'

'We also have an invitation to run a couple of Jean's 4.7s at Beddington.'

'Where's that?'

'Hampshire. Invitation only. They have asked Rudi and Mercedes. Stuck and Auto Union. There's appearance money. One hundred and fifty pounds a driver. Plus two hundred for the winner. Ettore says he will cover the rest of the costs.'

The last sentence faded and she smiled as she wondered if this was Bugatti's little consolation prize for depriving her husband of Le Mans glory.

'What's funny?'

'Nothing. Do you want to go?'

'To race against Rudi again? Maybe Nuvolari? Yes. Would you come?'

Eve could see the fire burning in his eyes once more, the need for the chance to feel adrenaline pump through his veins. The moronic English quarantine laws would mean she couldn't take even one of her dogs. But she could see this meant a lot to him. She nodded and he kissed her forehead.

'Beddington it is, then.'

Thirteen

BEDDINGTON, ENGLAND, 1937

The September sun bounced off the fields of wheat stubble and haystacks, bathing the English countryside in a comforting, golden glow. Eve shifted in her seat as Maurice contemplated his cards and let her eyes wander down the vista the way the designer intended, taking in the lake and its faux-Roman temple and the water gardens beyond, ending at the dark copse before the farmlands began.

Behind her was Beddington House, a grand eighteenth-century Palladian villa, trying hard to keep its dignity with a fan of rude racing cars parked on its lawns – the usual Alfas, ERAS, Rileys, Delahayes, MGs, Talbots, Maseratis and, right next to where she sat at the folding table with Maurice, a brace of gleaming new Bugattis.

To one side of the house a group of drivers and mechanics, including Robert and Williams, were playing football on a makeshift pitch. The pair of them were running that bit harder to keep up with the younger men, and she hoped they remembered they had a gruelling set of pre-race trials the following day before the race proper in the afternoon.

The innocuous new asphalt road to her right snaked around the house and, out of sight, connected to the racetrack the Duke had carved out of the glorious landscape at the rear of his house, across the gardens, through the forest, round the deer park, into the field he had rented from a neighbouring farmer and back again. For three miles, 125 yards, it twisted and rolled around a slumbering English countryside unaware of the kind of mechanical mayhem about to be inflicted on it.

The course bristled with hastily constructed stands, a press box, a commentary platform, feeding into a speaker system the engineers were struggling to perfect, hence the occasional howl of feedback or a hideously distorted voice drifting over the mansards of Beddington House. Now and then they heard a bark of German. The radio station Deutschlander was due to send back bulletins of the race to the home country.

Tomorrow the crowds would start to arrive, perhaps up to thirty thousand, drawn by the carrot of seeing the new Mercedes and Auto Union Silver Arrows, scourge of the continental raceways, at work on a field of English and French rivals. They would pay their 4 shillings (children 2/6, parking 2.0s). The *Light Car*, the *Sporting Life*, *Motor Sport* and the *Autocar* correspondents – including the famous 'Grand Vitesse' – were already here, sitting in deckchairs with owners and competitors, sipping Pimms served by the white-gloved staff and waiting for the bulk of the Germans to arrive.

There were whispers, of course, that the Germans weren't coming. There were rumbles about an annexation of Austria, Sudetenland and Leipzig and ever since Hitler marched into the Rhineland unopposed, the mood in Britain had been jittery. The possibility of war was even mentioned at the wonderful RAC club on Pall Mall, where they had had dinner before travelling to Beddington.

Eve heard a strange giggle and looked up to see two young, freckle-faced mechanics sneaking away from the rear of Williams' Bugatti. She stood up and moved around to see what they had done. An L plate had been taped to the elegant rear of the car. She plucked it off, bringing a flake of blue paint with it and cursed. Some distance away the two young Englishmen guffawed at their prank.

She tore the sign into a dozen pieces and threw it on to the Duke's already ruined lawn.

'I hate this country,' she said to Maurice, 'if they're not snobs they're imbeciles.'

'Or both,' he said as he grabbed a passing Pimms and sipped. 'At last. A drink that doesn't taste as if it came straight from a tradesman's bladder.'

Encouraged, she took one from the tray just as the sound of a high-powered sports car bounced through the trees lining the driveway and off the Portland stone of the house. 'Ah. Here comes Rudi and the stiff arm brigade,' said Maurice.

The little Mercedes roadster swept on to the gravel path then bumped its way over the grass to stop near them. At the wheel, as Maurice had correctly identified, Rudi. Beside him was a uni-formed officer of some description.

Rudi beamed when he saw them and climbed out. He was wearing a canvas jacket over white overalls, as if he expected to leap straight into a car and start competing. 'Eve. How nice to see you. Maurice.' He pointed at the rather stiff, correct figure hovering behind. 'May I introduce Assistant Sportskorpsführer Keppler.'

Keppler gave the soft, half-hearted version of the Heil Hitler salute, bending his elbow and nodding his head.

Maurice sniffed. 'What's an Assistant Sportskorpsführer?'

Keppler stepped forward and smiled. He was not a handsome man, his face slightly puffy and the eyes too small, but there was a liveliness about it that was somehow engaging. 'I am the person who makes sure you all lose.'

Eve laughed and Keppler beamed and went off to look at the rival cars, walking around the Bugattis with his hands clasped behind his back.

'Where's Baby?' asked Eve. Rudi's wife Alice, whom everyone called by her nickname, was famed as the best timekeeper in Europe, a devil on the twin chronometers. He rarely travelled without her.

'Switzerland.' He lowered his voice. 'House hunting.'

Eve raised an eyebrow.

'Just in case.'

'How is racing for Adolf?'

He unzipped his jacket and showed her the swastika on his breast pocket as if it were some kind of festering wound. 'They've made me a Sturmführer now.' He pulled a face but wiped the expression when he realised Keppler was coming back.

'Do these have the new rear axles?' Keppler asked authoritatively.

Eve and Maurice looked at each and shrugged. 'You need to speak to a driver or mechanic,' said Maurice. 'We're just along for the ride.'

All looked over when they heard the hiss of air brakes and a huge silver truck edged its way in through the stone gates, its sides centimetres from the twin pillars and metalwork. 'Ah,' said Keppler. 'The first of the trucks,' and strode over to direct the great lorry.

Eve looked quizzically at Rudi. 'How does he know about Jean's new axles?'

'There's a spy at Molsheim,' replied Rudi flatly.

'What? Are you serious?'

'There's a spy at every race works across Europe. And some in America.' He smiled at Maurice. 'In answer to your question, that's what an Assistant Sportskorpsführer does.'

Keppler stood proudly on the lawn, hands on hips, and waved the truck to his side. The cab doors opened and out jumped a stream of tall, handsome lads, all in steel grey overalls, who began to prepare the reception area.

'The pits are round there,' said Eve to Rudi, pointing along the slip road.

'I know. But Mercedes always has a second pits, away from prying eyes.'

Eve could see the football game was forgotten, and Robert, Williams and the others were drifting over to witness the spectacle. As the transporter ropes were untied, cords pulled and from the top of the truck a massive banner unfurled, proudly displaying the German eagle.

'My God,' said Williams when he reached Eve's side. 'What is this?'

Rudi turned and offered his hand and Williams pumped it. 'This,' said Rudi slowly, 'is the future of motor sport.'

Robert snorted. 'Well they can count me out.'

Rudi laughed. 'They intend to,' he said.

The Mercedes mechanics had produced a floor area made of strips of articulated aluminium and unrolled it. Tubular steel barriers were erected. Two ramps emerged from the rear of the trucks and down them came a covered shape, the green tarpaulin masking the outlines of some sleek, silver machine. The car was wheeled on to the metal flooring and the cover whisked back.

The W126 Mercedes seemed to suck up the rays of the English sun and fling them back defiantly. It was all riveted alloy, fluted air intakes, wire wheels, a race car stripped to bare aerodynamic essentials, a perfect synergy of form and function. And the function was to win. The swastika on the tail told whom that victory would serve.

As the German mechanics began fuelling, using pumps and pressure hoses, Williams sniffed. There was a strange, sweet aroma, not the usual benzol smell, drifting over. 'Christ, Rudi, what does she run on?'

'State secret.'

'Probably Hitler's piss,' suggested Maurice.

'Sshh,' said Rudi nervously.

'Why are they fuelling her? You're not taking her out?'

'The Auto Unions are three hours behind. They got held up at Dover. There was no crude oil for their trucks.' That meant Rudi's great rival Bernd Rosemeyer would be late arriving, too. 'It'll be dark when they get here. So I can get a couple of trial laps in.'

Rudi walked over, inspected the car and climbed in. Before he put his helmet on he fiddled with something at each side of his head. Rudi then signalled one of the mechanics who sprinted forward with a small trolley and plugged a metal cylinder into the side of the Mercedes. Robert and Williams glanced at each other knowingly. No hand cranking. Electric start.

The first roar of the exhaust seemed to shake the very earth. Now Williams knew what Rudi had been doing prior to putting his helmet on. Ear plugs. The exhaust note was a deep, low thrum, a thudding, chest-wobbling boom that powered up to an agonising scream as Rudi pressed the throttle and the super-chargers pushed air through the carburettors.

The strange odour of the secret fuel drifted across the grounds of the house, and Rudi slowly took the car down the slip road towards the track, blipping the throttle. Like the children of

Hamelin they all followed, mesmerised, half running, but too late, he was a disappearing speck by the time they reached the circuit proper. They could hear him, though, the angry note of the engine softening and rising again with each gear change, Rudi working hard through the box. He had what the Germans called *Fingerspitzgefuhl* – instinctive feel – and it sounded as if the car was responding to his thoughts.

In an astonishingly short time he reappeared, drifting the back end and correcting out of the hairpin, before aligning himself for the long run up the straight. Williams checked his watch. 'Two minutes fifteen,' he said, calculating that meant a lap time of over 80 mph – incredible on such a winding course.

'I had two eleven,' said Robert.

'Christ.' Williams ran a hand through his hair. 'What time is the next boat back?'

Fourteen

For Eve's birthday they went to La Pagode, the Japanese cinema and tea house on rue Babylone, and watched *Angels with Dirty Faces*, which made Eve sob, although Robert thought the noble ending a cop out. Afterwards the Gaumont-Pathé newsreel came on of goose-stepping German soldiers and Robert said loudly: 'Look at them. The pricks.'

A patron behind him hissed at him to be quiet and that he only wished France's army looked like that. 'Shut up,' snarled Robert, 'or I'll knock you down and piss in your ear.'

Afterwards they went for drinks at Drouand's near l'Opera, although Maurice, disliking the smug crowd the fashionable restaurant attracted, was keen to head off to the Sphinx. However, Robert protested that it was Eve's birthday and a brothel was perhaps the most appropriate of venues. Eve wasn't sure whether she was disappointed or not, as she had seen the magazine advertisements for the Egyptian splendours of the place and was curious.

Once settled, wine and brandies before them, they sat in

silence for a while, lost in their own thoughts. Eve scanned the room, looking for famous faces. Charles Lindbergh was there, with his wife Anne, no doubt back from another tour of Germany and telling anyone who'd listen about its wonderful Air Force.

'What if it is war?' asked Maurice finally, swirling the wine in his glass. 'You think the Maginot line will hold?'

Robert shook his head. Robert was sick of talk of defences, politics, was disgusted by the funeral of Rosemeyer, killed trying to break the Autobahn speed record for the Führer, which was choreographed as if he had been a war hero. He indicated Lindbergh. 'That man got one thing right. You saw what happened in Spain. They'll fly right over it.'

'What will you do?' asked Eve. 'If we fight?'

'Me?' asked Robert, as if the idea had never occurred to him. 'Grab some Chablis, head down to Menton and wait until it blows over.' He lit a cigarette and gave a thin smile. 'Or see if my old squadron will have me back. What about you, Will?'

'England. Enlist.' Firm and unwavering. 'The French don't have a war leader.'

'And England does?' sneered Maurice.

'The British are absolutely awful at having a good time.' He could see Eve nodding enthusiastically. 'Give them hard times, misery, give them war . . . they'll rise to the occasion. You want to fight a war? Over there is where you have to be.'

Despite the implied slur on his country, Robert nodded approvingly. He was beginning to feel a line had to be drawn, even though he was sure that Williams' mother country was behaving as perfidiously as always, manoeuvring to save its own neck while using France, Belgium and the others as a shield. 'Eve?'

Williams, mistaking the direction of the question, said forcefully, 'She'll come with me.'

He didn't catch the small, quick, rebellious wink she flashed at Robert.

Jean-Pierre Wimille spent 3 September 1939 getting slowly, inexorably drunk. It was the day he should have raced the Tank at La Baule. He had, however, declined to test the car and let Jean Bugatti do it. Late at night, on roads he thought empty, Jean had swerved to avoid a cyclist and was killed. Wimille's stubborn indolence had cost the brilliant young man his life. And, he knew, Ettore's. The old man would never recover from the blow.

Eve spent it at the desk in the bedroom, composing a long letter to the shocked and fragile Bugattis, trying to piece together some consoling thoughts, but mostly failing.

Robert was with his mistress in Nantes, a woman who adored having a sporting hero as a lover, but who at the same time demanded material proof of his devotion. He had travelled to deliver a gold cigarette lighter.

Williams worked at Avenue Montaigne, covering for Robert's absence, and although buying was the last thing on people's minds, cars were coming in and out of stock, some being shipped out of the country, others being mothballed until the political temperature fell once more.

Maurice nursed a hangover. The previous night he had spent carousing with friends around rue Blondel near Les Halles marketplace, a model of French inefficiency and bureaucracy, where goods imported from the regions were sold, and then often transported back to the very same district at hugely inflated prices. At night, filled with the calvados-breathing workers in blue salopettes manhandling vast mounds of fruit and vegetables, the Baltard ironwork of the great sheds glowing from the flames of burning crates, the streets around the metal parasols were filled with the kind of sexually licentious establishments that the bourgeois liked to dip a well-scrubbed toe in after the opera or theatre. During the course of a lesbian tableaux in a grubby bar, Maurice had made some excellent contacts in the market trade.

That day, hangover notwithstanding, over cervelat sausages at Balzar, Maurice negotiated to buy a small candle-making business. He also met with some of his friends who ran a small butcher's. Light and food, he believed, might be two important commodities soon. In the evening he began negotiations with a coat manufacturer and a coal merchant. Warmth, that would be much sought after, too.

Elsewhere, other, more important, people put the wheels of purgatory into slow, grinding, bone-breaking motion. Britain, and then France, declared reluctant war on the country already pounding Poland into submission.

Across in England, over a drink at Jules Bar in Jermyn Street, a friend of Rose Miller's mother asked if she would like to pursue some interesting work for her country.

Fifteen

FRANCE, SEPTEMBER 1939–JUNE 1940

Like waiting for test results you know will reveal a terminal disease, the confession of an unfaithful partner, the death of a loved relative, the announcement of war at least came with the blessing of certainty after four years of stomach-churning vertigo as France stared over the abyss and somehow did not fall. Now it had, headlong, and they were all waiting for the impact.

Williams came back from the Bugatti HQ in Paris on the fifth of September; he and Eve clung to each other for the longest time, snuggling and pressing as if trying to fuse into a single organism, as scared as either could ever remember.

That night he cooked a huge slab of lamb, which they devoured hungrily with a bottle of red Loire wine, each speaking in mundanities until they went outside to the dying day and, as twilight faded and the first stars appeared, spoke softly in the darkness, sitting under the big tree at the edge of the garden.

'You meant what you said that time. About returning to England?'

Williams lit them a cigarette each. 'I have no alternative.'

A snort. 'How is Paris?'

'The theatres have closed. Cafés are busy trying to put up black-out curtains. The Louvre is being emptied. Everything shipped into storage. They've killed all the poisonous reptiles in the zoo. Nervous.'

'I can't go with you.'

'Communists are being hounded. As allies of Hitler.'

'Did you hear what I said?'

'There will be rationing I expect. To conserve stocks.'

'I can't go to England with you, Will.'

'Sirens go off so often everybody ignores them. One day they'll be for real and the entire population will be out on the streets.'

'Stay here.'

Williams turned and faced her, waiting for his eyes to adjust fully to the darkness so he could see her face clearly. There was moisture glistening in one eye. Maybe he was only worth a half-cry. She blinked and now both sparkled wetly. 'I can't. I'll be arrested. Interned.'

'You are assuming we are going to lose. Maurice says—'

'Maurice?'

'Maurice says with the British we can hold them.'

'Come with me.'

'I can't. My parents. My dogs.'

'We'll take your parents.'

'Father is too ill to uproot.'

'You don't want to go, do you?'

She hesitated, wondering whether to fudge the truth. In the end she blurted out: 'To England? No. You'll go off and fight and I'll be left alone again, just like when you were racing.'

'You'll be free.'

'Better a prisoner in France than free in England.'

'That's insane.'

Eve touched his shoulder. 'Is it? I have friends I can turn to here. Family. Over there? We could hide in France. It's a big country.'

Williams stood up. 'I thought about that. Every option. The thing is, we'd have to live with ourselves afterwards.'

'I'd manage.'

Williams flung his cigarette butt off into the darkness, watched it flare briefly as it bounced along the gravel in the courtyard. He thought about sitting and waiting, perhaps hiding for weeks, months, years while other men fought the war, the just war. It reminded him of those long hours in the pits at Le Mans while others drove the Tanks out on the circuit, itching to be behind the wheel himself. 'I don't think I could.' He pulled Eve to her feet, lifted the hair away from her face and kissed her, feeling the salt of her tears run into his mouth as he did so.

'You're really going?' Robert asked. 'Definitely?'

They were in the comfortingly ornate Ritz bar, where the very prospect of war, invasion or bombing seemed absolutely absurd. In fact, in this part of Paris it was being treated as, at worst, an inconvenience – as they passed the fashion shops around Place Vendôme they had laughed at the mannequins sporting gas masks, chicly tied with coloured bows rather than ugly coiffure-threatening straps.

Williams nodded.

'And Eve still isn't?'

Hammering started from the corner and they both looked around, irritated at the intrusion. 'Black-out curtains,' explained the barman. So it was even creeping into these hallowed halls after all.

'I think,' continued Williams, 'I have exhausted everything short of kidnapping.'

Robert raised an eyebrow. 'Well . . .'

'No. Thanks all the same. What about you?'

'Huh. The Air Ministry . . . you wouldn't believe men can be so foolish, Will.' Robert took a drink of his whisky, pausing to gather his thoughts. 'You know, I was always so jealous of you.'

'Me? Jealous of me?'

'That you had Eve. That you had such skill. That you did it on your own. A chauffeur. That you didn't need it the way I did. You had a real life . . . you always reminded me that there was another way. I could never quite reach it.'

Embarrassed, Williams snorted derisively. 'Listen, perhaps some of that is true. How do you think I felt? You were the great Robert Benoist. Just to be on the same team . . . don't get me started. Grown men shouldn't cry at the Ritz.'

He laughed. 'Well, the great Robert Benoist wants to say this. He will miss you.' He kissed Williams noisily on both cheeks. 'Now fuck off.'

Williams and Eve didn't say much at the station. Every argument had been rehearsed, every weakness probed, every possibility exhausted, but two intractable people found no compromise. She had bought him, and carefully packed, a new Louis Vuitton trunk, as if to say 'no hard feelings'. If only that were true.

The whistle blew, there were frantic goodbyes along the platform as the passengers squeezed on to the crowded train. He kissed her, a quick, glancing one this time, as if anything longer would be unbearable.

'I have to go.'

'I know.' But the voice said she didn't. They were jostled by fellow travellers, eager to be away, as if Hitler was already knocking at the door. Another whistle. Williams stepped down from the train.

'I won't go.'

She felt her heart lift, lost in that one moment, knowing she had him back. Then her mind quickly spooled ahead, to a pacing, angry Williams, his opportunity lost, the slow corrosion of waiting and inactivity eating into him. She spoke words that were heavy and slow to come. 'I think you must. It's too late to stop now.'

He nodded, knowing that she had seen through the gesture for what it was. The train shunted forward a few centimetres and hissed impatiently. 'I'll miss you,' he said. It didn't seem enough, somehow.

'You better had.'

Williams stepped on to the train, reached out and brushed a blonde strand from her face. The locomotive jerked once more and his hand was snatched away. She began to walk slowly alongside, trying to hold back the tears that were stinging the corners of her eyes, as he leant forward to touch her cheek once more.

'Look after Robert. He's down at the Air Ministry every day demanding a new commission. At his age.'

She stopped, smiled and raised a hand as the train took her man away, heading west with gathering speed, its carriage windows framing a flashing cavalcade of relief, anguish, despair and hope. As the guard's van creaked by her, she said quietly to herself: 'And who's going to look after me?'

As she quickly turned and strode back towards the platform entrance the familiar intense stare came back at her and she froze. Robert.

'I thought you might need some company,' he shouted over the bobbing heads.

Eve managed a grateful grin she tried to invest with at least a simulacrum of happiness. As she walked up his arm came out and she slid hers through his and wondered what was going to happen now.

JUNE, 1940

Robert came back to the workshops and showroom on Avenue Montaigne to change. It was deserted as he expected. The mechanics had been taken by the *mobilisation generale*, the secretaries to the exodus, and the customers to other countries. In his office he stripped off his Air Force uniform in disgust and threw it into the waste. He had spent days badgering officers to be allowed to fly sorties, to support the troops, but confusion overwhelmed everything. Planes that could be harassing German troops and convoys stood on the Tarmac, idle.

Finally, as the Germans came closer, Robert had asked permission to take the planes back to a safe field to continue the fight. Permission refused. He attempted to take one anyway and was threatened at gunpoint. That was when he realised it was futile. France wasn't going to fight after all, not as a cohesive force.

Changed into civilian clothes, he locked up the premises and began to walk north towards the Champs Elysées but hesitated. He couldn't stand to see the great street humbled by the ugly steel barriers strung across it to prevent German gliders landing.

Robert turned and headed south down the Avenue Montaigne, past two gendarmes, rifles slung over their backs, looking nervous and jittery, scanning him for signs of subversion, as if he might have a hammer and sickle tattooed about his person.

The pavements were gritty beneath his feet, the last of the sand that had been dumped outside each apartment, waiting for the concierges to carry it to the roof as protection against bomb blasts. Only someone who didn't live in Paris could have come up with that plan, he thought. The concierges refused to a woman and a man to undertake such a menial task. The sand was left to be dispersed by the few children left in the city and pissed in by the packs of abandoned cats that now roamed the streets.

Posters everywhere proclaimed the city's fate; those torn down in disgust stirred lazily in the breeze.

Notice
To Residents of Paris
Paris having been declared an OPEN CITY, the military Governor urges the population to abstain from all hostile acts and counts on it to maintain the composure and dignity required by these circumstances.

The Governor General of Paris
Dentz.

How, wondered Robert, can you maintain dignity and composure when your trousers are round your ankles and your arse is stuck in the air, just waiting for the German army to shaft you? He cut through to the Avenue George V and, round the corner from the Crazy Horse, found a café open. The walnut-faced proprietress glared at him when he asked for a cognac with his coffee and pointed at the sign. No alcohol, Tuesday, Thursday and Saturday.

'Aren't you Robert Benoist?' she asked.

He nodded. It was amazing people still remembered him, two years after his last, twilight victory at Le Mans.

'Why aren't you off in England with your rich Jewish friends?'

He paid for the drink without it touching his lips and crossed the river. As he traversed the Alma bridge he could see clumps of black smoke hugging the river and taste the vile chemicals in the air. The sun suddenly became as hazy as the Paris streetlamps in their blackout veils, its light and warmth turned down several notches. It was true, then. Someone had torched the oil tanks at St Cloud.

A lone plane flew overhead and the few people on the bridge ducked under the parapet but Robert could see it was just a 108. A spotter plane.

It banked over the Île de la Cité and headed north. Robert guessed it was flying up the rue Sebastopol against the stream of the second river Paris had suddenly acquired, the one of people, flowing like thick molasses, coming in at the North and East gates, moving down Sebastopol and St Michel, exiting the city at Orleans and Italie. Cars, motorbikes, carts, bicycles, horses, all crawling at the same achingly slow speed, driven on by fear and desperation.

As he reached the Left Bank of the river, there were perhaps a dozen others in view, a few strolling, like him, most grim faced, hurrying about their business. A city of five million had suddenly become a semi-ghost town, with perhaps 750,000 people left: those too old, young or, like him, stubborn to move. His wife and children were safe out in one of the Rothschild houses – those rich Jews the café owner talked about had made sure friends were well provided for. Maurice was still here, busier than ever, Eve had decamped to Normandy and her dogs and he still saw Wimille now and then, grumbling about how the war had struck just as he was finding the best form of his life. Which was, he had to admit, tragically true.

Some of the gutters were inky black from the millions of singed fragments of the government papers burned by the ministries on the nearby Quai d'Orsay. Now a light soot began to fall, speckling the pavement and Robert could feel the lining of his lungs burning as noxious chemicals attacked the tissues. The fuel depots were blazing, bleeding their filth into the city's sky.

He looked around, wondering if the Metro was working then,

like an apparition came that rarest of mythical beasts, a cab. He ordered the phlegmatic driver to take him to the Dome, where the sight of Peggy Guggenheim sipping champagne convinced him he could get his cognac. The heavy black-out drapes were pulled back, but the terrace was emptying as the air became more sulphurous. Robert went inside, sat down, gave his order and listened to the radio, where the constant repetitions of the glutinous song 'J'attendrai' were interrupted by gloomy pronouncements on travel restrictions and exhortations to stay put.

Maurice, looking flushed and happy, sat down in front of him. With his pastel-coloured jacket and boater he looked like a boulevardier, in strangely gay dress for a city descending into twilight. 'Brother. I thought I'd find you eventually.'

There was a dark spot on Maurice's sleeve, Robert rubbed his fingers on it and sniffed. Gasoline. 'What have you been doing, Maurice?'

His brother looked around and from his pocket produced a handkerchief, which he slowly unwrapped. Robert caught a glimpse of brilliant colours dancing before the treasure was quickly returned to safety. 'For ten litres of petrol. The things I was offered.' He smirked. 'Including a real marquise.' A decree published in *Le Matin* had forbidden the removal from French soil of gold, platinum, silver and finished jewellery. Those heading for Portugal, Spain and Switzerland were happy to divest themselves of valuables if it meant fuel or food.

Seeing Robert's look of disapproval he changed tack. 'Who betrayed us, Robert?'

'We betrayed ourselves.'

The 108 came back, low, the engine noise thrumming percussively down the boulevard. 'Where are the English fighters?' asked Maurice.

'In England,' said Robert. 'Along with the British troops.'

'And precious few French ones.' Maurice had been assured that the British troops were given loading preference at Dunkirk, an action which simply confirmed his view that their so-called ally cared little for anything but the fate of Albion. The English will fight to the last Frenchman, was the widely held view with which he concurred. 'I suppose Williams won't be coming back now.'

Robert shook his head. 'No, even Will isn't that big a fool.'

He thought of Eve, alone, out in Normandy and tried to stop his mind wandering any further.

Sixteen

SCOTLAND, OCTOBER 1940

'Where do you think you are going with that, m'lad?'

The sergeant major loomed over Williams, almost blotting out the entrance to the Bridge End Hotel. He was tired now, and didn't need any more army games. It had taken two and a half days of riding overcrowded, delayed and misrouted trains to get up here to Kinross, and his temper was fraying dangerously.

He had been in the army for eight months, and he had hoped that Scotland would be a change for the better after the grinding, depressing uncertainty of London. They had acted as if he were an octogenarian when he had volunteered his services. After weekly, daily, then hourly appearances at the Strand recruiting office, they had found him a position in the RASC, running errands, ferrying officers, not what he had in mind at all. He was driving, at least. It kept his mind off Eve, kept away those cramping pains in his stomach, the feeling of nausea, the hideous realisation of what he had done now France had fallen.

He welcomed the transfer to the clean air and promised good, simple food of rural Scotland, and tried not to dwell on the fact it was taking him further than ever away from his wife.

'With what, Sergeant Major?'

'That.'

Williams didn't have to look. He had already received ribbing and reprimands about the fact he preferred his Vuitton trunk to the standard kit bag. If he'd been shipping overseas, then maybe he'd have acquiesced, but shuttling around the British Isles, the trunk-on-wheels served just as well. He didn't see what the fuss was about.

'It's my case.'

'Is it? And what do you think this is?' He nodded at the large, grey stone building behind him. 'The Ritz?'

It isn't the Ritz, he wanted to say, I know the Ritz. This is just some large dull provincial hotel taken over by 4th Liaison RASC and where he would be billeted in the basement while the general he was to ferry around would no doubt be swanning around in the Chairman's suite. He knew he was already two sentences beyond where Robert would have hit the uppity bastard. His snapping point was always a little further on, but it was coming up fast. He was tired. He wanted a drink. Not this idiot.

Both opened their mouths to speak at once and nothing came out but a honking sound. They both turned to stare at the source of the horn, a sleek Humber staff car that drew up a few yards away. Out stepped a brunette, in a uniform Williams didn't recognise right off, with an RAF flying jacket over the top. She walked slowly round the car, looked over at the pair of them, waiting for the salute they gave and she returned.

'Trouble, Sergeant Major?'

'This man has non-regulation kit, ma'am.'

He felt the eyes rake him. 'The sergeant major's right, you know. I don't think it's going to be a Louis Vuitton kind of war.'

'What sort of war did you have in mind, ma'am?'

'Corporal Williams?'

The question threw him and he could see the sergeant major frowning. How did she know who he was? Mind you, the phrase, 'can't miss him, only man fool enough to wheel around a LV trunk' might explain it. 'Yes, ma'am.'

'That's what I'd like to talk to you about.'

'Mind if I get rid of this first, ma'am?'

She inclined her head at the bolshie sergeant major who sighed and stepped aside. 'There's a pub down by the river. Four hundred yards. Shall we say half an hour?'

The warm beer tasted suspiciously thin, but Williams drank a whole pint of it before she arrived at his table in the small garden out the back with the fast-flowing river gurgling by at the end of the slope. The northern sun soon heated him up in his thick, coarse woollen uniform, and he was relaxing, almost forgetting the summons, when she slipped into the seat unheralded, gin and tonic in hand.

'Don't get up, Williams,' she said quickly. 'We won't be disturbed. I've requisitioned the garden for the war effort.'

'I didn't catch your name, ma'am.'

'No you didn't, did you?' She smiled and it transformed her face into something altogether more soft and friendly. Then it went, flicked off. What was she? Twenty-five? Six? Yet there was a hardness about her, possibly just a defensive carapace, although all of them were in the process of developing that. Her accent was top drawer, arrogant, yes, snobbish, certainly, used to being obeyed and served, but there was something else, too. The Sergeant Major, he knew, had felt it as well. An extra dose of self confidence, the assurance that comes with knowing you have absolute power on your side. 'Captain Rose Miller.'

Which outfit? He wanted to ask, but something told him he shouldn't.

Eventually she said, 'I'm with the Inter-services Research Bureau. Tell me, have you been out of France long?'

'Nine . . . no, close to eleven months.'

'Miss it?'

He nodded, thinking of the difference between London and Paris. 'Not too bad. Only every day.'

'I have had a word with your General. He was rather looking forward to having a race driver as his chauffeur.'

'Was? Or is?'

'I suggested to him you were rather overqualified.'

Williams didn't like this. Didn't like people who suddenly seemed to know an awful lot about him. Like the chap in Ireland all those years ago, he'd had the same air of authority. He began to feel uneasy, and as if reading his mind she said, 'Why didn't you contact your old friends in SIS when you got to London?'

'I don't have any old friends in SIS.'

'You helped them in Dublin.'

He laughed at this. 'Is that what they told you? They tried to get me to play piggy-in-the-middle. I didn't fancy my chances.' Then he realised she must have had access to some file about the whole affair. 'Is that who you are with? SIS?'

She shook her head but didn't answer directly. 'I am afraid we are rather making this up as we go along. We need some people who know France, who speak French like natives. We are not sure what for yet. Maybe translation, perhaps writing propaganda leaflets.' A long pause while Rose drank. 'What do you think?'

She pulled a rather crumpled envelope from her pocket and smoothed it out. 'Initially, returning to London for an informal chat. At the Victoria Hotel. Whitehall. Do you know it?'

Williams shook his head and tried to keep the exasperation

from his voice. 'I've just come from London.'

She smiled again, but this time he was disappointed to see her face didn't transform, but remained cold and impossible to read. 'As I said, we are flying by the seat of our pants. If it is any consolation, the chat is in two weeks' time, so no rush.'

'You came all this way for me?'

She waved a hand airily to dismiss such a notion. 'Good God, no. Several likely chaps up here.'

'Still, an awful lot of effort to pick up a few leaflet writers.'

'Hm.' He tried to interpret the expression. Nothing. 'There's something else might tempt you. If all went well, you'd be commissioned. Second Lieutenant initially. And you know what that means.'

He certainly did. No more sergeant majors querying his choice of luggage for one thing.

'What do you say?'

Williams took a big slug of beer and picked up the envelope. He rather liked the idea of any outfit that could sequester a pub at a moment's notice. The fact they knew that he'd been a driver for hire in Dublin suggested something other than leaflets was on the agenda. He slurped the last of his beer and licked the foam from his lips. 'Yes,' he said softly, 'why not?'

Part Two

From: SOE LONDON
To: Captain Rose Miller
Interim report. Stations STS 51/STS 23b/STS 51a

William Charles Frederick GROVER-WILLIAMS
General List Officer 231189
Born 16 Jan 03
Racing driver with Bugatti

Joined RASC Feb 40 as driver No T/174143. While at 4th
Liaison HQ RASC, Kinross (Bridge End Hotel) was selected
for employment in commissioned rank with SOE (Second
Lieutenant). Known as Vladimir Gatacre while training.

Initial training reports comment on his hard work and
anxiety to do well, describe him as an efficient soldier who
likes discipline, was fond of planning things and seeing that
the plan was carried out meticulously. His training as a WT

operator has been handicapped by his dislike of Morse and lack of confidence in learning it.

Further training has emphasised his loathing of signals but noted his extreme keenness on demolitions, which he considers his pet subject. He is described as a 'very good all round man' the 'star turn of this party'. Keen, shrewd and popular; strong sense of humour in adversity. A real good fellow who might overdo it if allowed to. A resourceful individual who would probably work best on his own.

Now Acting Lieutenant
Currently at STS 61c: Beddington House Finishing School

Seventeen

BEDDINGTON, AUGUST 1941

The late dusk was falling over the familiar scenery. Williams took two paces on to the asphalt of the old track and heard that terrible nerve-pinching screech of the superchargers, one which now reminded him, horribly, possibly unfairly, of the sirens attached to the Stuka dive-bombers to generate terror in the victims below. Was the Mercedes team trying to execute an early version of that terror? No, it was just a function of the blowers, surely.

The track was cracked and patchy now, part of it torn up as the farmer's field was reclaimed for cereals, the grandstands stripped down to mere wooden skeletons, the Castrol and Esso signs faded and flapping, but he could still smell the sweet, cloying aroma, like burnt sugar, of the German fuel.

All changed now. The Duke moved to London to do his bit, having lost his domestic staff anyway – a million servants suddenly unyoked and put into uniform had meant running a stately home wasn't quite the pleasure it had been – and the precious furniture and portraits had been put into storage while government oiks did whatever government oiks do. There were so many large country piles available it was no wonder that Special Operations Executive, the very name of which was meant to be top secret, was referred to by some of the instructors as Stately 'Omes of England.

Behind him in this particularly echoey shell of an 'ome, Williams could hear the gramophone music. The FANYs, the girls who were essential to the functioning of the STSs, the Special Training Schools, had reappeared in long evening gowns after a day of cleaning, cooking and driving and an ad hoc party had developed, with tangos and foxtrots.

He wasn't in the mood. And there was always the nagging thought that perhaps this was just another test, a check for sociability. Every detail was considered vital to success, and the sad fact was if you couldn't pass muster on any aspect, one morning you simply weren't at breakfast. Williams' group had already lost one chap who hit the whisky a bit too hard in Arisaig, another two who had failed the interview with the psychologists and yet another who declared that loud bangs made him jump when they were planting the new plastic explosives. The rumour was they went to a cooling-off house somewhere deep in the Highlands where they stayed until their secrets no longer mattered. Now he was left with a perfume salesman, a travel courier, a debutante, a nurse, a banker from Coutt's and a tailor.

Weeks of training had grown into months, with delays as various experts were found to fill in the gaps in their instruction – one so-called explosives expert had managed to blow his hand off, leaving a large vacancy in the ranks – as parachute courses were hastily arranged at Ringway, new safe houses brought on line.

All the time Williams was expecting a hand on his shoulder, a quiet word from Sykes or Fairburn or one of the other instructors as they finally figured out what was buried deep, deep in his psyche. Yes, he liked the action. Demolition was even fun.

Whereas the others in the group seemed driven by a desire to single-handedly liberate France and harass Germans, Williams had just one real aim, an ambition burning so bright everything else was a mere silhouette in comparison. To see Eve again.

Just to be able to do that he had lost three quarters of a stone, could strip and reassemble everything from a Sten to a Schmeisser in total darkness, knew from two old Shanghai policemen the fastest way to kill an opponent, how to derail an express train and survive in hostile country, foraging off the land for weeks on end and the simplest way to blow up a bridge. He only hoped Eve could somehow sense he was moving heaven and quite a lot of earth to get back to her.

Then he heard the soft sound, just hovering across the breeze. A sob. He walked out into the darkness and, over to his left, saw her sitting in front of a once well-pruned bush, now growing wild for want of a gardener.

Virginia Thorpe looked up and quickly dried her eyes. A waft of her Chanel perfume drifted across to him. It was not his favourite scent.

'Hello? Another one who thinks it's a vulgar charade in there? Or are you frightened you won't be able to control yourself with such gorgeous creatures?' Virginia Thorpe – or at least that was the name she used – was the deb of the party. She was beautiful in a languorous, sinuous way, but also, he was sure, a fearful snob. Being high and mighty enough to look down on the exceptionally well bred FANYs was certainly quite an achievement.

'Are you all right?'

'I just needed some air and . . . well, it gets to you sometimes, doesn't it? I saw you standing there and didn't want to disturb you. You seemed so lost in your own thoughts. So I just crept by.'

'I didn't even hear you. Nice quiet approach,' he said approvingly. 'Didn't hear so much as a twig snap.'

'Perfected when you have two older brothers. Spying on them got me where I am today.'

'Where are you today?'

She stood up. 'Cigarette?'

'Thanks.' He took a Craven A from her and lit them both.

Williams hesitated for a moment before confessing, 'I raced here once.'

'Raced what?' asked Virginia.

'A Bugatti.' Careful, man, he told himself, no good trying to impress this one. 'A car' would have done, but something made him rise to her bait.

'Really?' Just a hint of being impressed. 'Did you win?'

'No. The Germans did.'

She laughed, a deep throaty sound. 'Not very encouraging.'

'Why are you doing this, Virginia? I'm sure the FANY would have you like a shot. There's no need to risk your neck with all this derring-do.'

'Derring-do? That's a quaint expression for it. You boys all think you are Richard Hannay or Sandy Arbuthnot don't you? Isn't that the appeal?'

In the gloom she could almost pass for Eve, albeit an Eve of ten years ago. More refined and polished, with a confidence his wife didn't acquire until relatively late, and the thought made him ache for the real thing even more. But finally he said; 'I'm an Eric Ambler man myself.' The music stopped and there was a burst of applause. 'We'd best go back. Be marked down for not playing the game.'

'I don't think this is a team players' game, Gatacre. Do you?'

For once he gave an honest answer. 'Right now, I'm not sure what kind of game it is.'

They came for him at three that morning. Two big chaps he

hadn't seen before and never wished to again. It began with a shock of iced water in the face and an involuntary inhalation, which made his sinuses feel as if they were on fire. While he was still choking the blows began, one to the head and an expert one to his testicles which seemed to open up a tap, so that his strength drained from every limb. Rubber legged and confused he was dragged out and down the corridor, a third man appearing to poke him in the kidneys with a stick as they went.

Dragged downstairs he found himself in a room he never knew existed, some kind of wine cellar perhaps, the walls thick and damp, oozing a 'don't bother screaming, nobody can hear you' solidity, where he was tied roughly into a chair by the green-uniformed thugs.

Name.

Use your code name. The one on your papers. Charles Lelong.

What do you do?

Electrical engineer.

Why aren't you in Germany working for the Reich?

I repair factories after bom— after terrorism raids.

Twenty minutes of mouths shouting so close to him he could feel the warm spittle spraying him and he was back to his bed. Someone had thoughtfully changed the damp sheets and pillowcase. He smiled and snuggled down. Bet the Geheimstaatpolizei didn't do that. All in all, didn't go too badly, he felt.

Thirty minutes later they were back, rougher. No water in the face this time, just a yank on his hair and he was on the floor. Back to the same room. This time he could see blood on the floor. Was it real blood? It had the sickly claret-coloured sheen of actual arterial contents. More questions, but of a less general nature. Who are your friends in Paris? Who is Robert Benoist? Jean-Pierre Wimille? Where is your wife? And guns, pistols pressed against the side of his head, held under his nose, the

131

terrifying twin SS lightning bolts and the SD patches inches from his eyes.

By the third time, his head was completely clogged. He wanted to sleep, to feel those sheets again, to just tell them everything and get it over with, but his tongue wouldn't let him. To his horror he realised they had almost won. Even though he simply gave his false identity over and over again, he had let a small chink in, had toyed with the possibility of compromise, failure, treachery. That was how it worked. Needle away until almost involuntarily the survival centres of the brain do what they have to do. He tried to shut down his higher levels, to think about something else to mask the shouting. So loud, so piercing.

Then he had it. He focused on engine noises, the distinctive signature of all the cars he had known. He let them sing in his head, the deep throb of the Alfa, the scream of the early Mercedes, the strange ripping sound of the Bugatti, on and on they went, a cavalcade of the most cacophonous vehicles ever built, filling the room and his skull to the exclusion of all else.

Eventually, somewhere near dawn, they threw him back into bed and left him, shaking and sweating, wondering how much worse the genuine article could be. And how much weaker he would be when the time came.

Williams managed two hours of fitful, anxious sleep before the soft voice of his room-mate in his ear told him it was time for breakfast. Blearily, feeling faintly ashamed of his performance, even though his weaknesses and betrayals were all in his head, he lined up for eggs with the others. The queue was chatting and joking as usual, occasionally looking to him for a comment, but he felt dizzy and disoriented. Then he saw Virginia looking alabaster pale, her eyes shrunken, a dark crescent newly arrived under each one. They caught each other's stare and both knew. She winked first, the conspiratorial contact of fellow sufferers.

★ ★ ★

Five days and two more nocturnal interrogations later, his temples throbbing from a mild hangover, he watched Virginia doggedly swim length after length of the Beddington pool, a mock Greco-Roman temple, complete with columns, busts, and mildly erotic mosaics.

He went down on his haunches as she came in for the turn. 'Where did you learn to swim like that?'

She smoothly executed the change of direction and said over her shoulder. 'At home. In a pool much like this one, actually.'

On her return she said: 'Come in.'

'I can't swim.'

She laughed as her arms knifed into the water. They knew from parachute training that lakes make good navigational aids in a drop zone. So good, in fact, that the over-enthusiastic pilot might send you straight down into one. He had managed to avoid the inflatable dinghy training drop.

'I'll teach you.'

'Vladimir Gatacre?' the voice boomed off the tiles and he found himself springing up to almost attention. One of the gnarled instructors, this one a whippet-thin man in his fifties, strode over. 'Get your kit off, Sir. Time to earn your water wings.'

He looked down at Virginia. 'Sorry, looks like I'm already spoken for.'

After a month at Beddington there was little that could surprise Williams or his colleagues. One afternoon, following a particularly good lunch of what turned out to be wood pigeon, he was invited to the Carrington suite in the west wing. When he arrived he hesitated outside. The Sergeant reading the *Express* newspaper opposite with its usual grim headlines ('Miners' strike in Kent.

Leningrad under siege.') looked up.

'It's OK, sir. No boxing gloves this time.'

The last time he had burst into a room during an exercise a large red glove had landed on his temple, warning him always to check who is lurking behind a door. Williams, despite the Sergeant's assurances (the new motto 'Trust nobody', echoed in his brain during most waking hours), knocked.

'Come in,' said a muffled female voice.

On the other side of the door the heavy curtains were drawn, plunging the room into a curious half-light. Before him was a large desk, illuminated by an overhead light, and upon that desk was a large cloth which, judging by its contours, concealed an array of items underneath.

The woman who had spoken to him was sitting in a corner, visible mainly from the glowing tip of her cigarette. Without taking it out of her mouth she muttered, 'Remove the cloth. You have ten seconds. Put it back. Tell me what the items were and tell me how they connect to each other.'

Williams stepped forward and, feeling like a cheap vaudeville magician, got ready to reveal what was underneath the cover. He pulled it away and his eyes scanned the motley assortment, mouthing them to himself, trying to put together a little mnemonic as he had been taught, or failing that burning the image of the tray and its contents into his visual cortex.

'Ten,' said the voice, and now he realised he knew the woman. 'Tell me.'

He replaced the cloth. 'A piece of glass. Venetian. Murano? A rose. A tartan biscuit tin with what looked like red paint on it. A stuffed animal. A vole? A tape measure. Postcard of Windsor Castle. A piece of writing paper with all the words scrawled out. A couple of model village houses. A snowstorm paperweight of . . . was it the Acropolis?'

The woman stood and stepped forward so that she was at the edge of the pool of light. Rose Miller, in uniform, with flying jacket. 'Not bad. And the connection?'

His mind desperately shuffled the pack, first checking the initial of each to see if there was a word there, thinking what he would really like to do is have the Brains Trust standing next to him. A stuffed animal? Why? Then it came to him.

'It isn't a vole. It's a shrew. They are all references to Shakespeare. Merchant of Venice, War of the Roses, Macbeth, Taming of the Shrew, Measure for Measure, Merry Wives of Windsor, Love's Labours Lost, Hamlet . . . the snow thing? The Tempest?'

'Timon of Athens. But very good.'

Williams sighed with relief, suddenly wary. The constant testing and examination was draining. But perhaps that was the idea. 'So what's the point?'

'Do you know your Kipling?'

'No, I'm more of—'

'An Eric Ambler man,' she finished. Williams felt a jolt. He'd said that to Virginia out in the open air. Suddenly other little insights the instructors had had came back to him. Microphones. They are listening. All the time.

'It's a test. An observational and intuition test. We call it . . . Kim's Game. After Kipling.' She turned on the ceiling light, but it still left the room a gloomy yellow, as if smog had somehow crept in. 'Come on. I want to show you something.'

Williams watched the two Bugattis pull away from the line, marvelling at the acceleration, irritated at the puff of smoke coming from the rear wheels of the one on the left. Not enough power to the floor, too much wasted in wheel spin. Brakes too early, allowing the other to nose ahead, makes it up with fluid acceleration through the banking, and a clean exit, into top gear and along the straight. He awarded himself eight out of ten.

'How fast are you going?'

The abrasive sound of Rose's voice shocked him out of his reverie. Kim's Game was the first time he had seen her since that day in Kinross when she had commandeered the pub. Then there had been a come-hither edge to her, a spider-like seduction as she drew the potential recruit into her shadowy and beguiling world. Now that he and the others had discovered that spying, or at least the preparation for it, was, like much else in wartime, ninety-eight per cent mundanity, two per cent excitement, she was much more brisk and business-like. In front of them, projected on a small screen, was the footage shot by Maurice of the duel at Montlhery all those years ago. Now he could see all his mistakes in blurry, shaky black and white, realised how he was lucky even to come close to Robert.

'How fast?' Irritation in the voice.

'Oh. Sorry. About one-fifty along the straight.'

'Miles per hour?'

'Yes.'

'Looks bloody dangerous.'

Williams laughed. 'It's a damn sight safer than your parachute course.'

The camera jerkily swung around off the track and on to the spectators, making Williams feel slightly nauseous. His heart juddered when the image steadied and sharpened on to Eve, clutching a terrier to her breast, looking as if she was going to squeeze the life out of the poor dog in her anxiety.

'She looks worried.'

'She always did,' said Williams, thinking of how she grew to hate him risking his life. And now he was risking it to get back to her.

Rose twigged. 'Ah. That's Eve is it? She's very beautiful.'

'Yes.'

'Tell me. Why didn't she come with you? Married to a British subject, she would have had no problems.'

On screen the flag came down on Robert as Williams tried a last minute piece of slipstreaming. 'It's a long story.'

'Lights.'

Williams was suddenly blinking in the glare of bare bulbs. 'Where did you get the footage?'

'From the Prescott Hill Climb Bugatti Club. Drink?'

Williams nodded and they walked through rooms stripped bare of ancestral portraits and antique furniture to a well-appointed bar, where David, the white-coated barman, dispensed spirits, beer having disappeared a week before.

Unusually, it was deserted, the other recruits attending a lecture updating them on French politics in the thirties. Williams having been over there for all of that decade was excused in favour of the impromptu film show.

They ordered double scotches and sat down at a small table out of David's earshot, a consideration which, he was both pleased and alarmed to discover, was becoming second nature.

'I've read your interim report. Hopeless at Morse. Suspicious of all communications. Slow at lock picking. Swims like a house-brick. Runs into rooms without checking behind doors.'

'So I've failed.'

'Cheers.' She took a sip. 'On the other hand, likes blowing things up, works well alone, drives like a demon. I quote: "a tough, resourceful individual". Three nights of mock interrogations and you bore up well. You'll do, Williams. So far, at least. You have your passing-out test yet.'

Williams knew he would be required to get inside some high security installation or police station or steal a military car or a weapon, some little assignment that would show he could pull off a stunt in a country on a war footing. 'Why the movie?' he asked. 'I was there, remember?'

'So was Robert Benoist.'

'Robert?'

'You are a lucky man, Williams. You have friends in that country. Friends I think might help you. And a wife. The others will never know who to trust, will get desperately lonely . . . might make mistakes.'

She was going too fast for him. 'You want me to recruit my friends?'

'Robert Benoist. I read his press cuttings. I would imagine here is another tough, resourceful individual.'

Williams laughed. 'I can't argue with that. But he is his own man.'

'Meaning?'

'I don't know if he'd like being under anyone else's control. Especially mine. Number two driver suddenly number one? Never a happy situation in a team.'

Rose took out a Woodbine, Craven A having suddenly been supplanted in the tuck shop by those and Players. She offered him one and smiled. 'So you think he's a waste of time?'

'No, not necessarily. He's a brave man—'

Rose snorted and quoted in her very cultured voice: 'The man who can most truly be accounted brave, is he who knows best the meaning of what is sweet in life, and what is terrible, and then goes out determined to meet what is to come. Pericles. History of the Peloponnese War.'

'I'm an Eric Ambler man myself.'

She smirked. 'You get my drift. I have the feeling Robert knows the sweet things in life. Would he help? Would he put that in jeopardy?'

A few other recruits drifted in, but kept their distance. He could see Virginia talking animatedly to one of the instructors, a craggy Irishman clearly busy falling in love. She laughed, a little too loudly. 'Why Robert? I don't understand.'

'There will be missions where we need the talents of men like you and Robert.'

'Racing drivers?'

'At a hundred and fifty miles an hour, a tyre bursts, a deer runs out, you hit oil . . . how can you survive, when everything happens so quickly?'

Williams paused, wondering what she was getting at. 'It is only happening quickly to an outsider, an observer. The trick is to slow the world down, so that when things happen at one-fifty, one-sixty, they seem to be occurring at normal speed to you.'

'Precisely,' Rose said, 'that's why I want you and Robert. Men who think fast is slow.'

That's an answer? he thought, but didn't voice.

'There is one other thing.'

'What's that?'

'You drivers know what it is like to undertake a pursuit, and undertake it again and again, when you know the odds of you surviving shorten each time.'

'That was never my favourite part.'

'But it's true.'

'You never go out intending to be killed. Well, I never did.'

'Good.'

There was a silence while she considered whether to go on. 'It's started over there. God only knows it took them long enough.'

'What has started?'

'Resistance. Fourteen, fifteen months since they invaded. Since then, nothing. Then four weeks ago a German was shot at the Barbes-Rochechouart Metro. A week later someone tried to kill Pierre Laval of the Vichy government at Versailles. Another week, a German soldier shot at Gare de l'Est. Twenty killings in all, and growing. They are ready to fight now, especially the communists. We can hardly keep up with the new names being bandied about – Liberation-Nord, OCM, Front National, FTPF – they're the communists – and Armée Secrete . . .'

The list droned on and she saw his brow furrowing. It was as bad as pre-war politics. Actually, it was probably the same as pre-war politics – dozens of factions each with its own agenda. 'You'll be getting a lecture on them all, don't worry. Whoever we decide to back, they will need guns. They will need instruction. They will need examples. They might even need the odd racing driver.' She winked at him, an unnerving experience. 'So, Robert. Where is he now?'

Williams thought and replied: 'Probably brushing up his Pericles by enjoying the sweet things in life.'

Robert Benoist had grown used to the sight of Germans swarming across his city like a plague of green insects, but the shock of so many in a confined space, almost outnumbering civilians, took him aback. He looked at Eve on his arm and pulled her tight to his side. Over his shoulder he turned to the gaunt, worried-looking Dr Ziegler and whispered, 'Stay close. We won't stay long.'

Maurice's apartment was fit to burst. As Robert threaded his way through the crowd towards the drinks table he picked up snatches of conversation that went over the usual topics. The price of lightbulbs – if you can find one – the black market, how to get an *Ausweiss* – a travel permit – the new rations, the best collaborationist leaflets to make fuel briquettes out of, the coming winter. The latter exercised most people. The one of forty–forty-one had been bad, and now temperatures were dropping again. The autumn sound of Paris was no longer the rustle of leaves in the

Luxembourg garden – now given over to vegetables – but that of newspaper shoved into overcoats as insulation.

He heard his brother's distinctive low level whisper, urging a guest to come and see him if he needed . . . but at that point the words became inaudible.

'Maurice.'

'Robert. Eve.' His eyes raked her up and down with practised assessment. 'You look lovely. No trouble getting here?' Maurice had pulled some strings to arrange Eve's journey to Paris, and he beamed when she shook her head. 'Ah. Dr Ziegler. So glad you could make it. Drinks?' Maurice swept glasses of champagne from a passing tray. 'Robert. A word. Mother isn't very well again. We should have her looked after.'

'Anything I can do?' offered Dr Ziegler.

Maurice smiled: 'No, no. As you know, she's a stubborn woman.'

Maurice steered Robert to a corner and hissed: 'Are you out of your fucking mind bringing him here?'

'He's our doctor.'

'He's our very Jewish doctor.'

'Yes. And he doesn't have a telephone.'

'What?'

'They've cut off his telephone. I want you to get it back on.'

'Me?'

'Yes, you. Come on, Maurice. In return for a girl. Or a dirty show. A painting. I don't know how you do it, but you must help him. How can he work?'

'I think that's the general idea.'

Recently the first *rafle*, round-up, of Jews had occurred, with more promised. Jewish property and enterprises could now be confiscated. 'Just do it, Maurice.'

Robert glanced back over the heads of the partygoers and saw a tall, blond man had moved in on Eve. 'Who's that talking to Eve?'

'Ah,' said Maurice, relieved to be off the subject of Ziegler's telephone. 'Neumann. Joachim Neumann. Assistant to Keppler. You remember Keppler? The Sportskorpsführer? Out in the open now. SD. Neumann's not as bad as he looks. Quite a civilised chap, really.'

'We all are, Maurice.' It was Keppler, a man made doughy by many months of high living. 'Robert Benoist. How nice to see you again. The last time was in England.'

'And the last time you'll see it,' said Robert. Maurice blanched.

'Oh, I don't know. Mind you, I spend the day compiling lists of Wehrmacht men who will not use the official whores. I think we may have to postpone invading England altogether because our army have sore pricks.' Maurice joined in the laughter. 'We have decided to send anyone who catches VD to a Punishment Battalion. That should make them more careful where they dip their wieners, eh?'

Keppler followed Robert's gaze over to Eve, who was looking at her feet as Neumann spoke in her ear. 'Joachim. The ladies love him. I think it is the uniform.' Keppler patted his large belly. 'Somehow seems to fit him better than me.' He saw the look on Robert's face and said quietly, 'Don't cause any trouble, Robert. Striking a member of the SS is a capital offence. Tell me, whatever happened to that English driver, Williams? Where is he now?'

'Keeping better company than me I hope. Excuse me.' And he went to rescue Eve from Neumann, SS or no.

Eighteen

LONDON, NOVEMBER 1941

Williams had last visited Quaglino's in 1938. Then it had seemed slightly stuffy and formal after La Coupole and Fouquet's. Now, with evening dress for men the exception rather than the rule and civilians and servicemen in equal numbers, it exuded a slightly desperate jollity.

Williams, Virginia and Rose had taken a cab from the small flat near Baker Street where the women were staying – Williams was in a dingy hotel around the corner from them – and arrived to a backdrop of low rumbles and flashes as the East End of London flared fitfully under another raid. 'Don't worry,' said Rose. 'I hear if there is an alert they let you bed down in the basement.'

Virginia curled her lip. 'I'll take my chances in the street, thank you, ma'am.'

'No "ma'am" tonight. Rose.'

They checked their coats – Rose revealing a svelte black-beaded dress and Virginia a silk brocade gown with a ruched bodice – and were shown to a table. Williams, who had opted for uniform (the safest dress for a male these days), pondered the reason for the evening. They were obviously on the home straight now. Williams had passed his test of obtaining a classified document by blatant bribery of a government official – it turned out to be a vital map of the Tunbridge Wells sewer system – and had been in a holding house near Guildford for more weeks than he cared to remember, occasionally brushing up on fieldcraft and weapons, but otherwise cooling his heels and fighting boredom instead of Germans. Virginia was billeted elsewhere, but on a similar regime. At least while in the city he got to use the London Transport rifle range, which was conveniently buried under Baker Street tube station, and was able to take his frustration out on paper targets.

As they sat down Rose said, 'What a treat.'

'Is this our last supper, as it were?' asked Virginia.

'Not exactly. It's a bit of a tradition that, as your Conducting Officer, I take out my charges for an informal chat. Just to see if you have any worries. Count yourself lucky. Normally it's a ghastly bistro on the Edgware Road.'

'How do you stand it?' asked Williams.

'Well, the owner sometimes gets a chicken from his brother in the country.'

There was a pop of champagne corks and they looked over at a cheering group of young men and women. Another engagement announced, with the wedding day delayed, possibly indefinitely. 'That's not what I mean. How do you stand sending people off knowing they won't come back.'

Rose snapped a breadstick irritably. 'Might. Not won't. A certain ratio may not . . . but look at our pilots. Do they think about casualty rates every time they go up?'

'If they want to stay alive.'

'Hmm.'

144

Virginia interrupted by asking: 'So how is it we have been promoted to Quaglino's?'

Williams shuffled, embarrassed. It was his shout, as they say. He had access to a Bugatti entertaining account for clients held at Coutt's which had never been closed. It had sat there untouched for more than two years. Seemed a shame. But for some reason he didn't want Virginia to know that. He was relieved when Rose just glanced up from the menu and said; 'Oh, I fiddled some expenses for Vladimir here. Said he needed another bribe to corrupt yet more local policemen.'

Williams ordered a bottle of astonishingly overpriced Margaux, Orpen's favourite, and they plundered the menu. There was smoked salmon, chicken, mushroom pâté, various rabbit dishes. A cornucopia compared to what regular folk were getting, he knew. No whale meat at Quaglino's. Although if the Atlantic blockade got much worse, it might come to that, even here. Resentment against 'posh' restaurants was building, and he had heard talk of a five-shilling ceiling per person on meals. He scanned the prices as they ran through their orders with the waiter and realised they would burst well through that tonight.

The band started. Al Bowly with the Ray Noble Orchestra and 'The Very Thought of You'. A few couples from the engagement table got up to dance.

'I have something for you both.' Rose fished into her clutch bag and produced two tissue-wrapped items and deposited one in front of each of them.

'Do we open it now?' asked Virginia, already unwrapping the delicate layers. 'Oh,' she said, with an expression a few notches short of enthusiasm. 'How lovely.'

It was a gold powder compact, in a deliberately anodyne style that could have come from anywhere in western Europe. From his wrapping Williams produced equally plain but elegant gold cufflinks which he weighed in his hands. Their heftiness suggested quality.

'Thank you,' he said, and began turning one link over, trying to slip a fingernail into the hidden seam or concealed catch or whatever the boffins had dreamt up.

'What are you doing?' asked Rose.

'Looking for the gadget,' he said. 'I assumed these contain a map, a compass or our L Pill.' The latter was the cyanide suicide tablet each agent would carry, just in case.

'Sometimes,' smiled Rose, 'a pair of cufflinks is just a pair of cufflinks and a powder compact is just a powder compact. Another fledgling tradition. But one with a purpose. No distinguishing hallmarks, of course, but solid gold. You can pawn them if need be.'

The food arrived and it was clear that some kind of rationing was being applied in the kitchen after all. The portions were tiny. 'Best fill up on bread,' warned Rose.

They ate in silence for a while, enjoying flavours and textures far more delicate than they had become used to. Rose had just finished her chicken with the *Maître d'* approached and whispered in her ear.

'Excuse me,' she said, standing. 'A call.'

Virginia waited until she was out of earshot before taking a slug of wine and asking, 'What do you make of her?'

It was a very leading question. Did she mean personally or professionally. 'I wouldn't want to be in her shoes,' he finally offered, noncommittally.

No. Rather clumpy I thought.' She took another gulp. 'I think we'll need a second bottle. Anyway, I think she's a phony.'

'A what?'

'A fake. Something not quite U about her. The shoes, maybe.' He realised she was well on the way to getting drunk.

Rose strode over, her face dark, and for a second Williams thought she had heard them. He half considered checking the flower for hidden microphones. 'Look, I'm sorry, you two, but something's come up. Quite serious. I have to go back to Baker Street. You'll be all right, won't you?'

They both nodded and wished her good luck and Virginia suddenly burst out laughing. 'God, I feel like you used to when teacher left the classroom. Don't you?'

Williams couldn't help but grin. It was true, Rose Miller had the ability to be an oppressive presence when she wanted, quite the school ma'am, no matter how she wanted to be addressed. 'You still want that other bottle?'

'Oh, absolutely.'

They had taken the last Margaux, so Williams settled for a rather inferior St Emilion.

'How've you been these past few weeks?' he asked her.

'Bored. Bored, bored, bored. Bored. That about sums it up,' she said with feeling. 'You?'

'Much the same.'

'I know I shouldn't ask you this, but when do you go?'

He shrugged. She was right. She shouldn't ask.

'But it'll be soon, won't it? I think it'll be soon. This dinner. The cufflinks. The ghastly compact. Look, I know this is terribly forward of me.' More wine. 'But dear ol' Rosie had absolutely forbidden me to look up any of my old chums in town. Says I have to get used to isolation. But it's been so wretched in that bloody house. I wondered if . . .'

Williams wasn't entirely sure if he was meant to jump in here, and if so, with what exactly. But he felt the hairs on his neck prickling.

Virginia smacked the table in mock anger. 'Oh, do I have to spell it out?'

'I think we should go.'

Her face brightened. 'Now?'

'Separately.'

'Oh, for God's sake, man. We could dance. At least that.'

So he took her round the floor in a desultory foxtrot, trying hard to hold her chest away from his for fear that something might leach through to him, corroding his resolve like spiritual acid.

'Do you know anyone over there? I do. My old teacher lives in Lyons. I hope I get sent there.'

He grunted.

'Look, Vladimir. That can't be your real name, can it? You don't look like a Russian.' She said this in a low stage voice. 'Tell me the real one. At least that. Mine's really Veronica Taylor-Stapylton. I thought having the same initials would help.'

'Jenkins. Ron.'

She pinched his arm and he winced. 'No, it's not. I know it – I heard one of the instructors use it at the beginning by mistake. It's something Williams, isn't it?'

'Good Lord, no,' he said with conviction, the penny finally dropping. 'It's Seymour Kuntz,' he smirked, stealing an old punchline from a Maurice joke. Her brow furrowed as she tried to read his face.

Williams applauded as the music finished and briskly walked back to the table and asked for the bill, scribbling in the Coutt's cheque book. 'There's still half a bottle of wine,' said Virginia.

'Finish it,' he said, putting down a pound note. 'Here's the cab fare back. The *Maître d'* will look after you. Sorry.'

She jutted out her lower lip, threw the bill across the table and watched him leave in pouting silence.

He half stumbled into the fresh air, realising that he, too, was unused to such a quantity of red wine with hardly any food. Rose was across the street, leaning on her staff car, driver behind the wheel, smoking a cigarette. The air was tinged with the acrid fumes of burning buildings far away down the river, the sky smeared with red as if sunset had been called back for an encore, disrupting the otherwise velvet-black of the darkened city. He walked across to her.

'I was going to give you five minutes more.'

'And if I'd fallen for her cut-glass charms and tottered out arm in arm with her?'

'You'd be on a train to the Highlands where you'd be eating haggis and tossing the caber for the next year. Lift?'

'Another charade?'

'No. Show's over for tonight. This is off duty. What do you want to do?'

'It's your town more than mine.'

She opened the door to the Humber. 'Hop in.'

The place was half the size of a tennis court but Williams could have sworn five hundred people were crammed into the space. It was a basement somewhere not far from Leicester Square, with no external sign he could discern, and a retired pugilist with an interesting nose on the door, although he didn't seem too keen on turning anyone away.

The band, nearly all octogenarians, apart from a negro sax player, were playing fast jazz, and the crowd – everything from spivs to serving officers and all points in between, danced as best they could in the constricted space.

After ten minutes of feet and elbow they gave up and Rose shouted in his ear. 'There is a quieter bar up top.'

He followed her up a back staircase to a small, rather smelly room done out in purple velvet. The only other customer was a snoozing sailor. Rose fetched a couple of scotches from the barmaid and tucked them into a corner booth and, to his surprise, whipped a curtain across. 'In case clients want a bit of privacy.' Now Williams realised the girls who looked like tarts working the dancefloor were probably just that. 'But it doesn't usually get busy till later.'

Williams looked down at the seats, but they seemed clean enough.

'No, not here, you fool. They just soften them up in the booths. Promise them the world. Deliver the rather tarnished goods next door.'

'How do you know about this place?'

'John Gilbert?'

'The lock-picking instructor?' Gilbert ran the Beddington breaking and entry course.

'The problem with the racket is that almost everyone comes from a very nice background.' She made the word harsh and truncated. 'And this isn't a nice war. Johnny is a former safe-cracker and burglar. He brought me here to meet some of his friends. When you go over your identity and ration card will look just like the real thing. One of Johnny's friends. You will have a great deal of money at your disposal, thanks to Ronnie Cann. Took him a while to switch from fivers to francs, but I think you'll agree he does a nice job. Johnny's got us a first-rate pickpocket, too. He'll be starting as an instructor. As soon as we can get him out of Dartmoor Prison.'

Williams started to laugh. 'So, you employ everyone from debs to dips?'

'Rogues to racing drivers.'

Williams swallowed some scotch and loosened his jacket. The body heat from below seemed to be bleeding through the floorboards. 'So. Is this really pleasure?'

She shrugged. 'I'm having a good time.'

'That's a nice frock, by the way.'

'Frock?' She flicked some of the beads. 'Frock? It's a Molyneux, I'll have you know. And bloody expensive.'

Williams wondered if she was drunk, or if this was an act like Virginia's. 'So no business?'

She gave a lopsided smile. 'Perhaps a teensy bit.'

'Go on.'

'Two things. What do you make of Virginia?'

'As a seductress? Or a spy?'

Rose laughed. 'I'll settle for special agent.'

'A disaster.'

'Why?'

'Too good looking. Every man in every room she enters will look at her. Germans will offer to carry her bags . . . and if the bags are full of radio . . .'

'I take your point.'

'And she's got English written through her like a stick of rock. Oh, she can speak the part, but there is something very brittle about her, something the French haven't got. Furthermore, I have absolutely no idea why she would want to do something like this when there must be a thousand other ways to help the war effort . . .' There was a silence. 'You did ask.'

'I know. Thank you.' She didn't want to tell Williams it was too late. Her own doubts, especially over why such a young beautiful girl would put herself in such danger, had been overruled. Virginia had the green light.

'What was the second thing?'

'Less tricky. Could you kill someone? In cold blood?'

The switch in tone took him aback. 'Less tricky? What's that supposed to mean?'

'Just answer me. Cold blood. No warning. No reason. We say – he has to die. You do it.'

151

'I don't know.'

'Your Irish friends did it.'

'I had no part of that.'

'Oh, don't be so naïve. You think you can pick and choose which parts of a struggle like that apply to you? Just because you drove on a few raids where nobody got killed, you don't think you have any responsibility for anything else that went on?'

Williams nodded. 'No, I realised that. Which is why I got out. I grew up. Fast.'

He told her what she already knew, about the envelope Slade handed a young man called Grover that was the death warrant for one of his friends. How he was sure there was more to it than the smooth-talking SIS man had suggested and had burned the package without opening it, infuriating both O'Malley and Slade when they discovered what had happened. It was the only way out – his handing over the package would have been in itself a compromised act, an act of betrayal. It was then he realised he was just a boy messing about in things that had taken three hundred years to fester and finesse. All he had wanted was an escape from the suffocating normality of his family. Afterwards, he grabbed the chance to sink into Orpen's equally claustrophobic world for a few months.

'So then I had two lots of people hating me. The Irish and the British. My family were still in France and I went back, the prodigal son with his tail between his legs, and my father knew a man who knew a man who knew Orpen . . .'

'William Grover became just Williams. And now Grover-Williams. You're not very original with names, are you?'

'Maybe not. But you can see I'm none too keen on assassination.'

'This will be different.'

'Will it,' he said flatly.

'Anyway, that's for the future. I'm sending you in, three weeks time. Full briefing starts tomorrow. I want you over there and ready.'

'Ready for what?'

'As I told you. Whatever we want.'

Williams looked at his watch and Rose grabbed his wrist with a surprisingly firm grip. She angled it so the meagre lights flickered across the diamonds.

'And you can't take that. Too damn conspicuous.'

He slipped off the Cartier and handed it over. Rose examined the back and raised an eyebrow.

'We always meant to get it engraved . . . you know how it is. I'll be back for that,' he added firmly.

Rose slipped it into her clutch bag. 'Good. Then you'll know where to find it, won't you?'

Robert sat on the edge of the terrace at the Auffargis house, pulling petals from a withered rose head, letting them drop on to the gravel, brooding over yet another row with his estranged wife. When all this was over, he would contemplate the dreaded divorce. The arguments and recriminations that would cause didn't bear thinking about. He envied Williams his simple monogamous outlook, even if it was probably being sorely tested by separation.

It was a cold, sharp day lit by a low, jaundiced sun, but he was enjoying even that feeble warmth on his face. He had spent the day polishing and checking the last Bugatti Atlantic now sitting in the garage-cum-barn out back. It should have been turned in, but the papers Maurice had secured allowed him to keep it on the pretext he would be touring the country impounding all of Ettore's cars still in France. He despised Maurice's cosying up to the Germans, but he had to admit, when it came to playing both ends against the middle, Maurice was a master.

He had thrown the rubberised cloth over the Bugatti when the

Economic Police Patrol, with a small unit of German troops, had arrived only minutes later. The Sergeant in charge had looked in the barn and moved on. It wasn't cars they were looking for, but evidence of food hoarding, provisions to steal.

The small figure who appeared at the end of the drive snapped him out of his thoughts. She hesitated at the gates, the bicycle still between her legs, as if unsure of the address. He raised what he hoped was a reassuring hand and she pedalled in, swerving to avoid the pot holes now forming in the untended road surface. No gardeners or handymen or chauffeurs left now. He'd have to get off his arse and do it himself if he wanted a decent approach to the house.

She must have been around seventeen dressed in a rather threadbare overcoat that might have been fashionable five years ago. Her red hair was tied back with a bright purple scarf, and she wore a look of determination on her flushed face as she pulled to a halt, dismounted, and carefully laid the bike against one of the terrace pillars, careful to avoid crushing the wisteria. He could tell she had come from Paris, and city folk only ventured into the countryside for one thing these days.

'You're too late,' he said.

'I'm sorry?'

'You're too late. The Germans were here an hour ago. Took away a sack of potatoes and two chickens. Cleaned me out. I have nothing to give. You could try the farm down that way.' A pretty girl had some chance of getting something from old Pierre Marchant, one of the farmers who revelled in the shift in the balance of power that meant urban dwellers went cap in hand to their rural cousins, rather than vice versa.

'I haven't come for food.'

Robert stood up, a little suspicious. Surely she wasn't . . . 'Coffee?'

'No thanks. I have to give you this. You are Robert Benoist?'

He nodded and she held out a thin envelope. He ripped it open. It was one of the single sheet letters introduced shortly after the occupation with options to cross out: Dear . . ., Hope you are well/better/coming here – and so on. He read it three times before the message finally clicked and he felt a grin spread over his face.

'Are you sure about the coffee?'

'I have to get back.'

He walked out on to the driveway with her as she collected her bike. 'Thank you. You're very brave.'

She flushed a little and smiled shyly. 'Oh, the Germans never stop us.' She indicated the note. 'Not for that kind of thing, anyway. Doesn't occur to them that women could be up to no good.'

Robert felt a sudden chill, an intense feeling of concern for her, this vulnerable child swimming into unknown depths. 'I'm sorry, I didn't ask your name.'

'Beatrice.'

'Well, Beatrice, long may they continue to believe that. Be careful.'

'*Vive la France.*'

Now Robert felt awkward replying after the innocent intensity she invested in the tired old phrase. 'Yes, *Vive la France.*'

Without a backward glance she was gone, pedalling furiously into the darkening afternoon. He looked at the note again. He'd have to tell Eve. In person.

Robert was aware of the envious and suspicious glances as he drove west, through Dreux and towards Alençon. The roads were mostly empty, with just a few horse-drawn carts, a smattering of cars newly converted to run on compressed coal gas, with a

155

dangerous brazier created in the boot, and, in the larger towns, the velo-taxis, an upmarket version of the rickshaw. But a man driving a car? And a beautiful streamlined car at that? Nazi bigwig, that was the assumption most people made. Or a black marketeer.

He gunned the car, letting the fearsome noise wrap around him. Above sixty kilometres an hour the lack of soundproofing made conversation difficult in the Atlantic, but, with no passenger, he didn't care. The engine made its own delicious conversation and he let it talk at length on the spookily empty roads.

He was near Alençon when he came across the convoy, a long snake of half-tracks, Mercedes trucks, Kubelwagens and staff cars, plodding along at around forty or forty-five kilometres an hour. The troops in the rear vehicle all turned to look at him, their eyes dark under their coal scuttle helmets. At one time they would have worn field caps, but now that the British were making sporadic strafing sorties across the Channel, they had armoured up.

One of them waved and gave a thumbs-up in admiration of the Bugatti, but the majority of the boys – most were less than half his age – remained stony faced. He wondered where they had been. Russia maybe, where already six inches of snow covered the countryside, slowing down an advance that had once taken Rzhev, Belgograd, Stalino and Taganrog – less than three hundred miles from the Volga – in forty-eight hours? No, Robert thought, according to reports from both the conventional and the newly emerged underground press those units were still pushing for Moscow, hoping to take the city before everything froze solid. Perhaps the look on the prematurely lined faces was the thought that they could be the next to be shipped east.

After five minutes of unrelenting staring from the back of the Mercedes, Robert, cursing the fact that every Bugatti was right-hand drive, decided to risk overtaking. He dropped a gear, pulled out, relieved to find the way ahead clear, and floored the accelerator.

The drab military colours of the vehicles flashed by, and now he just had glimpses of open jaws and scowling faces. He felt himself smile, counting off the metres till he was clear of these gormless barbarians. He was half a dozen trucks away from freedom when the lead staff car swerved out, blocking his side of the road. He automatically glanced at the speedometer even as he stamped on the pedal. He was travelling at over a hundred and the Atlantic's brakes weren't its best feature. A tall, spindly hawthorn hedge made it impossible to swerve round this sudden obstruction so he pumped the brakes, once, twice, then full down, feeling the wheels lock, correcting the skittish rear end, bracing himself as the military car came closer and closer, feeling the Bugatti decelerating with agonising slowness, until with a smoking screech and a stench of rubber it stopped centimetres away from the occupants of the staff car, rocking on its suspension. Robert realised he was holding his breath and let out a long thin stream of air.

The tall, elegant Lieutenant who stepped out of the rear seat of the staff car offered a thin smile as he walked over to the driver's window. Robert rolled it down. 'A Bugatti,' the German said admiringly.

'Well read.'

'An Atlantic, I believe.'

Robert allowed himself to be a tiny bit impressed. 'Indeed.'

'Lovely.'

'Aren't they?'

'Why do you have it?'

Robert handed over the *Ausweiss* that Maurice had provided and then the identity card. 'Ah. You work for the company. I see.'

Still holding the papers the Lieutenant walked around the machine admiring its low-slung lines. When he returned he bent down. 'My Colonel would love to see this.'

Robert started his cover story, that he had just picked it up and was taking it to the large warehouse in Dieppe where many of the best cars had been spirited away. 'I'm afraid it has been requisitioned by—'

The Lieutenant cut him off with a snarl and threw the papers back at him. 'Fall in, in front of that half-track. Now.'

The German walked over and spoke quickly to the half-track crew. Robert watched as the forward machine gun was manned and swung in his direction. The convoy restarted with a grinding of gears and the low grunt of engines and Robert slotted in between the half-track and a Kubelwagen.

The lumbering column of vehicles swung south, away from where he wanted to go, had to go, heading for Le Mans. Robert could feel the Atlantic juddering unhappily in second and third, gears it simply wasn't used to hanging around in.

It was ten kilometres before he hit on the solution, another five of tricky driving with one hand before he had managed to sabotage his own car and a further seven before he began flashing his lights and honking his horn. Eventually the vehicle ahead slowed and after they had all rolled to a halt, the Lieutenant strode back into view, clearly irritated.

'What is it?'

'How much further?'

'Another eighty kilometres.'

Robert tapped his fuel gauge. 'I'm all but empty. I was meant to fill up at Alençon.'

The Lieutenant put his head in suspiciously. He turned the engine on. The needle juddered but didn't rise. Which was hardly surprising because Robert had disconnected it.

'Very well. You,' the Lieutenant pointed to the truck. 'Put some fuel in this car.'

The Lieutenant went back to his vehicle as the soldiers fetched jerry cans and started to slosh it into the Bugatti's cavernous tank. Robert waited until the machine gunner slid down for a moment before he rammed the car into reverse and let in the clutch. There was a scream as both soldiers' legs were crushed against the solid girder-like bumper of the half-track. He spun the wheel, thankful for the tight turning circle Jean had given the Atlantic and accelerated out, deliberately spinning the wheels, leaving a shower of dust. The Lieutenant, leaning against his car, smoking, gasped as the low coupé rocketed by him, holding in his stomach, feeling the metal wings pluck at his trousers.

The first bullet came after Robert within five seconds, but it took time to manoeuvre the bigger half-tracks into a clear line of sight. The convoy was already receding when he saw the muzzle flashes in his mirror, but at that moment he glimpsed the farm track running off to his left and he slid the car into it, hoping the suspension could cope with barreling over ruts at a hundred and thirty kilometres an hour. The track led him to a small lane, the lane to a road heading north, and as darkness fell he switched on the blue-painted black-out headlights and hoped nobody else took a fancy to his car that night.

Arthur Lock checked his watch by the feeble light of the moon and lit the third bonfire in the triangle. He wondered if the plane was coming. This was the third time of asking. On one occasion weather had stopped the drop, on another the plane had simply not appeared. This was the last chance, he felt, tonight or it was time to think again.

He hurried over to the edge of the field to join two of the half-dozen Frenchmen scattered on the edge of this dark wood and stood with them stamping his feet. He gratefully accepted an offer of brandy, rough though it was, and shuddered with pleasure as it scorched its way down into his stomach.

What a game to play. Dropping agents into the dead of night, hoping they don't break their necks or drown or fall straight into a German patrol. Then expecting them to disappear into the populace and somehow, against all the odds, make a difference. He wouldn't blame them if they weren't coming, not one bit.

Even as he began to have his doubts, he heard the low throb of the Halifax engines and could sense, rather than see, the great four-engined plane banking to circle back round over the DZ. That was unusual. A pilot who cared enough to give the jumpers a decent chance of landing on target. Most of them seemed happy enough to turf their charges out and head home.

He waited impatiently as it made the turn, levelled, and started the dropping run. He could imagine the first agent sitting on the edge of the hatch, remembering all that training. Push forward and straighten, arms by side, clean through the hole or your face bangs on the opposite side of the hatch. Wait for the static line to pull. Hope the jump master had remembered to hook it up. Feel the painful jerk as silk grabbed the air. Check canopy. Check lines. Twist slowly. Head for the fires.

The plane flew overhead, the noise faded and he started to scan the sky. 'There,' said one of his companions, and he could hear wind through silk as the first of the delicate mushrooms turned towards them and came rushing down at the earth. The other two blossoms were over to the south, one of them perhaps a mile away. Lock dispatched his colleagues to intercept, checked the pistol in his belt for easy access, just in case, and strode out to where the first drop had crumpled into the earth.

As he approached the jumper got up rather stiffly and began

hauling in the chute. Tentatively he said: 'There are two tragedies in life.'

The figure jumped then spun round and Lock had two shocks. One, it was a woman, and two there was a large streak of blood down her face.

'God, you gave me a fright,' Virginia Thorpe gasped. She looked him up and down, noting his very un-French ginger hair and freckles.

'There are two tragedies in life,' he repeated.

'One is not to get your heart's desire.'

'The other is to get it,' Lock completed and held out his hand. He used his code name as instructed. 'Captain Eric Colson. Welcome to France. You all right?'

She touched her face. 'Yes. Damn thing.'

Lock reached over and gently felt her pretty, delicate nose. 'Not broken I don't think. It'll just feel like it for a while. Come on, shouldn't hang around out here.'

The fires were doused, the chute rolled and stored for later retrieval, along with the baggy overalls which she stepped out of, revealing the drab skirt and jacket she had on underneath. There were three canvas bags plus a handbag. Lock took the former, one on each shoulder, carrying the third, and ushered her away from the field down a narrow footpath.

'What about the others?'

'Don't worry, they'll be taken by a different route. Can't put all your agents in one basket, eh? Did you have a radio?'

'No. Martin—' she carefully used the code name – 'he's the pianist.'

With his free hand Lock felt the bags slung over his shoulders. No weapons. Just documents. And money. She was one of those who'd come in with payroll and bribes. Good.

It was two kilometres to the draughty old barn, full of old straw

161

and duck droppings. The ducks themselves were huddled in a metal shed to the left, keeping themselves warm. Lock flicked on a torch and indicated a corner, where there were two uninviting blankets.

'Someone will be along eventually. We have to wait here. Sit down.'

Virginia looked at the blankets closely, decided they were old but clean enough and wrapped one round her. Lock slumped down a few feet away. 'Cigarette?'

'Should we?'

'Don't worry. You think the Germans patrol every lane in France? You forget how big a country it is.'

She took one and gratefully accepted the light and felt better as soon as the smoke hit her lungs. For the past twenty-four hours she had gone over and over her reasons for doing this. Nothing made sense. It had seemed like an adventure to begin with; now she was here the butterflies and sickness in her stomach were telling her that much more was at stake.

'Marilyn, isn't it?'

'Code name. Yes.'

'What do your papers say?'

'Yolande Laurent.'

'Occupation?'

'Dress designer with Piguet.'

The name meant nothing to Lock, but he knew a story that was checkable when he heard it. 'And will they vouch for you?'

'Oh yes.' She had worked there for a year before the war, helping reinvent the house's trademark gowns, so she knew the drill. A Yolande Laurent certainly had worked there, but had moved to New York to marry one of the clients who came in to buy a dress for his wife and left with more than he bargained for.

She suddenly felt cold and flat as the cigarette finished and she

162

pulled the rough, animal-scented blanket round her. 'How long have you been over?'

He hesitated. She should know better than to ask questions like that. 'A while.' In fact, Lock had been in France since before the invasion and stayed on after the Germans overran the country.

'How is it?'

'Grim for most people. Getting grimmer. You do what you have to do to survive . . .'

As if on cue three figures appeared at the entrance of the barn, silhouetted by the moonlight. Lock stood up and Virginia did likewise. Lock flicked the narrow beam of his torch over the men so Virginia could see the Germans' uniforms. The light glinted off the threatening barrels of the MP 38 submachine guns levelled at her. Lock heard her juddering intake of breath, imagined the cold, dead feeling gripping her insides and shrugged apologetically.

'. . . even if it means the odd sacrifice now and then.'

Eve opened a bottle of Bourgueil, recorked it, put it and two tumblers into a wicker basket, along with a piece of cheese and what was left of the bread she had made earlier in the day, threw a cloth over the contents and headed out into the courtyard of the water mill.

The four German soldiers billeted with her snapped to attention as they always did, although this time she could feel the eyes following her. The over-correct formality was slowly melting away eventually, she was sure, to be replaced by the standard issue arrogance of conquering soldiers. One of them muttered something and another laughed. Eve ignored them. It was only for a week longer and they were being pulled out to God knows where.

She cut left, down through a tangle of brambles, scratching her bare legs as she went, and picked up the river path. The ground was hard – there had been a frost the night before, and the fallen leaves were still brittle and crunchy underfoot.

Eve climbed over the low fence that marked the boundary of her property and carried on along the bank, paralleling the wide, sluggish river, now a deep, earthy brown from all the rain. The path dipped and became muddy, so she picked her way carefully until it started to climb again to firmer ground. She could smell the cigarette smoke now, and knew he'd be there.

Robert was sitting on a fallen log at the base of a soaring oak tree, just finishing the last of his cigarette. He smiled and rose slowly, stiffly, to his feet, kissing her on both cheeks. He'd spent the night parked in a field, tight against the hedgerow, before daring to continue on to see her.

'Eve.' He tried hard to keep the emotion from his voice, but he was pleased to see her. She sat down next to him and he indicated his cigarette butt. 'I'd offer you one, but I think it's mainly old nettle leaves. With maybe a cabbage in there. Maurice has promised me two hundred real cigarettes by next week.'

Eve poured some wine for each of them. 'How is Maurice?'

Robert laughed. 'I tell you, thriving. He's having a good war. I found my forte before all this happened . . . he's found it now. Mr Big BOF.' Eve looked puzzled; the acronym for black marketeers clearly hadn't spread outside Paris yet. '*Beurre, Oeufs, Fromage*. Although with Maurice it's more practical things—'

'And how are you?'

'All the better for being here.' She smiled at the compliment and Robert felt the familiar wariness from her. She never quite believed his intentions were honourable. Or maybe that was just paranoia on his part. He sipped the wine. It was lightly chilled, just right and he nodded appreciatively. 'I had a visit the other day from a young lady named Beatrice.'

'Do I want to hear this?'

'Oh yes, nothing like that. She brought a message. Don't know who from, I don't think I was supposed to ask.'

'What was it?'

He slugged back the wine and held out the tumbler for a refill. 'Well, there was some good news and some bad news. Which do you want first?'

Slowly she said, 'The good.'

'OK. Will's coming back.'

She almost dropped her drink as the realisation that he wasn't joking broke over her and she found herself gasping for breath, as if all her airways had suddenly constricted. 'Will . . . when?' Then she remembered the second part of the news. 'And the bad?'

Robert's mouth turned up at the corners. 'Will's coming back.'

She leapt forward with such a force Robert barely had time to brace himself as she slammed into him, arms round his neck, her squeal of delight echoing through the naked branches of the trees, dancing all the way back to the house.

When it opened in 1932 The Sphinx was the most glamorous brothel in the world. Famed for its gilded Egyptian motifs, the giant slit-eyed cats framing the doorway, and the opulence of the main salon, it advertised widely across Europe. It was the pinnacle of a *poule*'s career to get one of the slots on the drawing-room's sofas, and such was its fame that many believed the popular rumour that when Hitler visited Paris after its fall he wanted to see the Arc de Triomphe, the Eiffel Tower, Sacré Coeur and The Sphinx.

Whether Hitler admired the exterior or not, now the salon and bar were the haunt of his German officers, not all of whom came to sample the goods, a social club where rivalries and ambitions were, more or less, put aside. On this chill October night a huge, profligate fire was roaring in the fireplace, which formed the mouth of the enormous eponymous Sphinx itself, helping to keep a rosy glow on the near-naked girls who prowled the room.

At one of the tables on the left-hand side – which denoted that they were not to be bothered by the women unless summoned across the invisible barrier – sat a group of German intelligence officers. Three branches were represented, the Abwehr, the Gestapo and the SD, all nominally separate organisations yet all overlapping in their sphere of interests, especially when it came to tracking down the British spies who had suddenly started to appear, like an eruption of acne across the face of the country. Strictly speaking the SD should concentrate on French organisations, the Abwehr on British infiltrators and the Gestapo on subversives and Jews but they were discovering that enemies could not be so neatly compartmentalised. And, contrary to what Berlin thought, they did speak to each other, even if it was over bottles of Taittinger.

Keppler and Neumann of the Sicherheitsdienst faced Kommissars Stuppel and Kock of the Geheimestaatpolizei and Staffenburg and Pitsch of the Abwehr, the military intelligence currently, in residence at the Hotel Lutetia.

They were passing round the house pillow books, loosely bound collections of erotic postcards, which were intended to help clients get in the mood. Keppler rotated his to try to find a reference point for what was going on. He was fairly sure that they could only put you into the mood for a visit to the circus or some other contortionist's venue.

'So is it true, Keppler?' asked the portly Staffenburg, puffing on a cigar.

'Is what true?' Ah, he had it now. Very athletic.

'That you have a tame Englishman.'

Keppler looked up at Staffenburg and smiled. The Abwehr

man had a reputation as something of a buffoon, a mere hedonist who got where he was because he was married to a distant relative of Admiral Canaris. Maybe so, but Keppler knew that underneath that lipid-rich exterior, there was a shrewd, and eminently selfish, mind. Like Goering, whom he resembled, Der Dicke Staffenburg had to be watched lest you allowed the clown-like behaviour to lull you into a false sense of security.

'Where did you hear that?' asked Keppler warily.

'My man Bleicher. A little pillow talk.' Staffenburg winked lasciviously.

'I should steal him from you. Neumann here has finally found a nut he couldn't crack.'

The table laughed and Neumann said: 'I haven't finished squeezing yet.' He knew it was misplaced confidence. The woman Eve had proved totally immune to his blandishments.

'So do you?' asked Staffenburg.

Before Keppler could answer, a negro waiter – tolerated by the Germans in such exotic environments – approached and bent to whisper in his ear. Keppler instinctively leant away in case any of the man's spittle should touch him. Keppler nodded and announced, 'Excuse me, gentlemen, but I have business upstairs.'

Staffenburg tipped all but the last few dregs of champagne into his glass. 'Don't worry, Keppler, I'm sure we'll still be on this bottle by the time you have finished.' They all guffawed, but Staffenburg picked up the exchange of knowing looks between Keppler and Neumann and came to the conclusion that no woman was involved in this transaction. He was wrong.

Virginia Thorpe paced the room, her head throbbing with confusion. After being handed over to the Germans she had been driven for what must have been three hours in the back of a truck, sandwiched between two big men who smelt of stale sweat and rancid meat. They had not talked to her, although one of them had put a strip of plaster across her nose with remarkable gentleness. She had been kept for most of the day in a windowless room in a house on the outskirts of Paris, some kind of temporary prison. Again, no mistreatment, even some quite decent food.

Then a new set of men, two dour Frenchmen and a plainclothes German overseer, had delivered her into an alley and marched her roughly up to this ridiculous bedroom, all red velvet and purple wallpaper, with terrible reproduction furniture – if she didn't know better she would think this was some kind of bordello – and taken away her jacket and all her possessions.

Her main task now was to keep a pressure cap on the panic welling up inside her, to try to remember what the instructors said. There will be interrogation, *Anschauzen*, the yelling, bully-ing shouting inches from the face, mind games, intimidation, perhaps even torture. This was what went through your mind in the small, dark hours at Beddington. How will I do when it's the real thing? When there isn't a small part of your brain telling you these guys are just play-acting at being Nazis? Will she crumple and fold or keep her dignity and her secrets? Although what secrets she had, she wasn't quite sure. She must resist, she knew that. And she must try to escape. Shakily she got to her feet. Better to keep busy than start brooding on the Gestapo's methodology.

Virginia checked the wardrobe. Empty but for a feather boa and some kind of black corset. And a whip. She flung back the shutters, but the window was barred, heavy substantial rods of iron set close together.

She heard footsteps and low voices in the hall and sat down quickly on the edge of the bed, trying to compose herself. Don't look scared, they'd said. Any weakness—

'Ah. Miss Laurent. If that is your name. Welcome.' She looked up and the fleshy face beamed at her. 'I am Sturmbannführer Keppler of the Sicherheitsdienst. This –' he indicated the tall handsome man next to him, 'is my colleague Obersturmführer Neumann.'

Neumann glared at her, and she was shocked to see such hatred coming from such beautiful blue eyes.

'I apologise for the unusual surroundings,' continued Keppler, 'but you have arrived outside office hours.'

'My name is Yolande—'

'Stop it,' barked Neumann in heavily accented English, making her start. 'Do not insult our intelligence. Your name is nothing of the sort.' He pulled up a chair and sat astride it. 'You have a training name, a code name and a cover name. And a real name.' He waited for this to sink in. She was beginning to shake slightly. Above them a bed began to move rhythmically, unmistakably, as the business of the house went on as usual. 'You think you are the first spy to come here?'

There was moaning now, a woman. She tried to figure out if it was French or English moaning before she realised she was being ridiculous. Or perhaps it was the best thing to do, to keep concentrating on the absurdities.

Neumann sensed her drifting and shouted: 'Spy! What a disgusting occupation for a woman. Beneath the lowest, disease-infected whores in this place. Spies. You know what we do to spies? Do you? What fun we can have?'

Her throat was dry but she managed to say: 'My name is Yolande Laurent, I work at—'

The blow took her by surprise, spinning her half off the bed and bringing tears to her eyes. She pushed herself back up, sniffed and said, 'My name is—'

The second blow threw her to the floor and she stayed there, waiting for the stinging and throbbing to subside, coughing as she tried to catch her breath.

'Neumann,' said Keppler calmly. 'That's enough. Get out.'

'I—'

'Out. Go and enjoy yourself somewhere else.'

Then she knew what this was. Even as she rubbed at the burning patch on the side of her face, she heard the voices of the instructors at Beddington break through the shock and the terror. Expect the brutal young interrogator and the kindly older one. Except kindly wasn't a word she would apply to those piggy eyes in a jowly face. But that was the routine they were running through, for sure. Her spirits lifted a notch. Knowledge was control.

'I know what you are thinking. That old bad-man, good-man routine.' Keppler smiled weakly at her, and she felt the little knot of courage dissipate. 'Sorry. We are both bad men as far as you are concerned. Neumann, you know, was the son of a concierge in Hamburg. All those comings and goings. Grew up spying on people. And with a dislike of the rich, privileged Jews who looked down on his mother. Just think how he felt when he was given the chance to be paid for getting his own back on such people. Me? Born in Austria but joined the German police force, even though they ridiculed my accent. I was a detective in Karlsruhe before I joined the party in 1935. So, I suppose my methods are more traditional than Neumann's. But the fact is, we both want our questions answered . . .' He helped her from the floor on to the bed, and she composed herself.

'My name is . . .'

'Please,' he barked at her, raising his hand, causing her to flinch. He dropped it to his side. 'Please. If you can't say anything else, don't say anything at all.'

Keppler began to pace and allowed a warm glow of satisfaction to fill his belly. This was something he enjoyed, showing his colleagues that, although he knew their more extreme methods had their place, his ten years as a cop had taught him there were less invasive ways. The salted food/no water trick, for instance. It took a little longer than the current favourite of dunking spies in scalding and freezing baths and holding them under till they nearly drowned, but it had an elegance such crude brutality lacked. A man dying of thirst can be most eloquent when a glass of water is just out of his reach.

'The Hotel Victoria in Northumberland Avenue.'

She looked up at him.

'Interviewed there by a Major. Didn't give his name. Am I right? That was your recruitment into SOE. From there, a month or so of observation, to check you were the "right sort", fitness training at Arisaig Commando School. Then on to Guildford for tradecraft or Ringway for parachute training or vice versa. Finished at . . . Beaulieu? No, Beddington probably. Kept in holding house at Farnham. Orchard Court near Baker Street just before dispatch. Do they still have Parks the butler there? So English. Even the spies have butlers. Let's see, who would have been dispatching officer? Vera Atkins perhaps? Bodington? Miller? No matter, always the same drill – check you are French down to your fingertips.'

He reached out and snatched her hand before she had a chance to hold back and admired her nails. 'Very nice. So. You see, as my friend suggested, there is little we don't know.'

'My name is Yolande—' she began weakly.

'Your name is not important. Look, how do you think we know all these details? We have Arthur Lock, an Englishman, a hero to half the misguided Resistance, a loyal worker to us. We have at least three other SOE agents helping us. Five radio operators transmitting back under our guidance. The only reason we don't arrest every damn one of you is that you would send in another lot. This way, we get to keep you under observation until we are good and ready to haul you in. It's a game, Miss whoever you are. And we are winning. Your choice is to talk to me, or spend some time with Neumann.'

The woman upstairs was panting now, loud exhalations building to a theatrical climax.

'And if I tell you to go to hell?' she said with a bravery she tried to summon up from her twitching insides.

'Ha.' Keppler threw the brown envelope on the bed next to her. He waited until her eyes flicked down to the small package. 'From your jacket lining. What I believe you call your L pill. Cyanide, isn't it? Fast and painless. At least – that's what they tell you. I wonder how they know. Who has come back to say – "actually, old chap, hardly hurt at all". But if you want to find out, be my guest. I won't try to stop you. Another drop of agents is due next full moon. I can wait for them.'

As the panting became faster she reached out for the envelope, her hand hovering over it. The L pill. All of them had listened solemnly while they were told when and where and how to use it. Better to die silent, like a good Englishwoman.

She flipped open the envelope and took the pill in her fingertips, wondering if the poison was already seeping through into her bloodstream. She looked straight at Keppler, trying to calm the howling within, so she at least looked defiant, opened her mouth as wide as she would at the dentist and tossed the cyanide to the back of her throat. He didn't so much as blink.

Her dry throat tried to swallow, get the pill down, to let it take her before she changed her mind. But her body had already decided for her. Virginia's oesophagus had crushed itself flat, refusing to accept the deadly parcel. As she gulped and gulped, pushing the tiny tablet to the back of her throat, the retching reflex kicked in and she began to choke and cough.

Her eyes felt as if they were bursting out of her head and a metal band closed on her temples. She leaned over the bed and watched the half-dissolved pill slide off her tongue and onto the carpet.

God, had she taken enough into her bloodstream? Or was she going to live after all, because suddenly, irrationally, looking at the small, effervescing white disc, she wanted to live more than ever and hated herself for it.

Keppler picked up the harmless, saliva-covered piece of chalk, smiled, and popped it into his own mouth. 'Well done. A good try. But you don't want to die, do you? It would be such a waste of a young life.'

She began to cry just as the woman overhead orgasmed with a ridiculous flamboyance, the hideous loveless sound filling Virginia's brain to the exclusion of all else.

Nineteen

PARIS, MARCH–APRIL 1942

Robert exited the Metro at Raspaill, having stayed on past Montparnasse when he saw the amount of gendarme activity on the platform. A couple of greasy-haired *zazous*, the long-haired, jazz-loving youths, were being roughed up and, as a spin-off, papers demanded from random passers-by. Not that he had anything to worry about, strictly speaking, but like most people he had no desire deliberately to expose himself to the whim of the police, especially when their gander was up after the insolence of the *zazous*.

He emerged out on to the street, his breath coming in clouds as he walked across the frost-crisped grass of the Montparnasse cemetery. Spring was a long time coming. Many months had passed since the message from Beatrice, so long he was beginning to think it was a hoax, until this cryptic message arrived to send him back to Montparnasse for the first time in over a year.

His route took him through the cemetery, past the fluttering notices pinned to the trees warning about cooking cats – the cemeteries had become a favourite hunting ground for the contents of feline stews – and past benches with their 'Forbidden to Jews' plaques and into Avenue du Maine, slowly making his way north to rue de Vaugirard.

A few foolish feeble buds were showing on the plane trees, but for the most part it could still be deepest January. It was as if Paris was hibernating. The dark mornings, thanks to the switch to Berlin time, the power cuts, the blackout, it felt like living in a city of perpetual twilight, its spark permanently dimmed. Not even the news of the Americans entering the conflict had brightened the coldest months or brought a glimmer of cheer to Christmas.

Now he was at the small series of dead-end alleys, the *impasses*, that ran off rue de Vaugirard, and he could feel eyes staring at him from the long, grey queues that had formed outside the butchers' shops as he glanced down each cul-de-sac, looking for his rendezvous. The lines didn't move, except perhaps to contract and expand slightly, like a human concertina, as gossip and rumour and innuendo flowed back and forth.

The Café Cuisse was a long, dingy corridor of a place down the last *impasse*, its presence signalled by a shabby sign of a happy butcher. Robert waited outside the entrance for a second, peering into the gloom, then entered. The smell hit him immediately, the metallic, coppery tang of blood. A few of the regular clients were at the bar, manfully sipping what passed for coffee and washing it down with rough brandy. All wore large leather aprons, stained with red blots of accumulated equine blood, and wicked-looking knives hanging from the belts that were slung under their ample guts.

One of them eyed Robert cautiously and, apparently satisfied, went back to his drink. It was a good place for a meet. Given the choice of hanging round the Coupole or Select or taking your chances with surly cleaver-carrying horse butchers who were the main clients of the local cafés, most Germans and their stooges would opt for the former.

The proprietor gave Robert a coffee without his asking and indicated towards the rear, where, past the chipped and scuffed furniture, a lone figure sat reading a newspaper, the pages held out, obscuring his face.

The first Williams knew of Robert's presence in the café was when the little yellow flame sprouted at the bottom of his *Figaro*, quickly spreading like a brown stain up the spine, and he had to leap to his feet and stamp out the conflagration.

Robert watched the performance with a bemused grin, leaving Williams almost too exasperated even to offer a greeting to his old friend. He held out his arms and Robert fell into them and Williams thumped his back until he felt his ribs would crack under the onslaught. He pushed Will away, and put his hands on his shoulders, marvelling at the physical change, the muscular, honed figure before him.

'What?' asked Robert. 'You expected me to say all that "Giraffe Has A Long Neck" shit?' He pulled out a chair and sat.

Williams hesitated and joined in the laughter, which drew a few sidelong glances from the counter. Such expressions were rare these days, as if joy were a culpable offence.

'Good to see you, Will. How long have you been back?'

Williams sat down, gave his coffee a stir, even though there was no sugar to be had for it, and hesitated before telling the truth: 'Four months.'

'Four . . . you've been here four months? And you didn't contact Eve?' Robert felt a bolt of anger as Williams shook his head. 'What the hell have you been doing?'

Williams leant forward and lowered his voice while increasing its intensity. 'I am a pestilence, Robert. A plague. A vile disease. I can wipe out whole families, whole villages, just by my presence.

Just talking to you puts you at risk.'

'But—'

Williams raised a hand to silence him. 'I had to get it right, Robert. I had to know which days you could order alcohol, that pastries are only available Mondays, Tuesdays and Wednesdays, get used to the ration books, know that only Germans can drive on Sunday. You've no longer noticed all the changes, you've come in so gradually. But it's a minefield for a new arrival. Ordering a *café au lait* can be fatal.' Robert nodded. He knew there was no milk around that month. A stranger might not. And such a blunder might draw the attention of a V-Mann of the collaborationist rue Laurent Gestapo, or the real thing.

'So, where've you been?'

'The Citroën factory. Remember Bernard the mechanic? Foreman. Got me on the assembly line for six weeks. Thanks to him all the bearings on the tank turrets go out with caccolube grease on them . . .'

'Caccolube?'

'It contains carborundum powder. The turrets work well for a few weeks, maybe months, well enough that nobody suspects sabotage, then one day . . .'

Robert slapped the table with joy at the thought of a Panzer tank seizing up in the heat of battle, jammed solid as a Russian tank battalion appeared over the ridge of the Steppes.

'Same with the wheels, with ball bearings . . .'

They both chuckled. 'What now?'

'Now I need help. Now I need a truck. *Ausweiss*. Petrol.'

'Petrol, leave that to Maurice . . .'

'Maurice?'

'Maurice. And *Ausweissen*. He has his methods.' A thought suddenly came to Robert. 'Do you have a radio?'

Williams shook his head. 'No, nor a big flag with "Secret Agent – Come and Get Me" on it.'

Robert furrowed his brow, and Williams thought that the older he got the more hawk-like he became. 'Meaning?'

'Meaning the best way to get caught is to start broadcasting your position to the world.' Williams smiled ruefully. 'Besides, my Morse is diabolical. We'll use cut-outs.' The system of couriers with limited knowledge of all parties was by no means water-tight, but it was far less damaging if a messenger was caught – he or she could only take so many down with him. 'You have a cigarette?'

'Don't you?' Robert asked disappointed. 'You didn't bring any across?'

'Yes. But too good to smoke in public. If you catch my drift.'

Robert offered him one of the *tabac national* cigarettes, appreciating that smoking real tobacco might also attract the curious. They lit up.

'I'm using letter drops and couriers to communicate with England. That way if the link is blown, we should be buffeted. So, what chance of a lorry of some description?'

'I can get you a truck. But I'll have to drive it.'

'Why?'

'Because the better driver should take the wheel.'

Williams laughed softly. 'I thought we'd settled that.'

'We did. I won.'

'Thirteen years ago, old man. Anyway, you told me I was the victor.'

'I was being kind. And less of the old man – you aren't a boy any longer. We toss for it, then. Agreed?' Williams nodded. He was surprised by the excitement in Robert's voice. He'd been expecting an uphill struggle to get him involved. 'What are we doing?' Robert asked eagerly.

'It's dangerous.'

'Good.'

'What about Wimille?'

'You got any money?'

'Around two million Francs.'

'Then he'll play. You know Jean-Pierre. He's a cash-on-delivery boy. One more thing.'

'What?'

'I told Eve I had a meeting. I suspected the message was from you. She's in the rue Weber apartment.'

Williams felt his head swirl at the thought. For four months he had kept the whole idea of seeing Eve sealed in a corner of his brain, like a trunk in the attic, full of anticipated pleasures, but not to be opened. Not yet. Now it burst the stays, spilling its contents into his cerebrum and a mixture of love and terror almost overwhelmed him. Even before he realised it he was starting to rise from the seat, drawn to her, to the thought of her. Robert, ever practical, pushed him back down.

'Are your papers in order?'

Williams nodded. Robert removed his arm.

'Then go to her. She's still the most beautiful woman in Paris.'

Now he hesitated, fearing the magnitude of the task, the rediscovery of each other, that was before him.

'Before I take your place,' his friend added.

Williams stood, squeezed Robert on the shoulder and said, 'I'll be in touch about the . . . things we need.'

'Sure. But get this one right first, eh? She's missed you.'

'Me too,' Williams replied flatly.

Robert laughed and punched him on the arm. 'I would practise saying that a few times on the way over. Now go.'

After Williams had left Robert smoked another bitter cigarette, trying to work out what he had in mind. Dangerous. Not like

179

racing cars then? How many people had been claimed by that
during his time at Delage and Bugatti? Soon, the Germans would
have been in France for two years. In that time they had gone
from tourists and 'very correct' to an occupying army whose real
role had become very apparent – to strip France of men and
goods and redirect them to the Reich. He stubbed out the
cigarette. The thought had been circling in his head throughout
the harsh winter – it was time to do something about it.

Hans Keppler strode across to the window of his office on
Avenue Foch and looked down on the broad double-
carriageway thoroughfare. The chestnut and plane trees finally
looked as if they were going to make an effort to pretend it was
spring after all. The roads were quiet, just the odd charcoal-
burning car chugging asthmatically by or a smoother Citroën
Light 15 arriving or departing the courtyards at numbers 72, 82
and 84 that the SD had requisitioned. He was at 82 in the best
office in the entire complex, he felt. Dominated by a huge
chandelier, with an Aubusson carpet and ormalu desk, it was
elegant and civilised, even if the business he carried out wasn't
always.

He heard Arthur Lock cough and was reminded of just how
base some of the activities were.

'Anything?' he asked.

'Personal shit,' said Lock, and sneered, 'I love you so much,
darling. Kiss little Jimmy for me. Most of their women are
probably kissing big Jimmy next door.'

Keppler drummed his fingers on the window sill. 'Show her.'

'Laurent?'

'Yes. Show her how much we know. Tell me how she reacts.
You know what I need from her.'

'Pleasure.'

The enthusiasm with which Lock ensnared his fellow country-men left even Keppler with a sense of disquiet. He had no illusions about how Lock would act if ever it became expedient to switch sides. The man had deserted even before France fell, taking with him the mess funds. He had popped up as Major Lock of MI9 helping downed airmen in late 1940, while also helping himself to escape line funds. When discovered he had contacted the SD at Lille and betrayed everyone, including his young bride and her family. Having paused only to pawn their jewels, he was taken to Keppler to see if he could be of any use.

'After you've finished with Yolande Laurent get down to the Champs Elysées cafés. I have reports of English being spoken. Pump the waiters for all you can. Take some marks with you.'

Lock nodded and made his way to the door.

'Oh, and Lock.'

'Yes, Sturmbannführer?'

'And make sure you account for every last one of those marks. In writing.'

'Of course, Sturmbannführer,' Lock said innocently.

The Germans had made Virginia relatively comfortable on the fifth floor. Her cell was small, but they had managed to squeeze in a bed and a desk and chair, a selection of books in French and some basic toiletries. She was allowed to use a sitting room during the day, and had even been offered dinners out, which she had, of course, refused.

Since the night when she had tried to swallow what she had thought was an L pill, they had treated her with surprising civility. She knew this wasn't always the case. She glimpsed other prisoners who bore marks of beatings, heard both men and women sobbing in the night, lay awake listening to the distant shouts and screams of interrogation, of the slamming of doors and the angry bark of guards. Not for her, though. Not yet.

In a strange way she wished it would hurry up and happen. Waiting made it worse. The day would come when she was tested and she needed to know how she would react, whether the training in any way helped her to face up to what was in store. The longer they delayed, the more some part of her began to hope that it would never happen, that it would all turn out OK in the end, as if this were an Angela Brazil novel. That stupidly optimistic part of her brain was, she knew, slowly corroding her resolve, weakening her.

Lock knocked on the door but entered without waiting for a reply. Instinctively she shuffled back on the bed, away from this reptilian creature. He smiled and sat, placing a pile of documents on her desk and then ignoring them.

'How are you, Yolande?'

'Please, get to the point.'

'You're his now, you know. Keppler's.'

'What on earth do you mean?'

'Once he knew you couldn't go through with killing yourself.'

'It was chalk.'

'That wasn't the point, was it? We now all know your desire to live is stronger than your sense of duty.'

She glared at him but he just smiled back in his oily way. Lock was a creature she just couldn't place, as if he was some strange new species brought back by an expedition and was yet to be classified. He looked English, he sounded English but some basic part of him was missing. The humanity, she decided. 'That is rather rich, coming from you, Lock.'

'Me? I've never made any bones about who I look out for. Your lot come over here with all this noble cause claptrap and the moment they tickle your toes, you roll over.'

'Nonsense.'

Lock tapped the stack of documents. 'Do you know what these are?'

'Your memoirs?'

'Not quite.'

He handed a sheet across and she cast an eye over it. It was a letter, a personal letter, from a husband to a wife or sweetheart. 'Very touching.'

'It will be flown out on tonight's Lysander. All of this will be. It just so happens that, in return for safe passage, the flight controller lets Keppler read the mail.'

He let this sink in.

'All the mail. All the requests for arms, radio operators, maps, advice . . . all of it. Everything passes through the SD before it reaches London.'

Virginia shook her head in disbelief. The rules they had been taught at Beddington and Beaulieu with such certainty no longer seemed to apply. Was such a sordid arrangement worth it? Compromising security in order to get agents in and out without harm, agents who may be put at risk by the very action that secures their safe passage? Her head started to spin.

'So you have to realise, being the stubborn one won't do you any favours. Not when everybody else is busy cutting a deal with old Hans. He never asks anything unreasonable, you know.'

'What does he want?'

'First of all, a list of who you trained with.'

She laughed. 'Well, that won't do him any good. We all used false names. I have no idea who these people were.'

Lock took the time to roll himself a cigarette and look up at her occasionally. 'You know that's not true.'

'Do I?'

'You were trained with the same people for what? Six months? Eight? People aren't watertight. They leak. Little snippets at a time, perhaps, but it all comes out eventually. Now, I know you don't know where they are now, don't know where or why they were sent across. That's his job. Keppler's. All we need is the list and . . .'

'And what?'

Lock scooped up his documents, retrieved the letter from her and opened the door.

'And you get to keep those lovely nails for a while longer.'

The door closed and Virginia swung her feet on the bed, staring at the ceiling, trying not to think about the clumsy threat. A terrible feeling of hopelessness descended on her, a cloud of despair that everything, all the training, the sleepless nights, the fear she battled every single waking moment, everything had been a complete waste of time. Outfoxed and outflanked, sold up the river by men like Lock and the Lysander organiser. Hopeless. She closed her eyes and felt a hot tear roll out on to her cheek. Hopeless.

Williams pulled Eve closer to him, squeezing the breath from her lungs, as if he was trying to envelop her.

'Careful,' she gasped. 'I'm thinner than when you left.'

The air was thick and swirling, as if the apartment were about to erupt into an electrical storm. Questions and suspicions and apologies and recriminations and love and lust jostled with each other for pole position, the detritus of a long separation. Williams was aware of emotions locked behind enormous gates on both sides, frightened that to open them even a crack would sweep them away under a torrent.

Then, finally, they spoke in unison.

'I'm sorry.' A moment's pause and then the first carefree laugh.

'You first,' said Eve.

'I should have stayed.'

'I should have gone with you.'

'Does that make us even?' he asked.

'I think it does.'

There was a war going on outside he reminded himself. He was in an enemy-occupied city. The Gestapo or the SD might be searching for him even now. They were certainly arresting other agents, tightening their grip on the city. Yet he couldn't make any of it register, take hold. All that mattered was the room and the woman in front of him.

He pulled her down on to the bed, and she unbuttoned his shirt and began to sniff at his chest. 'What's all this?'

'What?'

'This.' She prodded his pectorals and felt her finger bounce back.

It was a moment before he realised she was referring to a physique changed and hardened by assault courses and push-ups and old colonial hands who liked nothing more than giving their men a 5 a.m. run. 'That? I think it's called muscle.'

She sniffed at his chest again and prodded, marvelling at the elastic skin, springy again after losing the adipose layer that had slowly accumulated underneath in their years together. 'I think I like it.'

'Why do you keep doing that?'

'What?'

'Sniffing me.'

Eve pulled herself up level with his eyes and he smiled into her face, thinner, it was true, but then so was what Robert said. As far he was concerned – maybe both were concerned – she was still the most beautiful woman in Paris.

'I want to know where you've been.'

He laughed and pulled her head to his neck and said very softly: 'Don't worry about where I've been. Worry about what we are going to do.'

Eve sat up, shook her head and shuffled back to work on his belt buckle. 'I know exactly what I'm going to do, Mister Williams.'

It took Maurice six weeks to find a decent truck with adequate documentation and a supply of petrol. He seemed pleased to see Williams, keen enough to help, but there was always a bill, always expenses. To Maurice, Resistance was a business like any other.

Meanwhile supplies came in. Sten guns, two Thomsons, pistols, some plastic explosive and timers. More money, always welcome. The team grew, much against Williams' better judgement, but picking up parachute drops needed organisation. A few of Robert's old farmworkers, Jean-Pierre Wimille, Thérèse Lethias, an old friend of the Benoist family, all helped with the clandestine activity.

Most of the materiel was hidden around Auffargis, some, including nearly all of the cash, at the Lethias' villa on the outskirts of Pontoise. Until it was needed. Thérèse started calling herself Banque du Liberation. And still the coded messages came from London: you need a radio operator. And still Williams replied: no. Then one day, when winter had finally given up the ghost, the plucky Beatrice came cycling down the drive with a single word as her message. Caravan. Williams heart gave an enormous judder, a surge of excitement cut with thin veins of fear. It was time to get off their arses and do something.

'Is there a reply?' asked Beatrice, anxious to be gone. She smiled as Robert walked from the house and raised a hand.

'No,' said Williams, but as soon as she remounted her bicycle he suddenly changed his mind. 'Actually, yes. Gelignite.'

'Gelignite?'

'Gelignite and *plastique*. And more pencils.'

She couldn't keep the curiosity off her face this time. Was he going to write the Germans to death?

Williams smiled. 'They'll know what it means.'

Keppler growled as Maurice won another hand of *casino*. He, Neumann, Lock – now wearing a SD uniform – and Maurice had been sitting around for an hour now, with a slow steady flow of money towards Maurice. The Sphinx was only half full this evening. Many officers and their units had been withdrawn from Paris and were heading east for the big summer offensive. Their replacements were not always the kind of gentlemen The Sphinx preferred. On stage two naked redheads performed a rather desultory version of the sand dance, accompanied by an elderly clarinet and piano duo. Keppler wondered if perhaps he should find a new venue. It wasn't as if he ever used any of the girls.

Maurice suddenly launched into one of his endless stream of jokes and Lock leant forward, his French still being a little shaky. 'So it's this guy's fiftieth birthday and he's feeling pretty good, certain he doesn't look his age. He goes to his wine merchant and says, I'll have a bottle of the twenty-seven Margaux. In fact, it's my birthday. If you can guess how old I am, I'll pay you double. Forty-five, says the merchant. Ha, no, I'm fifty, the man says. He goes to the butcher's and asks for a nice steak to go with the wine. He does the same thing to the butcher. If you can guess how old I am, I'll give you this fine claret and you can eat the steak. Forty-five, says the butcher. Ha, no, I'm fifty. And off he goes. On the Metro on the way home he says to the little old lady next to him: It's my birthday. If you can guess how old I am you can have this wonderful claret and this excellent steak. The old woman furrows her brow, unbuttons his trousers and has a good rummage around. She takes her hand out and says: You're fifty. Good Lord, says the man, how did you do that? Easy, says the woman, I was standing behind you in the butcher's.'

Neumann banged the table and Lock smiled weakly, possibly because he hadn't quite caught the ending when Maurice's words tumbled together into a single stream. Keppler nodded and lit a cigarette.

'By the way, Maurice, did you have any luck with that little task we talked about?'

Maurice passed the cards to Neumann to deal. Neumann raised an eyebrow in question, but Keppler waved it away.

'Not exactly, Sturmbannführer.'

'Not exactly,' he said coldly, letting his displeasure show in his voice, enjoying watching the ferrety Maurice shrink back into his scarab-shaped chair. 'Not exactly. Well, I haven't exactly got any more *Ausweissen* for you to run your little racketeering organisation.'

'Sturmbannführer,' he protested, 'I have nothing to do with the black market.'

'Your very blood runs black, Maurice. And if I choose to shut you down . . . you know the penalty for trafficking. Shall we say my office? Next Wednesday? Ten o'clock. I have the census lists, perhaps that will help.'

'Of course, Sturmbannführer,' said Maurice, as brightly as he could muster. But, from that moment on, he lost all his winnings, and more.

Twenty

JUNE 1942

Feldwebel Technician Otto Bruninghaus moved the dials in front of him, straining his ears to make out the ethereal voices that crackled and spat and drifted in and out of aural focus, as if he was eavesdropping on the spirit world. Finally he got a clear signal and flicked on the loudspeaker so the half dozen men in the room – four guards taking a break and two other technicians – could hear.

'I have a contact. Big contact. Ten thousand feet. Closing.'

And another voice. 'Something on your tail. One-ten. Break right. Break right.'

Bruninghaus said loudly, mimicking perfectly the rising panic in the voice: 'Something on your tail. A one-ten.'

Radio silence. He could picture the strange black combat, the shapes of planes barely glimpsed in the starless sky, the navigators hunched over primitive radar sets, the Me-110s swooping to protect the Dorniers and Heinkels, playing tag with the Bristols and Boulton Pauls lunging blindly into the night, the sudden glare of tracer fire and the sickening judder as cannon shells tore through metal and fabric and maybe flesh.

Bruninghaus's job was simple. To confuse the British night fighters, to disorientate them even more, so they would no longer trust their eyes, their ears or their screens. He was sitting in what he thought of as a giant, angular albino insect, a metal capsule attached to a trailer, its legs formed by the struts that splayed from each corner to give stability, its head by the giant radio mast that was raised into the air, enabling signals to pass unimpeded from the bottom of the chalk quarry where it sat.

Everything was white – the scarred walls and soil of the pit, the structure itself, the tents where they slept, their overalls, a world devoid of colour, at least on the outside. Every two or three days they packed up the rig and moved to another of the big pock-marks in the earth that dotted this part of France, to the far north west of Paris, just outside the Forbidden Zone, the huge swathe of northern France out of bounds to all but essential workers. Every few days the spotter planes would come over, searching for them, to be chased away by the protecting Messerschmitts.

'Have contact.' The radio buzzed again. 'Dorniers I'd say. I'll go under. Have a go.' There was the sound of gunfire, crackling, unreal.

'Damn. I'll turn again. Watch out for one-tens.'

This was probably a Boulton Paul, a single-engined fighter with a rather ungainly gun turret placed behind the pilot whose hapless occupant managed to miss the Dorniers. Bruninghaus flicked the transmit switch.

'Am getting low on fuel here. Returning to base. Over.'

'Who's that? Say again?'

His audience began to titter and Bruninghaus turned to face them and said in a sing-song voice, 'Time for tea. Tea time. Everything stops for tea.'

The others began to guffaw.

Then, more urgently, he said: 'Dornier 17s. Dozens of them. Dive, dive.'

The radio waves became full of confused jabbering, and after a few more baffling interventions Bruninghaus stood up and stretched and gloated, 'That should make sure our boys get an easier ride through to London. I need a piss.'

He went outside into the night and unzipped his overalls to relieve himself against one of the trailer tyres, careful not to splash the electrical wires snaking across the earth to the clanking generator. In fact, the machine seemed excessively noisy tonight, its low hum joined by a tappety burbling. Then he realised that the sound was coming from behind him. He turned, felt his jaw drop at what he could just make out in the gloom, and ran for the doorway to warn his companions.

Williams eased the truck into low gear and winced as he passed the guardhouse. Two amorphous shapes could be seen in the light of the few stars that were out, the apparently black splashes on the dirty white track their lifeblood draining away. All those days and nights of practising eye gouging and throat slitting and neck snapping, and there it was before him, the first evidence of cold-blooded murder, performed by Wimille's little coterie of mercenaries.

This was it, this was real, he thought and reminded himself that the explosives packed behind him, surrounded by enough black-market petrol to keep Paris running for a month, that was real too, as were the pot holes and ridges in the crude road he drove towards the quarry.

He looked in the wing mirror as he turned on to the hairpins of the cliffside road that would take him to the bottom of the giant gash in the earth. He could just make out the low shape of the Atlantic in the glass. He was glad it was there. Eve had thought them mad. She'd suggested the Renault van or the Citroën as the follow car, but both he and Robert felt speed would be their best ally. 'You'll be spotted in the Atlantic,' said Eve, adding with impassioned crudity, 'it's like driving round with your dick hanging out.'

'Spotting us is one thing,' Robert had said.

'Catching us is another,' finished Williams.

He guided the truck round the first of the hairpins, peering through the slot cut into a piece of steel welded across the windshield, hoping that the load in the back was secure and stable. He glanced at the primitive system of levers they'd welded on to the dashboard, praying they would work as well as they had in the dry runs.

This was no dry run. Sweat was beginning to stream down his face as he took the second bend, trying to use the throttle as little as possible, hoping not to lose the element of surprise. He'd been given this target before leaving England, assured that he would only be needed if the RAF failed to find and destroy the mobile masts. They clearly had.

Next bend, and suddenly the wheels were slipping on the edge of the road, sending flurries of grit and chalk into the air. He corrected, pulled the lorry back on to the centre, settling into the ruts made by hundreds of other trucks over the years. Better to endure the bouncing than risk plunging over the edge and detonating the load without achieving anything. Final turn, then a long ramp down to where he could just make out the spectral shape of the camouflaged transmission unit.

This was the part he had been dreading. The wait.

Williams lined the truck up at the top of the ramp and wiped his damp hands on his shirt. He pulled the six make-shift levers on the dash, watching the wires pull taut, praying that behind him half a dozen pencil timers had just broken. The problem was, all that had been sent were four-minute timers. Four minutes was three minutes too long as far as he was concerned.

He sat there, waiting for the seconds to crawl by, waiting for the searchlights to suddenly blind him, the bullets to start hitting the cab, the grenades to ignite the load behind him. Then he began to breathe long and slow. This was like a race. Life or death. Similar odds. You did that for ten years. You can manage this.

One minute.

Was he crazy? Should he have just come back and stayed with Eve, and sod those mad bastards in London who think that pinpricks like this one could affect the course of the war? A symbol, they always argued. No matter what you do it will be a symbol, a rallying call. Which presumably it would be even if he died. But he wasn't going to die. He was going to slow time down. He closed his eyes, felt the tachycardia kick in as, against the constant urging of adrenaline, his heart rate fell.

Two minutes.

With measured calm and steady hands, Williams moved the throttle brace into position, the steel rod that would fix the accelerator in the fully depressed position, and slid the retaining bolt through the steering wheel, which would keep the truck on a direct course for the wireless station ahead.

Three minutes.

There was someone outside who had spotted him. A technician. Sprinting to raise the alarm. Chequered flag time. He pressed the throttle to the floor, felt the ancient engine twist and jerk in its mounting as if trying to break free, engaged the throttle brace and let in the clutch, and in one smooth, flowing movement was out the door and heading for a hard landing.

Fifty seconds left.

The air exploded from his body as he hit the ground with a puff of choking chalk dust.

Forty-one, forty, thirty-nine . . .

Then he was on his feet and running, counting down, sprinting up the slope towards the Atlantic, willing his legs to pump faster.

Twenty, nineteen . . .

He waited for the explosion to lick its warm breath over him. Keep running.

Ten, nine, eight . . .

He was level with the car when he heard the crumple of metal as the truck punched into the German unit, its engine screaming in its red-lined death throes, the building itself half torn from its housings with a teeth-clenching shriek, bracing wires pinging free from the ground and spinning through the air with a lethal whistle.

Three, two, one . . .

Williams ducked.

Nothing.

He stared in panic at Robert who mouthed, 'Get in.'

Williams looked again at the twisted pile of truck and radio station. He could see a figure crawling from the wreckage. Something in his hand. Gun.

Williams opened the Atlantic door and reached into the back for the Thomson. 'Will. Get in. It's a dud. The pencils mustn't have snapped.'

'There's still the gelly . . . and the petrol.'

'Get in, you idiot.'

Another figure, and Williams felt the crackle of air as a bullet flew past him. He pulled back the bolt on the Thomson. He knew you couldn't ignite petrol with a bullet. Not an ordinary bullet. But you might with tracers, and the thirty-round magazine had seven of those in there, big .45 slugs that burned bright and hot.

He set the gun to auto fire. A pain seared through his ear, and his shoulder. Then he heard, way off to his left, a gunshot and saw a muzzle flash from the corner of his eye. Sniper. Wimille or one of his lads. Good people. Value for money.

Williams squeezed the trigger and felt the submachine gun judder up to the left and noticed the two fiery angels flying towards the truck.

More cover fire from the clifftop, pinning down the Germans. But still he could hear the air snapping near him.

Second burst, three tracers out into the truck. Still nothing.

Now Robert was firing, holding the Sten all wrong, hand on the magazine, sure way to jam it, but the damn thing didn't have the guts to jam on an angry Robert and the nine-millimetre slugs zinged into the wreckage ahead of them.

All or nothing. Williams squeezed the trigger to empty the magazine and at seven hundred rounds per minute the bullets were gone in an instant. Not a dicky bird. He turned to get the hell out of there.

The explosion of fuel knocked him back against the Atlantic as a fireball rolled and boiled around the truck, greedily engulfing the damaged radio station as well. Whether the timing pencils clicked in or the gelignite went – the plastic was pretty inert – a second, deeper, more energetic detonation spun pieces of metal and debris high into the air. Finally, reluctantly, with a high-pitched tearing sound, the radio mast started to lean, shift and turn as it fell on to the pyre, generating a dense cloud of metallic fireflies which spiralled up into the dark night.

Williams was already in the Atlantic, its wheels smoking as Robert yanked it round and sped up the track, sliding the back dangerously on each bend, while Williams smiled at a third explosion, consuming what was left of the complex.

They made the main road and headed into the forests, retracing their route through the backroads and unused pathways that

Robert had picked out to circumvent any patrols and road blocks. The trees blurred by at terrifying speed, Robert risking a flash of dim lights only when absolutely necessary. Williams let out a long breath of stale air, slumped down in the seat and closed his eyes, confident that his friend wouldn't wrap them round a trunk.

'Arm,' said Robert.

Williams looked down at his torn shirt and winced as his fingers found the wound underneath, a one-inch gouge through the muscle.

'All right,' he said with more hope than conviction. The trough of raw meat was beginning to sting.

Robert glanced across. 'Yeah, you'll heal.' He pointed to the cracks and starring at the corner of the windshield where two bullets had passed through and said with mock anger, 'Do you know how much a new one of these fucking things costs?'

Hans Keppler, a handkerchief over his face to try to filter out the worst of the smell of burnt rubber and human flesh, surveyed the tangled ruin of what had once been a fine piece of German technical engineering but was now a smouldering piece of scrap metal with the chassis of a truck embedded in it. Medics were extracting what charred remains they could from the mess, and laying them out on stretchers. Only one completely intact body had been located, and that was blackened beyond recognition. The day was already warm, thought Keppler, by the next day this charnel house would stink worse than ever.

Keppler looked at Neumann. 'Organised. Daring. Anything?'

'We have one sentry who saw a car. Low, fast. Two men, he thinks. But he died before he could say much more. Lost too much blood.'

'What's the nearest village?' asked Keppler.

'Place called Boissy. We've already shot four of them.'

196

Keppler raised an eyebrow. Hitler had ordered reprisals for acts of terrorism in the previous September, but this seemed a little too hasty.

'Two Jews and two Communists,' said Neumann by way of explanation. People who deserved to die whether Boissy was implicated or not. 'Just to help the recollection process of the rest.'

'I want the village fined a million francs. No more retaliatory measures for the moment.' Keppler used the approved term *Vergeltungssanktionen*, retaliation rather than reprisal. General Karl Heinrich von Stulnagel, the Militarbefehlshaber of France, had forbidden the word reprisals and even hostages from being used to describe the response to terrorism. 'If we find the expiators—' – *Suhnepersonen*, another new term – 'used the village and villagers in any way, then I suggest we transport all the males for labour work in Germany. Better than wasting bullets.'

And a safer, more elegant solution, thought Keppler. Sabotage on the scale of this attack was rare. But when it did happen, all concerned knew that the Germans would take revenge on the population. Keppler wondered if that was part of the aim of the perpetrators – to radicalise the population by having the Occupiers seen as brutal thugs. If so, it was a callous, but effective policy on behalf of the Resistance. Which is why Keppler preferred what General Keital called *Nacht und Nebel* – the disappearance of the Reich's enemies into the Night and Fog, leaving their loved ones in ignorance of their whereabouts or state of health, and as an important bonus, snuffing out the opportunity to create martyrs for their futile cause.

'Do you think the Laurent woman might have any knowledge of this?'

Keppler shook his head, disappointed. 'No.'

'You indulge her. Sir.'

'She'll break. I know the type. You don't have to touch them. Her mind does it all for you.' Keppler also quite enjoyed the rumour over at the Hotel Lutetia where the Abwehr were convinced he had acquired himself a British spy as a willing mistress.

Keppler took the handkerchief away from his mouth and walked briskly towards his white-spattered Opel staff car. He turned to Neumann. 'Everything ready for *La Grand Rafle*?'

'Yes. I have ordered a hundred extra coffins. Two hundred pairs of handcuffs. Black-out curtains for the buses which will take those not to be transported to execution and two thousand litres of fuel for burning the corpses of the dead.'

'Burning where?' asked Keppler, out of curiosity.

'Père-Lachaise. Most adults for resettlement will go to Drancy, families and children to the Velo.'

Drancy was an unfinished housing estate near Le Bourget which had been operating as a holding camp for Jews since May 1941; the Velo was the cycle track, the Velodrome d'Hiver. All would eventually be put on transports to the east, where God alone knew what awaited them. Although, in this case, Keppler could second guess the deity.

They climbed inside the car and Keppler ordered his driver to proceed. The *rafle*, Keppler had decided, was folly. The Jews were not going anywhere. They had no radios, no bicycles, longer curfew hours and, since May, all over the age of six were required to wear the yellow star. Keppler would forget the Jews for now, and work on cases such as this act of destruction. He took one last glance back at the carnage and said to Neumann: 'I don't want you wasting days on this Big Round-up. Just do it quickly. And remember – use gendarmes where you can, that way it will be seen as a French operation. And we can get on with catching these terrorists.'

Twenty-one

AUGUST 1942

In the darkness Williams pulled Eve closer to him and she stirred.
More than a month since the attack at the chalk pit. No new
instructions, not so much as a 'well done' from London. Probably
punishment for not having a radio. Now it was back to waiting.
Waiting for a young girl to turn into the drive, or a half-track full
of soldiers or a black Citroën full of Sonderkommando. It was
getting to Eve more than him, he knew.

Robert was travelling to Paris more and more to see his
mother, who had a suspected liver ailment and was in and out of
hospital. At least it kept him occupied. Wimille had gone back to
living it up as best he could in Paris, swearing he would be ready
whenever he was called upon. In a strange way, he said, he had
enjoyed it. Nothing strange about it, thought Williams. They just
all needed whatever stupid drug risking their lives generated.
Some more than others, that was all.

'Will.'

Eve had opened one eye.

'Hmm.'

'I want to go to Normandy for a while.'

'Why?'

'To see the dogs.'

'They'll be all right.' A neighbour was feeding and exercising the terriers.

'They'll forget who I am.'

'They're dogs,' he said. 'They love whoever feeds them.' She poked him hard and he sighed. 'If you wish. You'll need travel documents.'

'Maurice said he can fix me up.'

'When did you see Maurice?'

'In town. A week ago.'

Williams sat up. 'You've been plotting this for a week?'

'Plotting? Don't be ridiculous. I've been thinking about it. I could go and see my parents, make sure the dogs are fine. I'll be away a week or two at most.'

'I don't want to be without you.'

'Come with me.'

He looked into her eyes to see if she was serious, but the smirk told him she was just echoing another situation where he had been the one doing the leaving. And for a lot longer than two weeks. She knew that him travelling around was an unnecessary risk. Women still attracted less attention than men young enough to be working in the Reich's munitions factories. 'How is Maurice?'

'Fine. Funny thing, he offered me a refrigerator.'

'Why?'

'He said he had come into a couple.'

'What did you say?'

'I said we'd think about it.'

'Say no.'

'Why?'

Williams slid out of bed. Dawn was breaking, streaking the sky a deep orange. At one time the return of the sun meant the end of nightmares, the solar angel driving away the demons. Not any longer. The horrors seemed to go on, day or night now. Not so much here, in the country, but Paris was like a wounded animal turning on itself, devouring its own rancid flesh in a desperate bid to survive. 'Because you don't know where it's come from.'

'You don't mind taking his *Ausweissen*.'

'That's different. That's for a good cause.'

He turned to face her, and even in the gloom she could tell by the set of his jaw he was deadly serious. She decided that one victory, his acquiescence over her travelling, was enough for one morning. 'Okay, Will. No refrigerator.'

In the soft early dawn light he saw the figure at the gate and reached down for the Colt pistol beside the bed. He looked back. Gone. Then he saw her again, pushing her bicycle down the drive. Beatrice. Or one of her friends. A year ago the Germans would let a pretty young girl come and go with near impunity. It never occurred to them that young French women would be part of a clandestine organisation. Now, since they had uncovered dozens of underground printing presses and Resistance cells, they had realised the glue holding them together – the runners, messengers, lookouts, distributors – were, as often as not, the same smiling girls they whistled at in the street.

Williams pulled on some clothes, shoved the gun in his waistband and went down to greet the courier. No, he couldn't go on risking their young lives. Maybe London was right. Time to get a pianist in.

Maurice looked down the list on the desk in front of him and ticked two names, Pierre Tavel and Jean Leffe. He glanced up at Keppler who was staring out at the splendid chestnuts in the central ribbon of the boulevard and the grand *poules*, the high-class prostitutes who had always lived on Foch, sunning themselves on the grass.

'Tavel, I am pretty sure,' said Maurice softly. 'Leffe's real name is Szlifkes. Polish Jew.'

Keppler nodded. This was tedious work, but each department had been given a quota of Jews to identify. RSHA, the mother organisation of the SD and Gestapo in Berlin, estimated 800,000 Jews in France, perhaps a quarter or a fifth of that in Paris. The numbers didn't add up. The *rafles* had failed to find anything like that amount. Rather than accept that they might have inflated the figures, Eichmann had told the Gestapo and SD to flush out those hiding under aliases or being harboured by sympathetic French families.

Keppler walked over and examined the list. He flicked the pages. There were eight ticks in all. 'Not many, Maurice.'

This was the third time Maurice had visited the office, the third occasion he had had to shut his mind to the consequences of his actions, identifying people he knew were naturalised Jews, who would fail the Nazi criteria on parentage, and be resettled along with the thousands of others. Still, if he didn't do it . . .

'Well, I've already given you most of the ones I know. Surely there can't be many left in the city?'

'Berlin thinks there must be. They think they are out there somewhere, waiting to cause trouble.'

'What do you think, Sturmbannführer?'

Keppler laughed and fished himself a cigar from a beautiful red mahogany and brass humidor, recently arrived on his desk from an apartment over in the 7th that had been vacated the day before the round-up. A tip off, he suspected. Either a sentimental gendarme or one who charged exorbitantly to supply news of impending actions.

He swivelled the container to Maurice, who selected a fat

Jamaican. 'I don't think about things like this. Orders come from RSHA, I obey them, then get on with my real job. Which, I should remind you, is the pursuit of enemies of the state. At least, those more dangerous than Jewish doctors and bankers.'

Maurice nodded. He knew Keppler was a reasonable man.

'So, what is it to be this time, Maurice? Eight names ... a couple of *Ausweissen* for you to continue your scurrilous smuggling activities or another visit to the warehouse?'

The great storage sheds near Gare de Lyon were stuffed full of the possessions of Jews who were caught in the big trawl-in on 16 and 17 of July. Sure, Maurice felt sorry for them, but there was everything from tables to refrigerators going begging. Shame to let it rot. But in the end he said: 'The *Ausweissen* would be most useful. My mother is not well and—'

'Stop. Spare me the weasly excuses.' Keppler signed the paperwork and handed it over to Maurice. 'Let's see if your memory improves next time you have to visit poor ailing Mama.'

Maurice grabbed the permissions to travel, which he would split with Robert, and hurried out, closing his ears to some of the more extreme sounds echoing down the corridors and out into the fresh air, ignoring the protests of his bad leg.

The meeting was on the banks of the Canal St Martin, up near La Villette. As with the horse butchers in Montmartre, the cafés hereabouts were the haunts of the slaughtermen and the herders, and probably as safe as anywhere in Paris, but Williams knew that the army of collaborationist eavesdroppers had grown as rations had shrunk. People had to eat, feed what was left of their families. So meetings were best arranged in the open air, away from the cafés where random raids were becoming more and more common.

Williams had to be careful in Paris for other reasons, too. As a healthy man in his late thirties he was eligible for working in the Reich. His papers proclaimed him as an electrical engineer, a reserved occupation, especially when so many factories were being hit by allied bombing or, more rarely, sabotage. Even so, one false move during a routine check and such niceties could be forgotten and he could be heading east. He slowed as he came past the gushing lock gates and into the wide Basin La Villette. An elderly couple sat on the benches on the Quai de la Seine, throwing a few precious crumbs to the pigeons.

A little cluster of teenage girls, their wooden clogs clacking ferociously to the rhythm of their gossip, hurried by. The same noise could be heard all over Paris – the Wehrmacht had taken the nation's entire leather supply, and decent shoes now only appeared for special occasions. At the far end of the Quai a lone woman studied a magazine – sunglasses, hair tied back, wearing a jacket and skirt made from thick felt-like material that were fashionable, despite their unsuitability for the summer weather.

Twenty metres away he slowed, unable to believe what he was seeing, then remembered himself. Don't act surprised. Do not draw attention to yourself. He strode up and uttered his part of the pre-arranged greeting.

'Mam'selle. I believe you have a bicycle for sale.'

Rose Miller looked up over her glasses. 'Yes. Would you like a ride?'

'I'd prefer to know how much first.'

'Sit down and we can discuss a price.'

Williams quickly took his place beside her and whispered, 'What on earth are you doing here?'

'We had some accidents at Ringway. Terribly short of people this month.'

'But you . . . if you are caught . . .'

She pointed to her brooch, a green emerald set in an arrangement of gold leaves and he understood that, somehow, it was lethal. Her L pill. 'Listen, Bodington has been over twice.'

'Bodington?'

'Nick Bodington. Buckmaster's deputy. Knows Paris from before the war. If *he* can chance it, so can I.'

Williams was unconvinced. It seemed like unnecessary bravado. Rose put a hand on his knee, briefly, as if to reassure him.

'Besides, I needed to see what it is like. Changed, hasn't it?' She waved a hand to indicate the whole of Paris. 'Even since you came over. How can I do my job unless I really know what conditions are like? You can't beat first-hand experience.'

'All right, all right. You are here now. Listen, I've changed my mind. I need a radio operator.'

Rose nodded. 'You'll have to wait. As I said, we are desperately short. The courier system is still working, obviously.'

'For the moment,' said Williams. 'I think it's time to change.'

'Have you contact with any other groups. Prosper?'

He shook his head. He had heard of one group who met in cafés in central Paris who occasionally lapsed into English. Maurice told him they were being watched, hoping to snare others. If that was Prosper, Williams wanted no part of it. 'So why are you here?'

'I need a recce done. Something funny is going on. On the railways. Some trains heading east are stopping at a factory at St Just. You know it?'

'No.'

'It's a chemical works. I need to know what's going on.'

'Is that it?' he asked, disappointed. 'You came all this way to tell me that?'

Rose snapped. 'Yes that's it. Except I want you to film it.'

'Film? With what?'

'I have the equipment. I will show you. And afterwards Robert
– he's to come back with me.'

He felt a sudden panic at losing his friend. 'What? Why?'

'Training. See if we can make him a better radio man than
you.' She arched an eyebrow. 'Not that it will be very difficult.'

Some way down the towpath a pair of German officers
appeared, the familiar muddy green identifying them as
Wehrmacht.

'Are you in order?' asked Williams, using the now automatic
shorthand.

Rose nodded.

'What's your name?'

'Claudette Duclos.'

They stood to walk casually away from the Germans, who
seemed simply out for a stroll. But you could never tell. 'What's
your cover?'

'Typically French,' Rose smiled, and stood on tip-toe to kiss his
cheek. 'You're a married man, and I'm your mistress.'

Rose Miller spread the small rigid attaché case stamped SNCF
out on the table and went through the mechanism once more.
Outside a ferocious summer storm raged; raindrops like lead
pellets rattled the windows, and low thunder sporadically under-
pinned it.

Rose, Robert and Williams had before them a selection of
weapons, including a new Colt .45 auto that Williams had
bagged as his, and three Sten guns plus Bakelite limpet mines,
pencil sticks, plastic explosive. Behind them Chiquita, Robert's
Portuguese maid who had finally come back to work for him
after reaching Lyons and getting stranded there during the
exodus, was preparing a chicken stew with a stringy bird she
had managed to barter from a nearby farm. She didn't bat an

eyelid at the hardware being tossed about.

Rose pointed at the concealed camera. 'Focus, about fifteen feet. It's a fixed lens, wide angle. All you do is set the aperture according to the amount of light. Trigger here. Point the case at what you want to film. Load and unload in this bag here.' She held up the black velvet sack.

'How noisy?' asked Robert.

Rose shrugged. 'The case has been blimped. Soundproofed,' she added when she saw the quizzical look on their faces. 'I also have a new poem code. We are changing all of them. I know you don't like it, Williams, but when you get an operator, I want you to use this. Not very cheery, but they are far less likely to know it than the Yeats you chose.'

The poems were the grids upon which the messages could be coded and decoded. The Germans knew this, and were aware that some poems were more popular than others. So the more obscure the better – one chap in SOE codes was even writing his own, although he was having trouble keeping up with demand, his muse not always working to the exact period of full moons. She cleared her throat and began to recite. 'Sweet sister death has gone debauched today—'

The kitchen door flew open and crashed back on its hinges, making Chiquita jump. Williams pushed back his chair and levelled the Colt at the doorway. Eve, wet and bedraggled, stood there, eyes blazing, surveying the scene before her. Chiquita rushed over and eased her out of her coat. Williams looked at his watch. He should have met her at the station. He began to apologise but was cut off by the torrent of words spat at him.

'You know what I heard in Normandy? Oh, the dogs are fine by the way, Will, thanks for asking. Last week the Germans raided the Leroux house. The son had a radio on the table. So they shot him. Shot the mother. Carted the daughters off to Christ knows where. You sit here with this pile of shit in plain view and you don't post a look-out . . .'

Rose said. 'I'm Claudette—'

But Eve hadn't finished. She strode over to Rose. 'I can guess who you are. These two idiots spent ten years trying to get themselves killed on the racetrack. Then you come along with your half-baked secret war. And they say, oh, how wonderful. An even more dangerous game to play. You, of course, think they are doing this for England and France.' Eve picked up the Colt and flung it at the window. They ducked as it crashed through the glass and into the shrubbery.

Williams glared at her then turned back to Rose. 'Finish giving me the new code.'

'Now?'

'Now.'

Rose cleared her throat. 'Sweet sister death has gone debauched today and stalks on this high ground with strumpet confidence—'

'Strumpet?' asked Robert distractedly as he watched Eve pirouette towards the doorway, her arms outstretched in some wild theatrical gesture. He wondered if she had been drinking. Perhaps that Normandy cider.

'Strumpet,' confirmed Rose.

'As in tart,' offered Eve.

Rose ignored her. 'With strumpet confidence, makes no coy veiling of her appetite but leers from you to me with all her parts discovered.'

They jumped again as the door slammed once more. Robert touched Williams' arm. 'Better go after her, Will.'

Williams, embarrassed by the wilful display, said, 'Let her stew.'

Rose got to her feet. 'She'll catch her death. I'll go.'

She opened the door and blanched at the driving rain hitting her face. The wind wrapped something round her foot. A blouse. Rose followed the trail of discarded clothing, carefully picking up shoes, skirt and underwear as she went, squinting into the blackness until a flash of lightning illuminated in stark blue-grey, the chilled flesh of Eve, standing naked looking up to the heavens, a smile on her face, imagining it was ten, twelve years ago and all she had to do in life was disrobe now and then for a nice old man to paint her.

Eve was aware of someone to her side and looked around, surprised to see Rose. She looked the woman carefully up and down in grudging admiration, and said quietly, 'He's mine. I don't care who you are. Touch him and I'll rip your guts out.'

Before Rose could give any sort of reassuring reply Eve snatched the bundle of clothing from her hands and marched inside, leaving her standing, wondering what she had just witnessed, as rivulets of water streamed down her face and into her open mouth.

Twenty-two

LAKE SENLITZ, OCTOBER 2001

Deakin could tell the old woman was tired now. She sat slumped in the canvas chair while yet another body shrouded in black rubber was taken away. She had promised the police a full and frank statement, and they were happy with that. Nobody wanted to detain a fragile old woman about crimes that may or may not have been committed fifty-odd years previously.

The technician handed her a tightly wrapped box containing the rusty canister. 'There is a plastic film over the label, which should protect it from further degradation, but I've taken photographs as well, just in case.'

'Good man. Thank you.'

She glanced up at Deakin and caught the look on his face. 'You have a question?'

'We all have a million questions. Such as what are you going to do with that?' He pointed at the box containing the cylinder.

'Oh, finish off a few things. Loose ends, you know. Been nagging at me all these years.'

'About Williams?'

'And the others.'

'How did he end up in the lake?'

'All in good time, Deakin, all in good time.'

The first heavy drops of rain splattered around them and Deakin looked up at the black sky. 'We should be going.'

Rose stood. 'I have one last thing to do. Put that in the car will you?'

Deakin took the package and placed it in the boot of the hire car while, heart in mouth, he watched Rose struggle down to the shoreline, stepping gingerly over the rough stones, any one of them capable of breaking her thin, brittle ankles. Deakin said his goodbyes to Warner, promising him a full report back in London, and waited for her to make the journey back, relieved when she reached solid ground. Exhausted by the effort, she gratefully took his arm. Deakin looked down and saw the Cartier watch was missing from her wrist.

Twenty-three

AUGUST–SEPTEMBER 1942

Williams crept up the stairs and into the spare bedroom, tiptoed up behind Eve as she darned a stocking and put his hands over her eyes. It was two days since her little exhibition. Robert had billeted Rose with Madame Lethias and gone off to visit his mother. Williams and Eve were alone, something everyone seemed to think was a good idea.

'You don't know what it's like, do you?'

She grabbed his wrists and pulled the fingers from her face and turned, the mad anger no longer in her eyes. 'To have your stomach knotted all the time? To feel the fear eating into you, lining your face, destroying your heart? I used to feel it just once or twice a month when you were racing, I could manage that. But now, every time someone appears at the door, every time you go out . . .'

'It's important, Eve.'

'How many of you do you think there are over here? A hundred? A thousand?'

Williams shrugged. He didn't know. Whenever he sat in a café he wondered if the surly, unshaven guy at the bar, the woman near the doors checking herself in the mirror every five seconds, the travelling salesman, which one of them might have passed through Arisaig and Beddington and been seen off by Vera Atkins or Rose Miller.

'And you think you can make a difference. We need an army – a real army, not a secret army – to drive the bastards out.'

'Every little helps.'

Eve stood up. 'How will it help if you get yourself killed? Help the allies? No. Help me? No.' She hugged him as hard as she could. 'Tell that woman to go away. Tell her you'll sit out the war till the second front starts. Let's go to Normandy.'

'I can't do that.'

'Which part?'

'Any of it. Look.' He turned her face up, brushed stray hairs out of her eyes. 'Robert feels the same. OK, she is sending us off to do something that looks stupid, but what do we know? Do we see the big picture? No.'

'Does that woman?' Eve spat the words out.

'That woman? Is that what your little show was about?' he asked. 'Was it about Rose?'

Eve looked down at her darning again. 'Of course not.'

'Not even a little bit?'

She looked up and held her thumb and forefinger a couple of centimetres apart. 'Maybe this much.'

Williams put a hand under her chin. 'Why? What are you thinking? That we are, were . . .'

'Don't say it. Don't. It's not that. It doesn't have to be sex, you know.' She paused to examine why her insides were still slowly, corrosively boiling. 'I suppose I am jealous because she gave you this part of your life and I have no say in any of it. I can feel you excluding me, even when she isn't here. You and Robert. It's worse than when you were racing. Seeing the three of you, cooking something up like witches, forgetting all about me . . . it was too much.'

'I don't mean it to feel like that. I value what you do, what you think. You know that.'

'Then do me a favour.'

'What?'

'Stop using that stupid car.'

Williams laughed out loud. 'Stupid?'

'It's stupid to be seen in. Anywhere. Anytime.'

'That car could save our lives.'

'Or it could get you killed. I know Robert is reckless, but he really doesn't need a partner in idiocy.'

Williams ran through the task they had been given by Rose, and, it was true, speed was not going to be essential. Robert's argument would be this: driving fast cars is what we do, have always done. But Eve's was the wiser counsel. 'We'll give it a try. This time.'

Eve kissed him, hugged his chest again and said quietly, 'Thank you. And I'm sorry about the other night.'

Williams led her by the hand into their room across the landing and lowered her on to the bed. 'I'm sorry too.'

She looked up at him and smiled. 'Show me . . .'

The Alphachem offices at St Just were located upwind of the actual chemical plant, so that the exposure of the clerks and managers to the vile odours and eye-stinging emissions were minimised. The building wasn't anything grand, just a concrete box, really, but within Raymond Berri had insisted on an office every bit as well appointed as if he had been on the Champs Elysées. Heavy red curtains, leather sofas, a big desk, a wonderful padded swivel chair. The picture of him painted by Orpen had pride of place on one wall. Thinner in those days and grander. For the last five years he'd been climbing back up through Alphachem. Now he could climb no more. From the window he could see the single track rail spur that came from the mainline east of Paris and where, once a week or more, a train of boxcars would shunt down to pick up a consignment of delousing powder.

At least, that was what the inventory said. For weeks, no, months, now Berri had been having doubts, ever since he had taken a closer look at the trains and heard the heart-stopping noises from within. Sobbing. Babies crying. Low moans. The hacking of sick people. Human misery in small parcels of sound.

Whatever it was he wanted no part of it and had said so to the man sitting opposite him, Georges Legine, the owner of the company and therefore his boss.

Georges took a cigar, clipped it and lit it. 'Raymond. The things is, if we don't do it, someone else will. And someone else will make millions of francs a month. And we'll have lost that for what? Some vague liberal unease on your part.' He waved the cigar dismissively and exhaled. 'It's madness.'

'It's collaboration.'

'Oh, Raymond. You make it sound like a dirty word. Didn't Petain himself use the term? Everyone collaborates. It's just a matter of degree. Should you boycott the baker who serves Germans? Or the butcher? You'd starve if you started applying such criteria. I consider what we are doing as the necessary business to stay alive. There is only one customer now, Raymond – Germany. We supply or die.'

'There are Jews on those trains.'

'So? What concern is it of ours?'

Raymond cleared his throat. 'I am Jewish. At least, one of my grandparents was. In some people's eyes that is enough to get me a corner of a cattle truck.'

'Is that why you went to the Resistance?'

It hit Raymond like a slap and he squirmed in the chair, causing the leather to squeak. It was true. One of the foremen from before the war had been a vocal communist. Raymond was sure he would be part of this Franc-Tireurs et Partisans outfit. He'd tracked him down in Senlis and, although admitting nothing, the foreman promised he'd speak to 'some people'. Raymond regained his composure. 'Nonsense.'

'You know there is a rumour that Rene Peugeot sabotaged his own works. I wouldn't want anything like that to happen here, Raymond.'

The door opened and the swarthy officer called Meyer, who co-ordinated the Alphachem shipments with the Drancy trains, entered without knocking, two German soldiers flanking him. Berri heard the high whistle of the approaching train. He suddenly realised what was happening.

'I don't suppose I'll need to pack?' he said quietly.

Meyer shook his head.

Berri grabbed a fistful of cigars from the box and stuffed them in his inside pocket. Georges Legine shrugged, an it's-your-own-fault gesture of reasonableness and Berri walked out with his escort to find his place in the scruffy, rattling cattle trucks now slowly snaking past the window into the works' sidings.

Williams and Robert stepped out of the small car, aware of the stares of workers and German guards. The train had just pulled in and now sat four hundred metres down the track, huffing and hissing impatiently, dwarfed by the knotted steel pipework of the chemical complex and its cavernous storage warehouses. The pair were absolutely calm. Their documents said they were railways safety inspectors for the SNCF. And the documents were entirely genuine, thanks to Ettore Bugatti, who used his contacts in the industry to secure the real thing, official stamps and all.

Robert carried the blimped case, held as casually as he could, finger on the trigger which would start the film rolling. He had to use it sparingly, as there was only around five minutes of actual film time on it. He asked directions to the office from one of the workers and they entered a rather stark reception room, with a desk and two threadbare chairs. The receptionist, a small, balloon-faced woman in her fifties, was eyeing them suspiciously. Williams flashed his ID. 'SNCF Inspectorate. Can we see Monsieur Berri please?'

'Monsieur Berri is no longer with us,' said the receptionist.

'Really?' said Robert, puzzled. They had been given the name only last week, and Williams was convinced it was Orpen's old friend, a man he was sure they could trust. 'So who is in charge?'

'That would be our chairman, Monsieur Georges Legine. I shall tell him you're here. Do you have an appointment?'

'This is a snap inspection,' said Williams with as much SNCF-style pomposity as he could muster. 'Having an appointment would rather defeat the object. We'll be outside.'

They left the building and walked across to the track, slowly following it down towards the train, a ragbag of scabrous mismatched trucks. They could see a clump of German guards, including a couple on the roof of the train, all brandishing submachine guns. Williams concentrated on getting his stride as easy and unworried as possible. Robert bent down to brush his shoe and came up with a small square of paper he had palmed. After a few more metres he unwrapped it, studied the contents and passed it across to Williams.

The writing was tiny, spidery and very, very young.

I was picked up in the street in Toulouse on 12 July by the police. Held in a gymnasium there and transported to a big place called Drancy. It is near Paris. Am now on a train travelling east. Whoever gets this, please tell my parents I am alive. They will reward you. They are at 7 rue Pergola in Toulouse. There is no phone. Please write to them. Tell them I love them. And I love my sisters. God bless, Armand Simone.

Williams swallowed hard. The message was so measured, so calm. A young boy snatched before he could tell his parents, thrown into a rancid, overcrowded gymnasium with dozens, perhaps hundreds of other equally confused and scared men, women and children, then shipped north to Drancy. He knew, everyone knew, that conditions there were squalid beyond belief, that after a few days in the vast, filth-ridden dormitories, of scrabbling for inedible food, trying to use the primitive, diseased sanitation, suicide became a viable option, the best way out.

But he'd thought only Parisians ended up there. Now Jews from the ZNO – the Vichy non-occupied zone – were being brought up as well. Williams could see a sprinkling of other scraps of paper beside the track, the senders clearly hoping that friendly factory workers would find them and pass them on, a desperate dead-letter drop. Even that action spoke of terrible despair. Williams made to pick one and Robert stopped him, aware that the guard on the roof was peering down at them.

'Maybe later. There is nothing we can do. Not now.' Williams hesitated and Robert grabbed his friend by the upper arm and squeezed as hard as he could, pulling him upright. 'You want to join them in there? Don't be stupid, Will. Pull yourself together.' He said slowly: 'We're SNCF inspectors, Will. Remember. We don't care. We don't care. We mustn't care. Not now.'

Williams checked his heartbeat. It was wild and erratic, and he slowed it, taking in big gulps of air, letting the calm of the race circuit shroud him. After a minute or so he finally nodded, fully back into character and raised a placatory hand to the German guard, who waved back.

They moved close to the last two cars, new additions which had been shunted up from a siding. Beyond a ragged line of soldiers at the rear of the train they could see white-overalled men heaving a cargo into the gaping sides of these boxcars. At first the workers looked to be hideously deformed, but Williams said: 'Gasmasks.'

Robert nodded. Gasmasks. He pressed the trigger on the case handle and heard the faintest whirring as the reel started to spool.

'Hey, you two. What the hell are you doing here?' The German officer burst out of the ranks and strode towards them. 'Who are you?'

'SNCF,' said Robert coolly.

Meyer snatched the ID and flicked his eyes from photo to face rapidly. 'You have no authority over the trains of the Reich.'

'They are not trains of the Reich. They are SNCF trains while they are on French soil.'

'And we have authority when hazardous materials are transported.' Williams indicated the gasmasked men.

Meyer dismissed the idea with a wave and handed the IDs back. 'Not hazardous. The masks are just a precaution. Delousing powder.'

'Gentlemen, gentlemen.' The soothing voice of Georges Legine came from behind them. 'Excuse me. Herr Meyer, is there a problem?'

'Yes. This train has to be on its way in,' he checked his watch, 'twenty minutes. Exactly'

'It will be. Allow me to talk to these gentlemen.' Meyer turned on his heel and went off to shout at the workers to get a move on. 'Ah, the Germans. Such slaves to the timetable. Now, what can I do for you?'

'We wish to check that the safety regulations as regards the transportation of toxic material are being adhered to.'

'Of course. Come.'

He led them through the line of soldiers, who grudgingly parted. Robert was now next to the men and the cylinders they were loading and pressed the trigger once more, rotating the case to catch the label, with its prominent skull and crossbones, on film. He hoped.

'As you can see,' said Legine, 'proper padding between layers and netting to hold them in place. This stuff isn't that lethal in fresh air. Only in confined spaces. So once the clothes are treated, and the lice dead, they are laid outside and the toxin evaporates.'

They walked on to the second truck and ahead the battered old cattle cars stretched, the stench of human waste and sweat and fear oozing from them. A barrier of four soldiers standing abreast prevented them going any further along the low platform, but the expression on their faces told Williams they could smell it too. Robert nudged Williams ever so gently. He was staring at one of the Germans, his eyes boring into the man, as if he was personally responsible. Williams broke off contact.

Beyond this barrier of soldiers, four gendarmes walked the train, occasionally stopping to shout or bang their sticks on the side of the trucks. A voice occasionally reached them, a plea, asking, Robert could just make out, for water. More thumping on the sides, fresh threats from the gendarmes.

Now Williams could hear terrible coughing from within the nearest boxcar, a thin feeble sound, the sound of small lungs infected with something slowly filling them up with mucus. The youngster began to cry, a little girl, and he could hear soothing words from an adult. Still no response from anyone else, not Legine, not the guards. A gendarme was up to the chained doorway now, and he rapped on the side. 'Quiet in there. Be quiet.'

The hacking became muffled as if a hand was over a mouth. The gendarme moved on. Robert thought of the gun in his inside pocket, constructing a dangerous fantasy of him and the policeman and a dark alley.

Legine, alarmed by the pair's excessive interest in the trucks, steered them away. 'Just these two trucks are our responsibility, gentlemen. Not the rest of it. Now let me assure you about safety. We've been making this stuff for five years. Never had an accident yet.'

The wailing started slowly, this time from a truck some distance away from them.

'This stuff being?' asked Williams.

Now the wail was echoing along the platform, climbing the register.

'Zyklon B, they call it. Prussic acid. A delousing agent. Heading for the Russian front, I believe. I'll show you the dockets.' Legine was agitated, anxious to move away from the chilling sound. 'They're in my office.'

'Shut that damned woman up.' It was Meyer, irritated at the commotion.

Legine started to fuss, ushering them away from the train, but the screech of metal rollers as a cattle truck gate slid back made Williams stop and spin round. The cries of relief from those within as fresh air flowed into the truck were drowned by the cries of the hysterical woman, but again, the workers refused to look up and carried on loading.

Within the mass of vertical bodies, where faces crushed against faces, limbs entangled with each other, chests were pressed tight, and everyone breathed only the exhalations of their neighbour, there was a ripple as the woman forced her way to the front, her baby clasped in her arms. The gendarmes screeched at her to shut up, but she carried on wailing.

Her companions slowly prised the dead child from her arms, pinning her limbs as she thrashed about in the madness of grief, and passed it down to a gendarme, who, with surprising gentleness carried it across the platform and laid the body down in the shadow of the factory wall covering the tiny body with a paper sack.

The screams lessened then, spiralling down into sobs. The gate clanged home, the bolts were secured, but the image of those haunted faces framed in the doorway wouldn't leave Williams. It was burned on his cortex in stark black and white, a composition of faces, hollow-eyed men and women who have already passed beyond this life and are waiting for death to save them.

Twenty-four

MAY–JULY 1943

The eight months were purgatory for Williams. Robert went back with Rose to England, picked up by a Hudson near Le Mans. Sporadic drops of weapons and supplies came in and had to be intercepted and dispersed around the estate with the help of Eve, Maurice and Jean-Pierre Wimille. However, stashing supplies for some vague far-off event was hugely frustrating – and judging by the débâcle of Dieppe, the second front was a very long way off indeed.

It was getting more dangerous to move around. The occupiers had introduced a scheme, the Service du Travail Obligatoire, the STO, forced labour for nearly all able-bodied men. Now Paris was a city of women, old people and young children, the middle band of males gone, as if wiped out by an age-sensitive plague.

With agonising slowness, that savage snapshot, the faces at the door of the cattle truck, slowly faded, to the point where Williams could close his eyes at night and not have it leap out at him, not cause the anger to rise again. He just hoped that one day, when he needed it, it would be there again to remind him.

Robert returned in March, leaner and fitter, with the new, lighter B2 radio, a decent enough grasp of Morse and a welcome innovation – codes on silk sheets and one-time pads. The poem codes were quietly being retired for something more professional and harder to break.

Maurice, Eve and Williams celebrated Robert's return with a meal at the restaurant in Dreux that Maurice supplied with decent wines. The owner, a man of surly demeanour, explained that, by sheer luck, he had a decent cassoulet they could share with real, not sawdust sausages. And to follow, a *tarte tatin*.

Maurice, of course, knew what was in the cellar and ordered Brouilly and Pouilly Fumé, in a voice that caused the owner to shush him. Exactly what was and wasn't in stock was a closely guarded secret, to be manipulated according to the cut of the customer's jib.

There were a few other clients, all of them smart businessmen, who, thought Williams, looked as if they wouldn't know a ration book if he slapped them round the face with one. He had misgivings about even being there, but the others had overruled him.

'How is it over there?' asked Eve.

'Well, the food is worse than ever. And there's hardly any of it,' smirked Robert. 'I saw Philippe Rothschild.'

'Ah,' said Williams. 'How is he?'

'Well. He's working with a similar outfit to us. Urged me to join them. Gaullists.'

Williams knew this was the SOE branch under the control of the Free French, the one that was supposed to have the pick of French nationals. Robert would be quite a prize. 'What did you say?'

'I said I didn't care for de Gaulle. Just because he was right about tanks, and actually did some fighting against the Germans, doesn't automatically make him the best man to lead France.'

'What did Philippe say?'

'He understood. He told me to be careful. Of SOE. We aren't always told the full story.'

Williams laughed. 'It's a secret service. That's what they do. Keep secrets.'

Eve asked: 'How is the city?'

'London . . . well, London's taken a pounding. Makes me glad that it didn't happen to Paris.' He looked at Williams. 'Don't believe all that pulling-together propaganda shit. People are dying. There are deserters robbing banks. Food shortages like France . . .' He tailed off while wine was poured then continued. 'But there is a feeling since Africa that the tide has turned.'

'Doesn't feel like it here,' said Maurice.

'I don't know,' said Williams. 'You look for the signs you'll see them. Maybe you should lift your head from the black-market trough now and then.'

Maurice furrowed his brow. 'Listen, without me—'

'Without you what?' Williams snapped, pushing his plate away. 'We might not get to eat this shit? All it does is give me gut ache anyway . . .'

'It's not gut ache, it's your prissy guilty conscience—'

'Stop it,' said Robert firmly. 'Just stop it. What's got into you two? Don't fall apart now.'

There was a silence while wine was twirled in glasses.

'What's next?' asked Williams. 'For us? More waiting?'

'Mostly. Two things. There is a line of pylons that feed power to dozens of factories, from Michelin to Aluminium Nord. We are to blow those at some point.'

Williams broke into the baguette, wondering about its strange flaky consistency. You just didn't know what you were eating these days. 'And?'

'Georges Legine has to die.'

Eve asked: 'Why? They'll only replace him.'

'Then we do the next one.'

'And the next?'

'If we have to. As an example to others. And, being a Frenchman, it's unlikely there'll be reprisals.'

Williams said: 'Why don't they bomb the St Just plant if they want to do some real damage?'

'I suggested that,' said Robert and affected an English accent. ' "Not a top priority, old boy", apparently.'

No, trainloads of Jews heading east, just a fact of war. And, thought Williams, it ties up all those guards, all that rolling stock. Jews heading east meant no fresh units heading west, he supposed. 'Do they know where the trains go?'

Robert shook his head. 'Like here. There are rumours.'

The cassoulet arrived and they ate for a while in silence. It was good. Better than any of them had tasted for a long time. Even Williams, despite his earlier protest, tucked in, earning himself a smirk from Maurice which he ignored.

'Did they have any suggestions as to how to get to him?' he asked.

'Oh yes,' said Robert quietly. 'He's been assigned a Milice escort.' The Milice were the volunteer militia formed in what was once the unoccupied zone, a ragbag assortment of thugs, bigots and criminals. 'There is only one time in the week when he dumps them.' Robert went back to slurping his food.

'And?' asked Williams.

'And I think we'd better toss for this one.'

Georges Legine peered into the darkness and damned the blackout lights of his car, sending their feeble slits of blue-ish light into the gloom and fading away to nothing. As he dropped down to second gear he spotted his first one in the trees, just a glimpse. Big, maybe too big. The last one had been unshaven and stank of cheap perfume and he'd felt like he was fucking a docker. Not the idea at all. Something more delicate. But it looked like a bad night tonight. Perhaps there had been another raid by some high-minded Germans or the gendarmes were out to extort some more protection from the girls' purses.

It wasn't fair. He had one simple pleasure in life, a quick taste of anonymous transvestite sex and that was it. Back to the wife, children, work, the unholy trinity of his life. He was just contemplating giving it up as a bad job, when he saw her.

Tall again, but not too heavy, a muscular body sheathed in a yellow dress, his favourite colour. A shock of curly hair, and from what he could see, nice legs. Not as petite as he was hoping for, but this was no night to be fussy. He gave two flashes of the lights, the agreed invitation and she raised her arm in agreement. He pulled over.

Georges stepped out and looked around. Nothing, possibly the shape of another car in the gloom, but it didn't look like cop or Gestapo. He squished across the wet grasses to the bushes and his quarry. Skittishly she stepped back into the shadows of the tree.

'How much, Madame?' he asked.

'Two thousand,' said the low voice, trying hard to climb to a higher register, but failing.

Extortionate, but it was a seller's market tonight. 'Show me your arse,' Georges said matter-of-factly.

She turned around, stuck her rear out and slowly wiggled the dress up and over her hips, to reveal the lace-covered buttocks underneath.

'Lovely. It's a deal. Come here.'

Georges took off his overcoat, stepped to the shrubbery he knew so well and selected a small, well-trammelled clearing. He laid the coat on the ground and beckoned her over. She hesitated and he wondered if this was his/her first time.

It was sheer stroke of luck that Georges stumbled on a root just as the knife flashed out, grazing his adam's apple rather than opening up a second mouth. Mary, Mother of God. A robbery. Georges tried to shout but only a dry, strangled yelp emerged and she was back on him.

'Help.'

Georges lashed out wildly with a strength born of desperation, catching the creature a good solid blow in the face. Ha. Another. He swept a short, heavy branch from the ground and began to swish it back and forth. Williams waited until it was at the far arc of travel, confidently stepped in and drove the blade up under the ribs and twisted. He felt the warm blood trickle over his hands. Already the light was fading in the man's eyes and Williams made sure he got the dedication in before the curtain fell once and for all. 'This is from Raymond Berri.'

The Atlantic started up and purred down the road and Williams sprinted to the kerbside as best he could, the blood spatters on his dress glistening black in the moonlight. Wimille and friends had done a good job of driving off all the competition, leaving him the only show in town for Legine, but he knew the creatures would be back soon. He fell into the car beside Robert, panting, and they drove off. Robert glanced in the rearview mirror. He could see a couple of dark figures on the road. The curious, alerted by Legine's cries, coming out once it was safe.

Out of the park and heading south, back towards Auffargis, Robert taking the car on to the warren of backroads he knew so well. Williams tore off the wig and rubbed his chin where Legine had managed to hit him. He was rusty. He would have done better than that at Arisaig. But then that was all make-believe, with rubber knives. How did he feel now he had done it for real, knifed a human being in cold blood? Rose Miller had asked him if he could. Now he knew. He tried to examine his thoughts. Nothing. Except for the burning anger a scribbled, despairing note could still ignite in his guts. It had to be done. It was done.

'Next time,' Williams said wearily, 'you get the frock.'

'But, darling, it was your arse he liked.'

Williams punched Robert so hard his upper arm went numb, but that only made him laugh even harder.

Twenty-five

FRANCE, JULY 1943

'Life must go on,' said Maurice as they were waved through a roadblock after he had produced his travel pass. They were in a Hotchkiss tourer, another of Maurice's recent acquisitions, with the hood down, as they headed north to the picnic site at the Forest of St Germain.

Williams and Maurice were in the front, Eve and Robert in the rear. Williams had suffered a restless night, because inside he wasn't as at ease about the death of Legine as he had thought he should be. He was sure it would pass. That morning Robert showed him a badly printed copy of *Combat*, the underground paper. In it were strange pictures of the camps that the paper suggested were the final destinations for the trains, camps that made the hellhole of Drancy look like the Elysian Fields, so it claimed. It could be propaganda of course. The thought of those trains told him otherwise. Exactly why they took so much delousing powder along, though, was a mystery to him. Probably to stop typhus outbreaks.

'Did you hear about the guy on honeymoon in Mexico?' began

Maurice. 'Well, the local police chief, he warns him, he says, Señor, Speedy Gonzales, the fastest dick alive, is in town. It is essential that you sleep the night with your hand firmly planted upon the pussy of your beautiful bride. So the guy does exactly this. But in the middle of the night he needs to scratch his nose. When he puts his hand back a voice says: "Please-a Señor, to take-a your hand-a off-a my arse." '

Robert and Williams laughed despite themselves – Maurice's jokes may not have been top notch, but his delivery was. Then Eve said quietly: 'I don't get it. Why didn't he scratch his nose with the other hand?' At which point they all guffawed.

Williams pointed when he saw the line of pylons marching aggressively across the countryside. 'Those?'

Robert nodded. 'That line. But we have a problem.'

'What?'

'Tell him, Maurice.'

Maurice became serious for a second. 'Berlin has ordered fifty hostages for each act of sabotage. Ten to be executed. Forty to be transported to Germany. Which, I have heard suggested, is much the same thing. Only slower.'

Williams nodded.

Robert leaned forward. 'Which means we are looking at a large number of avoidable casualties.' He put his hand on Williams' shoulder. London had urged him to destroy the line as soon as possible, but that seemed ridiculous to him. The Germans were becoming very adept at carrying out running repairs. Bombed factories were up and functioning again within days, sabotage often corrected within hours. Surely if it was all co-ordinated properly, if the Resistance attacks were timed across the country to coincide with the second front, that would make any blow twice as effective. 'Oh, don't worry, Will, you'll get your big bang OK. But not until the Allies have landed. You'll just have to wait.'

231

'Wait, wait, wait. That's all we fucking do. Wait.'

'Yes and you could be in Paris getting your toes tickled by the SD. Plenty of people will be. I met Madeleine the other day, SOE's radio operator. Beautiful, too beautiful for this job, and not overburdened with brains.'

'What were you doing? Swapping Morse tips?'

'I was trying to tell her not to write the messages down every time. And to keep moving. They'll DF her before long if she carries on with her routine.'

'I told you,' said Williams. DF was the aggressive direction finding the Germans were indulging in, along with tricks of sequentially cutting the power supply to streets and even houses in an area where a pianist was operating, knowing that when the radio went off air, they had pinpointed the agent. At least Robert had bought one of the newer sets, which could be operated from batteries. 'Every time you use that radio, you make sure you go as far away from the house as possible.'

'Don't worry we've got a proper operator coming. Name of Chandler. I'll put him in Pontoise with Thérèse Lethias. Is that far enough away for you?'

Williams grunted. The real answer was no, but he couldn't see any alternative.

Maurice took a small track into the forest that had closed around them, bumping the Hotchkiss down a rutted sand road, churning up a plume of dust. The trees parted almost theatrically to reveal a wonderful, almost perfectly circular lake, with a dilapidated wooden jetty running from the shore and a tethered swimming platform bobbing in the centre.

Eve squealed in delight and Maurice crowed: 'Welcome to Chez Maurice, a spot known only to the fortunate few. This is an official no-war zone, mention of the Germans is forbidden, as is brooding too much.' He turned to look at Williams. 'This means you.'

Williams managed a smile. They had decided the previous night that the Atlantic had to go. Eve had won. It was to be put out of action for the duration of the war, safe from plundering Germans. 'I hope you don't mind,' continued Maurice, 'but I borrowed your portable gramophone.'

There was five minutes of furious activity. Eve unloaded the player and cranked it up to give them a soundtrack of Jean Sablon. Maurice spread out the blankets while Robert and Williams unpacked, with increasing disbelief, ham, chicken, a pie, tripe sausage and four bottles of wine.

Eve, revelling in the feeling of hot sun on her pale skin, took off her blouse. Then her skirt. And her slip. The water was calling her. The first the others knew was when they heard the splash of a body knifing into the lake and the heartfelt gasp as she surfaced, shaking the water from her hair.

'Maurice,' she shouted, 'you could have heated the damn thing!'

He shrugged. 'Too early in the season.'

Williams stood and undid his trousers, stepped out of them and unbuttoned his shirt. Robert looked on, puzzled, wondering what he was going to do. He answered by waiting until Eve had struck out for the platform then sprinting along the jetty, picking up a couple of splinters as he went, performing a rather heavy, inelegant dive into the water and striking out crudely but strongly.

Eve heard the splashing behind her, and redoubled her effort. She felt vulnerable in open water with what had to be Robert closing on her fast. She started to scream a little, like a pursued maiden, and in her haste her strokes became ragged. She was aware of the splashing directly behind her, could feel the hand scything through the little waves the breeze was creating, the hand almost touching her feet. Then he was alongside. She turned to say something and swallowed a great gulp of water, spitting and coughing and hacking and managing to splutter in surprise: 'Will . . .'

He trod water while she recovered her composure and they did the last fifteen metres in parallel, Williams hauling himself on to the platform and holding out a hand for her. He jerked her out of the water and they stood there, dripping and drying in the sunlight.

'I thought you couldn't swim.'

'I have to have some mystery in my life.'

'Not from me.'

He kissed her. 'Especially from you. Don't want you to take me for granted.'

The crooning of Sablon came across the water intermittently as the breeze blew, like a radio going in and out of tune. She could see Robert opening the wine and helping himself to a large glass.

'I feel sorry for Robert,' Eve said.

'Why?'

'He should have a woman.'

'He has a wife, a mistress in Nantes and the odd "friend" he can call upon.'

'Wife in name only. The woman in Nantes is a bitch. Robert told me he thinks she has a German lover, which is why he no longer travels there. And "friends"? Pah. No, he needs someone to love him properly.'

'Are you offering to fill the post?'

Eve slid an arm through his, leant on his shoulder and said teasingly: 'Would you mind?'

'Maybe after I'm gone.' He pulled her face round. 'Or have you comforted him already? While I was in England.'

She slapped his face lightly.

'And what about that Rose Miller woman with the big eyes and big chest?' Williams knew better than to protest that her chest wasn't all that big. That was a pit with sharpened stakes in the bottom, just waiting for him to stumble. 'There must have been many lonely nights in London.'

'There were,' he said, and kissed her again. 'And they stayed that way.'

She pouted to let him know she was prepared to accept this for the moment. 'She likes you. I can tell.'

'Everybody likes me.'

'Yes, everybody finds someone to like because there are so many of you. Irish gangster, faithful chauffeur – oops, chauffeur – top racing driver, dog breeder, secret agent . . .' She traced a line on his chest and Williams shuddered. He held her close, feeling her nipples pressing into his flesh and, as blood flowed into his groin, wondering how much they could see from the shoreline. 'I still don't really know your secret, Mr Williams.'

There was no build up. No faint whisper growing louder. The roar of powerful engines suddenly engulfed them, assaulting their ears with a thudding ferociousness. The Mosquito came over at tree-top level, the propeller blades almost crowning whole swathes of the forest, and burst over the lake. They could see the pilot, briefly, but he was looking straight ahead, all his energy and concentration focused on keeping the machine low and level.

Then it was gone, leaving only a ringing in their ears and their hearts pounding. 'That's it!' exclaimed Williams. 'What if we get the RAF to do a dummy raid on the pylons while we blow them. That way the Germans blame the airforce, not the locals. And no reprisals. What do you think?'

Remembering Maurice's restrictions on topics of conversation she turned and pushed him as hard as she could. Williams stood for a second balanced on the edge, windmilling his arms theatrically before allowing himself to topple.

'You broke rule number one,' she shouted as he crashed into the lake. 'No war talk.' Even so, she couldn't help considering it. No reprisals, she thought. As if anybody could guarantee such a thing these days.

In the sun-dappled courtyard of the Avenue Foch SD headquarters, Hans Keppler leant against his powder-blue Opel and lit a small cheroot. He had started smoking them to try to cut down on cigarettes. And he was perhaps drinking too much. A bottle of excellent wine seemed to be permanently open in his office. The belt of his uniform was beginning to slide under his burgeoning gut, as if he was an old man.

On the far side of the yard, Neumann paced up and down in front of the six men they had plucked from the streets of Villers, near where Legine had been assassinated. Six months ago they would not have bothered, but now there was an epidemic of clandestine killings – even the Milice were being targeted.

The firing squad marched out and assembled in front of the prisoners, some of whom only then began to appreciate just why the wall behind them was so badly pock-marked and stained. They weren't the first prisoners to be lined up here. They certainly wouldn't be the last.

'I have given you every opportunity to help,' announced Neumann in the pompous voice that made Keppler's teeth grate. 'One of you must know something. Gossip. Hearsay. Anything.'

The six, their jaws slack, their eyes full of pain from beatings, merely shuffled. 'Fine. Sergeant.'

The soldiers shouldered their weapons. Virginia looked at the floor. 'Take aim.'

'Nobody?' asked Neumann.

'Fire.'

Even though he had seen this pantomime dozens of times, Keppler still flinched at the sharp metallic click as firing pins fell on empty chambers. As expected, the men were quaking. One of them had lost control of his bladder. Ashamed, he stepped forward.

'I . . . I would like to talk with you.'

Neumann frowned. 'You left it a little late.'

The squad chambered the rounds into their Mausers and prepared to fire for real.

The short Frenchman shuffled forward, the ankle chains preventing him from making much headway. 'First save these men. Let them go back to their families.'

Keppler was suddenly interested. Neumann was not a man to let people go back to their families if he could help it. He saw that as defeat, evidence of weakness, rather than good public relations. Entrance to Foch should be a one-way ticket as far as he was concerned. 'Bring him here, Joachim,' he shouted.

Two of the firing squad frogmarched the man over to the Opel, his chained feet dragging on the brick flooring. Most of his top teeth were missing and livid bruises criss-crossed his cheeks, as if he had been whipped. One eye twitched uncontrollably. And he smelt of fear, sweat, blood and piss. Keppler stepped back from him in case some of the odour clung to his uniform.

'What do you have?' asked Keppler. He could see Neumann pacing, irritated that he had been usurped.

'A car. A very low car. Knee-high to a grasshopper, they said. Two men in it.'

'Did you see it?'

'No. A friend.'

'Which friend?' Keppler asked casually.

The eye starting twitching faster. 'I mean a man I met in a café. Didn't know his name.'

Keppler didn't have time to waste extracting the name of his gossipy chum from him, and admired the man for trying to protect him, so he simply asked: 'Anything else?'

'No.'

Keppler sighed. 'Back in line then.'

'Except he said, it was very strange. It had a fin down the back.'

'A fin?'

'Yes, like a fish. Big metal fin.'

'Back in line.'

He was dragged away and Keppler felt the old excitement rise in him, the kind of thrill he rarely felt these days, the frisson of the chase and the kill that had made him want to be a policeman. The solution to this matter was nearly all there in his head now, he knew it. He just had to order his thoughts. Plus he had a hunch, a strong instinct about where he could find the missing elements.

As he turned to hurry inside he hesitated and shouted across to his junior. 'Neumann, you can stop. Send them for labour duty—'

The flat slap of the rifle shots rang out around the courtyard, making Keppler start, and the six jerked grotesquely, before slumping into a heap, some of them still twitching. Neumann pulled out his Walther pistol to administer the *coupe de grâce* and shouted: 'Sorry, Sturmbannführer. What were you saying?'

Keppler flung open the door to Virginia's cell with a force that made her jump. Behind him stood Obst, his stenographer, a plump bespectacled man who looked as if he should be in a tax office in some provincial town.

'I didn't mean to startle you, but time is short.'

Virginia looked up at him and tried to compose herself. So this was it. She felt the blood drain from her face. 'Time for what?'

Keppler clicked his fingers and Obst handed over a light blue document, with black carbons attached. 'Do you know what this is?'

She shook her head.

'It is a *Nacht und Nebel* order. Filled out in your name. What it means is very, very simple. You go to Germany. You don't come back. We don't care what happens to you in the meantime. Here.' He held out the pages. 'How is your German?'

'Poor.'

She took the document and scanned it, from her cover name, Yolande Laurent, printed at the top down to the flamboyant signature of the Sturmbannführer.

'As you see, ready to implement.' The voice was harder than she had ever heard, making sure she knew the time for bluffing was over.

Virginia pointed to her spare dress and the toiletries. 'Can I take some things?'

'You can tear it up.'

Virginia waited, knowing that Keppler was about to offer her something, some way out.

'I have been looking at dates. There is someone I am after, someone I am fairly sure went through with your batch of agents. Had to have. It fits in with the time we started to see . . . to see a pattern emerge.'

'What pattern?'

He ignored her. 'I need that list. Just the men. Now.'

'I can't do that.'

Keppler sat down next to her on the bed. 'Listen, what you do will make no difference to my actions. I know exactly how to proceed. However, I just want some confirmation of a suspicion I have.'

'I can't give you a list.'

Keppler snatched the *Nacht und Nebel* order from her and

handed it to Obst. 'I have seen where you will end up, you know. Or at least, something very similar. The Kommandant was most proud of his work. I made my excuses and left. On the way home I had to stop my car to be sick. What happens here is as nothing. Nothing.'

Keppler watched a spark of fear flash in her eyes. It was there for a second, but he knew he had her, knew her imagination was doing his job for him. Slow it down, soften it. Play the trump card. 'Look, Virginia . . .'

Her head snapped up. Her Beddington name. How could he know that?

'Virginia Thorpe. We showed your picture to one of your fellow agents. He identified you not as Yolande Laurent, but Virginia Thorpe.'

'Then why not ask him for the list?' she said.

Keppler had anticipated the question. He flicked the N&N form. 'He is rather difficult to get hold of at short notice.' In fact he was extremely difficult to get hold of because the man from Coutt's was dead, falling from the roof of number 84 while trying to escape. All I need to know is this – was there a man who raced cars? A racing driver? A man couldn't keep that quiet for ever. Nothing else, that's all I need. No name, nothing. Just confirmation.' He let his voice harden slightly. 'In ten seconds Obst here will implement the order.'

Five of them ticked away.

'All you have to do is nod if I am right.'

Three more went by.

'A racing driver.'

The inclination of the head was sharp and fast, as if that somehow made it better.

'And he was called Williams, wasn't he? Not there and then, but that was his real name. Wasn't it?'

Another brief nod and even as he watched her blanch with self-loathing, inwardly Keppler gave a whoop of joy and let the warm glow of victory wash over him. The knee-high to a grasshopper car was a Bugatti Atlantic and the two men had to be Benoist and Williams. Now all he had to do was find out where they were hiding themselves and that car. And that was the easy part.

The day after the picnic Williams slapped thick grease over the bodywork of the Atlantic, thick gloops of it running off down on to the gravel driveway and lying there like so many beached jellyfish. Robert was inside, covering the seats with oiled tarpaulin.

Eve emerged from the house swinging the keys to the Renault van. 'I'll see you later,' she said, and they both raised a hand as she drove off.

'I'll miss her,' said Williams.

'Me, too,' said Robert. 'But she'll end up getting us both killed.'

Williams finished the protective coating and peered in at Robert. 'One last blast?'

'We shouldn't. But . . . you want to do the honours?'

Robert started the engine and moved across to the passenger side. Williams jumped in beside him, the tarpaulin crackling beneath him. For the last time for a long time he let the rear wheels spin on the gravel, splattering the entrance like buckshot, let in the clutch and took the car out on to the road, watching the speedometer swing up until they were going at more than a hundred and twenty kilometres. The countryside flashed by in a blur. Williams judged the turn perfectly, letting the back end drift as he took them on to the forest track, correcting the oversteer and accelerating again, until the trees became a solid wooden wall of trunks.

241

'We'll have to move as well,' shouted Robert.

'What?'

The noise was frightening, the whoosh off the vegetation mixed with the raucous scream of the engine.

'We'll have to move house. Been there too long.'

'Any idea where?'

'Uh?'

'Where?'

'Tahiti.'

'Sounds good to me.'

Realising that meaningful conversation was impossible, they both fell silent while Williams took them on a circuitous route through the forest, only stopping once to take a nasty dip in the road very slowly, rather than risk tearing off the exhaust as the suspension bottomed.

As Williams eased off the pedal on the final leg, they began to see figures in the trees, barely glimpsed flashes of sheepskin and sten guns. Mostly local farmers, the ranks had been swollen recently by the little team Robert had cautiously assembled from the waifs and strays from the forests around Auffargis. Eventually they arrived at the clearing.

Eve was stomping up and down, occasionally glancing at her watch, furious at what she saw as reckless tardiness. She stabbed a finger at her wrist in silent admonition. Around her were four of the farmers and six of their big, muscular shirehorses, harnesses attached to long ropes disappearing into a long, shallow pit which had been crudely excavated by the tractor-dozer at the edge of the clearing.

Williams guided the burbling car down the long slope, feeling the chill of the freshly uncovered earth as they reached the bottom. It was a little too like a grave for comfort, he mused, and one that could hold an awful lot of people. The top of the trench was about a metre above the precious car's roofline. He wondered how much a metre of earth weighed. Not too much he hoped.

The two drivers loped quickly back up the ramp and Eve got to work. She signalled the horses to be driven forward, and the sagging ropes tightened and hummed as the heavy tarpaulin was dragged over the car, wrapping it in a green cocoon.

'When do we move?' asked Williams.

The dozer started up, a raucous rasping sound, and it chugged forward, pushing the mound of excavated earth back into the hole, the soil forming the rough shape of the car, like an unfinished clay model.

Williams looked across the hole at Eve on the far side who shrugged in sympathy. Williams passed the key on its silver chain to Robert who looked at it thoughtfully and kissed it before tossing it over to Eve. She caught it and carefully looped it round her neck.

Robert looked at Williams. 'My mother has been moved to hospital in Paris. I must see her. But I'll take us to our new home after that.' He put an arm around Williams and steered him away from the burial. 'Tomorrow. We move tomorrow.'

Twenty-six

JULY–AUGUST 1943

Eve slumped down next to Maurice on the terrace of the café near Etoile, breathless and sweaty, and ordered a coffee. When it arrived he offered her a flask. 'Armagnac. Complements the taste of acorns perfectly.' She helped herself to a generous dose.

The day was cooling now. As if to mock the deteriorating fabric of daily life in the city, the summer of 1943 was turning out to be glorious. She shouldn't complain – the airless heat was preferable to the icy winter it had suffered. At least living was cheaper than in the cold months.

A charcoal-powered car chugged by, belching its filthy fumes, a billboard strapped to the top advertising that evening's perform- ance by Maurice Chevalier at Odeon.

'Is it true?' she asked.

'Is what true?' He looked at her admiringly. She looked good in the simple summer dress with the high neckline, a new silver chain round her neck disappearing into her hidden cleavage. Maurice had always been indifferent to Eve's charms, or at least more immune than his brother. He liked his women to be beautiful – Eve certainly fulfilled that criterion, even twelve years after he first met her – but she remained something of an innocent. Not stupid, not naïve, but she exuded a more whole-some view of humanity than Maurice could possibly counten-ance. He liked his women somewhat more earthy, soiled, compromised. Like himself.

'Sicily,' she said quietly.

Maurice shrugged. Rumours were rife that resistance to the landings in Sicily had collapsed, that Mussolini was finished. Even the word armistice was being bandied about. 'Ask them.' Maurice pointed to a group of two couples at a far table, laughing a little too loudly.

'Who are they?'

'I don't know,' said Maurice. 'But if I were the Gestapo I'd have them in the cells of rue des Saussaies in a flash. Every day they meet here. Sometimes one brings a case which the other leaves with. Stupid.'

Maurice lit a cigarette and offered Eve one. She refused. They were normally so adulterated – the smugglers like to boast 'as long as there is grass in Belgium, the French shall have tobacco' – that she had decided to give up.

'I asked you to meet me because perhaps you could convince my pig-headed brother it is time to give up his . . . pursuits. And your husband.'

'Why?'

'It is getting far, far too dangerous. Those people at Foch have stopped beating about the bush. The honeymoon is very, very over. Yet those two race around in that car as if they can whistle their way past the graveyard.'

'Not any longer.'

Maurice raised an eyebrow. 'Really? They got rid of the Atlantic?'

'They're in mourning for it.' She took a hit of the coffee and shuddered. She'd been over-generous with the Armagnac, and it wasn't the subtlest example of the liquor. She waited for the searing trail down her gullet to subside before she asked: 'Why the sudden concern, Maurice?'

'I saw a DF map in Keppler's office.' He caught the look of distaste that was clearly more than the effect of the brandy. She found it hard to accept that dealing with the enemy wasn't the same as supporting them. To him it was all a matter of checks and balances, and as long as the correct column came out in profit, then compromises were tolerable. 'I saw the areas they are concentrating on, where they have transmissions they cannot pinpoint exactly, but know someone is operating. A lot in Paris. One in Pontoise. Isn't that where Robert put the Englishman? And a few on the edge of the Rambouillet forest.'

Eve nodded. Robert always left the house to transmit, always drove into the forest, but clearly had a few favourite spots. Repetition, the radio man's worst enemy.

'Eve, you would be shocked if you knew how much they know.' He looked up as a car pulled into the kerbside. A powder-blue Opel. He felt a bolt of white hot pain shoot down his bad leg. He quickly whispered: 'Go inside. Now.'

Without asking for an explanation, Eve turned her face away from the car, stood, grabbed her bag and headed inside.

The window rolled down and there was Keppler, smiling. 'Maurice. We have a date.'

'We do?'

'Who was that with you?'

'My wife. She's just gone to . . .'

'Your wife? I didn't know you were married.' Neither did Maurice till that answer popped out of his mouth. 'I am afraid I only have one ticket.'

'For what?'

'Your namesake. Chevalier. Come along.'

Maurice stood and limped slowly over to the car, his leg more painful than ever. The door opened and he slid in beside Keppler. Framing the SD man on the far side was Neumann, expressionless. In the front, next to the driver, Arthur Lock, busy rolling a cigarette, turned and gave him a smile that made him wince. Arthur Lock was not the kind of man who you wanted smiling at you. At Keppler's signal the driver pulled away.

'We don't have a date, do we?'

'Only with destiny, Maurice,' Keppler replied sardonically with a little high laugh. 'And how is Mrs Williams?'

Maurice's mind raced. He sped it forward to the worst possible scenario. Why didn't they pull in Eve if they were after the Chestnut circuit? Because picking up Eve might forewarn Robert and Williams. This way, all Maurice had done was accept an invitation from his old chum Keppler. Nothing suspicious about that. Maurice felt his forehead prickle hot and cold, as if he was about to vomit.

'So where are we going?' asked Maurice. Because he knew if it had been straight to Foch or Saussaies, there would have been none of these niceties.

'To see how your poor old mother is.'

Sitting in the small café opposite the St Stephanie Clinic in the Republique district, to the south of the city, where his mother was being treated, Robert sipped at his third bitter coffee of the morning, trying to lift his energy levels. Despite a large quantity of red wine he'd been unable to sleep, his mind spinning about what he suspected. And about the dangerous game Maurice had embarked on. Three years previously the Germans had arrived behaving with an almost serene *noblesse oblige*. Now that the *noblesse* looked distinctly shaky, the rules had changed. He just hoped that Maurice had noticed.

Robert tried to stop the gnawing in his stomach, as if the acid was corroding the fleshy walls. Like everybody else, he didn't eat anything like as well as he had pre-war – although he did well in comparison to most – but it wasn't hunger causing his dyspepsia. It had been writhing away ever since he got back with his orders. Blow this, damage that. Meet the radio operator Madeleine – a woman so beautiful as to draw the attention of the dumbest of Germans. And once they got over that face, they were bound to wonder about that big case she was lugging around. Link up with this group there, bury more arms here. Something was very wrong. He just didn't know what it was.

Down the street the last of the housewives departed with a precious slice of bloody flesh. One of Paris's many overworked horses had collapsed between the shafts, and while the owner had gone off to seek help, a swarm of two-legged vultures had descended, brandishing their sharpest knives and largest enamel bowls. Great steaks of the stringy flesh were quickly sliced off, leaving the carcass glistening sickeningly. As the women scurried away, so a cloud of crazed flies descended. When the owner returned he would find his horse reduced to an undulating mass of black, interspersed with islands of darkening crimson.

The girl made him start. It was Beatrice, no longer the child who had once cycled up his path, but a young woman, albeit one with a lined, hollow face and eyes that darted jerkily from side to side. This time she was keeping an eye on her bicycle, her most precious possession. He hoped that the damage caused by fear and subterfuge and privation to this young lady was reversible and that once this was over she could go back to being frivolous and carefree. Somehow, though, he doubted it.

'I have a message from Jester.'

Robert nodded. Jester was in charge of the dead letter drops, and someone Robert trusted. Mainly because he had never met him, didn't know where he lived and had never met anyone who did. That was his kind of agent.

'Maurice is ill.'

Robert tried to keep his face impassive. The phrase meant Maurice was taken. It was known that a few brave Frenchwomen who worked in Foch and Laurent and Lutetia, the other Gestapo strongholds, kept their eyes and ears open and reported to Resistance contacts. But Maurice was a familiar figure around Foch at least; something must have changed to make them assume he was there under duress.

'Is it serious?'

'It could be terminal. You should go now.'

With that she mounted her bike and pedalled off, not looking back. One day, when all this was over, he must find that Beatrice and do something for her. Maurice taken. Go now. He scanned the street for suspect cars, men with hats pulled low, as the V-men did whenever they thought they needed to look inconspicuous. Nothing. Robert looked at the hospital opposite. Still nothing untoward.

He decided to take a chance, grabbed the precious chocolates he had found at a stupendous price – his mother had an astonishingly sweet tooth, and had suffered these last few years – and hurried across the road, bounding up the steps to the entrance.

Madame Benoist was on the third floor, but rather than encase himself in the claustrophobic lift he took the stairs, two at a time, occasionally glancing behind him. It may be early, but the hospital had been up for hours, and he could smell fresh carbolic almost masking the fading aromas of an untempting breakfast.

Robert stopped at the entrance of the room. A group of nurses were round his mother's bed, fluttering and twittering like sparrows. 'What's going on?' he boomed inadvertently.

'Ssshhh,' said the Sister. The group parted and when he saw her face he gasped. A livid bruise ran left to right, the ancient skin glowing hideously purple. One eye was closed, red and swollen, the lid marbled with veins.

'Robert,' she said thinly.

He walked over and held her and he was aware of the sister shooing the junior nurses away. Robert could feel the bones through his mother's nightdress and the wild beat of her heart. He fought hard to stop crying, to keep his voice steady as he held her at arm's lengths and forced himself to examine the poor, defiled face. 'Who did this?' he demanded.

'It was the Germans,' said the sister.

Robert spun round. 'And you let them do it?'

'It isn't a matter of letting them or otherwise, Monsieur Benoist,' she replied with surprising passion. 'Not with the SS. Your mother was very brave.'

He turned back to the bed. 'But why?'

'They had Maurice with them. Don't blame him. You'd have done the same.'

'Done what? Done what, Mother?'

'Please, he had no choice but to tell them.'

Robert felt the colour drain from his face and he laid her back on to the pillow as gently as he could, his arms shaking with the tension of not lashing out at something to vent the anger he felt building. He turned to the sister. 'I need a telephone. *Now.*'

Twenty-seven

Williams woke with a slightly thick head. Rather than transport the by-now meagrely stocked wine cellar of Auffargis they had decided to try to drink it. He, Eve, Robert and Jean-Pierre Wimille had got through far too many bottles. Wimille had finally volunteered to join Chestnut full time. Like many other Frenchmen, he was now beginning to think sabotage and subversion wasn't all pissing in the wind. With the Allies ready to take on the Italian mainland, perhaps they really could make a difference.

Eve had told them about Maurice's chummy exchange with Keppler, which she had heard from within the café. 'If you dance with the devil, sooner or later he gets to call the tune,' Williams had slurred enigmatically at this point.

Still, they were moving now. New house, fresh start, time to regroup. Wimille was sleeping it off across the hall. He was to help them move essential belongings to the new house Robert had chosen near Houdan, but he and Robert had carried on drinking after Eve and Williams had excused themselves to go and make lazy, drunken love and fallen asleep entwined. He untangled her arms from him, slipped out of bed and poured

251

himself a large tumbler of water.

'Good morning, Mister Super-lover,' she said.

He glanced over to see if she was being sarcastic.

'I'm serious. You should drink two bottles of wine more often.'

He threw the dregs of water at her and she squealed and dived under the covers. He pulled on trousers and a shirt. 'I'll get the coffee.'

He went downstairs, shaking his head, checking the physical damage of their late night, holding out his splayed fingers at arm's length, examining them for tremors. Not too bad. The house smelled, though, of stale cigarette smoke and vinegary wine. Chiquita, the maid, was already up trying to clean up the mess.

'Morning,' he said.

She nodded back with a smile.

'Robert up?'

'Monsieur Benoist has gone to Paris. See his mother at the clinic. Left very early.'

Williams walked over to the window and looked out across the lawn to the stand of trees that formed the edge of the forest. He thought about the men out there somewhere, scattered across the thousands of hectares, waking stiffly after another night in the open, quietly seething about what had become of them, vaga-bonds in their own country.

The phone rang and Chiquita went to get it. He looked back at the woods one more time, and was halfway through turning to take the call when his brain finally put together what the early morning sun had caught at the very edge of the tree line, his cerebrum magnifying it until he could see the air-cooling holes around the barrel.

Chiquita had picked up the phone. 'Hello?'

'Get down!' Williams yelled as he dropped to the floor, but it was too late. The heavy machine-gun slugs ripped into Chiquita's body and flung her back against the wall, sending big spurts of her blood across the rough white surface. The window imploded, showering him with glass and he shuffled to press his back against the heavy outside wall, feeling it shake and shudder as round after round blasted it, splintering the terrace, and he imagined the dancing rose petals torn from the trellis, floating on clouds of brick- and sawdust.

Even above the sustained racket of bullets he heard something upstairs. Wimille. He hoped he had the sense to get out the back. There were bicycles, a motor bike, places to hide. He also hoped he took Eve.

The upstairs window blew out as the gunners started to rake the rest of the building, and through the open doorway he saw Eve rolling down the stairs, falling into a heap at the bottom as the banisters and rails flowered into raw shards.

'Eve. Eve.'

She began to move, slowly at first, then quickly on all fours, ignoring the glass and debris that sliced through the flesh of her hands and knees, heading for him.

'Stay back. Stay down.'

More bullets hammered into the wall and through the window, zinging as they went, smaller calibre now, rifles and Schmeisser fire. Eve reached him and crawled up his body until she was level with his face. 'Always say goodbye. Isn't that what Robert used to say?'

The gunfire stopped, leaving their ears buzzing angrily after the onslaught they had suffered. Some crockery items fell lazily to the floor, smashing into pieces. Williams brushed the hair away from Eve's face. 'No more goodbyes.'

Then he heard the rumble of the half-track coming up the drive.

★ ★ ★

Keppler's blue Opel led the way. He was in the back seat with Maurice, who stared at the floor, ashamed even to set eyes on the house. In the front was Neumann, whose idea the fusillade had been. He was convinced that if this Chestnut circuit did have all the arms that Maurice had suggested, there was a good chance they might use them. Best soften them up first. Behind the Opel was a half-track with a contingent of troops to mop up the pieces.

They slewed to a halt outside the house and the soldiers were out and inside within a few well-drilled seconds. Good men. SS men. Not like some of the scum arriving these days, thought Keppler. Romanians, Croatians, Hungarians, all pouring in to defend the Atlantic wall from whatever it was the Allies were up to this summer. Something, that was for sure.

Keppler stepped out of the car and glanced down at Maurice. He wasn't moving. Neumann was already out, picking his way around the destroyed Renault van, collapsed on its frame after the machine guns had reduced the body to a metal mesh, across the ruined terrace and into the house.

Soldiers were breaking those big flower urns that hadn't been shattered by the gunfire, and every so often guns, explosives and timing sticks would fall out. A concrete trough yielded an intact parachute container, full of Stens and ammunition.

Keppler walked around the side to the barn-cum-garage which he had ordered not be targeted and threw open the doors. Empty. No Bugatti. He stifled the disappointment. This wasn't about such booty, this was about breaking a spy circuit, he reminded himself. He slammed the doors shut. Owning an Atlantic, one of just three ever made, that would be a bonus, though.

Williams and Eve were dragged out on to the terrace, where they were thrown down on the torn boards, the soldiers aiming machine pistols at their heads. Both glared at Keppler with hate, until Williams spotted Maurice in the car and his jaw began to work, clenching and unclenching, his teeth grinding noisily.

Williams wasn't scared now. This was like just before a race. He had to stay calm, detached. Every time he let that clutch in, he was embarking on a journey that could end in pain or injury or death. Now he was doing it again. And he had training to fall back on. But Eve. Please, God. Not Eve. If they laid a finger on Eve he'd make sure Maurice died, one way or another.

'Just these two and one dead girl, sir,' said the sergeant. So Wimille had made it.

As the man talked he heard a clink. The Bugatti key and chain had slipped from Eve's neck and fallen down through the cracks in the terrace. She'd undone it. She winked at him and he thought his heart was going to explode.

'No Robert Benoist or Jean-Pierre Wimille?' asked Keppler.

A smiling Neumann emerged with a gramophone and a stack of records. 'A miracle. Not one broken.' He proceeded to load it into the boot of the Opel. 'So the brother has flown the coop?' Neumann asked Keppler.

Keppler strode up and stared down at the pair, and signalled them to be dragged to their feet. 'No,' he said as ominously as he could to Williams' face. 'Not exactly.'

Robert listened to it all. Chiquita had picked up the telephone, he had heard her greeting and then that sound. At first he had thought it was interference on the line, a common enough occurrence these days, but then it resolved itself into the sound of a room, a house suffering a holocaust of gunfire. And some masochistic part of his brain, some evil primitive part, made him hold the phone to his ear for what seemed like hours, flinching as he heard the detonations and destructions and imagined what those bullets were doing to the flesh of his friends. To Eve.

With exaggerated care he put the phone back on its cradle and slumped in the chair at the nurses' station, putting his head in his hands. For a moment he began to cry, then caught himself.

'Are you all right?' asked the sister. 'Can I get you anything?'

Robert sat up, blinked, and took a deep breath. From his jacket he took a Browning pistol and checked the action, much to the young nurse's horror. 'Yes. Please. A glass of water.'

Robert gulped it back, dragged a forearm across his mouth and stood, his emotions in check again, all but for that bright, white spot of anger burning near his heart. Keep in there, he reminded himself, feed off it. The brighter it glowed, the easier this would be. 'Tell my mother I'll be back.'

He retraced his steps down to the entrance and stepped outside, hesitating for a second at the top of the steps. The first cosh hit him a glancing blow on the shoulder and he spun around, reaching for the Browning. The second caught him on the bridge of the nose, blinding out daylight with its wash of pain, and a third and fourth sent him crumpling down the stone steps into oblivion.

Twenty-eight

The police Citroën van came screeching from where it had skulked round the corner and the two gendarmes rushed down the steps after Robert and pulled the dazed man to his feet. Blood streaked his face from his contact with the rough stone, and, thanks to the lead-filled coshes, bruises more florid than his mother's were already blossoming across his face.

A brusque search revealed Robert's gun, which the gendarme called Didier slotted into his belt. He opened the rear doors of the van and with the help of Farnoux, his partner, they flung Robert in the back of the paddy wagon, stepped after him and banged the sides to tell the driver to go. Siren blaring it headed north, from Republique, heading through the heart of Montmartre, skirting the Les Halles markets, on its way to the Arc de Triomphe, and, ultimately, the deceptive grandeur of Avenue Foch.

Robert pulled himself up slowly, scrabbling for some kind of hold as the van swung this way and that. There were no benches or seats of any sort for prisoners, just some worn leather straps hanging from the roof and metal rings for attaching handcuffs. Painfully he slid himself up the bulkhead and managed to hold on.

The two policemen dangled at the far ends, like experts, swaying with the rhythm of the Citroën. Farnoux pulled a small folding metal seat down from the wall and perched on it. Didier looked the wild-eyed, blood-stained prisoner up and down. 'That's just for starters, Monsieur Big Shot,' he said, and grinned.

Robert examined Didier's bulging gut, and the Browning stuffed against it, and wondered how much the man weighed. More than he should as a police officer in these austere times, that was for sure. Himself and Didier probably made one-eighty, maybe even two hundred kilos. Robert waited until the van slowed, probably working its way around a velo or a horse-drawn cart or a knot of pedestrians – with only light traffic, people wandered into the road with impunity these days.

Robert already knew the man in the cab's clumsy driving style. He would jerk away from a near standstill and accelerate furiously until the poor engine ran out of steam, then brake with an equally heavy foot as soon as he saw some obstacle. He waited, letting his weight pull on the strap, trying to look suitably beaten and cowed. They mustn't notice. They mustn't realise. Until the moment came.

It came with an unexpected judder and screech of tyres, even though he had tried to anticipate the lumpen responses of the driver, and he hit the bulkhead with a painful thud. Using the momentum, Robert bounced back as the van picked up speed again and pumped all his energy into the two or three strides he would have before they finally cottoned on to the fact that, in the heady flush of a successful apprehension, they had forgotten to handcuff him.

He saw the shock in the faces as he came down the length of the van at them, the desperate scrabble for the gun holsters, Farnoux trying to rise from the seat and then Robert hit Didier like a sack of bricks, throwing all his mass straight into the gendarme's chest, their combined weight punching open the unsecured lock on the rear doors and sending them as one diving out on to the road.

Robert was on top when they hit the ground with a bone-jarring crunch and he felt the air explode out of Didier, ribs straining and snapping as his full weight drove the man into the road surface. Already he could hear shouting and banging as Farnoux screamed at the driver to stop. As he pulled himself up Robert jerked the Browning pistol free from the belt and levelled it at Didier.

Didier, sweating with the knifing pain in his sides and breathing hard and shallow, looked up in terror and began to push with his boot heels, crawling on his back to get away from the figure standing over him with the pistol, the man who looked as if he might just be crazy enough to kill a cop. The gun was rock steady, tracing his movements as he cockroached backwards.

'Please,' Didier gasped. 'I am only doing my job.'

Robert's eyes glanced down at a uniform defiled and degraded by what the *flics* had done for their masters over the last few years. He thought of those pathetic, heartbreaking little notes from the train, the swaggering cops banging on cattle trucks telling the starving, thirsty inhabitants to keep quiet.

'And I'm only doing mine,' said Robert softly before he shot him twice in the heart.

The first police bullet smacked past him and down the boulevard. Robert began to look around. Pedestrians, mostly old women, were frozen in position, wide mouthed with a mixture of horror and excitement, unsure of how to react.

The Musée Grevin, with its waxwork tableaux, was opposite. No escape that way. Another bullet. A shrill whistle summoning help, blast after blast. Robert raised the Browning and shot at the van where Farnoux and the driver were crouched, both blowing for assistance at the top of their lungs. A crowd was gathering. A charcoal-powered car had stopped, the driver unsure what to do about a gunfight in the Boulevard Montmartre. Sirens. Lots of them. Robert ran, south, through the art nouveaux-covered Galeries, elbowing aside the first shoppers scurrying out to snap up the day's meagre produce.

The noise and shouts behind him told him the police were giving chase. His heart thumping, he swerved left and right until he emerged from the arcade into a long, narrow street running east towards Boulevard Bonne Nouvelle, Williams' old stomping ground.

He began to run straight ahead, down the road, picking up his feet to make sure he didn't trip on the uneven paved surface. Another shot. Robert risked a glance behind and saw maybe six or seven uniforms powering after him. A round burned through the outer part of his leg and he felt himself stumbling headlong as the muscle jerked in pain. He hit the road, rolled, and came up with the Browning outstretched. Think. How many rounds? It's a High Power. German model. Nine millimetre parabellum round. He'd reloaded the bloody gun time and time again but his brain was mush. Seven . . . no, thirteen. Thirteen rounds. He'd already used three, or four. He had enough left to take a few with him.

On they came, eight of them, slowed now, getting ready to close in for the kill, like a pack that knows it has its prey cornered, relishing this moment. He had slain one of their number. They weren't going to take him alive. They weren't going to let him go slowly. No quick bullet for him.

Robert pumped two rounds at them and the cops stopped, hesitating. No hits. They were crouching, difficult targets at this range. He stood, ignoring the flash of agony in his leg. Look at that later. If there was a later. He fired another shot. One of the police groaned and clutched his shoulder.

The other seven started to yell and came at him, firing as they went, caution gone, bullets splaying round him. Robert dived to the wall as if it could wrap and protect him.

A vase came first. It shattered in front of the lead policeman and he blithely carried on, unaware of its significance.

The gramophone hit the cop full on with a deadly inert impact, sending the man to the floor as if poleaxed, a huge flap of red scalp dangling free. Robert looked up. A table was arcing through the air. Books. Another vase. All rained down like some strange biblical plague of household objects. Robert smiled to himself. Resistance.

A full chamberpot smashed into the cops, who began to huddle together like a Roman tortoise formation, but without the shields to protect their backs. A guitar. More vases. A sewing machine, breaking bones as it slammed into a shoulder. The air grew thick with domestic detritus, some of which must have been of great sentimental value. A small cupboard. Bottles of cleaning fluid exploded around them with muffled explosions. Some kind of caustic soda detonated in their midst and there were screams. Robert fired again, joining in the ritual assault on the men with something more lethal than bleach. One of the cops hit the floor, rolled and was still. A washstand hit him and the body arched, but no more. Dead. A radio, a precious radio, eviscerated itself on the cobbles.

From the apartments above more and more rained down and Robert backed off, heading for the streets where he knew he could find safety. There was an enormous groaning sound and a balcony gave way, an upright piano heaved over the edge tearing the metalwork and huge lumps of concrete free, disintegrating with spectacular echoing dissonance.

The police began to retreat, walking at first, then running, back to get their colleagues and return in greater numbers, leaving three sprawled in the road, slowly disappearing under random cairns created from the bric-a-brac of other people's lives. The shutters and windows began to slam shut, the stories of innocence already being concocted, the occupants only now beginning to wonder just what they had done. Robert raised his arms, tears in his eyes, proud of his countrymen for the first time since he knew not when and shouted: *'Vive la France!'*

Keppler took his charges to the police station at Rambouillet and Williams was transferred to a windowless van, chained to a ring in the side, two German soldiers guarding him. Keppler had said he would talk to him when they got Robert. 'When?' Williams had laughed. 'If.'

Keppler smiled back. 'When,' he repeated. Eve was loaded separately. The Women's Section was in a different building.

After a slow, jolting drive through the southern suburbs of Paris the van drew to a halt. He knew where he was. Fresnes Prison, the great hulking fortress on the outskirts of the city, was taking on the same symbolic mantle as the Bastille. This was a place where awful injustices happened, where all flesh was corruptible, malleable, where you lived and died by the whims of jailers more evil than any of their charges.

Williams was unlocked from the ring, handcuffed, and led into the outside world. The large cobbled courtyard was surrounded by towering walls with tiny slit windows. In the little amount of bright summer sunshine that managed to penetrate this well, the walls' rancid, diseased surfaces looked vile enough, thought Williams. God only knew what this place was like at the dead of night when most inmates arrived. In the corner were two bodies, crumpled and ignored, both bearing the marks and strangely angled limbs of savage beatings.

Williams was pushed firmly through the huge, over-sized

metal doors, clearly designed to make the prisoners feel insignificant, as if giants really walked this earth. He was marched into a cold, echoing hallway, where his details were entered into the prison log while a selection of French and Germans eyed him up, as if vying for the chance to lay into him. Williams stayed calm, answered the questions curtly but correctly, giving his name as Charles Lelong. He was then taken by a German NCO and two French warders downstairs, along a grim, sweaty passageway, and into an internal courtyard, this one lined and criss-crossed with galleries and gangways, resounding to the crunch of hobnailed boots, shouted orders and the odd thunk of wood and rubber on flesh.

Williams' cell was on the lower level, which meant it had no window. The darkness was probably a blessing. The NCO delivered a heavy punch to Williams' face and he stumbled inside, crashing into the opposite wall.

The door slammed on him, the NCO looked through the peephole and marched off. Williams checked his face, but the blow had merely cut his lip. He sucked back the blood and, still handcuffed, groped his way around his new home, locating a WC, a tap and an iron bed with a straw mattress. He sat gingerly on the latter, and, despite the near certainty that there were lice just waiting for him, he sank back and closed his eyes, trying to still his racing mind so he could get some sleep. Astonishingly, he dozed.

He was woken by the sound of a trolley rattling across the steel latticework of the galleries. An elderly German was escorting two orderlies who were dishing out soup and coffee, although, as Williams discovered, it was difficult to be sure which was which. More visits gave him a grimy blanket and some newspaper, which was torn into small squares in case there was any doubt about its intended use. Finally, his handcuffs were removed and he massaged some life into his numb wrists.

Nothing too drastic yet, he thought. But he knew what might be awaiting him. Suspension from hooks in the ceiling with his arms behind his back, constant beatings, the famous and dreaded *baignoire*, where victims were repeatedly held under water until they lost consciousness, a torture that could be repeated for hours. A torture that was rumoured to be something of a spectator sport at rue de Saussaies – the German female clerks were often invited to watch.

The afternoon passed slowly, the anticipation of Gestapo and SD delights eating at him, so Williams tried to get his mind off torture and began to play mental games, trying to recall every winner of every grand prix since 1925, something to stop him thinking about Eve, to leave no room, no part of his brain that dared dwell on what he had got her into.

At around four there was a commotion. Voices shouting in French. Then English. 'Is there an Englishman here?'

'Yes,' yelled another voice.

'Quiet.' Guards were trying to silence everyone, but the voices radiated off the hard metal surfaces so much it was hard to pinpoint who was speaking unless you were right next to the cell, and the conversations bloomed and died within seconds, every-one knowing they had two or three short sentences to make their point. Williams walked to the bars to listen, but not participate.

'Who are you?'

'Conrad. Vincent Conrad.' Code name, thought Williams.

'Chalambaud. You in the Racket?'

Williams knew what this meant, and so did Conrad. Wisely, he chose not to reply. Then the first voice said; 'Don't let the bastards break you, Vincent. The Allies have taken Sicily. It's started.'

So Sicily really had fallen? Christ, from there Italy. So not Calais or Normandy. Jesus. The news both exhilarated and depressed him. Fighting their way up Italy, through Hitler's heavily defended back door, meant they could forget the second front for at least a year.

An orderly appeared at the door, glaring. 'Was that you?' Williams shrugged, not wanting to give them an inch. 'If it was, just shut up. Last time we celebrated some Allied victory Fritz shot five of us. Just shut up.'

The noise gradually subsided, to be replaced by the odd muffled scream from somewhere down a subterranean passage. Then singing, in both French and English. Except the lyrics to the songs were coded stories of missions, betrayal, escape, recapture. There were a lot of agents in the prison, thought Williams, a hell of a lot.

As he sat down on the bed again Williams thought about his wife. Damn. Eve, alone in a cell like this, waiting for . . . he squeezed his eyes shut. Go away, he told the images. Go away. He lay down and began to chew the inside of his cheek till it bled.

Across at the Women's Section, Eve had been put in a higher, lighter cell with a scrawny, pinched woman who, the trustee delighted in telling her, was a prostitute, who looked at her with scant regard, and made it clear that over half the cell and all its contents were her property. Eve sat down quietly on her tiny cot and hoped Williams was OK. She couldn't help feeling that men risked being treated much worse in this hateful place. Although she had already seen women being dragged off by their hair and kicked and beaten as they were pushed along the gangways, so perhaps this was leaping to a false conclusion. For the first time in a long time, Eve began to feel scared for herself rather than Will or Robert.

'Resistance?' asked the prostitute.

Eve shrugged, aware that the woman could easily be an informer. 'A mistake. It'll be cleared up.'

The woman grunted. 'What's your name?'

'Eve.'

'Renée. You won't be here long.'

'Why not?'

'Resistance are usually taken to Saussaies or Foch. Sometimes they come back, sometimes they don't.'

'Why are you here?'

'Resistance.' Eve's expression must have shown her disbelief. 'Why do you look like that? You think only the bourgeoisie are allowed in?'

'No, I . . .'

'I heard what the trustee said. Whore. He's right. And I have a disease. And now so do twenty, thirty, forty German soldiers. And they'll be sent out of France to die on the eastern front. Tell me, Eve, how many Germans did you get rid of?'

Eve burst out laughing and when she realised she wasn't being mocked, Renée joined in. 'I'll make sure you get the Croix de Guerre.'

'Just get me some of that penicillin, dear.'

Eve stood up and crossed over to the other woman's bed. Renée hesitated and moved up. 'Listen, I am new to all this, Renée. Forgive me, I have a feeling you . . .' Eve stopped, struggling to find the expression.

'Know the system? Like the back of my hand.'

'My husband is also in here somewhere. I'm going to get him out.'

Renée rubbed finger and thumb together in the age-old symbol for money, but before she could elaborate, a key turned in the lock, the door swung out and in stepped Neumann, his gleaming, immaculate uniform and boots a stark contrast to the cancerous surroundings. Renée couldn't help an intake of breath.

'Eve.' He glanced around at the cell, which was clean and neat by Fresnes standards. He placed a block of grey, gritty soap on her bed, along with a toothbrush, a hairbrush and a tube of toothpaste. 'I brought you some things.' He looked at Renée and his lip curled with distaste. 'I will arrange for you to get your own cell.'

'I'm happy here.'

'I'm not happy you are here. I can get you out, you know. Very simple.' Neumann raised a querying eyebrow.

'And my husband?'

Neumann stood staring for a second, his face impassive, those blue eyes flashing, turned and left, slamming the cell door, bringing a fine shower of dust from the lintel.

Renée made the money gesture again, then pointed at her crotch. 'I was forgetting. There are two ways out.'

Twenty-nine

The shredded remnants of the *Nacht und Nebel* order were still on the desk in Virginia's cell. She had spent much of the last twenty-four hours in a coma-like state lying on the bed, refusing all food and offers of companionship. Now she wished she had an L pill; she would take it like a shot. She felt she had been bamboozled into a betrayal. But what had she done? What had she really done? Confirmed simply that Gatacre was Williams. Yet she had only discovered it by chance, she could have pretended the information had never come her way, but something, something weak inside had made her head nod of its own accord.

She looked over when a knock came at the door and stared back at the wall when Lock entered.

'Go away.'

'Keppler wants you.'

'Tell him to go to hell.'

She was aware of him moving closer. 'Look, little lady, you might as well face up to it. You're in as deep as me now. Thing is, Neumann has got your pal Williams. You know what that means, don't you? All you have to do is tell him he's wasting his time playing the silent hero. The game is well and truly up.

268

Save him a lot of pain. You owe him that.'

She snapped round and glared at him. Maybe he was right. Maybe she did owe him that. Virginia sat up, feeling her head swim as she did so and swallowing hard.

'You all right?'

'I need some water. Perhaps something to eat.' If you were going to be a traitor, she reasoned, you might as well do it on a full stomach.

It was nightfall by the time Robert reached Auffargis. He had come a very circuitous route over the back fields, looking for signs of sentries, an ambush, but there was none. He had managed to escape from the cops by taking to the rooftops, and eventually descending into an apartment block when the wound in his leg became too painful for the scrabbles and leaps. The concierge had surprised him on the second floor, pinning him to the wall, an ornate poker in hand.

'I am not a housebreaker.'

The elderly man had peered into his face and whispered, 'No. But I believe you are Robert Benoist.'

Robert swallowed hard and said: 'Yes, I am.'

The concierge had let him go. 'Then it would be an honour if you would join me for a drink in my room.'

After being forced to drink too much brandy and reminisce about his racing days while the man cleaned and dressed the wound in his leg – which was effectively a very deep rip through muscle – the concierge had loaned him his bike and sent him on his way. He had cycled slowly and stiffly out to his old house.

Robert had a torch but did not use it. There was a moon – more poor souls would be coming in from SOE, he thought – and he knew the paths well enough. He approached through

269

the woods and sat on the flattened grass and broken ferns where the machine gunners had lain half a day before him. He imagined the fire raking the house, the van shuddering as bullets wrecked it, the terrace collapsing, the plants torn asunder. Were they alive? He'd called in to see Bugatti's old secretary, Madame Teyssédre, a brave woman who he knew had links to the Resistance, just as she suspected his, although they never discussed them for security reasons. Find out for me if they are alive. She said she'd try. Then she whispered, 'Have you heard about Sicily?'

As he lay there watching his poor shattered house, waiting for signs of a trap, he thought about Sicily. A sudden influx of agents in Paris and northern France with orders to begin sabotage. Massive drops of weapons. Radio sets. Explosives. That would convince the SD and the Abwehr that something big was afoot. Messages would dribble back to the Wehrmacht and the RSHA where a picture would emerge of the Allies planning to attack northern France. While all the time they were sneaking up the back alley.

So London lost a few spies in the deception, a few tonnes of materiel, a dozen radio sets. Which the Germans turn. Or think they . . . his mind spun. Who knew the truth? Not him, not any of them.

After waiting thirty minutes Robert crept across the lawn, gun in hand, down to the last two bullets in the magazine. But nothing stirred except for an owl way back in the forest. He felt sick as he got closer to the house and saw the damage the heavy calibre guns had done, atomising huge sections of the wall, smashing every last piece of glass in a window frame. He sat down on the terrace and, beneath the broken boards, he saw something gleam. Reaching down between the splintered wood he managed to pull up the silver chain with the Atlantic key on it. Eve must have deliberately dropped it down there. He kissed it and placed it over his own neck.

Inside the wrecked kitchen he cleared the debris from a section of the floor and levered up one of the flagstones. Beneath was the B2 transmitter. He lugged it outside, strung the aerial over the wooden trellis half hanging from the wall and set up to transmit. This wasn't his sked, but he inserted the emergency crystal. Someone would be listening. And the Germans. Out there in the night a DF van would prick up its metal ears and slowly turn its attention to him. Let them try. He used the one-time pad to create the short, sharp communication.

He transmitted, received a recognition, did his security check and sent the message in full. Don't trust this radio any longer. Chestnut blown. Last secure transmission. A reply. He quickly put it into clear. We'll send a plane. He roughed out a final goodbye: Thanks. Perhaps later. Have housekeeping to do. Out.

Afterwards he took the B2 back inside, returned it to the hiding place. In the sink he burned the silk code sheet and the one-time pads while he smoked a welcome cigarette. Finally he put the crystals, two regular and one emergency, in their black velvet bag and, using the butt of the gun, smashed them to useless bits and hurled them through the open window. Ready. As he had said, time to clean house.

Some figures are so strange as to be unnoticeable, invisible. It was Madame Teyssédre's idea and Robert embraced the surrealness of it. So, late in the afternoon, a man in a stove-pipe hat and black frock coat cycled rather stiffly along Boulevard Capucines, looking neither right nor left, not bothering to take in the wonderful confection of Opera, the young men being dragged from the Metro by Gestapo, the Light 15s prowling

271

past him, the rickshaws and charcoal cars that crossed every intersection ahead of him. Paris was imploding now, the hated regime had become more violent, wild, thrashing out to try to suppress the groundswell building and building; but instead of suppressing it was compressing the people like a spring. Sooner or later they would bounce back.

The chimney sweep turned right by the Opera Comique, ignoring the Germans mingling on the pavement sipping pre-show drinks, past the row of horsedrawn taxis, and the little cluster of emaciated, desperate prostitutes hoping to catch an officer's eye.

Robert reached the apartment block, dismounted and locked the bike up with a chain. He rang the bell for the concierge. Nothing. He waited ten minutes until a young mother came out to give her baby some air before curfew and he slipped in as the door almost slammed shut. He climbed one flight of stairs, slowly, because of the still aching wound, found himself a deep, dark doorway and settled down for however long it took.

It wasn't a lengthy wait. He heard the door close softly and the lock being turned and the distinctive foot-dragging gait of his brother. He smiled bitterly to himself. Now they both had matching limps. Maurice descended the stairs, his stiff leg thudding down first each time. As he passed him on the landing Robert gave a low whistle and he saw his brother start and turn. Robert stepped into the light, the meagre bulb throwing the stove hat into a gross, elongated shadow.

'Williams?'

The sound of a guilty conscience. A man with something terrible on his mind. Robert stepped forward and raised the Browning. 'You know it isn't Williams. You know it can't be Will, don't you?'

'Rob—'

'Hush.' Robert came close, put a hand behind Maurice's head and forced the gun into his mouth.

'I coubbnnmmm,' Maurice tried to say.

'Hush now, brother. You broke my heart. Broke my heart. Just two bullets left. I hope the first one kills you, I really do. It'll be better than you have given Will. And Eve.' He pressed the gun down, forcing Maurice to his knees.

'Theyadmmuuvvver.'

'Hush. Doesn't matter now. Whatever.'

The gun began to shake. Slowly at first, then quite violently until it was banging against Maurice's teeth and Robert fought to pull the trigger against the sound of his mother's pleading. 'You'd have done the same,' her weak voice said. Would he? *Would he?*

Robert wrenched the barrel from Maurice's mouth, brutally cutting his top lip with the fore-sight, swung the gun back and slashed it across Maurice's temple, sending his brother sprawling to the floor with a groan. He lay there, panting, not daring to move, knowing the moment of blind hatred had passed for ever, unless he said or did anything to provoke Robert. He'd won. He'd survived. Do nothing.

Disgusted as much with himself as his brother, Robert repocketed the gun, went down the stairs and stepped out into the glare of headlights from SD cars. He thought about running back inside when he heard a Schmeisser being cocked somewhere behind him in the hallway. No doubt the soldier would love him to try something.

'Robert.' It was Keppler, taking in the strange disguise. 'A new career. Very good. Well, you'll be pleased to know the chimneys at Foch haven't been done for some time.'

Williams had lost sense of whether the water pouring down on him from the overhead spigot was boiling hot or freezing cold. His raw, pummiced skin reacted in the same way – screeching out in agony. In the interrogation cell of Fresnes the music played softly in the corner, one of his Jean Sablon records, while Neumann paced up and down in front of him, occasionally regulating the water that cascaded on to his head, running into his nose and mouth. Williams felt as if the constant streams had runnelled his face, etching deep furrows into it.

He couldn't actually see Neumann because, after binding him into the heavy wooden chair, they had slipped blackened motor-cycle goggles on to his head. And then the water started. Cold, hot, freezing, scalding. In a strange way, Williams could relax now. After all the gut-wrenching anticipation of torture, after thinking perhaps they weren't such bad guys after all, and it wouldn't happen, here was the proof that they deserved whatever they got.

His whole upper body was screaming out and he was compart-mentalising the pain, trying to make it distant, happening to someone else, cursing God, simultaneously denying Him and praying to Him that this wasn't happening to Eve.

Suddenly the water was turned off and the sickly crooning became much louder. Williams breathed a soft sigh of relief, but now the skin began to prickle and itch, something he could do little about with his hands firmly tied. Which was just as well, because within seconds he wanted to rip into his scalp and tear it off.

'Better, eh?' Neumann said. 'Now. You know what we need. Your contacts. The radios. Are you still using a poem code? If so what is it? If not, where are your one-time pads? Who is Jester? Where is Madeleine?'

The smell that drifted across to him seemed so out of place

here, so alien, he had a moment placing it. Then he had it. Perfume. Chanel. Number Five. From Coco who, of course, lived at the Ritz with her German lover. How appropriate. 'Williams,' said Virginia. 'Remember me?'

'I always hated that smell.'

'Chanel?'

'Treachery.'

Neumann laughed and Williams felt hands grab his arm and his fingers being splayed out on the arm of the chair. Virginia felt sick to her stomach. She had to convince him this was all for nothing, pointless. Lock was right, they were being played for fools.

'Williams, they are going to smash your right hand. Tell them,' Virginia pleaded. 'You know they know everything. Please.'

Williams was aware of cold metal on the back of his hand. A hammer face.

'Let me out,' Virginia said. 'Let me out, I want no part of this.'

Williams felt the hammer lift anyway. 'You are already part of it,' said Neumann.

He braced himself, wondering what would be left after it pulverised bone, snapped tendons and crushed muscles. Would he be able to drive again?

The door opened and Williams heard a heated, whispered conversation. A decision was made. He slowly let the tension drain from his body. He was being untied and unmanacled. He was dragged up and pulled out into the corridor. Neumann whispered: 'You're a lucky man, Williams. Keppler wants to see you. And he doesn't like damaged goods.' Foch, he thought. They're going to Foch.

Robert sat on the chaise longue in Keppler's office, his bad leg stretched out. It had been re-bandaged by the warders of the tiny cell on the fifth floor where he had spent the previous night. Nobody had really tried to pressure him to talk so far. He had a visit from an Englishman called Gilbert, who had done his best to convince him that co-operation was the only way. Then a more insidious conversation with some slippery sack of shit called Lock. That hadn't lasted too long.

But he had seen other men who bore the signs of heavy beatings, and he'd heard the guards in action, shouting and slapping and whipping. Clearly, the message was there are two routes we can go here. Your choice.

At a small fold-out desk next to Keppler's ormolu sat Obst, a stenographer. Two armed soldiers were on either side of the door, just in case Robert felt like walking over and strangling Keppler there and then. It was a tempting idea. He watched as the Sturmbannführer decanted a bottle of red wine, poured a glass and nodded appreciatively. 'Château Corton André. Superb.'

Robert asked, 'What year?'

'Thirty-seven.'

'Too young. You mustn't be impatient. Or do you think you're running out of time?'

Keppler smiled. 'Sicily?' He shook his head. 'It's a long way up Italy, let me tell you. A long way.' He sipped again. 'Six years. I think it's time enough.'

The door opened and in came Williams, still damp from his soaking, skin blotchy from scalding, the goggles firmly in place. Neumann pushed him into one of the gilded Louis XV chairs and snapped handcuffs in place. Virginia went and sat quietly near Obst.

Robert looked at Neumann and hissed: 'What's wrong? Run out of little old ladies to beat up, arsehole?'

'Perhaps. But their sons will do just as well.' He took a step towards Robert who swung his leg off the settee and half rose to meet him. The guards stirred, wondering how to react to the looming confrontation.

'Neumann. Enough. Go and send Lock in.' There was a beat before he added, 'And make sure Mrs Williams is comfortable.'

The junior officer hesitated and looked at Williams, hoping for a reaction to the news that his precious wife was in the building. He left disappointed.

Keppler took out his Luger pistol and laid it on the desk in front of him. 'When Virginia was turned over to me, I told her more about SOE than she knew. I could do the same for you. Prosper, Autogyro, Donkeyman and now Chestnut . . . all gone. We nearly caught Bodington last month. That would have been a prize. Your head of clandestine flights gives us these—' from his desk he produced a pile of mimeographed letters and communications. 'Everything going out on the Lysanders, copied to us. Very polite, eh? We know who is doing what where. Except you two decided that the normal methods of communications were unsafe. You were right. So you kept us in the dark. Very, very rude. Time to make amends.'

The door opened and Lock slipped in and stood next to one of the guards. Robert looked across at him with his hawk-like stare until the Englishman's eyes went down.

'What's going on here, Keppler?' Robert asked, 'Why don't you just pull out our toenails and have done with it?'

Keppler shuddered. 'My God, the very thought of it. That doesn't happen here. Not in this room.' He smiled. 'Not on this carpet. We can take you to eighty-six or seventy-two if we need to do that. But I prefer not to use such methods.'

'So what am I doing here?' asked Williams.

'Well, every now and then Neumann has to be allowed to

prove he can do better than me. I'm just an old copper to him, outdated, outmoded. He has science on his side, I have reason. Every time he proves me right.'

'How gratifying,' croaked Williams.

'Yes, I think so,' said Keppler as he sipped the wine again. 'You see, there isn't much I need from you. Arms dumps? Got them. Contacts? Got those, too. Wimille? Well, he'll have gone to ground. All that is left is just a few details, really. Not worth the effort of beating you all up.'

Robert got up, walked over to Williams and took the goggles off. Nobody tried to stop him. Williams blinked in the sudden light and his eyes began to water. Robert touched the burns on his head and smiled at his old friend. 'These need dressing.'

'They will be,' said Keppler.

'Now.'

'You are in no position to make demands.'

'And you think you are? They'll go septic. They need something on them.'

Keppler hesitated and clicked his fingers at Virginia. She went outside, fetched a first aid kit. On her return she began dabbing iodine on the wounds. Williams, wincing, avoided her gaze.

'So,' continued Keppler, 'there are three things I need.'

'Just three?' asked Robert.

'Yes.'

'And in return?'

'You go east as POWs. Not *N&N*.'

'*N&N*?'

'*Nacht und Nebel*. Night and Fog. *Veruckt unerwunscht*. Return not required.'

'*Nacht und Nebel*. Nice,' mused Robert. 'So why should we trust you, you cunt?'

Lock couldn't help a smile at the sheer audacity. Even Keppler was too taken aback to react angrily. 'Ask Arthur over there. Ask Virginia. Starr. Gilbert. Suthill. A dozen others. Look, Neumann is our resident thug. I make deals. And I keep them.'

'It's not good enough.'

Keppler banged the table in mock disgust. 'Benoist, you really are the absolute limit. Can I remind you, you are my prisoner, I have the power of life and death, yet you sit there as if it is the other way round.'

'I think it is.'

'Please, explain for us.'

Williams cleared his throat and answered for Robert. 'The Allies are in Sicily. Next Italy.' He looked at Robert, 'And if I got it right, the Germans seem to have been hammered at somewhere called Kursk. So now we know that one day, one day soon, you and your chums here will be called to reckon for us. How you treated us. Now, I can guess what will happen to Lock. But you . . .'

Keppler shrugged. 'So, my life in your hands? An interesting thought. Let's pretend you are right. How do we proceed?'

'Tell me the three things you want,' said Robert, 'and I'll tell you what I will trade for them.'

Keppler stood up and paced in front of his desk, a small smile on his face, fascinated and amused by the calmness of the man. 'I want your radio. Its code. And . . .' He looked a little embarrassed. 'The Bugatti Atlantic.'

Robert nodded. 'Seems reasonable.'

'Robert—' Williams croaked, suddenly disliking where this was going.

'No, Will. Let's see how it goes. Roll the dice, Keppler.'

The German nodded. 'The radio? I assume you have a radio?'

'Yes, I have one. And for that I want Eve Williams released.'

Keppler clapped his hands in delight. 'Very good . . . although

279

why are you bargaining for another man's wife?'

'*In loco maritus*,' said Williams.

'How modern.' Keppler took the yellow release form and signed it, handed it to Virginia and said, 'Do it.'

'But—'

'Just do it.'

Five minutes passed while Keppler paced and hummed tunelessly to himself. Eventually he went over to the window and looked down. He beckoned Robert to his side. Below he saw Eve and Virginia reach the high metal gates at the front. Eve, looking tired and bedraggled but as beautiful as ever, hesitated as she stepped through the small door cut into the larger one and scanned the building. Robert wasn't sure she caught the two-fingered kiss he made as Virginia bundled her out into the street. He imagined he could hear her running on the other side, sprinting for the small apartment round the corner, and sanctuary.

'You know that was easy for me. I hate women being involved in this,' said Keppler: 'So?'

'Don't do it, Robert,' said Williams.

'She can be picked up again very quickly,' snarled Keppler.

'A deal is a deal. And she's out, Will. That's all that matters,' said Robert heavily. 'Here we go. Go back to the house in the forest. Kitchen. Fourth flagstone from the door. You'll find a B2 transmitter.'

'And the frequency?'

Robert glanced at Williams and said: 'Over to you, Will.'

Williams tried to stay calm. There was a message here. Robert knew perfectly well what the frequencies were. He could tell Keppler. Unless he wanted to make him complicit in this dreadful compromise. Or was trying to tell him that it really didn't matter. Williams caught the softest, fastest of winks and, taking it as reassurance, said quickly: 'Four point five to nine megacycles. Three crystals. Two normal, one emergency.'

Keppler smiled and went back to his wine. 'Now let's try . . . for the coded poem. You are still using the poems?'

Both nodded at once, a tad too enthusiastically, but Keppler failed to notice.

'You want the code? You'll leave my family alone, once, and for all time,' said Robert.

'Maurice included?'

'Fuck Maurice. I should have shot him.'

'Did you know your brother helped us compile lists, lists of naturalised Jews in Paris? I gave him a travel pass for every ten names.'

Robert felt his spirits sink. They moved around on the backs of denounced and deported Jews. He felt sick to his stomach. He repeated softly: 'I said, fuck Maurice.'

'OK. You have my word. The family, left in peace.'

'No matter what?' insisted Williams.

'No matter what.'

Obst, the stenographer, asked: 'Which of you is the poet?'

Williams began the defunct code: 'Sweet sister death . . . has gone debauched today, and stalks on this high ground . . .'

'Repeat the last five words please,' requested Obst.

To Williams' surprise, Virginia picked up: 'Stalks on this high ground . . . with strumpet confidence . . .'

Obst stumbled at the sudden change. 'Strumpet?'

'Yes, strumpet. With strumpet confidence makes no coy veiling of her appetite . . . but leers from you to me . . . with all her parts discovered.'

Obst asked: 'Who wrote this?'

Virginia answered: 'David Jones. He saw you lot in action last time.'

'I prefer Irving Berlin,' said Keppler offhandedly.

'He's Jewish,' said Williams bitterly.

'I won't tell if you don't.' Keppler drained the last of his wine and said triumphantly, 'This seems to be going rather well. So finally, we come to the Bugatti Atlantic. What do you want for that?'

Robert pursed his lips and clicked his fingers, as if seeking the right conditions that would satisfy him before he said slowly, in his most cultured voice: 'How about you suck our cocks?'

Thirty

Eve let the feeble spring sun warm her back, stroking deliciously through the thin linen jacket she wore over a faded cotton dress, as she leafed through the postcards and books on the banks of the Seine, moving from stall to stall, marvelling at the pictures and prints of a city that seemed to exist in a half-remembered time, as if it really was sepia and brown tinged, the way her memory tended to play it back these days.

Eight months since the arrests. Eight months of arguing, cajoling and – above all – bribing. So many thousand francs to make sure they had decent cells, another ten for better rations, twenty for a message, a scrap of paper with almost illegible scrawl, written in the depths of winter with numb fingers, but still strong, the big X, the kiss, still defiant. Five thousand to take them new clothes. Twenty-five for a passage into that hideous inner courtyard and glimpse at a cell window, so high and so far it could be anyone, but she knew it was Will.

And she got a message from Robert. It told her he had spent the last two weeks inscribing something on his wall. Something

283

he still believed, something for her to cling on to. Never give up. Never confess. Never surrender. That he would look after Will for her, no matter what. It had made her weep for her friend.

Now, the ultimate bribe.

Paris felt like a powder keg or a steam cooker with no safety valve, heading for an explosion. More desperate deportations of Jews and undesirables, more workers for the Reich, more reprisals not only in the capital but at Lille and Tulle. There was a strong anticipation of ultimate liberation now. That included kicking over traces, losing any little conveniences. Like SOE spies. And of feathering nests. Hence the greed of guards and gaolers in Fresnes, there to be exploited.

So she had to make sure Will and Robert were on the right train, not labelled *N&N* but POW. So she had a deal, of sorts.

She felt a tap on her shoulder and turned round to see Neumann beaming at her, in sober civilian clothes for once. She managed to smile back with what she hoped was enthusiasm. He kissed her cheek and she tilted her head as if she welcomed it.

'They went out last night. To Germany. Both to Stalags for officers.'

Inside she felt like crying, the thought of Will and Robert moving even further from her, but she managed to say, 'Thank you, Joachim.'

'All this could have been done long ago if you had just come to me earlier.'

'I know. I was . . . stubborn. Silly.'

He held his arm out and she slipped hers through his. They began to walk north, crossing the river at the Pont Royal and wandering through the Tuileries, its once immaculate beds now churned up for precious vegetable production. Nobody seemed to notice the pair of them, nobody stopped and pointed, or hissed, 'Whore, slut, traitor', as she half expected. Just two lovers of indeterminate nationality out for a walk.

'You know, I don't always approve of Hans Keppler's methods,' said Neumann. 'But he has taught me two things. The power of negotiation, especially if you are doing so from a position of strength.' He bent down to kiss her again, this time on the lips. 'And patience. And I have to say, Eve, you were well worth the wait.'

Across the Rivoli, heading for Place du Vendôme to his apartment on rue de la Paix.

'Can I ask you about something? If you promise not to question me on it?'

'Questioning is my job, Eve.'

'You're out of uniform. And all this isn't really part of the job. Not strictly speaking.'

'True.' He considered for a moment. They were on the Vendome now, the shops that had been swarming with German officers and their mistresses two years before looking a little shabbier, more desperate now. The age of frivolity was over. Buying couture dresses and hastily pawned Jewish jewellery was no longer the priority it had been. Still, as ever, a line of Hotchkisses, Rolls-Royces and Delages attended upon the Ritz, where a form of good life continued apace, day and night. 'OK, no questions.'

She began to relay the rumour she had received from a sceptical Madame Teyssédre. 'An acquaintance told me an astonishing story. They heard that a group of French Canadian agents were met at Gare d'Austerlitz by someone who they were assured was a friend. The friend betrayed them to your people.'

'Go on.'

'The agents got word out of Fresnes—'

'How?'

'Uh-uh. You know Fresnes leaks like a sieve now. Anyway, no

questions. You promised.' She pinched him hard on the arm.

'Very well,' Neumann laughed.

'The message said their betrayer was a man called Williams.'

'Really?'

'Was it?'

'Was it what?'

'Was it Will?'

'What do you think?'

'I think you had someone impersonate him. It wouldn't be the first time, would it? You set up the meeting on a turned radio and sent a stand-in.'

He shrugged noncommittally. 'Such as?'

'You are about the right height and build. A little younger. Wrong colour hair. But with a hat . . .'

'Here we are.' Neumann stopped and opened the solid, ornate door of a grand apartment block. 'No questions and no answers either I am afraid. But I will tell you this.' She felt his hand low on her back, sliding on to her backside as he propelled her in. 'I have no objection to being in your husband's shoes right now.'

Eve had to gasp when she saw the scale of the apartment itself. An enormous living room, full of good-quality furniture, all in heavy reds and golds, with two bedrooms and a bathroom leading from it. 'My God.'

'Yes, excellent isn't it. I've only had it a month. The contessa had to, um, leave at rather short notice. There's a good view of the Opera from that window there. Drink?'

'Gin?'

'Uh, no. Scotch?'

'Perfect.'

'Coming up. Make yourself at home.'

Eve slipped off her jacket, draped it over a sofa and began to walk around admiring the furnishings.

'Music?' asked Neumann rhetorically. 'Strauss. "One Thousand and One Nights". You like Strauss?' She nodded. 'Good. I can see we are going to get on brilliantly.'

'Joachim. Do you mind if I take a bath first?'

The thought of Eve in a tub made him flush and he said, 'If you leave the door open for me.'

'Of course.' He watched appreciatively as she went in to the big marble space, bent over the bath and began running the water. 'My God, it's so hot,' she shouted over the gushings. 'I haven't seen such hot water since . . . since before you people came.'

'Well, you should have spent more time with us people.' He clinked ice in the glasses but hesitated while she unbuttoned her dress and let it drop, revealing underwear that had seen too many washes. He would do something about that. The drawers of the apartment were stuffed full of enough lace and silk to cause a riot along Avenue Montaigne.

'Can I have it in here?' she asked, snapping him out of a daydream of Eve in the finest of lace camisole tops.

He picked up the glasses and hurried across to her, not wanting to miss the final moment of the striptease. Her smile faded as he stepped across the threshold, and he thought perhaps she was frightened or modest but then he felt the metal snout of the Welrod against his temple and heard the hiss of the bullet as it brushed through the silencer baffles on its way to his brain.

The bullet exploded out of his temple, punching slivers of bone and eye socket out, leaving the eye itself dangling crazily in its ruined housing. The whisky hit the floor in a fury of glass and ice and Neumann buckled at the knees.

Rose Miller waited for him to fall, wishing the Welrod came with a second shot, reaching for another round when Neumann slumped into Eve, his head lolling to one side, slowly sliding down her, leaving a trail of bloody gristle down her front, until he lay curled at her feet, the last of life leaving him in two quick, powerful spasms.

Eve opened her mouth to scream but managed to suppress the urge and muttered a heartfelt: 'Jesus.'

Rose rolled the body to one side, turned the bath faucet off, pulled two towels off the neat stack on the shelf, laid them across the smashed tumblers and said: 'Mind the glass.'

'Oh yes,' said Eve slightly hysterically, 'wouldn't want to get blood on the towels.'

Rose looked at the gore congealing on Eve's body. 'We'd best get you cleaned up. There's a shower in the master bedroom.'

Sensing the numbness enveloping Eve, Rose took her by the hand, led her away from the gruesome body, through to the big glass cubicle in the bedroom, pulled off the remains of her underwear and pushed her under the wonderfully hot stream coming from the enormous shower head. She soaped the blood and bone and brain specks from Eve's neck and shoulders.

'What animals,' said Eve flatly.

Rose stripped off and climbed in. 'Us or them?'

'Both. God.'

'Well, the alternative was a piece of German sausage up your fanny.'

Eve looked shocked. 'I'm not saying . . . I just . . .'

Rose raised a hand. 'Neumann was becoming a threat. He'd begun to use his brain as well as his brawn.'

'At least he got Will and Robert out as POWs.'

Rose just nodded, as if she believed this were true. Keppler at least had some intention of keeping his invidious deals. With Neumann, she wasn't so sure. For the next few minutes there was only the hissing of water and the squelch of soap.

'Listen, Eve,' said Rose eventually. 'I know you wondered.

About Williams. And me. In London. Nothing happened.'

'Something happened to him there. He wasn't quite the same person.'

'Something has happened to all of us. You weren't the same. France wasn't the same. He loves you. Did then, does now.'

'Then I owe him an apology.'

To her own surprise Rose took Eve's face in her hands and kissed her on the lips, feeling for all the world at that moment like a protective mother to the older woman. 'The wardrobes out there are full of Fortuny, Balenciaga, Molyneux, Lelong, Paquin. Help yourself. When you see Williams, you can apologise in style.'

Eve turned off the water, stepped out and quickly wrapped a towel around herself, flustered and embarrassed. 'What now?'

'You go to Normandy. Stay out of Paris. I go back.'

'And then?'

'Then we wait. Wait for the Allies and Russians to meet up in Berlin.'

Eve nodded. 'And pray he lives that long.'

Rose accepted a towel from Eve and touched her face lightly. 'Let's pray they both do.'

Thirty-one

MARCH–APRIL 1945

The wind sliced through the coarse, blue-striped uniform and straight into Williams' bones. Not that there was much flesh to act as a barrier, that had progressively fallen away over the last ten months since his arrival at this place. Sachsenhausen–Oranienburg. May its name be spat upon for years to come, he thought.

Unusually, six of them from the officers' detention block had been assigned to repair a broken water pipe, and they hacked their way into the frozen earth still not touched by the spring thaw. At least he hoped it was a repair detail. Williams had seen many, many men digging their own final resting places over the last few weeks. But none this close to the elaborate main entrance. He stopped for a second and looked up at the guard and his three Lagerschutz – trusties – in charge of this bedraggled Kommando. One swing with the spade and he could take the German's head off. Robert would.

He thought about Robert a lot. He'd last seen him at Gare de l'Est, chained with other officers, being herded into a train, dozens of them into small carriages built for eight or ten. He himself had boarded a different train, for a different destination. Even the opportunity to die together had been denied them.

After Robert's arrogant rebuttal of Keppler, the Sturmbann-führer had washed his hands of them. There were beatings, solitary confinement, the usual casual brutality, withdrawal of rations and finally a ten-day transportation to Germany, during which any remaining valuables they had managed to cling on to were looted. They had been packed into a tiny hut on arrival before sorting into various groups, being shaved, showered and given the hideous uniforms and the chafing clogs. There had been nineteen of them in his shipment to Sachsenhausen. There were four left now. Some executed, some lost through illness, a few victims of the internecine fighting between rival groups of inmates, mostly over the dwindling food supply. But he'd survived.

He still had that picture in his head, the one of the faces at the cattle-truck doorway at St Just. And now he knew why it had seared its way into his visual cortex. To keep him alive. Those people, they had already crossed over. They had been through Drancy and the Velo and other tortures and they had accepted that they were simply on a long, slow road to death. And whenever he remembered those stares, the vacant, let's-get-it-over-with gazes, they jerked him back every time he felt like curling up and dying. Not yet. Not yet, damn you. Those people, he owed them a lot, they'd given him a touchstone for life. Had Robert got it, too?

One of the trustees motioned to continue digging. Had he been a Jew or a Russian such a pause would have caused Williams to have been shot there and then. But the group kept in the big concrete block that housed him were different.

291

Commandos, spies, politicals, some with *N&N* on them, true, others, like Williams, just with a letter displaying their nationality.

He went back to scraping at the earth, trying to minimise the jarring effect of permafrost on his shoulders and elbows. He had noticed three loose teeth that morning. His body had held up well, but unless it got better food soon it would start to digest itself, he knew, to the point of no return. Again, he'd seen that. Men locked in cages in the courtyard, weakening every day as the *Apells*, the roll calls, came and went, allowed to rot in full view as some kind of warning. As if anyone needed reminding just what a tenuous hold they all had on life.

Sachsenhausen was not one camp, but forty-four separate units, including satellites at the Heinkel factory and the grenade manufacturers a few kilometres down the road. Stories reached them from the latter of prisoners purposefully detonating explosives and taking guards with them. Now only trustees were allowed to do the final assembly.

A late flurry of snow began, bleakly beautiful swirls, dancing through the Breughelian landscape, mocking the grey-fleshed inmates with their dazzling purity. Williams' teeth started to chatter, loosening them further, no doubt. He could taste blood, too, where his gums had started to bleed. And still, he had to count himself lucky. All around him were the field of low, wooden huts, the various sections of the camps for Jews, and Russians and Gypsies and anyone else the Reich despised.

The Russians had always been killed on a savage scale, casually, brutally. Some went to the block known as Station Z, ostensibly for medical examination, actually for a bullet in the head, others were herded into the underground chamber on the corner opposite his cell window, where they were gassed. The smell of burning bodies was so all-pervading that few of them noticed the once-nauseating stench any longer.

Since the beginning of February, when a high-ranking Gestapo man called Müller had visited Commandant Kaindl, the killings had increased to a frenzy. A mobile gibbet had been constructed, which Jewish trustees had to wheel from end to end of the camp, hanging four inmates at a time and then moving on to their next appointment, like some grotesque telegram service. The guards had invented the 'hat' game, snatching prisoners' hats and throwing them over the do-not-cross line in front of the wire fences. Not going to get the hat, you were shot for disobeying orders. Stepping over the line to get it, you were shot for attempting to escape.

They were trying to empty the camp, to kill them all. He knew that now. There was another volley of shots from somewhere over in the Russian section. Firing squad. One every twenty, thirty minutes throughout the day. There were thirty or forty thousand prisoners, Williams had estimated. They were killing two or three hundred a day, perhaps more. The sheer scale of the undertaking was demoralising the guards, who seemed to be making hardly a dent in the morning and evening roll-calls, despite their best, murderous efforts.

Planes flew high over head, their frozen exhaust plumes vivid in the ice-blue sky. USAF planes probably, and perhaps up among them the new Nazi secret weapons the guards sometimes boasted about. They knew they were planes of some sort, fast and lethal, but could offer no more details. But, V-weapons or not, still the Flying Fortresses and the Superfortresses and the Lancasters came on, day after day, sometimes bombing the Sachsenhausen satellite factories, more often than not trying to find a target left untouched in Berlin.

The gates opened and a dilapidated truck limped in, its

293

canvas sides ripped and torn, one wheel on the rear double axle flat, floundering on its rim. Williams realised it had been strafed, casually sideswiped by a Mustang or a Typhoon or one of the other tank busters skimming the countryside like marauding bandits seeking prey. The tailgate came down and half a dozen bodies were thrown on to the hard ground with sickening casualness. The survivors stepped slowly down, hurried by impatient German guards, as if there was something worth rushing to, anything to achieve in Sachsenhausen other than your early death.

The men looked about as fit as he did, scrawny and bony, in the emaciated condition of most camp inmates that stripped away individuality, made it hard to recognise one human being from another. It was more like a medical syndrome than the mere result of starvation, all united in the same stance, the stoop, the slack jaw, all with the dull stares of men who had seen more horror than they could ever communicate. More than they would ever want to.

Then a pair of eyes that didn't look glazed or drugged. A pair that flashed and pierced and told you to go and fuck yourself. The frame was shrunken, how could it not be, but Robert was as straight backed and defiant as ever.

Williams dropped the pick and stood, stepping out of the shallow trench, aware of the guns swivelling to point at him, knowing he was taking a hell of a risk.

'Robert,' his voice felt weak, underpowered, smaller than he remembered. Years of whispering had left his vocal chords stiff and useless. He cleared his throat. A gun barrel was in his stomach.

'Robert.' The yell finally carried, flapping slowly across the yard, hitting Robert as he was about to pick up one of his dead companions to take to the crematorium. Benoist let go of the arm which flopped back to earth, straightened and stepped forward. A grin split his face when he recognised the voice, if not, yet, its owner. He took two fingers and raised them to his lips in a kiss and blew it across just as the rifle butt hit the side of his head and he spun down on to the bodies.

At the same time Williams was struck in his shrunken stomach, the blow punching straight through to his spine, causing him to fall to his knees in coughing agony. He heard a bolt pulled back on a machine pistol.

'Stop.' A voice rang out as a man stepped down from the cab of the truck and straightened the jacket of his SS Untersturmführer uniform. The guards froze, not used to being halted in the middle of their work. The newcomer looked at Robert, snapped his fingers and told him, in French, to get up. He waved the guard away. Then he strode across towards Williams, who was slowly unfolding himself from the bent double position. He looked up and the man said in English: 'Get up, Williams. I need you alive.'

Lock. Arthur Lock.

Except now, they discovered, he was Heinrich Locke, the new identity a reward for loyal service to Keppler at Avenue Foch. Along with Virginia and a few other traitors, Lock had managed to avoid the transports and had skipped Paris just before Liberation, to carry on the good work in Germany. Which meant camps, and more camps.

Sitting on the other side of Williams' bars – one wall of the cell was a grid of metal-framed squares which opened on to the concrete gallery – keeping an eye on Robert, whom he had put next door, Lock shamelessly explained that he had wanted to change sides before the Allies reached Paris, but knew that too many people in the city had a grudge against him.

He had put them on SS rations and offered them decent cigarettes which they consumed hungrily and guiltily, especially when fellow prisoners demanded they pass them along. They took three or four big drags and did so. There were other Allied officers in the block – RAF, SAS, SBS, SIS, Commandos, Parachute Regiment, all those whom the Germans thought deserved harsher treatment than a POW camp. But out of all of them, what did Lock want with Robert and Williams? On the third day he began to tell them, after a fashion.

'The Russians are coming. You know that. You can hear their guns at night. A week. Maybe two. Before the month is out, certainly. This uniform will be a death sentence when they get here.'

'You'll be here?' asked Williams.

'I hope not. I hope not. We'll talk again.'

'Lock?' asked Williams as he turned to go.

'What?'

'Keppler?'

'Oh, he's around. In charge of "liquidating" several camps. Keep out of his way. He's not the nice man you once knew.'

Williams heard Robert's snort of laughter.

Through whispered conversations and Morse tapped on the pipes or bars, Williams pieced together where Robert had been. Buchenwald, mostly, a grisly camp whose main aim was to provide labour for a munitions factory and to get rid of Russian prisoners. As in Station Z at Sachsenhausen there was a *Genickshuss*, a measuring device for checking height, which concealed a small calibre pistol in the wall, with which the prisoner was shot in the back of the head. The small, soft bullet never exited, so blood was minimal, and German patriotic songs drowned out the shots. But, as at Sachsenhausen, this was deemed too slow and hanging, shooting and gassing were stepped up.

A week previously he and thirty-six other Allied officers had been selected for slow hanging with piano wire. Several managed to swop identities with men who had died of TB or typhus in the infirmary. Robert hadn't. But Lock got him on a convoy transferring prisoners between camps. As far as he knew, the others had gone to their terrible deaths, strangulation that lasted ten or more minutes.

'Then we got shot up on the way here. Ironic, eh? Survive a year or more of German prisons. Get blown to bits by your own side. But one thing worried me. When I was checked in here, my name was logged in pencil.'

Williams laughed. 'Mine too. We all are. It means we can be rubbed out at a moment's notice. God, my stomach aches.'

'Too much food. Eat it slowly.'

Williams lay down on his bunk and said softly, 'What's Lock up to?'

He could almost feel Robert's shrug in the darkness. 'We'll find out soon enough.' There was a pause. They could hear the usual sporadic coughings and sobbing, the intimidating sound of hobnail boots, distant gunshots, the crump of bombs falling on some hapless target. 'Will.'

'Quiet!' A guard.

'It's good to be with you again.'

Williams smiled to himself. 'Yes. Yes it is.'

There were no more work details. For the next four days the pair were allowed exercise, food as good as the guards, even coffee, although it was all but undrinkable. They saw Lock looking at them every now and then, smiling as if at some kind of private joke.

That evening he came to them, had them released and

marched down to the interrogation cells, where he dismissed the guards and gave them both another cigarette. American cigarettes.

'God,' said Williams as the real tobacco made his senses explode. 'Where did you get these?'

Lock shrugged and said cautiously, 'We have some contact with the Americans. Go-betweens. Just putting out feelers.' He lit his own cigarette. 'It has some side benefits for the runners if they make it back. They get to sell us these. At prices that'd make you weep.'

'What could the Americans want from you?'

'Oh, they have a list. People they want to put on trial, people they want to find and keep from the Russians, people who can help them identify the good and bad Nazis.'

'And that would be you?'

'It would. I have been in what they call deep cover since 1940. An audacious agent of the crown. Burrowed deep into Gestapo HQ. Saved countless lives.'

'This is a joke, right?' asked Robert.

Lock shook his head. 'No,' he said with practised sincerity. 'I can prove it if some idiot doesn't lynch me first.'

'You were a double agent?' asked Williams, almost believing him.

'Of course. What kind of monster did you take me for? Who do you think told Keppler that deals were the best way of interrogation? Not torture.'

There was a snort of disbelief and derision from Robert. 'I wish you'd told Neumann,' said Williams rubbing his still scarred scalp.

'So. Gentlemen. I need character witnesses. People who saw me at Foch. Who will say nice things about me. Fellow secret agents.'

Williams put his bony elbows on the table. 'Why should we?'

'Because I can get you out of here. Over the next twenty-four hours thirty thousand prisoners will be marched north to the sea. Those that make it will be loaded on to ships. The ships will then be scuttled. Himmler's orders. You do not want to be on that trip, believe me. The remainder of you have been marked for special treatment. That's . . . well, you know what that is. I can keep you off that list as well.' He leaned over and said pointedly to Robert, 'Can't I?'

Robert nodded and said: 'Go on.'

'We take a half-track. There is one in the storage sheds. The morons they use for guards can't get it going. You two, I would think, easy. We head west to the Americans. You confirm my story, I join OSS, you go home. How does it sound?'

Williams closed his eyes and imagined Eve, at the kitchen table, looking up at the ghost in rags, unshaven, bleeding gums, protruding ribs, shot libido, wondering why this old, old man was bothering her. He opened his eyes. 'How does it sound? Sounds good to me.' But Robert just ground out his cigarette and sniffed.

Sleep was never very deep, but the roaring from the courtyard woke them, and the deep crimson shapes dancing across their cell walls took them to the window. A huge bonfire of documents was piled in the centre of the yard where the hated roll-calls usually took place, and they were being consumed by a gasoline-fed conflagration, the most damning of documents turning to ashes and floating up into the night sky. Williams watched the small figures moving around, throwing more and more files and directories on to the bonfire in an increasing frenzy.

Down in the yard itself Keppler stood back away from the heat, keeping to the shadows, selecting which documents were to be incinerated and which packed into the special steel containers he had been issued with.

Lock looked perplexed. 'Why keep any documents at all?'

Keppler shook his head. 'I don't know. Orders. Perhaps they want to learn from their mistakes for the next time.'

Lock laughed. 'You think you'll get a second chance at this?'

Keppler looked affronted. 'Who knows? We should be ready for the eventuality. Now, I want the huts emptied before dawn and the march to begin. You will then execute the remaining terrorists. Do you have a list?'

Keppler took the clipboard from Lock and ran his eyes down it, recognising several names, those who passed through his hands in Paris, and some later in Berlin. The squeamishness had long gone from him. He now knew what had happened to most of the men and women he had promised good treatment at Foch. Lethal injections. Shot in the head. Slow hanging with piano wire. Once it had happened to a few, who would believe him that it was beyond his control? 'I thought Williams was here? And Benoist, you told me?'

Lock cursed his big mouth. 'They are.'

'Add them, add them. I want them all dead. I'll be back to check after I have liquidated Eberslitz.' Another camp, just to the east, almost within sight of the Russians. 'Then we can plan our escape and our story. Agreed?'

'Agreed,' said Lock, as if he would be waiting for Keppler who, he was certain, had no intention of going to another camp and certainly no intention of returning. He knew he wouldn't in Keppler's place.

Williams and Robert were locked in their cells all the next day as they watched the camp emptied of most of its population. Not from the big cell block, but from the huts, Jew and non-Jew herded into raggedy lines and propelled forward through that hateful gate with its clocktower and its vile slogans exhorting work and cleanliness. Those who could not walk were shot on the spot.

All day long, the men and women in striped uniforms were lined and moved forward, too weak to resist, and driven forward by randomly wielded clubs, pushed to their death along the road. Even the hospital and guinea-pig blocks were emptied, their inmates contriving to make even the usual skeletal souls look positively healthy. It was amazing that such creatures could move at all.

As each column marched off they could hear an accompanying tattoo of pistol and machine-gun shots as every few yards another man or woman was murdered. And so, as dusk approached, the last stragglers left and the doors finally closed on the camp, now strangely silent for a moment, with no more wheezing and pacing and coughing and the million other little sounds of misery that filled every moment. Thirty thousand out on the road, a shuffling column of death. Perhaps three or four thousand left in the camp, mostly those too weak even to leave their filthy bunks. Some had been shot where they lay, and with the *Totenrager*, the corpse shifters, gone, they stayed there.

Now the dogs began to bark with a worrying urgency, picking up their handlers' mood. Williams heard the running crunch of boots and the opening of cells, the swish of clubs and the confused screams of men being dragged away. He ran to the doorway and shouted, 'Robert. What is it?'

'Don't worry, we aren't on the list.'

Gunshots, loud in the confined space. A ripple of machine guns. Someone had tried to jump a guard. More barking, getting closer on this landing. Williams backed away from the entrance, waiting for them to pass, like the Angel of Death, hoping he had a symbolic cross of blood on his cell. Next door now. No. Not next door.

'Robert.' He flung himself against the bars. He could hear the dog, snarling. 'Lock, Lock. Where are you, damn you? Lock.'

He glimpsed Robert being bundled out, his face set in determination. They caught each other's eye and Robert shouted his watchwords: 'Never give up. Never confess. Never surrender.' The club hit him between the shoulders and he slumped forward and was gone, whisked away.

Six SS guards appeared outside Williams' cell, two rifles poked through the grill. The door slammed back and the alsatian was in, teeth bared, rearing up on its leash, willing its handler to let it loose. Clubs were raised and he ducked and instinctively raised his arms to protect himself when the sergeant shouted an order he didn't catch. As rapidly as they had entered they withdrew, locking the door and moving on.

'Wait. Wait. You've made a mistake. Both of us. Two of us.' He fell to his knees. 'We're together. We stay together.'

The noises switched to outside his window. The big sodium lights came on and bleached the courtyard in their dazzling glare as the men were herded into a rough formation. Williams pulled himself to the bars and shouted Robert's name again. His friend looked up, shading his eyes against the dazzle and raised a hand.

'Goodbye,' said Williams softly.

The group were turned by the guards and marched across to the bunker in the corner, where the studded steel gates with the big rubber seals had been drawn back to welcome them into the dark tunnel.

Schutzhaftlagerführer Ressen stepped into his white overalls with the elasticated arms and legs and slipped the gasmask over his head, checking the fit carefully. He wriggled his hands into the big red rubberised gloves, put on the heavy boots, scooped up the canister and stepped out into the eerie silence of the courtyard. The only sound was the muffled yells of the men in the bunker, now closed tightly shut, and some lunatic yelling from the cell block. Damn fool. Should count his lucky stars he wasn't in there with the rest of them.

This was to be Ressen's last task. Do this job and catch that truck heading for Berlin, ostensibly for the final defence of the capital and the Führer. Ressen would make sure he was over that tailgate well before they reached the city limits. He might not be the sharpest dagger in the SS, but he knew when it was time to cut and run.

He climbed the six rungs of the steel ladder that took him on to the roof of the bunker and walked across to the nearest square wooden chimney. The voices were louder now, the sounds carrying up the ventilation shaft. They sounded calm, resigned, but he couldn't be sure. Ressen didn't speak English.

He reached the first chimney and levered off the big square cap. From inside he pulled up the long pole connected to the wire basket and set it down next to him. He took the steel canister and unscrewed the lid, holding it at arm's length. The moment the pellets hit air they began to smoke as the sublimation process began – straight from solid to gas.

He shook out half the pellets into the basket, then lowered it down into the darkness below, closing his ears to the sudden panic that ignited below, the yells and the shouts and curses and then the screams. They wouldn't last long. Ressen quickly replaced the cap and strode across to the second shaft, where he repeated the process. After the canister was emptied and the lid replaced he took it and flung it across the rear of the bunker to the pile of identical containers that had grown larger and larger over the last few years, a mass of yellow labels, some peeling and faded, others still bright yellow, but the type on most quickly fading, so that it was almost impossible to read all but the most recent, like the one he had just used: Danger de Mort. Alphachem-IG Farben, St Just, France.

Thirty-two

APRIL 1945

As much as anything was registering on nerves anaesthetised by sorrow, Williams was aware of Lock standing at the metal trellis work that formed the front of the cell. He didn't look up. Robert had been through so much, fought in the skies above France, raced at a time when the attrition rate was horrendous, resisted to the best of his ability. To die like that . . .

He mustn't dwell on it, on the airless chamber, its walls and floors stained with excrement and blood, marks that could never be rubbed clean. The smell of sweat and fear, the stoicism mingling with the panic. Those last few minutes when the air shaft opened and in came the pellets and the poison fumes ripped into the throat of the first man.

'Williams,' Lock said, and waited for a reply. 'Williams.'

It came through the cloud of grief like a dim, distant voice at the end of a tunnel. His own voice sounded metallic, inhuman. 'Fuck off.'

Not to see him again. Not to feel the power of that stare, not to hear him tell some fool he would knock him down and piss in his ear, not to watch him take a car into a bend at a speed that was far too fast and bring it round like a lamb. Not to share a glass of wine and a joke. It was corrosive, the very idea of a permanent separation, and it was burning through his insides.

'I couldn't save him, Williams.'

Neither could I, he wanted to shout. Neither could I. Why not? Why couldn't I save Robert? He kept asking himself.

'I said fuck off.'

'Keppler—'

That made his head snap up. 'Keppler?'

Lock was glad to have his attention and he spoke quickly before that bitter, tear-stained face went down again, back into catatonia. 'Keppler was here, yes. Not now. I think he's gone to the Americans.'

'Why would he do that?'

'Americans or Russians? Which would you choose? The Russkies are due within forty-eight hours. We have to go.'

'Fuck off.'

'No, wait. Look, he made me put you both back on the list. Both. I couldn't take the pair of you off. Too suspicious. I told the sergeant you were needed for further questioning. Williams, the guards are going. There are three thousand people busy dying in the huts out there. Don't make it three thousand and one.'

'If it's three thousand and two I'll be happy,' and he looked up at Lock from under heavy lids.

'I say the word and someone will come and shoot you where you sit.'

'No they wouldn't. Not for you. You'd have to do it yourself.' Again those brimming eyes, brimming with hate and tears. 'Could you do that?'

'It won't come to that, man. Look, we go west. You say nice things about me. You can get Keppler. We both win.' He tried to keep the desperation out of his voice. They'd abandoned him now. After all those years of service, he was just another Englishman they couldn't be bothered to waste a bullet on. 'What do you say?'

Slowly and stiffly Williams got to his feet, the inertia of many hours having almost fused his joints, and brushed himself down. 'I'll say nice things about you, Lock.'

'I have your word?'

Williams said evenly, the madness gone from his voice now: 'You have my word.'

Lock banged the bars in delight. 'Wonderful. I'll get the key.'

The vast barns at the edge of the camp held an astonishing assortment of booty. Williams estimated they were over a kilometre long, piled high with furniture, purloined art, clothes, jewellery, carpets, great mounds stacked indiscriminately, waiting for the day when they could be sorted. Which would never happen now.

He and Lock walked the length of the treasure trove, and Williams stopped to select a herringbone coat from a pile and slipped it on. Warmth. Real warmth. For the first time in a long time. He grabbed a scarf and wrapped that round his neck, relishing the feel of rough wool against his skin.

Lock had civilian gear over his arm, a smart tweed suit, plaid shirt and knitted tie and trenchcoat. But for the moment he kept on his uniform, his passport through the wreck of Germany until they reached the Allies. His manner was cheery, upbeat, as if he wanted to keep Williams on song too, keep him focused, make him realise that it was all about concentrating on getting out of this hell hole.

The half-track was at the very end of the warehouse, a scabby, neglected-looking thing, with empty gun mounts like missing teeth sprouting across the strange framework erected over the rear of it. Williams indicated Lock should get in and he lifted the bonnet. 'You tried it?'

'Yeah,' said Lock. 'Turns over. Won't fire.'

Williams quickly went through everything just in case, sucking fuel up the line, cleaning the carb, the points and checking the distributor. When he gave a thumbs-up, the motor lazily did a couple of revolutions, stuttered and then burst into noisy, clacking life. Timing was shot, one cylinder was misfiring, and blue oil was pumping out of somewhere, but it'd do.

'Excellent. I knew you were the man for the job.'

Williams slammed the bonnet down and moved to the door. 'Move over,' said Williams. 'I always drive.'

It gave Williams great pleasure to steer the half-track straight through the wooden gates of the entrance and feel them tear from their mountings and twist and buckle under the weight of the troop transport. It was the closest he had come to a happy feeling since he first walked through the same joyless portal. Apart from the moment he saw Robert.

He spun the lumpen beast through ninety degrees and headed west, trying to comprehend that this was the outside world. Except it looked like a continuation of the camp, desolate and foreboding, as hellish without as within. The road was lined with those executed on the death march, bodies carelessly tossed on the verge. A couple of miles down the road carrion-pecked bodies swung from the lampposts, illegible signs hung round their neck. Williams looked at Lock.

'It's what the SS do to deserters, mate,' he explained. There was other traffic on the road – carts, horses, the odd civilian car – but nobody paid any attention to them, except to move out of the way, unsure who was inside. Each was in their own cocoon, on a mission, trying to save their neck. They had no desire to find

308

themselves dangling from a lamppost.

Occasionally they heard shots, or the whumpf of an artillery shell landing, sending up a thin plume of black smoke. At one village Williams stopped the half-track and ran into a still-smoking house, emerging with a white sheet which he tied to one of the heavy duty aerials that sprouted from the cab. And on they went, thankful that the all-terrain machine could take to the fields when the road was blocked by refugees or burnt-out military hardware.

The landscape grew increasingly blasted and bombed, trees carelessly strewn across meadows and roads and houses, more bodies, some of them half chewed by scavenging dogs and rats. In the corners and shadows of the building shapes scurried. Children, he thought.

'What will you do now?' asked Lock as they hit an empty stretch of road at last. 'Williams? What will you do now?' He carried on regardless of the silence. 'You know I always wanted to be a writer. Funny, eh? Me? Hoxton lad writing books. Murder mysteries, I fancied. Your Agatha Christies. Shit, couldn't do that now. A body in the library? Big deal. We got three thousand behind the wire over there.' And he laughed until Williams silenced him with a hard glance. 'At least we know whodunnit, eh? No mystery there.'

On a long, steep hill Williams ground a gear, felt it jam and punched it irritably. The knob and the top of the shaft sheared off and he cursed as the remaining spike slashed open his palm. He looked at the stream of crimson blood, checked the wound wasn't too deep, wrapped his scarf around the stem and carried on.

'You all right, mate?'

Williams nodded.

The Mustang came out of nowhere, right down the road, head on, its belly bulge almost skimming the tree tops, the Pratt and

Whitney engine screaming. The half-track rocked in the prop wash and Lock ducked as the machine thundered overhead.

'Jesus. I thought we were dead.'

'He'll be back.'

They trundled on, weaving across the stumps of villages, and clusters of red-eyed inhabitants. There were the occasional Volksturm units, the home guard, but nothing threatening, mostly boys rattling around in men's helmets, clutching ancient Mausers. A cluster of Hitler Youth eyed them suspiciously, but did nothing. Lock made the bent-arm Heil Hitler, and several returned it, some with wild-eyed enthusiasm. Williams was glad to see the back of them. Their luck was holding out.

The Mustang returned, running at right angles this time, low and sleek and beautiful, its silvery skin aglitter as the low winter sun caught the thousands of rivet heads stitching it together. Williams shoved his hand out of the window and raised it in salute. The pilot stared impassively for the fraction of a second he was level with them, then gained height, banked and headed off.

Williams rewrapped the scarf around the jagged gear lever and pushed forward as fast as the terrain would allow, wincing as the potholes and shell craters threw them about, the vibrations passing straight from seat to spine, thanks to the scant muscle cushioning still clinging to his frame.

With the road clear of civilians and troops, Lock began to strip off his uniform, transforming himself from SS to escaped British agent. Williams wondered if he thought anyone would fall for such an idiotic cover story. Well, maybe. No crazier than the idea that racing drivers would become SOE agents.

The first indication that there were no American lines as such, just a fluid, mobile bridgehead, came with the still-smoking ruin of a carbonised Eager Beaver, the US workhorse truck, which was twisted and shattered at the roadside. Maybe a mine, thought

Williams, and instinctively slowed. The Yanks must be near, though. As if in answer two rounds zinged against the bodywork.

'Put both hands out in surrender,' said Williams, looking down at Lock, who had slid off the seat.

'And get my head shot off?'

More rounds, and a heavier thunk, maybe a BAR. Williams could see a muzzle flash from a stand of trees in the centre of a field off to their right. Just lazy potshots perhaps. A splattering of detonations hammered against the body work and he felt the door buckle inwards. Light machine gun, a Johnson or the like. Maybe they were serious. 'Sooner or later they're going to find a bazooka or something.'

Lock reluctantly pulled down the flimsy side pane and stuck the top of his body out, yelling, 'Don't shoot, don't shoot! English. English prisoners.' A bullet smacked into the corner of the windshield and he slithered back in but Williams pushed him back out. He yelled more desperately this time, and the firing stopped.

They rounded the bend and Williams could see two Shermans parked nose to nose across the road, a ragged pile of sandbags stacked up their sides. The sun flashed back from the lenses of binoculars being trained on them. One of the Sherman turrets slowly cranked and elevated its gun, drawing a bead on the half-track. Williams stopped, exhausted, letting the engine idle, feeling it pop and splutter roughly under his feet.

'That's it,' said Lock exultantly. 'You did it. You did it. We did it. Just remember the deal. You say nice things, we're both in clover.'

Williams turned off the ignition and the half-track engine ran on for a second before juddering to a grateful halt.

'What? What are you doing, man? Look. Four hundred yards. Home. Free. Drive on.'

Williams took a breath and willed strength into the poor abused strings of muscle he had left as he yanked the protective scarf away from the gear lever. In a movement as fast as a snake strike he reached up and grabbed the back of Lock's head, taking a handful of hair and forcing his face downwards in one smooth, fast arc. Lock screamed as he saw the bloody spike rearing up at him, but it was too late, there was a horrible squelching sound as it pierced his eye and the momentum took it on deep into his skull. He began to thrash, but that only mixed things up more, and the razor-edged shard sliced its way through nerves and capillaries and brain matter until the thrashing became a mad twitching and then he was still, a last groan as the air leaked from his lungs marking the passing of Arthur Vincent Lock.

'Don't worry,' said Williams quietly, patting the head, 'I'll say nice things about you.'

Williams opened the driver's door and slid out on to the road, his legs wobbling as they hit the ground. He steadied, pulled the coat around him and began to walk, raising his arms as he did so. He could see a flurry of activity ahead, observers, stepping from behind the tanks, a few with carbines levelled, and among them a woman.

His legs went and he hit the asphalt, the roughened surface gashing the skin from his chin. Strange. After all this time. That he should fall now, he thought. Up. Get up. He pulled himself to his feet, swaying, stepping backwards when he wanted to go forward. Almost two years since his capture. Now free. All those things he had done. And seen. Robert. He fell again, on to his hands and knees, almost not noticing the searing pain in his cut hand.

Robert. Couldn't save him. Could save himself, but not his friend.

On his feet again, but the world was spinning, the sky and

ground switching places with dizzying rapidity. His vision was imploding, as if someone were closing the world's aperture down, shrinking it to a tunnel of light, and the only thing coming up the tunnel was a woman's voice. Funny, he thought, as the ground rushed up once more, it sounded just like Rose Miller.

Thirty-three

APRIL-MAY 1945

The wind snapped at the thin canvas that formed one side of the bathroom wall, making it sing a mournful, icy song. The first signs of spring had retreated, winter was having a last rally before handing over the reins. Williams turned on the spigot and let more hot water run over his body as he sat in the tub, inspecting the damage of two years' incarceration. He was a horrible yellowy, parchment colour, with a mottling of bruises covering him. His ribs looked like a xylophone, and his knees and elbows seemed swollen to twice their normal size, but he was eight or ten meals down the road to recovery and already he could feel tissues rebuilding. Lucky. Lucky man.

In the other room he could hear Rose Miller sorting out his belongings. The woman was amazing. She'd cleared the way for his release from the Americans within hours, convinced them that Lock was a legitimate SOE target, managed to produce his Vuitton case, which he suspected she had been travelling with as her own anyway, and taken him through to a hotel around twenty kilometres west of Berlin. The city itself was still in its death throes, the Russians crawling all over the eastern districts like insects, the sounds of their artillery clearly audible. Two or three days and it would all be over. Or at least, the fighting would. There was lots of unfinished business.

'Do you mind if I put some things of mine in your trunk?' shouted Rose from the next room.

'No,' he replied, puzzled. 'What kind of things?'

'I have an Alphachem Zyklon can. Gold dust.'

'What will happen to Alphachem?'

'We'll see. The Degesch directors are to be put on trial. War crimes.'

'Degesch?'

'The people who discovered what you could do with the Zyklon B. To people, I mean.' That snapshot started to form in his brain again, the cattle truck and the faces at the St Just sidings, but it failed to hold, as if the fixing solution were defective. He knew why. He didn't need those people any longer to remind him where the French poison gas ended up. He had Robert.

'But Alphachem will plead ignorance,' Rose continued, mimicking their whinings. 'How were we to know what it was being used for?'

'If you'd seen the trains, you'd know.'

'Well, Alphachem were well aware they had something to hide – you know they buried thousand of tonnes of the cyanide pellets at St Just just as the Americans rolled up?'

'Christ. And when it leaks?'

'Ah. That's another story. For now we nail them for what happened to the canisters you saw going east on the trains.'

'You want me to testify?'

'If it comes to it. Although there is a slight problem there.'

'What?'

'Get out and I'll tell you.'

Williams heaved himself from the bath and wrapped a thin, threadbare towel around himself and looked at the collection of hollows that was his face in the mirror. 'Who are you going to be now, Mr Williams?' he asked of it.

Towel tied firmly in place he went through and stopped in the doorway to the austere room, with its peeling brass bed and grubby kitchen area. When he saw Rose twenty minutes earlier she had been wearing a WAAF uniform, rank of Squadron Leader, with a flying jacket over it. Now she was just wearing a flying jacket and nothing else.

'Aren't you cold?' he asked.

She laughed, embarrassed. 'Is that all you can say? Oh dear. Looks like I have lost all my charms.' She began to pull the sheets round her.

Williams felt blood move in ways and to places it hadn't for many, many months and his throat was suddenly dry. He took two steps towards the bed. 'No . . . I . . . It's . . .'

Rose held her arms out. 'Shut up and come here.'

Eve Williams paced the clearing, marvelling at how quickly nature had recolonised the ground. A small clump of local farmers waited for her decision, their horses' breath cloudy in the cool morning air. From her coat pocket she took the telegram and re-read it. Missing in Action. Regrets. She tore it up and threw it at the bushes. Williams wasn't dead. There was still something inside her breathing, waiting for him. He wasn't dead.

'Eve?'

She turned and saw the familiar figure of Wimille. 'Jean-Pierre!'

He took her by the shoulders and hugged her. She hadn't seen him since that night when he had escaped from the house, but she'd had messages. He had stayed active, building up weapon stocks for D-day. Nothing flashy, nothing too glamorous. No Gestapo chases, no torture cells, no big explosions. But the guns had been there when they were needed.

'How did you find me?'

'Madame Teyssédre.' Bugatti's old secretary had survived imprisonment and worse for her efforts. Many of her family and friends hadn't.

'How are you, Eve?'

'They say he's probably dead. Somewhere called Sachsenhausen.'

'Robert?'

'Buchenwald they think. One of . . .' She shuddered. 'One of thirty-seven.'

'Can I help?' asked Wimille.

'Can you dig?'

He laughed. 'I can dig, why?'

She pointed at the ground. 'The Atlantic is down there.'

'Where?'

'Under your feet.'

'My God. What state is it in?'

'We're about to find out.'

'Well, if it is even halfway decent, I can clean it up. I'll have it ready for when he comes back.'

'He is coming back, you know.'

Wimille kissed her lightly on the forehead. 'I know.'

Eve took a deep breath, pointed to the ground and said in a loud voice, 'OK, gentlemen. We excavate here.'

At the camp the libido went some time after the intangibles – dignity, shame, faith and hope. But disappear it did, as survival of the individual, rather than the species, took precedence. Even as he realised what was happening, part of Williams' brain questioned what Rose was doing. Was she trying to restore confidence to a starved, damaged man, or was something less altruistic at work?

But those questions got fainter and fainter, and an unfamiliar machinery kicked into action, hormones pumping, blood moving, and even the little voice telling him it was wrong, a mistake, was snuffed out for a while.

Afterwards she lay on top of him, humming a tune he didn't recognise. Rose looked at him and said, 'How do you feel?'

The voice was back, the same voice you heard after a long drunken night, admonishing you for the rubbish you talked, the idiotic things you did, making you blush with shame and remorse at the memory. Except this time there was no alcohol to blame. 'Better and worse. Guilty as hell.'

Rose kissed the end of his nose and rolled him over. Sitting astride his back she began to knead at the thin shoulders, her fingers seeking out the muscles, pushing blood into them. 'How's that?'

'Well the guilt's still there. But it feels great. Ow. Careful. Where did you learn that?'

'From my father. Or rather doing it to my father. After he came in from the fields.'

'What, beating the peasants?'

'No. *He* was a peasant. A Hungarian peasant.'

Williams half turned but she pushed him down.

'We came to England in nineteen-thirty. My father knew things were going to get bad. He wasn't prepared for the prejudice he found even in London. So he told me, the only way to deal with snobbery is to be more snobby than they are. He set up a restaurant in Knightsbridge with his brother. Made some money. I went to Roedean. Learned to speak like this . . .' She came down close to him. 'We are all fakes, Williams.'

Rose rolled off him and scrabbled in her bag, producing a jar of coffee beans and shaking them with glee. 'Look. How long since you had real coffee?'

'Even longer than I had a good fuck.'

'Mr Williams. Language.'

'Come on, you must have heard worse in the fields.'

She pulled on the flying jacket and went over to the kitchen area, searching for a coffee grinder. 'You tell anyone else that story and I'll throw you back to Keppler.'

The name gave him a jolt. 'Keppler? Is he still alive?'

'Look in my bag.'

He reached over and unhooked it from the bedpost and rummaged around until he found a framed photograph of a small cottage next to an Austrian lake. 'This was in Foch.'

'It was. It's his bolthole in Austria.'

'He's there now?'

She began to grind the coffee and he tried to stop watching the cute way her bottom wobbled as she did so. The windows rattled as something exploded near by and dust sprinkled from the ceiling. 'How did he get away?'

'The French had him. There was nothing on him. No torture, no executions. So he walked away, scot free.'

'That's absurd.' Keppler's little ploy of distancing himself was just that. A ploy. A way of making him seem above all that barbarity, while reaping its reward when need be. He had to pay.

'Plus, of course, the French are busy trying to forget the number of people who dealt with Foch. Put Keppler on trial, let him list all his informers and it'll be a can of worms for them.'

'Talking of worms . . . Maurice?'

'Ten years.'

'He should swing.'

319

'You can't hang every French collaborator. Not enough gallows. Not enough trees.'

Williams looked down at the photograph one more time. 'Why are you carrying this?'

'Rat week.'

'What?'

'Rat week. Keppler may not have done any killing himself, but he certainly sent dozens, maybe hundreds, to their death. But there is something else you need to know. I said there might be a problem with you testifying against Alphachem?'

She came over with the coffee and he sipped, blistering his lips but not caring because it was so rich and wonderful and pure. She saw the look of pleasure and said, 'American. I knew you'd like it.'

'What's the problem?'

'Keppler said you were under Gestapo direction for six months after your arrest.'

He felt his throat constrict. 'What?'

'Virginia Thorpe confirmed it. Obst, too.'

Williams was speechless.

'Deuxième Bureau have put a price on your head. You can't go back. Not yet.'

'Rose. I—'

'Don't say anything. Listen, I read the French interrogation transcripts. Rubbish. I could get more out of him in ten minutes than they did in two days. I had Gestapo officers like him crying like a baby within half an hour, begging to be hanged. But they wouldn't let me at Keppler. Denazified and sent home, quick as you like.'

'So what can I do?'

'FX has a station at Vienna—'

'FX?'

'My section.'

'I thought you were F section.'

Rose laughed. 'That was the idea.'

'What was FX?'

'Best you don't know.'

Williams spun the possibilities over in his mind. FX. Then he recalled how much she knew about Dublin. 'You were SIS? A plant in SOE by the secret service?'

Rose took a breath and let it out slowly. 'Kind of.' At a bar in Jermyn Street in 1939 a friend of her mother's had put her on the SIS payroll, while directing her towards employment with MI(R), one of SOE's prototypes, to keep a weather eye on it. When she joined SOE proper, her loyalty to SIS remained more or less intact.

'Kind of? Bloody hell. So tell me this. Robert was convinced that SOE sent in its agents willy-nilly in forty-three to bluff the SD and Abwehr into thinking some sort of build-up was taking place. A landing in Pas de Calais maybe. While really Sicily was where the blow would fall. I said SOE wouldn't do that, wouldn't sacrifice its agents. But, of course SIS might.' He thought of that slippery bastard Slade back in Ireland. 'Why should MI6 give a flying fuck about a few bumbling amateurs being snared. Is that right? Was Robert right?'

Rose drained her coffee, got up and washed the cup. She didn't turn when she said, 'Utter bilge. We never sacrificed anyone. My job was to work for SOE to the best of my abilities, except on the rare occasion when it conflicted with an SIS operation.'

'Bollocks.'

Rose spun round, tears in her eyes. 'No, not bollocks, the truth. You asked me once what it was like sending people off. People you got to know. Like. Love. It was bloody awful. Every minute of it. Ask Bodington or Buckmaster or Atkins. And I don't need you making pointless shitty accusations, thank you very much.'

If it was a performance, it was a good one, and Williams muttered an apology. It probably didn't matter now. They did what they had to to win. In the long run, he guessed the alternative was even worse than what a few hundred agents went through.

'You were saying. FX.'

She sniffed, recovered her composure and began to get dressed. 'Obst we've lost track of. Thorpe and Keppler, we know where they are. If you pick them up, I . . . can interview them. Off the meter, you understand. I can get signed depositions clearing you. And we can go dancing in Vienna to celebrate.'

'And I thought this was a one-night stand?'

'What sort of girl do you take me for, Mr Williams? You can take my Humber. I'll get the papers drawn up and weapons issued. They'll say you're on War Crimes Tribunal business. Which is pretty much the truth. Can you manage it?'

He thought for a moment. The hatred would get him through it, no matter how weakened he was. He nodded. From her pocket Rose took out the diamond-encrusted Cartier watch and held it out to him. 'Before I forget.'

And the voice in his head was loud and clear and it was his own, from many, many years ago: *If you were mine I'd never betray you.*

Williams watched the diamonds dance and sparkle and said slowly, regretfully, 'Keep it. I'm finished with it.'

Williams focused the binoculars out on the lake, bringing into sharp relief the face of the man he was after. The two others in the small boat were unknown to him. All were well wrapped against the wind rippling the lake surface, so he couldn't be absolutely sure he had never seen them before. But he really didn't care. Keppler was the one.

Awkwardly, like tired old men, they manhandled the steel cylinders that were at the bottom of the craft and heaved them overboard, a dozen in all. There were satisfied smiles all round and Keppler, dressed, rather incongruously, in an old British army greatcoat, restarted the engine and headed off back to shore.

Williams had pulled the Humber over to one side of the road which led down from the mountains to the dark, bowl-like Lake Senlitz where Keppler was depositing whatever records and goods they thought should be hidden from the Allies, yet saved for posterity. The alpine flowers were out, blooming across the upper meadows, where cows, released from winter quarters, were now roaming contentedly. Williams barely registered the stunning backdrop. He only had eyes for ugliness.

Williams ignored the desperate, muffled kicking from the boot and refocused on the party below.

The two unknown men leaped out of the boat as Keppler beached it on the small shingle shoreline that had been carved out of the low cliff that ran round this southern part of the lake. The trio shook hands, and his companions climbed into a battered Skoda and drove off, leaving Keppler to stow the gear. He only had a short walk, maybe two kilometres, to the small cottage so familiar from the photograph. It showed signs of repair – a freshly patched roof, a new coat of paint. No doubt it had been sadly neglected while the owner was off doing the Führer's work in Paris. Now he had all the time in the world to fix it up.

The kicking again and a muffled scream. Virginia. The drug had worn off. He'd have to readminister. He had picked her up near Salzburg and she had come quietly, convinced he was going to kill her. Instead, he had tied her, gagged her and injected her with the sedative Rose had provided while he went to complete the pair. She could breathe in there, he was sure. She could wait.

323

His heart racing at the thought of the confrontation, Williams pulled back the slide on the Colt pistol and laid it on the seat next to him, beside the handcuffs and a US army burp gun, the sort of machine gun that was a lethal shredding machine at close range. He hoped he didn't have to use it.

Williams selected first and set off down the hillside, carefully taking the bends at sensible speeds so no tyre squeal would alert the man busy stowing oars and ropes in the shed by the roadside.

He drove to within a hundred metres, then something made him pull over. Keppler. That stooped, arthritic creature, his skin grey, his hair thinning, that was an SD man? The man who sipped fine wines while he conjured up some new Faustian pact?

Yes it was, he reminded himself. The very same. The man still blighting his life with his lies. As he pulled away, Keppler, warned by the canny survival instincts that had kept him alive these last few months, looked up. He peered at the windscreen and again, although there was no way he could recognise Williams, he knew he had to defend himself. Calmly, Keppler pulled out a Luger pistol, levelled it and fired.

The bullet shattered the screen, and tiny slivers of glass peppered Williams' face, each one hot and stinging. He punched out the remnants of the windshield and headed straight for Keppler, foot flat down now, wheels spinning, engine protesting, right at him. A second shot. A third, and part of Williams' ear flapped open, squirting blood across the upholstery. Rose won't be pleased, said a stupid irrational voice in his head.

He hit Keppler full on, snapping a tibia with the bumper, and sending the man careering over the bonnet towards him. Williams raised his arms as the figure suddenly filled his vision, crashing into the space where the glass had once been. The car slewed to a halt.

Williams reached for the gun, but a bloody claw grabbed his

wrist. Keppler twisted in the space, bringing another arm on to his face, scratching at Williams' eyes. He felt a lid tear, and lashed out, punching, but the massive woollen coat absorbed his blows.

Now Keppler was also scrabbling for the gun. With his elbow Williams knocked the gear stick into reverse and floored the pedal as he let in the clutch. The car careered wildly backwards, bumping up the grass verge, and still the SD man clung on. Williams stamped the brake hard, but felt the wheels lock on grass made slippery by the recent thaw. The Humber slithered on, slipping and sliding, back towards the edge of the low cliff where it tipped over into the black waters with a stomach-turning free fall. Even as the icy mass closed over him, Williams could still feel the German's hands desperately trying to find his windpipe, to earn the satisfaction of choking the life from him before the lake had a chance to drown them all.

Thirty-four

OCTOBER 2001

Deakin has forgotten how ear-piercingly raucous Brighton's seagulls can be as they swoop down to dive bomb a ragged old man who throws bread on to the shingle for them. The sea is lively, the tide running and waves leaping up around the pillars that support the skeletal remains of the West Pier, now slowly being restored.

He is sitting in the Victorian shelter alone, watching the families enjoy what may be the last fine weekend of the year before winter closes in. He scans the promenade and finally sees the old lady appear in the distance, propelling herself along the prom towards them, threading through rollerbladers and dog walkers. She had told him on the telephone that she has finally had to accept a wheelchair.

She whirrs up to him, a smile on her face as if she is genuinely pleased to see him. She holds out a bony blue hand and as he takes it he is shocked to see the Cartier watch on her wrist. She catches the glance.

'Oh I know. I was going to do something melodramatic,

but . . . well, it's rather nice isn't it? Too nice to waste on a lake. Shall we walk? Or rather, you walk, I'll roll. We can get a cup of tea along there.' She points to the café at the end of the prom.

He stands and paces alongside her. 'Still on the payroll, Deakin?'

'Part time. Good to be back.'

'I told Sir Charles he was a damn fool letting people like yourself go.'

'I appreciate it.'

'I trained him you know. Back in the fifties.'

'Ah.' That explained his loyalty and indulgence.

'It's very kind of you to come down from London, Deakin.'

'It's not entirely a social visit, Dame Rose.'

'No?'

'Two things. The French have started digging up the Zyklon B at St Just.'

Rose chuckles. 'Good. You told them about the film?'

'I told the Alphachem CEO you still had Robert's images of St Just trains being loaded. And a genuine canister. All they had to decide was, did they want us to announce to the world what had happened? They decided full disclosure was the best policy. Caused a bit of a stir, I hear.'

'Excellent. Well done. And secondly?'

Deakin takes a deep breath, wondering whether he is going to shatter an old woman's sense of closure. A spanner into the works. 'We've checked the dental records of the bodies from the Humber. You were right about Virginia Thorpe. The man, however, didn't check out. It seems it wasn't Mr Williams after all.'

A rattly laugh. 'I know that.'

He can't keep the surprise from his voice. 'You knew?'

'Suspected shall we say. Why do you think I didn't throw the

327

watch into the water? I had a feeling Williams didn't die in that lake. Not that easy to kill a man like Williams, Deakin. They were extraordinary men, both of them. But chalk and cheese. With Robert, what you saw was what you got. Charming, cultured, refined, a lovely man, a real gentleman. Apart from the language. Whilst Williams . . . brave, resourceful, talented, certainly. But, of course, he turned out to be anything but a gentleman. As you will see.' She peers ahead to the café. 'Good. She's there. There is someone I would like you to meet.'

Deakin is trained not to like surprises and she hasn't mentioned a third party before. 'Who?'

'My granddaughter. Evie. Lovely girl.'

Deakin looks down at her and up at the café, where a woman, perhaps in her twenties, sits cradling a coffee, smiling at her approaching grandmother. Granddaughter? Deakin has checked the files on Rose, at least those sections he was allowed to access. She never married. There were no children. Deakin lets the news sink in, trying to get the flailing loose ends to knit together. When they finally do, he asks: 'Did you ever hear from him after Berlin? Did you ever hear from Williams?'

Rose shakes her head and the cloudy eyes look wetter than usual as she says quietly: 'Not a whisper.'

Thirty-five

FRANCE, SEPTEMBER 1945

Rose Miller consulted the map on the passenger seat and took a left at the cross roads. A few signs had been tacked back up, but for the most part the Normandy countryside was still denuded of decent directions. Occasionally she could spot the jagged stump of poles where the Germans had snapped off signposts to try to baffle the advancing Allies some fourteen, fifteen months previously. She had thought the place would be back to normal by now, but no, the fields had a sad, untended look, apple trees seemed to be growing through a dense carpet of rotting fruit, and precious walnuts lay uncollected on the ground. Too much land, too few people left.

Rose ground a gear as she slowed for St Arraton, taking in the little cluster of white houses, their stonework marked by the smallpox of rifle and machine-gun fire. On the far side of the village lay a scorched Sherman tank, its tracks unravelled like giblets, a gaping wound in its side.

He's dead. We have no idea where. I'm sorry, Eve.

Would she be able to say her name without her voice breaking?

Rose Miller rounded a bend and cursed when she saw a slow-moving lorry ahead, almost filling the narrow Normandy lane. Just what she needed. She accelerated towards the tailgate and then eased off when she saw the eyes looking at her. Peering over the top of the roof, heads swaying in rhythm with the truck, were two giraffe heads, attached, she assumed, to two real live giraffes. She burst out laughing. Here she was in so-called war-ravaged Europe, and someone was moving giraffes around?

Maybe they were there to restock the zoo. She hadn't heard of anyone eating giraffes in the desperate days of Occupation, but there was much went on that the tight-lipped French would prefer not to mention. A few cafés suddenly finding themselves with *fillet de giraf* on the menu would not surprise her one bit.

The truck belched smoke and wheezed as they hit a slight incline and the driver changed down, dropping to below thirty kilometres an hour.

'Come on, Noah,' Rose found herself saying. She pressed the horn and a hand appeared from the driver's window. For a moment Rose thought she was going to get an obscene gesture and she felt her anger rise, the fury of someone used to getting her own way, but the truck slowed even more and the hand waved her on. She went down to second and floored the Jeep, brushing within inches of the truck's side and flinching as the tendrils of the uncut hazel hedgerow flicked at the other side of her vehicle. She poked a hand through the space where canvas roof met door and waved her thanks. There was an answering flash of lights.

He's dead. No, we don't know . . .

Rose looked down at her wrist and gasped at her own stupidity. The diamond-encrusted Cartier winked at her, as if party to her near-miss. It was Rose's turn to slow down. She worked the watch from her arm and pushed it under the buff folders in the Jeep's map pocket. She suddenly felt her mood lighten. That was what had been worrying her, not her over-rehearsed speech to Eve. Some part of her subconscious had been sending alarm signals, trying to warn her, telling her she had to take off the watch. Relieved, she settled back and pressed the accelerator and watched the giraffe-truck recede in the rear-view mirror. Soon be over, she thought to herself. And then they could all get on with their lives.

She pulled into the driveway of the converted watermill and waited, the Jeep's engine ticking impatiently. Eve emerged from the kitchen, a couple of those hideous little dogs yapping at her feet. Rose climbed out, adjusted her jacket carefully, and approached Eve, shocked at how she'd let herself go. Where was the radiant beauty? The Yvonne Aubicq that men had supposedly done battle over in fast cars. Ratty hair, a shapeless housecoat, a tired, washed-out face.

'Hello, Eve.'

Eve smiled weakly and nodded. 'Any news?'

'None. I've just come off the line with Vera Atkins. If anyone knows what happened to our agents, she does. The trail ends at Sachsenhausen. I'm sorry. I've brought you a few of his things.'

Rose reached into her shoulder pack and produced some letters and photographs, one of which – the standard SOE head and shoulders shot, the one that would line the stairwell of the Special Forces Club like so many frozen in eternal youthful sepia – fluttered to the ground. They both bent to pick it up, but Eve followed it all the way down, collapsing on to her knees, impervious to the sharp gravel. She looked at the photograph and began to weep, bowing as if praying and then, with a sickening thud, banging her head rhythmically on the drive, picking up small pieces of stone every time she did so, driving them deeper and deeper into her skin with each blow.

'Eve,' said Rose, touching her shoulder. 'Eve, stop it.'

She began to wail and Rose looked around, desperate for relief, some kind of saviour. In the garage she glimpsed the unmistakable curves of the bodywork of the Atlantic. 'You dug it up? My God . . .'

'Could you go now please?'

'Eve, I miss him too. And Robert—'

'Go. Please. Leave me.' She looked up, the thin streams of blood running into her eyebrows and creeping down her cheeks. 'Please.'

Rose deposited the rest of Williams' things on to the ground beside Eve and backed away, suddenly anxious to be away from this crazy woman. She climbed into the Jeep, started it, and, careful not to spray Eve with gravel, turned it in a large circle and drove out of the courtyard, making a right.

A great feeling of relief washed over her, relief and guilt. It was over. Done. What did it matter where she thought her husband died, or what he had got up to in a half-ruined hotel in Bad Bleibau? In many ways Williams did die in Sachsenhausen, and died a hero. This way the Deuxième Bureau suspicion would be quietly buried, as would the Rat Weeks, all lost in the confusion of the post-war turmoil. Forty-two thousand airmen had not returned from missions and their fates were not known. What was a handful of SOE operatives against that?

Except the thousands were faceless. She had known the handful. It made a difference.

She came to the slow-moving lorry of giraffes bumping up the road, glanced at the bearded driver, and pulled over to let him pass. Return the favour. He honked as he slid by. The feeling of nausea hit her as the belch of exhaust filled the Jeep. Rose opened the door and vomited across the asphalt, once, then again, her stomach heaving on empty.

Rose took a slug of water from the canteen, washed it around her mouth and spat. She looked down and felt at the tiny lump swelling under her waistband. She knew what she had to do. Couldn't go home as an unmarried mother. So, a nursing home in Brittany. A change of surname for the baby. Adoption to a nice English family, maybe one which lost a child in the Blitz or the youngest son to the Germans. That would be good. Maybe even replace one of those thousands of missing airmen. Then back to work. She pulled the Jeep off the verge and on to the road. Rose Miller had a feeling that Europe was about to enter a 'peace' that didn't really deserve the term and she wanted to be part of the next battle.

Eve Williams was sitting cross-legged on the gravel when the big lorry inched its way in, indicators flashing, air brakes hissing as the driver sought to edge it in without demolishing the stone pillars. Clear of the gateway he edged forward, pulling the truck tight in against one of the paddock fences, away from where she sat. With a final shush the engine stopped and the driver climbed from the cab.

She looked up at him, then at the four wonderful doe-like eyes staring down at her from their crazy-paved necks. Giraffes. She pulled some specks of gravel from her forehead, feeling silly now. 'The zoo is another fifty kilometres.'

'I know.'

He stood there, arms folded, and Eve read the tag stitched on the overall's breast pocket. Tambal. 'Well, Mr Tambal, if it's coffee you want, I can help. Anything else . . .'

She held out her hand and he strode over and pulled her to her feet. As she came up his arms went round her waist and for the first time she looked beyond the beard and the thin network of scars and the bent nose and the misshapen ear and felt as if she were going to be sick. 'Ah . . .' was all that came out.

He reached up and pulled the hair from her face, the way he had seventeen years before on a lonely beach in the headlights of a Rolls-Royce. 'Hello, Eve.'

'Will.' Her voice was a frightened whisper. 'Will?'

'I was.'

'No, no, you are . . .' There was pleading in her voice. 'You're alive?'

'No. Will's dead.'

She took a step back, looking at him, making sure he was solid, not some tormenting spectre. 'Why?'

'Too many things. Just too many. Time to start over.' He had done it before, he could do it again. Grover became Williams who became Grover–Williams. Now he had to die, for the terrible things he had done. Rose, Lock, and . . .

'Robert?'

The worst sin of all. He shook his head.

'Tell me.'

And he did, mostly. A friend given and then taken away, leaving him behind. After he had finished he said quietly: 'Fresh start, OK? No questions, no recriminations. That's the offer.'

'I'll think about it,' she said and grinned. When he didn't react she pinched him. 'I'm joking.'

It would be a long time before he could really laugh out loud again, he knew. It was like after the King had died when he was a boy, and his father had turned them into a house full of whisperers. Now he felt the entire world should lower its voice in respect for and remembrance of what had happened to his friend.

'The giraffes?' Eve asked.

'Long story.'

Then he saw the Atlantic. She noticed his eyes dart over there, saw the small, expectant smile on his face. Knew he was recalling the madness of driving it with Robert, risking their lives because they wanted that speed. It was a kind of insanity, he could see that now, but in a world gone completely mad, it was difficult to pick out what exactly was sane and what wasn't. He looked at Eve again, disbelieving, and echoed Rose's words: 'You dug it up?'

'Long story. But it works.' She took him by the hand and pulled him across to the garage, yanking the barn door fully open and revealing the long, low shape he never thought to see again.

Eve climbed in, turned the key, pressed the ignition and the engine ripped into life, the familiar Bugatti signature, loud and raucous, in total contrast to the elegant wrapper. 'Move over,' he said.

She looked up at him and shook her head. 'Uh-uh. Dead men don't drive.'

Williams hesitated a moment, then jumped in the passenger side. Eve let in the clutch and the car leapt forward, wheels throwing up a storm of gravel, causing the giraffes to pull back in shock as she bumped the Atlantic out of the courtyard and turned left, away from Rose and everything she stood for, flooring the accelerator, throwing him back in the seat. Williams watched hypnotised as the line of plane trees rushed towards them, blurring together as the speedometer crept round the white face of the dial, the only evidence of gaps between the fat, peeling trunks the semaphore flashing of the early morning sun.

Author's note

Early One Morning is a novel and should not be regarded as a historical document, but at the core of it are a few remarkable truths. Williams (aka William Grover aka William Charles Frederick Grover–Williams), a former chauffeur for Sir William Orpen, Robert Benoist and Jean-Pierre Wimille really did form a Resistance circuit in France in 1942–3. The idea of the fastest men in the world against the German occupiers is what sparked this work. Like so many other clandestine groups, they were betrayed to the Germans, and many people suffered and died as a result.

Robert Benoist was actually apprehended much later than Williams. His escapades herein, driving a Bugatti from under the noses of a convoy he had been forced to join and leaping from a moving police car (it was a Hotchkiss, not a van), are true. There were so many other tales of Robert's bravery and resourcefulness that, for a while, SOE were suspicious of a man who could escape from the clutches of the Germans so often, until Robert came to England for training and they saw what he was made of. As far as we know, he was hanged by piano wire at Buchenwald, alongside 36 fellow Allied officers, by the SS on 12 September 1944.

Maurice Benoist was tried by a French court for collaboration. Due to ill health, he served only five years of a ten-year sentence. Still protesting his innocence, he died in 1955.

Some suspicion of betrayal also fell on Jean-Pierre Wimille, who was acquitted and exonerated by the court. After the war, racing for Alfa Romeo, he was well on his way to being belatedly recognised as one of the greatest drivers of his era, when he was killed at the 1948 Argentinian Grand Prix in Buenos Aires.

Yvonne Williams became a well-known dog breeder and a judge at Crufts Dog Show in London. The two Scotties on the Black & White whisky bottle were reputed to be hers. She died in 1973.

Although Williams was officially notified as executed at Sachsenhausen in March 1945, in May 1947 a communication was sent from Berlin by MI5 to SOE asking for help in relocating a former Bugatti race driver, Grover–Williams, to the USA. Sometime later a man calling himself Georges Tambal, closely resembling Williams, an expert on race cars and with the same date of birth, moved into Yvonne's farmhouse. She was to claim he was her cousin. Tambal was knocked off his bicycle and killed by a carload of German tourists in 1983.

Keppler is modelled on Hans Kieffer, who was hanged by the French. His crime was signing the execution order for a group of British commandos later in the war, not running the SD in Paris. SOE admitted there was little they could have pinned on him for his activities at Avenue Foch – he really was a man who preferred a deal to torture. Of course, that certainly wasn't true of all Gestapo, SD and Abwehr officers.

Rose Miller is in no way based on the wonderful Vera Atkins of SOE, whom I had the privilege to meet shortly before her death. She told Jack Bond and I that she interviewed Kieffer after the war and managed to reduce him to tears within a short time. This did not endear him to her. Jack asked her over dinner at the

Special Forces Club how she viewed the Germans sixty years after the events. There was a long pause while she drew on a cigarette and she eventually said, very softly, with great feeling: 'As disagreeable as ever, really.' Out of Williams and Benoist, both of whom she met, we got the impression that it was Robert she admired more.

Vera would not have approved of the way I have played with dates, for instance for how long the deeply flawed poem codes were used and the timetable of SOE operations (I have them up and running a little faster than reality). She would certainly have exploded at the suggestion of an SIS plant in SOE. I can only plead, once more, that this is a fiction with a bedrock of actual events.

However, a French company (which survives today as part of a US multinational) did manufacture Zyklon B during the Second World War as well documented in France by journalist Annie Lacroix-Riz, who has suffered much vilification for this and other exposures about industry's role in the occupation.

Arthur Lock is based on Harry Cole, a British renegade, his career much as described, apart from his death.

It is likely Williams escaped from Sachsenhausen by striking a deal with an SS officer called Meyer to give a testimonial to the Allies. The famous Yeo-Thomas (The White Rabbit) used a similar method, as described in Mark Seaman's excellent book *Bravest Of the Brave* (see below).

Virginia Thorpe is a total fiction, but several SOE agents did find themselves relatively comfortable homes in Avenue Foch and appeared to have a far too cosy relationship with the SD. Henri Dericourt ('Gilbert'), who controlled Lysander flights for SOE, certainly did let the SD look at the mail. The debate over whether he was simply a traitor, a double agent or a triple agent has raged since the 1950s. There is no doubt, however, that being shown such documents seriously weakened the resolve of several agents when they were in Avenue Foch.

Around 480 SOE agents went into France by plane, parachute or boat. One hundred and thirty were captured. Twenty-six returned. This is thought to be the tip of a very large iceberg – the official numbers take no account of collateral damage to the French population caused by a circuit's collapse. There were many brave French and English men and women involved in the Chestnut circuit, including Lieutenant Roland Dowlen, an SOE radio operator who was sent to help Chestnut on 31 March 1943 and was billeted with Thérèse Lethias in Pontoise, away from the house at Auffargis, for security reasons. Nevertheless, he was captured on 31 July by DF vans, and his radio was subsequently operated by the Germans until 31 October. Dowlen was executed at Flossenburg. Other circuit members, too numerous to mention here, were also arrested and many died in concentration camps and prisons. *Early One Morning* is dedicated to all of them.

Both Benoist and Williams, whose enigma survives him, were awarded the Croix de Guerre and to this day trophies in both men's names are raced for.

Sources

My initial research into the Williams/Benoist story was with Gervaise Cowell (now deceased), the SOE advisor for the Foreign and Commonwealth Office, and Richard Day, curator of The Bugatti Trust in Gotherington, Gloucester. The results were published in *Arena* magazine as the short story *The Man With One Name*, for which I am grateful to the then editor Peter Howarth, who encouraged me to present it as fiction.

That was 1995. Two years later, after a meeting engineered by Duncan Stuart of SOE, I was fortunate enough to have use of the unstoppable energy and drive of the inimitable Jack Bond, film director and producer, who worked closely with Beatrice van Lith, Robert Benoist's granddaughter, to uncover many of the details used herein, principally Williams' survival of Sachsenhausen plus Beatrice's insights into the character of Robert. Jack also showed a remarkable facility for prising out information from both the UK and French security services, the latter regarding the Zyklon B issue (and picked up a warning that digging too hard might be detrimental to his health). Jack also unearthed, from Eve's neighbours, the tale of Tambal turning up with the giraffes.

Richard Smith, a man with a mission if ever I met one, trawled through the Public Records Office at Kew and dropped many pieces of the jigsaw puzzle into place, proving beyond any doubt that Williams was not executed at the camp. To get an admission from SOE/MI6 that the files are wrong is a remarkable feat.

Again, I have played fast and loose with all these people's exemplary work.

For those who wish to find out more about the characters and events without the gloss of fiction, I would direct you towards the bibliography which follows.

Bibliography

Orpen: Mirror to an Age by Bruce Arnold
The IRA by Tim Pat Coogan
Memories of Montparnasse by John Glassco
Americans in Paris by Brian N. Morton
The Twilight Years: Paris in the 1930s by William Wiser
Paris and Elsewhere by Richard Cobb
The Josephine Baker Story by Ean Wood
Driving Forces by Peter Stevenson (a book about the Silver Arrows).
Hitler's Grand Prix in England (Donnington 1937 and 1938) by Christopher Hilton
Ettore Bugatti by W.F. Bradley
Bugatti, The Man and The Marque by Jonathan Wood
The Bugatti Story by L'Ebe Bugatti
The Power and the Glory, History of Grand Prix Racing Vol 1 1906–1951 by William Court
The Monaco Grand Prix by Craig Brown/Len Newman
Alfa Romeo: The Legend Revived by David G. Styles
London at War by Philip Ziegler
SS Intelligence by Edmund L. Blandford

Occupation: The Ordeal of France 1940–44 by Ian Ousby

Occupied France by H.R. Kedward

The Fall of Paris June 1940 by Herbert Lottman

The Prime of Life by Simone de Beauvoir

Swastika over Paris by Jeremy Josephs

SOE by M.R.D. Foot

SOE in France by M.R.D. Foot

Inside SOE by E.H. Cookridge

Noor-un-nisa Inayat Khan by Jean Overton Fuller

Secret War by Nigel West

Between Silk and Cyanide by Leo Marks

Flames in the Field by Rita Kramer

The Secret History of SOE by William Mackenzie

An Uncertain Hour by Ted Morgan

The Death of Jean Moulin by Patrick Marnham

Bravest of the Brave by Mark Seaman

Sabotage and Subversion: Stories From The Files of SOE and OSS by Ian Dear

Undercover: The Men and Women of the SOE by Patrick Howarth

Industrialists and Bankers Under the Occupation by Annie Lacroix-Riz

Sisters in the Resistance by Margaret Collins Weitz

Paris After the Liberation by Antony Beevor and Artemis Cooper

THANKS TO: Jack Bond, Richard Smith, David Miller, Bill Massey, Martin Fletcher, Peter Howarth, Don Hawkins, Susan D'Arcy, Dylan Jones and Christine Walker. Extra thanks to Rita Kramer for inspiration and the Pericles.